WELCOME, CHAOS

By Kate Wilhelm

Welcome, Chaos
Oh, Susannah!
Listen, Listen
A Sense of Shadow
Better than One (with Damon Knight)
Juniper Time
Somerset Dreams and Other Fictions
Fault Lines
Where Late the Sweet Birds Sang
The Clewiston Test
The Infinity Box: A Collection of Speculative Fiction
City of Cain
Margaret and I
Abyss: Two Novellas
The Year of the Cloud (with Theodore L. Thomas)
Let the Fire Fall
The Downstairs Room and Other Speculative Fiction
The Killer Thing
The Nevermore Affair
The Clone (with Theodore L. Thomas)
More Bitter than Death
The Mile-Long Spaceship

WELCOME, CHAOS

KATE WILHELM

Houghton Mifflin Company Boston 1983

A portion of this book was first published in slightly different form in the September 1981 issue of *Redbook* under the title "The Winter Beach," and appears in *Listen, Listen,* a collection of Kate Wilhelm novellas (Houghton Mifflin, 1981).

Library of Congress Cataloging in Publication Data

Wilhelm, Kate.
  Welcome, chaos.

  I. Title.
PS3573.I434W4 1983   813'.53   83–6181
ISBN 0–395–34431–X

Printed in the United States of America

S 10 9 8 7 6 5 4 3 2 1

For Mary Ann, Jean, Maisie, and Kitty,
with love.

WELCOME, CHAOS

HUGH LASATER stood with his back to the window, watching Lloyd Pierson squirm. They were in Pierson's office, a room furnished with university-issue desk and bookshelves, as devoid of personality as Pierson himself was. He was one of those men no one after the fact could ever identify, so neutral he could vanish into a mist, become one with a landscape, and never be seen again.

Lloyd Pierson stopped fidgeting with his pencil and took a deep breath. "I can't do it," he said primly, examining the pencil. "It would be unethical, and besides she would appeal. She might even have a sex discrimination case."

"She won't appeal. Believe me, she won't make a stink."

Pierson shook his head. He glanced at his watch, then confirmed what he had learned by looking at the wall clock.

Lasater suppressed a laugh.

"You do it, or I go over your head," he said mildly. "It's a funny thing how people hate having this kind of decision shoved at them when it could have been handled on a lower level. You know?"

"You have no right!" Pierson snapped. He looked at Lasater, then quickly away again. "This is insufferable."

"Righto. Dean McCrory, isn't it? I just happen to have his number here somewhere. I suppose your secretary would place the call for me?" He searched his notebook, then stopped, holding it open.

"I want to talk to your supervisor, your boss, whoever that is."

Lasater shrugged. "Got a piece of paper? I'll write the number for you." Pierson handed him a note pad and he jotted down a number. "That's a Washington area code. Dial it yourself, if you don't mind. You have an outside line, don't you? And his is a direct line, it'll be his private secretary who answers. Just tell him it's about the bird of prey business. He'll put you through."

"Whose private secretary?"

"Secretary of Defense," Lasater said, as if surprised that Pierson had not recognized the number.

"I don't believe you." He dialed the number.

Lasater turned to look out the window. The campus was a collage of red brick buildings, dirty snow, and too many people of an age. God, how tired he would get of so many young people all the time with their mini-agonies and mini-crises and mini-triumphs. Unisex reigned here; in their dark winter garments they all looked alike. The scene was like an exercise in perspective: same buildings, same snow, same vague figures repeated endlessly. He listened to Pierson parrot his message about bird of prey, and a moment later:

"Never mind. Sorry to bother you. I won't wait. It's all right."

Lasater smiled at the bleak landscape, but when he turned to the room there was no trace of humor on his face. He retrieved the notepaper, put it in an ashtray, and set it afire. After it was burned he crushed the ashes thoroughly, then dumped them into the wastecan. He held the pad aslant and studied the next piece of paper, then slipped the pad into a pocket. He kept his amusement out of his voice when he said, "You will never use that number again, or even remember that you saw such a number. In fact, this entire visit is classified, and everything about it. Right?"

Pierson nodded miserably.

Lasater felt only contempt for him now; he had not fought hard enough for anything else. "So, you just tell her no dice on a leave of absence. You have about an hour before she'll get here; you'll think of a dozen good reasons why your department can't do without her services."

He picked up his coat and hat from the chair where he had tossed them and left without looking back.

Lyle Taney would never know what happened, he thought with satisfaction, pausing at the stairs of the history department building to put his coat on. He went to the student union and had a malted milkshake, picked up a poetry review magazine, bought a pen, and then went to his car and waited. Most of the poetry was junk, but some of it was pretty good, better than he had expected. He reread one of the short pieces. Nice. Then he saw her getting out of her car. Lyle Taney was medium height, a bit heavy for his taste; he liked willowy women and she was curvy and dimply. Ten pounds, he estimated; she could lose ten pounds before she would start to look gaunt enough to suit him. He liked sharp cheekbones and the plane of a cheek without a suggestion of roundness. Her hair was short and almost frizzy it was so curly, dark brown with just a suggestion of gray, as if she had frosted it without enough bleach to do a thorough job. He knew so much about her that it would have given her a shock to realize anyone had recorded such information and that it could be retrieved. He knew her scars, her past illnesses, her college records, her income and expenses . . . She was bouncy: he grinned at her tripping nimbly through the slush at the curb before the building. That was nice, not too many women were still bouncy at her age: thirty-seven years, four months, sixteen days.

She vanished inside the building. He glanced at his watch and made a bet with himself. Eighteen minutes. It would take eighteen minutes. Actually it took twenty-two. When she reappeared, the bounce was gone. She marched down the stairs looking straight ahead, plowed through the slush, crossed the street without checking for traffic, daring anyone to touch her. She got to her car and yanked the door open, slid in, and drove off too fast. He liked all that. No tears. No sentimental look around at the landscape. Just good old-fashioned determination. Hugh Lasater liked to know everything about the people he used. This was data about Lyle Taney that no one would have been able to tell him. He felt that he knew her a little better now than he had that morning. He was whistling tunelessly as he turned his key, started the rented car, and left the university grounds. She would do, he told himself contentedly. She would do just fine.

Lyle put on coffee and paced while she waited for it. On the table her book looked fragile suddenly, too nebulous to support her entire weight, and that was what it had to do. The book had a flying hawk on the cover; sunlight made the rufous tail look almost scarlet. The book was about hawks, about the word *hawk*, about hawklike people. It was not natural history, or ornithology, or anything in particular, but it had caught on, and last week it had made the best-seller lists. A fluke, of course, such a long shot it could never happen again. She was not a writer, and she really knew nothing about birds in general and hawks in particular, except what she had researched and observed over the five years it had taken her to do the book. The book was so far removed from her own field of history that it was not even counted as a publication by her department.

Her former department, she corrected herself, and poured coffee, then sat down at the table with it and stared at the book, and went over the luncheon one more time.

Bobby Conyers, her editor for the hawk book, and Mal Levinson from the magazine *Birds* had insisted that a follow-up book on eagles would be equally successful.

"Consider it, Lyle," Mal had said earnestly, on first-name basis instantly. "We want the article. I know ten thousand isn't a fortune, but we'll pick up your expenses, and it'll add up. And Bobby can guarantee fifteen thousand up front for the book. Don't say no before you think about it."

"But I don't know anything at all about eagles, nothing. And Oregon? Why there? There are eagles in other places, surely."

Mal pointed to the clipping he had brought with him: a letter to the editor of a rival magazine. It mentioned the bald eagles seen along a stretch of Oregon beach for two years in a row, suggesting they were nesting in the vicinity.

"That part of Oregon looks like the forest primeval," he said. "And eagles, bald eagles, are on the endangered list. That may be the last nesting site on the West Coast. It'll make a terrific article and book. Believe us, we both agree, it'll be even better than *Hawks*. I'd like to call it *Bird of Prey.*"

Bobby was nodding. "I agree, Lyle. It'll go."

She sipped her coffee, her gaze still on the book. In her briefcase were contracts, a map of Oregon, another one of that section of coast, and a photocopy of an article on eagles that Mal had dug out of a back issue of his magazine.

"What if I can't find the nest?" she had asked, and with the question she had realized she was going to do it.

"It's pretty hard to hide an eagle's nest," Mal had said, grinning, knowing she had been persuaded. He began to talk about eagles then, and for the rest of the hour they spent together, it had been as if they all knew she would go to Oregon, search the jagged hills for the nest, set up a photography blind, start digging for facts, tidbits, myths, whatever else took her fancy to make up a full-length book.

And she did want to do it, she told herself again firmly, and tried not to think of what it would mean if the book failed, if she could not find the nest, if the eagles were not nesting there this year, if . . . if . . . if . . . She would have to face Pierson and ask for her job back, or go somewhere else and start over. She thought briefly of filing a claim of discrimination against Pierson and the university, but she put it out of mind again. Not her style. No one had forced her to quit, and no one guaranteed a leave of absence for a job unrelated to her field. Pierson had pointed this out to her in his most reasonable tone, the voice that always made her want to hit him with a wet fish. The fleeting thought about the statistics of women her age getting work in their own fields went unheeded as she began to think seriously about the difficulties of finding an eagle's nest in the wooded, steep hills of the coast range of Oregon.

Presently, she put the book on a chair and spread out the coastal map and began to study it. The nest would be within a mile or two of the water and the exact places where the birds had been seen were clearly marked — an area roughly five to eight miles by two miles. It would be possible, with luck, and if the bird watcher had been right, and if the eagles came back this year . . .

Lyle sat on the side of her bed talking on the phone. During the past week she had packed up most of the things she would take with her, and had moved into her study those things she did not want her sublessees to use. She would lock that door and keep the key. Almost magically the problems had been erased before her eyes. She was listening to her friend Jackie plead for her to reconsider her decision, and her mind was roaming over the things yet to be done. A cashier's check to open an account with in the village of Salmon Key, and more film and printing paper . . .

"Jackie, it's not as if I were a child who never left home before," she said, trying to keep the edge off her voice. "And, I tell you, I am sick and tired of teaching. I hadn't realized how tired of it I was until I quit. My God! Those term papers!"

She was grateful a moment later when the doorbell cut the phone call short. "Lunch? Sure. I'll be there," she said and hung up, and then went to open the door.

The man was close to six feet, but stooped; he had a big face. She seldom had seen features spread out quite as much as his were: wide-spaced eyes with heavy, long lashes and thick sable brown brows, a nose that would dominate a smaller face and a mouth that would fit on a jack-o'-lantern. The mouth widened even more when he smiled.

"Mrs. Taney? Could I have a few minutes to talk to you? My name is Hugh Lasater, from the Drug Enforcement Administration." He handed her his identification and she started to open the door; he held it to the few inches the chain allowed.

"Ma'am, if you don't mind. You study the I.D. and the picture, compare it to my pan, and then if it seems okay, you open the door." He had a pained expression as he said this.

She did as he directed, then admitted him, thinking he must be looking for an informant or something. She thought of the half-dozen vacant-eyed students in her classes; the thought was swiftly followed by relief that it no longer concerned her.

"What can I do for you, Mr. Lasater?" She motioned to a chair in a halfhearted way, hoping he would not accept the quasi-invitation.

"No one's here with you?"

She shook her head.

"Good." He took off his coat and hat and put them down on the sofa, then sank down into the chair she had indicated. "You almost ready to go?"

She started, but then, glancing about the apartment, decided anyone with an eye could tell she was going somewhere. "Yes. Next week I'm going on a trip."

"I know. Oregon. Salmon Key. The Donleavy house on Little Salmon Creek."

This time when she reacted with surprise, the chill was like a lump of ice deep within her. "What do you want, Mr. Lasater?"

"How'd you learn that trick?" he asked with genuine curiosity. "You never had any intelligence training."

"I don't know what you're talking about. If you'll just state your business. As you can see, I'm quite busy."

"It's a dandy thing to know. You just step back a little and watch from safety, in a manner of speaking. Useful. Damned off-putting to anyone not familiar with it. And you're damned good at it."

She waited. He knew, she thought, that inside she was frozen: her way of handling anger, fear, indignation? Later she would analyze the different emotions. And Hugh Lasater, she realized, was also back a little, watching, calculating, appraising her all the way.

"Okay, I'll play it straight," he said then. "No games, no appeal to loyalty, or your sense of justice, or anything else. We, my department and I, request your help in a delicate matter. We want you to get fingerprints from a suspect for us."

She laughed in relief. "You aren't serious."

"Oh yes, deadly serious. The Donleavy house is just a hop away from another place that sits on the next cliff overlooking the ocean. And in that other house is a man we're after quite seriously. But we have to make certain. We can't tip him that we're onto him. We need someone so innocent, so unlikely that he'll never give her a second thought. You pass him a picture to look at; he gives it back and you put it away carefully in an envelope we provide. Finis. That's all we want. If he's our man, we put a tail on him and let him lead us to others even more important and nab them all. They're smuggling in two thirds of all the coke and hash and opium being used in the States today."

He knew he had scored because her face became so expressionless that it might have been carved from wax. It was the color of something that had died a long time ago.

"That's contemptible," she said in a low voice.

"I'm sorry," he replied. "I truly am. But we are quite desperate."

She shook her head. "Please go," she said in a low voice. In a flash the lump of ice had spread; her frozen body was a thing apart. She had learned to do this in analysis, to step out of the picture to observe herself doing crazy things — groping for pills in an alcoholic fog, driving eighty miles an hour after an evening in a bar . . . It was a good trick, he was right. It had allowed her to survive then; it would get her through the next few minutes until he left.

"Mrs. Taney, your kid wasn't the only one, and every day there are more statistics to add to the mess. And they'll keep on being added day after day after day. Help us put a stop to it."

"You have enough agents. You don't need to drag in someone from outside."

"I told you, it has to be someone totally innocent, someone there with a reason beyond doubting. You'll get your pictures and your story, that's legitimate enough. The contracts are good. No one will ever know you helped us." He stood up and went to his overcoat and took a large insulated envelope from the inside pocket. "Mrs. Taney, we live in the best of times and the worst of times. We want to squash that ring of genteel import- ers. People like that are making these the worst of times. It's a dirty business; okay, I grant you that. But Mike's death was dirtier. Twelve years old, overdosed. That's pretty damned filthy." He put the envelope down on the end table by the sofa. "Let them make the first move. Don't try to force yourself on them in any way. There's Saul Werther, about sixty-two or -three, cultured, kindly, probably lonesome as hell by now. And a kid he has with him, cook, driver, handyman, bodyguard, who knows? Twenty-one at the most, Chicano. They'll want to know who you are and why you're there. No secret about you, the magazine story, the eagles, it's all legitimate as hell. They'll buy it. You like music, so does Werther. You'll get the chance. Just wait for it and then take advantage of it. Don't make a big deal of not messing up his prints if he handles a picture, a glass, whatever. Don't handle it unnecessarily either. There's some wrapping in the envelope, put it around the object loosely first, then pop it in the envelope and put it away. We'll be in touch."

Now he put the coat on. At the door, he looked back at her. "You'll do fine, Lyle. You really will. And maybe you'll be able to accept that you're getting back at them just a little bit. It might even help."

◧ **2** ◨

BRILLIANT GREEN moss covered the tree trunks; ferns grew
in every cranny, on the lower dead limbs, on the moss, every
inch of space between the trees. Nowhere was any ground visible,
or any rock; all was hidden by the mosses and ferns. Evergreen
bushes made impenetrable thickets in spots where the trees had
been cut in the past, or a fire had raged. Logging had stopped
years ago and now the trees were marching again, overtaking
the shrubs, defeating them, reclaiming the steep hills. Raindrops
glistened on every surface, shimmered on the tips of the emerald
fronds; the air was blurred with mist. The rain made no sound,
was absorbed by the mosses, transferred to the ground below
efficiently, silently.

Lyle sat on a log and listened to the silence of the woods
on this particular hill. The silences varied, she had learned; almost always the surf made the background noise, but here it
was inaudible. This was like a holding-your-breath silence, she
decided. No wind moved the trees, nothing stirred in the under-
growth, no birds called or flew. It was impossible to tell if the
rain had stopped; often it continued under the trees long after
the skies had cleared. She got up, and for another half-hour,
climbed to the top of the hill. It had been a steep climb, but a
protected one; here on the crest the wind hit her. Sea wind,
salt wind, fresh yet filled with strange odors. The rain had
stopped. She braced herself against the trunk of a tree twisted
out of shape, with sparse growth clinging to the tip ends of its
branches. She was wearing a dark green poncho, rain pants of
the same color over her woolen slacks, high boots, a woolen
knit hat pulled low on her forehead and covered with the poncho
hood. A pair of binoculars was clipped to her belt under the
poncho. She took them out and began to study the surrounding
trees, the other hilltops that now were visible, the rocks of a
ledge with a drop of undetermined distance, because the gorge,
or whatever it was, was bathed in mist. She did not spot the
nest.

She turned the glasses toward the ocean and for a long time

looked seaward. A new storm was building. A boat so distant that it remained a smudge, even with the full magnification, was stuck to the horizon. She hoped that, if it was a fishing boat, it made port before the storm hit. There had been two storms so far in the sixteen days she had been in Oregon. It still thrilled and frightened her to think of the power, the uncontrollable rage of the sea under storm winds. It would terrify her to be out there during such a storm. As she watched, the sea and sky became one and swallowed the boat. She knew the front would be racing toward shore, and she knew she would be caught if she returned to her house the way she had come. She stepped back under the trees and mentally studied the map of this day's search. She could go back along the western slope of the hill, skirt the gorge (it was a gorge cut by a tiny fierce stream), and follow it until it met Little Salmon Creek, which would lead her home. It was rough, but no rougher than any other trail in these jagged hills that went up and down as if they had been designed by a first-grader.

The wind blew harder, its cutting edge sharp and cold. Her face had been chapped ever since day one here, and she knew today would not improve matters. She started down the rugged hillside, heading toward the creek gorge. The elevation of this peak was one thousand feet; her cabin was one hundred feet above sea level. She began to slide on wet mosses, and finally stopped when she reached out to grasp a tree trunk. Going down would be faster than getting up had been, she thought grimly, clutching the tree until she got her breath back. The little creek plunged over a ledge to a pool fifteen or twenty feet below; she had to detour to find a place to get down the same distance. "A person could get killed," she muttered, inching down on her buttocks, digging in her heels as hard as she could, sliding a foot or so at a time.

The trees were fir, pine, an occasional alder, an even rarer oak, and at the margins of the woods, huckleberries, blueberries, blackberries, Oregon grapes, raspberries, salmonberries, elderberries . . . She could no longer remember the long list of wild plants. They grew so luxuriantly that they appeared to be growing on top of and out of each other, ten feet high, twenty feet. She never had seen such a profusion of vines.

Down, down, slipping, sliding, lowering herself from tree trunk to tree trunk, clinging to moss-covered rocks, feeling for a toe-hold below, sometimes walking gingerly on the scree at the edge of the creek when the berry bushes were impenetrable. Always downward. At last she reached a flat spot, and stopped to rest. She had come down almost all the way. She no longer had any chance of beating the storm; she would be caught and drenched. Now all she hoped was that she could be off the steep hill before it struck with full force. She looked seaward; there were only trees that were being erased by mist and clouds, leaving sugges-tive shadows. Then she gasped. There was the nest!

As Mal Levinson had said, it was hard to hide an eagle's nest. It was some distance from her, down a ravine, up the other side, a quarter of a mile or perhaps a little more. The rolling mist was already blurring its outlines. Impossible to judge its size, but big. It had to be old, used year after year, added to each new season. Eight feet across? She knew any figures from this distance were meaningless, but she could not stop the calcu-lations. Half as deep as it was wide, four by eight then. It crowned a dead pine tree. A gust of wind hit her, lifted her hood, and now she realized that for some time she had been hearing the roar of the surf. She got up and started to make the final descent. In a few moments she came to the place where the little creek joined the larger one, and together they crashed over a rocky outcropping. Now she knew exactly where she was. She stayed as close to the bank of the creek as she could, searching for a place where she could cross. Farther down, near her cabin, she knew it was possible, but difficult because in its final run to the sea the creek was cutting a deep channel through the cliffs.

How lucky, she was thinking, to find the nest this close to her own place. The two creeks came together at the two-hundred-foot altitude, child's play after scrambling up and down one-thousand-foot peaks. Less than a mile from the cabin, it would be nothing to go back and forth, pack in her gear . . . She stopped suddenly and now felt a chill that the wind had not induced in her. There was the other house, Werther's house. The nest was almost in his back yard.

The boy appeared, coming from the garage carrying a grocery bag. He waved and, after a brief hesitation, she waved back, then continued to follow the creek down to the bridge where tons of boulders and rocks of all sizes had been dumped to stabilize the banks for the bridge supports.

The rain started as she approached the bridge, and she made her way down the boulders with the rain blinding and savaging her all the way. The creek was no more than a foot deep here, but very swift, white water all the way to the beach. Normally she would have picked her way across it on the exposed rocks, but this time she plunged in, trusting her boots to be as water-proof as the manufacturer claimed.

She had forgotten, she kept thinking in disbelief. She had forgotten about Werther and his young driver/cook/bodyguard. At first it had been all she had thought about, but then, with day after day spent in the wet woods, climbing, slipping, sliding, searching, it was as if she had developed amnesia, and for a week or longer she had not thought of them at all. It was the same feeling she had had only a few days ago, she realized, when she had come upon a bottle of sleeping pills and had looked at it without recognition. Then, as now, it had taken an effort to remember.

She made her way up her side of the boulders; five hundred feet away was her cabin dwarfed by rhododendrons. Wearily she dragged herself toward it, turning once to glance briefly at the other house, knowing it was not visible from here, but looking anyway. The boy had walked to the edge of the creek, was watching her; he waved again, and then ran through the rain back toward his own house, disappearing among the trees and bushes that screened it.

Spying on her? That openly? Maybe he had been afraid she would fall down in the treacherous shallow stream. Maybe he thought she had fallen many times already; she considered how she looked: muddy, bedraggled, dripping, red-faced from wind-burn and cold. She looked like a nut, she thought, a real nut.

She found the key under the planter box and let herself in. The cabin was cold and smelled of sea air and salt and decay. Before she undressed, she made up the fire in the wood stove and put water on to boil for coffee. She wished she had not seen the boy, that he had not spoiled this moment of triumph, that the nest was not in Werther's back yard almost, that Lasater had never . . . She stopped herself. She wished for golden wings.

"Don't waste perfectly good wishes on mundane things," her father had said to her once when she had still been young enough to sit on his lap.

She was smiling slightly then as she pulled off her boots; her feet were wet and cold. Ah well, she had expected that, she thought sourly. She made the coffee, then showered, and examined new bruises acquired that day. She had not lost weight, she thought, surveying herself, but she was shifting it around a lot. Her waist was slimming down, while, she felt certain, her legs were growing at an alarming rate. She would have legs like a sumo wrestler after a few more weeks of uphill, downhill work. Or like a mountain goat. She pulled on her warmest robe and rubbed her hair briskly, then started to make her dinner.

She sniffed leftover soup, shrugged, and put it on to heat, scraped mold off a piece of cheese, toasted stale bread, quartered an apple, and sat down without another thought of food. As she ate, she studied her topographic map, then drew in a circle around the spot where she knew the nest was. As she had suspected, it was less than half a mile from Werther's house, but not visible from it because of the way the land went up and down. There was a steep hill, then a ravine, then a steeper hill, and it was the flank of the second hill that the eagle had chosen for a building site.

She started in surprise when there was a knock on the door. No one had knocked on that door since her arrival. She looked down at herself. She was in a heavy flannel robe and fleece-lined moccasins. Her hair was still wet from the shower and out every which way from her toweling it. Her wet and muddy clothes were steaming on chairs drawn close to the stove. Everywhere there were books, maps, notebooks; her typewriter was on an end table, plugged into an extension cord that snaked across the room. Mail was stacked on another end table; it had been stacked, now it was in an untidy heap, with a letter or two on the floor where they had fallen when the stack had leaned too far.

"What the hell," she muttered, stepping over the extension cord to open the door.

It was the boy from Werther's house. He grinned at her. He

was a good-looking kid, she thought absently, trying to block his view of the room. It was no good, though, he was tall enough to see over her head. His grin deepened. He had black hair with a slight wave, deep brown eyes, beautiful young skin. A heart throb, she thought, remembering the phrase from her school years.

"I caught a lot of crabs today," he said, and she saw the package he was carrying. "Mr. Werther thought you might like some." He held out the package.

She knew he had seen the remains of her dinner, her clothes, everything. No point in pretending now. She held the door open and stepped back. "Would you like to come in? Have a cup of coffee?"

"Thanks," he said, shaking his head. "I have to go back and make our dinner."

She took the package. "Thank you very much. I appreciate this."

He nodded and left in the rain. He had come through the creek, she realized, the same way she had come. Actually it was quicker than getting a car down the steep driveway, onto the road, up her equally steep driveway. Over a mile by road, less than half a mile on foot. She closed the door and took the package to the sink. The crabs, two of them, had been steamed and were still warm. Her mouth was watering suddenly, although she had eaten what she thought was enough at the time. She melted butter, then slowly ate again, savoring each bite of the succulent crab meat. Werther, or the boy, had cracked the legs just enough; she was able to get out every scrap. When she finished, she sat back sighing with contentment. She was exhausted, her room was a sty, but she had found the nest. It had been a good day.

And Lasater? She scowled, gathered up her garbage and cleared it away. Damn Lasater.

◻ 3 ◻

FOR THE NEXT three days she studied the area of the nest minutely. There was no good vantage point actually for her to stake out as her own. The pine spur was at the end of a ravine that was filled with trees and bushes. Nowhere could she see through the dense greenery for a clear view of the nest. She had to climb one hill after another, circling the ravine, keeping the nest in sight, looking for a likely place to put her lean-to, to set up her tripod, to wait. She finally found a site, about four feet higher than the nest, on a hillside about one hundred feet from it, with a deep chasm between her and the nest. She unslung her backpack and took out the tarpaulin and nylon cords, all dark green, and erected the lean-to, fastening it securely to trees from all four corners. It would have to do, she decided, even though it stood out like a beer can in a mountain brook. She had learned, in photographing hawks, that most birds would accept a lean-to, or wooden blind even, if it was in place before they took up residence. During the next week or so the lean-to would weather, moss would cover it, ferns grow along the ropes, a tree or two sprout to hide the flap . . . She took a step back to survey her work, and nodded. Fine. It was fine and it would keep her dry, she decided, and then the rain started again.

Every three or four days a new front blew in from the Pacific bringing twenty-foot waves, thirty-foot waves or even higher, crashing into the cliffs, tearing out great chunks of beach, battling savagely with the pillars, needles, stacks of rock that stood in the water as if the land were trying to sneak out to sea. In the thick rain forests the jagged hills broke up the wind; the trees broke up the rain, cushioned its impact, so that by the time it reached the mosses, it was almost gentle. The mosses glowed and bulged with the bounty. The greens intensified. It was like being in an underwater garden. Lyle made her way down the hillside with the cold rain in her face, and she hardly felt it. The blind was ready; she was ready; now it would be a waiting game. Every day she would photograph the nest, and compare the pictures each night. If one new feather was added, she would know. The eagles could no more conceal their presence than they could conceal their nest.

When she reached her side of the bridge again, she crossed the road and went out to the edge of the bluff that overlooked the creek and the beach. The roar of surf was deafening; there was no beach to be seen. This storm had blown in at high tide and waves thundered against the cliffs. The bridge was seventy-five feet above the beach, but spray shot up and was blown across it again and again as the waves exploded below. Little Salmon Creek dropped seventy-five feet in its last mile to the beach, with most of the drop made in a waterfall below the bridge; now Little Salmon Creek was being driven backward and was rising. Lyle stood transfixed, watching the spectacular storm, until the light failed, and the sounds of crashing waves, of driftwood logs twenty feet long being hurled into bridge pilings, of wind howling through the trees, all became frightening and she turned and hurried toward her cabin. She caught a motion from the cliff on the other side of the bridge and she could make out the figure of a watcher there. He was as bundled up as she was, and the light was too feeble by then to be able to tell if it was the boy or Werther.

The phone was ringing when she got inside and pushed the door closed against the wind that rushed through with her. Papers stirred with the passage, then settled again. She had to extract the telephone from under a pile of her sweaters she had brought out to air because things left in the bedroom tended to smell musty. The wood stove and a small electric heater in her darkroom were the only heat in the cabin.

"Yes," she said, certain it was a wrong number.

"Mrs. Taney, this is Saul Werther. I wonder if I can talk you into having dinner with me this evening. I'd be most happy if you will accept. Carmen will be glad to pick you up in an hour and take you home again later."

She felt a rush of fear that drained her. *Please*, she prayed silently, *not again. Don't start again.* She closed her eyes hard.

"Mrs. Taney, forgive me. We haven't really met, I'm your neighbor across the brook," he said, as if reminding her he was still on the line. "We watched the storm together."

"Yes, of course. I'd . . . Thank you. I'll be ready in an hour."

For several minutes she stood with her hand on the phone. It had happened again, the first time in nearly four years. It had been Werther on the phone, but she had heard Mr. Hendrickson's voice. "Mrs. Taney, I'm afraid there's been an accident . . ." And she had known. It had been as if she had known even before the telephone rang that evening; she had been waiting for confirmation, nothing more. Fear, grief, shock, guilt: she had been waiting for a cause, for a reason for the terrible emotions that had gripped her, that had been amorphously present for an hour and finally settled out only with the phone call. No one had believed her, not Gregory, not the psychiatrist, and she would have been willing to disbelieve, yearned to be able to disbelieve, but could not, because now and then, always with a meaningless call, that moment had swept over her again. She had come to recognize the rush of emotions that left her feeling hollowed out, as the event was repeated during the next year and a half after Mike's death. And then it had stopped, until now. "Mrs. Taney, I'm afraid there's been an accident. Your son . . ."

She began to shiver, and was able to move again. She had to get out of her wet clothes, build up the fire, shower . . . This was Lasater's doing. He had made the connection in her mind between Werther, drugs, Mike's death. He had reached inside her head with his words and revived the grief and guilt she had thought was banished. Clever Mr. Lasater, she thought grimly. He had known she would react, not precisely how, that was expecting too much even of him. He had known Werther would make the opening move. If Werther was involved with drug smuggling, she wanted him dead, just as dead as her child was, and she would do all she could to make him dead. Even as she thought it, she knew Lasater had counted on this too.

Hugh Lasater drove through the town of Salmon Key late that afternoon, before the storm hit. He and a companion, Milton Follett, had been driving since early morning, up from San Francisco in a comfortable, spacious motor home.

"It's the hills that slowed us down," Hugh Lasater said. "The freeway was great, and then we hit the coastal range. Should have been there by now."

Milton Follett was slouched down low in his seat; he did not glance at the town as they went through. "Could have called," he grumbled, as he had done several times in the past hour or so. He was in his midthirties, a blond former linebacker whose muscles were turning to flab.

"Thought of that," Hugh Lasater said. "Decided against it. Little place like this, who knows how the lines are connected, who might be listening? Anyway I might have to apply a little pressure."

"I think it's a bust. She's stringing you along."

"I think you're right. That's the reason I might have to apply a little pressure."

He drove slowly, collecting information: Standard Gas, attached gift shop; Salmon Key Restaurant and Post Office, a frame building painted red; Reichert's Groceries, having a canned food sale — corn 3/1.00, tomatoes, beans, peas 4/1.00; Tomseth Motel, closed; a sign for a lapidary shop; farmers' market and fish stand, closed . . . Tourist town, closed for the season. There were a few fishing boats docked behind the farmers' market, and space at the dock for four times as many, unused for a long time apparently. A dying fishing town, surviving now with tourist trade a few months out of the year. Lasater had seen numberless towns like this one; he touched the accelerator and left the dismal place behind and started up another hill.

"Sure could have used a road engineer and a few loads of dynamite," he said cheerfully, shifting down for the second time on the steep incline. The hill rose five hundred feet above sea level, reached a crest and plunged down the other side. He did not shift into higher gear as he went down. The wind was starting to shake the monster, forcing him to hold the steering wheel around at an unnatural position for a straight road. The wind let up, and the vehicle rebounded. He slowed down more.

"Another mile's all," he said. "We'll be in camp in time to see the storm hit."

"Terrific," Milton growled.

Lasater made the turn off the highway onto a narrow gravel

road that was steeper than anything he had driven that day. The trees had been shaped here by the nearly constant wind and sea spray; there were stunted pines and dense thickets of low, contorted spruces. The motor home was vibrating with the roar of the ocean and the explosive crashes of waves on cliffs. There were other people already in the state park; a couple of campers, a van, and even a tent. As they pulled into the camping area a sleek silver home-on-wheels pulled out. Lasater waved to the driver as they passed in the parking turn-around; he took the newly vacated spot.

Milton refused a walk with him, and he went alone to the ridge overlooking The Lagoon. That was its name, said so on the map, and there it was, a nearly perfect circle, a mile across, surrounded by cliffs, with a narrow stretch of beach that gave way to a basalt terrace which, at low tide, would be covered with tide pools. The lagoon was protected from the sea by a series of massive basalt rocks, like a coral reef barrier. Although they ranged from twenty to forty feet above water, the ocean was pouring over them now; the lagoon was flooded and was rising on the cliffs. Waves crashing into the barrier megaliths sent spray a hundred feet into the air.

He looked at the lagoon, then beyond it to the next hill. Over that one, down the other side was Werther's drive, then the bridge over Little Salmon Creek, and then her drive. Here we all are, he thought, hunching down in his coat as the wind intensity grew. Time to go to work, honey, he thought at Lyle Taney. You've had a nice vacation, now's time to knuckle down, make a buck, earn your keep.

He had no doubt that Lyle Taney would do as he ordered, eventually. She was at a time of life when she would be feeling insecure, he knew. She had chucked her job, and if he threatened to pull the rug from under her financially, she would stand on her head on any corner he pointed to. He knew how important security was to a woman like Lyle Taney. Even when she had had a reason to take a leave of absence, she had held on grimly, afraid not to hold on because she had no tenure, no guarantees about tomorrow. He had imagined her going over the figures again and again, planning to the day when her savings would be gone, if she had to start using that stash, trying to estimate royalties to the penny, stretching that money into infinity. He understood women like Taney, approaching middle age, alone, supporting themselves all the way. It was fortunate that she was nearing middle age. The kid was too young to interest her, and Werther too old; no sexual intrigues to mess up the scenario. He liked to keep things neat and simple. Money, security, revenge, those were things that were manipulable. They were real things, not abstracts, not like loyalty or faith. He did not believe a woman could be manipulated through appeals to loyalty or faith. They were incapable of making moral or ethical decisions. They did not believe in abstracts. Maternal devotion, security, money, revenge, that was what they understood, and this time it had worked out in such a way that those were the very things he could dangle before her, or threaten. Oh, she would do the job for him. He knew she would. He began to hum and stopped in surprise when he realized it was a tune from his boyhood, back in the forties. He grinned. Who would have thought a song would hang out in a mind all those years to pop out at just the right moment? He sang it to himself on his way back to the motor home: "They're either too young or too old/ They're either too gray or too grassy green . . ."

□ 4 □

WERTHER'S HOUSE was a surprise to Lyle. It was almost as messy as her own, and with the same kind of disorder: papers, books, notebooks, a typewriter. His was on a stand on wheels, not an end table, but that was a minor detail. Carmen was almost laughing at her reaction.

"I told Mr. Werther that I thought you would be very simpatico," he said, taking her coat.

Then Werther came from another room, shook her hand warmly, and led her to the fireplace.

"It's for a book I've wanted to do for a long time," he said, indicating the jumble of research materials. "A history of a single idea from the first time it's mentioned in literature, down to its present-day use, if any. Not just one idea, but half a dozen, a dozen. I'm afraid I keep expanding the original concept as I come across new and intriguing lines of inquiry." His face twisted in a wry expression. "I'd like to get rid of some of this stuff, but there's nowhere to start. I need it all."

He was five feet eight or nine and stocky; not fat or even plump, but well muscled and heavy boned. He gave the impression of strength. His hair was gray, a bit too long, as if he usually forgot to have it cut, not as if he had intended it to be modish. His eyes were dark blue, so dark that at first glance she had thought them black. He had led her to a chair by the fireplace; there was an end table by it with a pile of books. He lifted the stack, looked about helplessly, then put it on the floor by the side of the table. *A History of Technology*, Plato's *Republic*, a volume of Plato's dialogues, Herodotus, Kepler . . . There was a mountainous stack of the *New York Times*.

Many of the books in the room were opened, some with rocks holding the pages down; others had strips of paper for bookmarks.

"My problem is that I'm not a writer," Werther said. "It's impossible to organize so much material. One wants to include it all. But you . . ." He rummaged through a pile of books near his own chair and brought out her book on hawks. "What a delightful book this is! I enjoyed it tremendously."

"I'm not a writer either," she said quickly. "I teach — taught — history."

"That's what the jacket says. Ancient history. But you used the past tense."

Although there was no inflection, no question mark following the statement, she found herself answering as if he had asked. She told him about the magazine, and the book contract, the nest.

"And you simply quit when you couldn't get time off to do the next book. Doing the book on eagles was more important to you than remaining in your own field. I wonder that more historians don't lose faith."

She started to deny that she had lost faith in history, but the words stalled; he had voiced what she had not wanted to know. She nodded. "And you, Mr. Werther, what is your field? History also?"

"No. That's why my research is so pleasurable. I'm discovering the past. That's what makes your hawk book such a joy. It sings with discovery. It's buoyant because you were finding out things that gave you pleasure; you in turn invested that pleasure in your words and thoughts and shared it with your readers."

She could feel her cheeks burn. Werther laughed gently.

"What capricious creatures we are. We are embarrassed by criticism, and no less embarrassed by praise. And you have found your eagle's nest after all those days of searching. Congratulations. At first, when you moved in next door, I thought you were a spy. But what a curious spy, spending every day getting drenched in a rain forest!"

"And I thought you were a smuggler," she said, laughing with him, but also watching, suddenly wary again.

"The lagoon would make a perfect spot for landing contraband, wouldn't it? Ah, Carmen, that looks delightful!"

Carmen carried two small trays; he put one down at Lyle's elbow on the end table, and the other one within Werther's reach, perched atop a stack of books. There was wheat-colored wine, a small bowl of pink Pacific shrimp, a dip, cheese, crackers . . .

"I've never tasted such good shrimp as these," Werther said, spearing one of the tidbits. "I could live on the seafood here."

"Me too," Lyle agreed. The wine was a very dry sherry, so good it made her want to close her eyes and savor it. The fire burned quietly, and Carmen made cooking noises that were obscured by a door. Werther had become silent now, enjoying the food; outside, the wind howled and shook the trees, rattled rhododendrons against the windows, whistled in the chimney. It was distant, no longer menacing; through it all, behind it, now and then overwhelming the other sounds, was the constant roar of the surf. She thought of the pair of eagles: where were they now? Were they starting to feel twitches that eventually would draw them back to the nest?

Werther sighed. "Each of us may well be exactly what the other thought at first, but that's really secondary, isn't it? How did you, a history professor, become involved with hawks?"

She brought herself back to the room, back to the problem Lasater had dumped in her lap. Slowly she said, "Five years ago my son, he was twelve, took something one of the boys in his class had bought from a drug dealer. There were twenty boys involved, three of them died, several of them suffered serious brain damage. Mike died."

Her voice had gone very flat in the manner of one reading a passage in a foreign language without comprehension. She watched him as she talked. She could talk about it now; that was what she had accomplished under Dr. Himbert. She had learned how to divide herself into pieces, and let one of the pieces talk about it, about anything at all, while the rest of her stayed far away hidden in impenetrable ice.

Werther was shocked, she thought, then angry. One of his hands made a movement toward her, as if to touch her — to silence her? or share her grief? She could not tell.

"If you're not with young people, children, you don't realize," she said slowly. "They've changed. They don't seem to value life the way my generation did. I used to ask my class what they saw themselves doing in five years, ten years. They looked at me as if I had gone mad. They wouldn't be around that long, they said, again and again. The world was going to be blown up before then; if they were alive at all, they'd be scratching for a living, digging in the ruins . . ." She shook herself. "Mike thought that. We talked about it. I tried to make him believe there was hope, a future. I don't think I ever got through to him. They had a game they played, Mike, his friends. It was called After the Bomb. An adventure game where they had to survive any way they could. It was horrible. I realized later that he hadn't believed a word I said. My students don't — didn't — believe me. They see a different world. Maybe a realer world. I don't know. It's a world of hatred and destruction and evil. A world where experimenting with drugs doesn't seem to be taking such a terrible chance. Today, or next year . . . It's all the same to them."

"And you turned to the world of hawks where there is no good or evil, only necessity."

She felt bathed in the warmth of his words suddenly, as if his compassion were a physical, material substance that he had wrapped around her securely. He knew, she thought. He understood. That was exactly what she had looked for, had needed desperately, something beyond good and evil. Abruptly she looked away from his penetrating and too understanding gaze. She wanted to tell him everything, she realized in wonder, and she could tell him everything. He would not condemn her. Quickly then she continued her story, trying to keep her voice indifferent.

"I found I couldn't stay in our apartment over weekends and holidays after that. My husband and I had little reason to stay together, and he left, went to California, where he's living now. I began to tramp through the woods, up and down the Appalachian Trail, things like that. One day I got a photograph of a hawk in flight, not the one on the cover, not that nice, but it made me want to get more. Over the next couple of years I spent all my spare time pursuing hawks. And I began to write the book."

Werther was nodding. "Therapy. And what good therapy it was for you. No doctor could have prescribed it. You are cured."

Again it was not exactly a question; it demanded no answer. And again she felt inclined to respond as if it had been. "I'm not sure," she said. "I had a breakdown, as you seem to have guessed. I hope I'm cured."

"You're cured," he said again. He got up and went to a sideboard where Carmen had left the decanter of wine. He refilled both their glasses, then said, "If you'll excuse me a moment, I'll see how dinner's coming along. Carmen's a good cook, but sometimes he dawdles."

She studied the living room; it was large, with a dining area, and beyond that a door to the kitchen. The west wall was heavily draped, but in daylight with the drapes open, it would overlook the sea, as her own living room did. Probably there was a deck; there was an outside door on that wall. One other door was closed, to the bedroom area, she guessed. The plan was very like the plan of her cabin, but the scale was bigger. Both were constructed of redwood, paneled inside, and broad plank floors with scatter rugs. She began to look through the piles of magazines on tables: science magazines, both general and specialized. Molecular biology, psychology, physics . . . History journals —

some probably had papers of hers. There was no clue here, or so many clues that they made no sense. It would be easy to pick up a digest magazine or two, slip them in her purse, put them in the envelope, and be done with it.

But he wasn't a smuggler, she thought clearly. Lasater had lied. She picked up a geology book dog-eared at a chapter about the coast range.

"Are you interested in geology?" Werther asked coming up behind her.

"I don't know a thing about it," she admitted, replacing the book.

"According to the most recent theory, still accepted it's so recent, there are great tectonic plates underlying the rock masses on earth. These plates are in motion created by the thermal energy of the deeper layers. Here along the coast, they say, two plates come together, one moving in from the sea, the other moving northward. The one coming in from the west hits the other one and dives under it, and the lighter materials are scraped off and jumbled together to make the coast range. That accounts for the composition, they say. Andesite, basalt, garnetite, sandstone, and so on. Have you had a chance to do any beach combing yet?"

She shook her head. "Not yet. I'll have more time now that I've located the nest."

"Good. Let me take you to some of my favorite places. South of here. You have to be careful because some of those smaller beaches are cut off at high tide, and the cliffs are rather forbidding."

Carmen appeared then. "I thought you were going to sit down so I can serve the soup."

Carmen dined with them and his cooking was superb. When she complimented him, he said, "No, this is plain everyday family fare. I didn't know we were having company. Next time I'll know in advance. Just wait."

There was a clear broth with slices of water chestnut and bits of clam and scallions; a baked salmon stuffed with crab; crisp snow peas and tiny mushrooms; salad with a dressing that suggested olive oil and lime juice and garlic, but so faintly that she could not have said for certain that any or all of those ingredients had been used.

"And take Anaxagoras," Werther said sometime during that dinner, "nearly five hundred years before Christ! And he had formulated the scientific method, maybe not as precisely as Bacon was to do two thousand years later, and without the same dissemination, but there it was. He wrote that the sun was a vast mass of incandescent metal, that moonlight was reflected sunlight, that heavenly bodies were made incandescent by their rotational friction. He explained, in scientific terms, meteors, eclipses, rainbows . . ."

The ancient names rolled off his tongue freely, names, dates, places, ideas. "Empedocles identified the four elements: air, earth, fire, and water, and even today we speak of a fiery temper, an airy disposition, blowing hot and cold, an earthy woman, the raging elements, battling the elements, elemental spirits . . . An idea, twenty-five hundred years old, and it's still in the language, in our heads, in our genes maybe."

Before dinner there had been the sherry, and with dinner there was a lovely Riesling, and then a sweet wine she did not know. She told herself that no one gets drunk on wine, especially along with excellent food, but, once again before the fire, she was having trouble following the conversation, and somewhere there was a soft guitar playing, and a savage wind blowing, and rain pounding the house rhythmically.

She realized she had been talking about Prometheus and Epimetheus, about herself, her lack of tenure and seeming inability to get tenure. "I'm not a hotshot scholar," she said, thinking carefully of the words, trying to avoid any that might twist her up too much. She thought: hotshot scholar, and knew she could never say it again. She knew also that if she repeated it to herself, she would start to giggle. The thought of breaking into giggles sobered her slightly.

"You're interested in what people thought," she said almost primly, "but we teach great movements, invasions, wars, successions of reign, and it's all irrelevant. The students don't care; they need the credit. It doesn't make any difference today, none of it."

"Why don't you do it right?"

"I'd have to go back to Go and start over, relearn everything. Unlearn everything. I've always been afraid. I don't even know what I'm afraid of."

"So you bailed out at the first chance. But now I think Carmen had better take you home. You can hardly keep your eyes open. It's the fresh air and wind and climbing these steep hills, I suspect."

She nodded. It was true, she was falling asleep. Suddenly she felt awkward, as if she had overstayed a visit. She glanced at her watch and was startled to find that it was eleven-thirty.

"Ready?" Carmen asked. He had her coat over his arm, had already put on a long poncho.

Werther went to the door with them. "Come back soon, my dear. It's been one of the nicest evenings I've had in a very long time."

She mumbled something and hurried after Carmen to the car. The wind had died down now, but the rain was steady.

"He meant it," Carmen said. "It's been a good evening for both of us."

"I enjoyed it too," she said, staring ahead at the rain-blurred world. The drive was very curvy; it wound around trees, downward to the road, and only the last twenty-five feet or so straightened out. It would be very dangerous if the rain froze. Down this last straightaway, then onto the highway, across it and over the cliff to the rocks below. She shivered. Carmen had the car in low gear, and had no trouble at all coming to a stop at the highway.

"Is he a doctor?" she asked. "Something he said tonight made me think he might be, or has been, a doctor." She shook her head in annoyance; she could not remember why she thought that.

"I think he studied medicine a while back, maybe even practiced. I don't know."

Of course, Carmen probably knew as little about his employer as she did. They had an easy relationship, and Carmen certainly had shown no fear or anxiety of any sort, but he was a hired man, hired to drive, to cook, to do odd jobs. They had arrived at her door.

"I'll come in and fix your fire," Carmen said, in exactly the same tone he had used to indicate that dinner was ready. There was nothing obsequious or subservient in him.

He added wood to the fire, brought in a few pieces from the porch, and then left, and she went to bed immediately and dreamed.

She was in a class, listening to a lecture. The professor was writing on the blackboard as he talked, and she was taking notes. She could not quite make out his diagrams, and she hitched her chair closer to the front of the room, but the other students hissed angrily at her and the teacher turned around to scowl. She squinted trying to see, but it was no use. And now she no longer could hear his words, the hissing still buzzed around her ears. The professor came to her chair and picked up her notebook; he looked at her notes, nodded, and patted her on the back. When he touched her, she screamed and fled.

She was on a narrow beach with a black shiny cliff behind her. She knew the tide had turned because the hissing had become a roar. She hurried toward a trail and stopped because Lasater was standing at the end of the beach where the rocks led upward like steps. She looked the opposite way and stopped again. Werther was there, dressed in tails and striped trousers, wearing a pale gray top hat. She heard a guitar and, looking up, she saw Carmen on a ledge playing. Help me, she cried to him. He smiled at her and continued to play. She raised her arms pleading for him to give her a hand, and the eagle swooped low and caught her wrists in its talons and lifted her just as the first wave crashed into the black cliff. The eagle carried her higher and higher until she no longer could see Werther or Lasater or the beach, the road, anything at all recognizable. Then the eagle let go and she fell.

◘ 5 ◘

HUGH LASATER waited until the Volvo came out of Werther's drive and turned north, heading for town, before he went up Lyle's driveway. There was heavy fog that morning, but the air was still and not very cold. The front of her house had a view of the ocean that must be magnificent when the weather was clear, and no doubt you had to be quick or you might miss it, he thought, gazing into the sea of fog, waiting for her to answer his knock.

Lyle was dressed to go out, boots, sweater, heavy slacks. She had cut her hair even shorter than it had been before. Now it was like a fuzzy cap on her head. He wondered if it was as soft as it looked. Silently she opened the door wider and moved aside for him to enter.

"How's it going?" he asked, surveying the room quickly, memorizing it in that one fast glance about. A real pig, he thought with a touch of satisfaction. It figured.

"Fine. I've found the nest."

He laughed and pulled a chair out from the table and sat down. "Got any coffee?"

She poured a cup for him; there was another cup on the table still half filled. She sat opposite him, pushed a map out of the way, closed a notebook. Her camera gear was on the table, as if she had been checking it out before leaving with it.

"Pretty lousy weather for someone who has to get out and work in it every day," he said. "Your face is really raw."

She shrugged and began to put the lenses in pockets of the camera bag. Her hands were very steady. She could keep the tension way down where it couldn't interfere with appearances. Lasater admired that. But the tension was there, he could feel it; it was revealed in the way that she had not looked at him once since opening the door. She had looked at the coffee cup, at the pot, at her stuff on the table. Now she was concentrating on packing her camera bag.

"Met Werther yet?" he asked casually.

"Yes. Once."

"And?"

"And nothing."

"Tell me about him." The coffee was surprisingly good. He got up and refilled his cup.

"You know more about him than I do."

"Not what he's like; how he talks, what he likes, what he's like inside. You know what I mean."

"He's educated, cultured, a scholar. He's gentle and kind."

"What did you talk about?"

He caught a momentary expression that flitted rapidly across her face. Something there, but what? He saved it for later.

"Ancient Greece."

"Lyle, loosen up, baby. I'm not going to bite or do anything nasty. Open up a little. Tell me something about the time you spent with him."

She shook her head. "I'm not working for you, or with you. I'm here doing a job for a magazine, and for my publisher. That's all."

"Uh-huh. It was the cover story, wasn't it? You don't buy it." He sighed and finished the last of the coffee. "Don't blame you. After seeing that state park I don't blame you a bit. Have to be an idiot to try to smuggle anything into that cove. Who'd of thought there'd be dopes camping out all winter. It's February for Christ's sake!"

"You admit you lied to me?" She knew he was playing with her, keeping her off guard, but she could not suppress the note of incredulity that entered her voice. She knew he was a master at this game, also, and she was so naive that she didn't even know when the play started, or what the goals were.

"What'd you talk about?"

She started again. There was more than a touch of confusion in her mind about what they had talked about for nearly five hours, and somehow she had revealed something to Hugh Lasater. Almost sullenly she said, "Philosophy, cuisines, the coast, geology. Nothing. It was nothing of any importance." She finished packing her camera case and stood up. "I have to go out now. I'm sorry I can't help you."

"Oh, you'll help," he said almost absently, thinking about the changes in her voice, subtle as they were. Although she had learned to step back, her voice was revealing in the way it changed timbre, the quickness of her words. He had it now, the cue to watch for.

"Have you read your contracts for the article and the book?"
She became silent again, frozen, waiting.

"You should. If you didn't bring copies with you, I have some. I'll drop them off later today, or send someone else with them."

"What are you threatening now?"

"You've got no job, kiddo, and the contracts have clauses in them that I doubt you'll be able to fulfill. I doubt seriously that you can get your story together within ninety days, starting nearly a month ago. And I doubt that you really meant you'd be willing to pay half your royalties to a ghostwriter. But you signed them, both of them. Honey, don't you ever read contracts before you sign them?"

"Get out of here," she said. "Just get out and leave me alone."

"People like you," he said, shaking his head sadly. "You are so ignorant it's painful. You don't know what's going on in the world you live in. You feel safe and secure, but, honey, you can feel safe and secure only because people like me are doing their jobs."

"Blackmailing others to do your jobs."

"But sometimes that's part of the job," he protested. "Look, Lyle, you must guess that this is an important piece of work, no matter what else you think. I mean, would anyone invest the kind of effort we've already put into it if it weren't important? We're counting on your loyalty — "

"Don't," she snapped. "Loyalty to what, to whom? In the middle ages the nobility all across Europe was loyal to nobility. The guilds were loyal to guilds. Peasants to peasants. Where's the loyalty of a multinational-corporation executive? Or the Mafia? Loyal to what? What makes you think there's anything at all you can tell me that I'd believe?"

"I'm not telling you anything," he said. "I know you won't believe me. Except this. He's a killer, Lyle. I didn't want to scare you off before . . ."

She pressed her hands over her ears. "So let the police arrest him and take him in for fingerprinting and questioning, the way they do other suspects."

"Can't. He has something stashed away somewhere and we want it. We want him to lead us to it. If he's our man. First that. Is he our man? We can't go inside his house for prints. There are dozens of ways of booby-trapping a place to let you know if someone has entered. A hair in a door that falls when the door's opened. A bit of fluff that blows away if someone moves near it. An ash on a door handle. A spiderweb across a porch. He'd know. And he'd bolt, or kill himself. That's what we want to avoid. A dive off a cliff. A bullet through his brain. A lethal pill. We want him very badly. Alive, healthy, and in his own house where he keeps his stuff. We'll put a hundred agents on him, follow him ten years if it takes that long. If he's our man. And we expect you to furnish something that'll let us find out if he is our man. Soon, Lyle." He paused, and when she did not respond, he said, "So you like the old fart. So what? Even the devil has admirers. There's never been a monster who didn't have someone appear as a character witness. You see it every day, the neighbors describing a homicidal psychopath as a nice, quiet, charming man, so kind to the children. Balls! Your pal is a killer resting between jobs. Period. You're in no danger, unless you blow it all in front of him. But I'll tell you this, I wouldn't underwrite life insurance on the kid with him."

She regarded him bitterly, not speaking.

He got up and went to the door. "I know, you're thinking why you. You didn't ask to get mixed up in something like this. Hell, I don't know why you. You were there. And you are mixed up in it. And I tell you this, Lyle baby. When it gets as big as this is, there's no middle ground. You're for us or against us. That simple. Be seeing you."

Hugh Lasater had known Werther/Rechetnik would turn up at the most recent molecular-biologists' conference in UCLA this past fall. He had counted on it the way he counted on Christmas, or income tax day. And Werther had not let him down any more than Santa had done when he was a kid. Werther had been there and left in his white Volvo with the kid driving him as if he were a president or something. Since that day in November he had been under surveillance constantly. Twice they had tried ploys designed to get positive identification, and each time they had failed. The kid paid the bills, did the shopping, drove the car. Werther wore gloves when he went out, and the house was booby-trapped. Turk had spotted a silk thread across the porch the first day Werther had left, and Turk had backed off exactly as he had been ordered.

The first time they tried to get his prints indirectly, it had been through the old dog of a routine telephone maintenance visit. The kid had refused the man admittance, said they didn't want the phone in the first place and didn't care if it was out. Period. No one insisted. The next time a young woman had literally run into Werther on the beach. She had been wearing a vinyl cape, pristine, spotless, ready to receive prints. Werther had caught her reflexively, steadied her, then had gone on his way, and Milton Follett had received the cape. Nothing. Smudges. Just as reflexive as his catching the girl had been, his act of smearing the prints must have been also.

There were two men in the Lagoon State Park at all times, one of them on high enough ground to keep the driveway under observation through daylight hours, and close enough at night to see a mouse scamper across the drive. Farther south there were two more men in the next state park. He was bottled up tight, and they still did not have positive identification.

They could have picked him up on suspicion of murder, staging the arrest, mug shots, prints, interrogation, everything, but Mr. Forbisher had explained patiently that without his papers Werther was simply another lunatic killer. He would surely commit suicide if cornered. They wanted it all in a neat package undamaged by rough handling. They wanted his papers.

It irked Lasater that no one would lay it all out, explain exactly what it was that Werther had. But Christ, he thought, it had to be big. Bigger than a new headache capsule. He suspected it was a cancer cure; the Nazis had used Werther's/Rechetnik's mother for cancer experiments, and he was getting his revenge. It had to be that, he sometimes thought, because what could be bigger than that? The pharmaceutical company that owned that secret would move right into the castle and be top of the heap for a long time to come. When he thought of the money they were already spending to get this thing — money they were willing to keep spending — it made his palms sweat. He did not really blame them for not telling him all of it; that was not how the game was played. All he needed to know, Mr. Forbisher had said primly, was that they wanted Werther, if he was actually Rechetnik; they wanted him intact with his papers. And Hugh Lasater had gone off looking for exactly the right person to put inside the house next door. Step one. He had come up with Lyle Taney.

◘ b ◘

SHE SAT with her knees drawn to her chin, staring moodily at the nest. She did not believe Lasater, and she knew it didn't matter if she did or not. She might never know the truth about him, she thought, still bitter and angry with Lasater, with herself for stepping into this affair.

She had read the contracts, and she had asked Bobby about the time, about other things Lasater hadn't brought up yet, but no doubt would if he felt he had to. Formalities, Bobby had said, don't worry about them. Basically, he had said, it was the same contract as her first one, with a few changes because the work was not even started yet. And she had signed. She had drawn out so much of her savings to pay for this trip, for the three-month's rental on the house, for the car she had leased. It takes a month to six weeks to get money loose from the company, Mal had said. You know how bureaucracies are. And she did know.

They must have investigated her thoroughly; they knew her financial situation, the bills she had accumulated during those wasted, lost years; they knew about Mike; they knew she would be willing and even eager to leave her job. She remembered one thing Werther had said, about historians losing faith in what they taught. He was perceptive, Lasater was perceptive, only she had been blind. She put her forehead down on her knees and pressed hard. She wanted to weep. Furiously, she lifted her head and stared at the nest again.

The sun had come out and the day was still and warm. Down on the beach there would be a breeze, but up here, sheltered by hills and trees, the air was calm and so clear she could see the bark on the pine spur that bore the eagles' nest.

"Mrs. Taney?" It was Carmen's voice in a hushed whisper.

She looked for him; he was standing near a tree as if ready to duck behind it quickly. "It's all right," she said. "The nest is still empty."

He climbed the rest of the way up and sat down by her, not all the way under the tarp. The sun lightened his hair, made it look almost russet. "You said last night that I could join you, see the nest. I hope you meant now, today. I brought you some coffee."

She thanked him as he took off a small pack and pulled a thermos from it. The coffee was steaming. He wore binoculars around his neck. She pointed and he aimed them at the nest and studied it for the next few minutes.

She had forgotten that he had asked if he could join her. She frowned at the coffee, trying to remember more of the conversation. Nothing more came.

"It's big, isn't it? How soon do you expect the eagles to come?"

"I'm not sure. They'll hang around, fixing up the nest, just fooling around for several weeks before they mate. Sometime in the next week or two, I should think."

He nodded. "Mr. Werther asked if you have to stay up here this afternoon. There's a place down the beach a few miles he'd like to show you. Beach combing's great after a storm, and there's gold dust on the beach there."

She laughed. "I don't have to stay at all. I took a few pictures, I was just . . . thinking." She started to check around her to make sure she had everything. "Have you been with him long?"

"Sometimes it seems a lifetime, then again like no time at all. Why do you ask?"

"Curious. You seem to understand him rather well."

"Yes. He's like a father. Someone you understand and accept and even love without questioning it or how you know so much about him. You know what I mean?"

"I think so. It's a package deal. You accept all or nothing."

"He's very wise," Carmen said, standing, reaching out to pull her to her feet. He was much stronger than his slender figure indicated. He looked at her and said, "I would trust him with my life, my honor, my future, without any hesitation." Then he turned and started down the hillside before her.

Just like Werther, she thought, following him down. He side-stepped questions just as Werther did, making it seem momentarily that he was answering, but giving nothing with any substance.

Lyle left her camera bag at Werther's house; they all got in the Volvo and Carmen drove down the coast a few miles. Here the road was nearly at sea level; water had covered it during the storm and there was still a mud slick on the surface. Carmen parked on a gravel turnoff, and they walked to the sandy beach. In some places the beach on this section of the coast was half a mile wide with pale, soft sand, then again it was covered with smooth, round, black rocks, or a sliver of sand gave way to the bony skeleton of ancient mountains; here the beach was wide and level, and it was littered with storm refuse.

"We'll make our way toward those rocks," Werther said, pointing south. The outline of the rocks was softened by mist, making it hard to tell how far away they were.

It took them five hours to get to the rocks and back. All along the way the storm detritus invited investigation. There were strands of seaweed, eighteen feet long, as strong as ropes; there were anemones and starfish and crabs in tide pools, all of them colored pink or purple, blue, green, red; there was a swath of black sand where Werther said there was probably gold also. It was often found in the heavy black sand; washed from the same deposits, it made its way downstream along with the dense black grains. They found no gold, but they might have, Lyle thought happily. She spied a blue ball and retrieved it. It was a Japanese fishing float, Werther said, examining it and handing it back. He talked about the fishing fleets, their lights like will-o'-the-wisps at sea. They had not used glass floats for thirty years, he said; the one she had found could have been floating all that time, finally making it to shore.

At one point Carmen produced sandwiches and a bottle of wine from his backpack, along with three plastic glasses. They sat on rocks, protected from a freshening breeze, and gazed at the blue waters of the Pacific. A flock of sea gulls drifted past and vanished around the outcropping of granite boulders.

"It's a beautiful world," Werther said quietly. "Such a beautiful world."

Carmen stood up abruptly and stalked away, he picked up something white and brought it back, flung it down at Werther's feet. It was half a Styrofoam cup.

"For how long?" he said in a hard furious voice. He picked up the wine bottle and glasses and replaced them in his backpack, then turned and left.

"You could bury it, but the next high tide will just uncover it again," Werther said, nudging the Styrofoam with his foot. He picked it up and put it in his pocket. "Speaking of high tides, we have to start back. The tide's turning now, I think."

They watched the sunset from the edge of the beach, near the car. The water covered their footprints, cleaning up the beach again of traces of human usage. It was dark by the time they got back to Werther's house.

"You must have dinner with us," he insisted. "You're too tired to go cook. You'll settle for a peanut butter sandwich and a glass of milk. I feel guilty just thinking about dinner while you snack. Sit by the fire and nurse your images of the perfect day and soon we'll eat."

Lyle looked at Carmen, who nodded, smiling at her. It was he who knew what she would eat if she went home now. She thought of what he had said about understanding and accepting Werther, and she had the feeling that he understood and accepted her also, exactly as she was, nearing middle age, red-faced, with frizzy hair going gray. None of that mattered a damn bit to him, not the way it mattered to Lasater, whose eyes held scorn and contempt no matter how he tried to disguise it. She nodded, and Carmen reached out to take her coat; Werther said something about checking the wine supply, and needing more wood. She sank into the chair that she thought of as hers and sighed.

Perhaps she could say to Werther, please just give me a set of good fingerprints and let's be done with that. She could explain why she needed them, tell him about the hook Lasater had baited for her and her eagerness to snatch it. He would understand, even be sympathetic with her reasons. And if he was the man Lasater was after, he would forgive her. She snapped her eyes open as a shudder passed over her. Lasater was sure, and she was too. She felt only certainty that Werther lived under a fearsome shadow. She felt that he was a gentle man, whose gentleness arose from a terrible understanding of pain and fear; that underlying his open love of the ocean, the beach, the gulls, everything he had seen that day, there was a sadness with a depth she could not comprehend. She believed that his compassion, humanity, love, warmth, all observable qualities, overlay a core as rigid and unweathered and unassailable as the rocky skeletons of the mountains that endured over the eons while everything about them was worn away. He was a man whose convictions would lead him to action, had already led him to act, she thought, and admitted to herself that she believed he was wanted for something very important, not what Lasater said, because he was a congenital liar, but something that justified the manhunt that evidently was in progress. And she knew with the same certainty that she had been caught up in the middle of it, that already it was too late for her to exclude herself from whatever happened here on the coast. Unless she left immediately, she thought then.

"You're cold," Carmen said, as if he had been standing behind her for some time. He was carrying wood. "These places really get cold as soon as the sun goes down." He added a log to the fire, tossed in a handful of chips, and in a moment it was blazing. "You're in for a treat. He's going to make a famous old recipe for you. Fish soup, I call it. He says bouillabaisse." He stood up, dusting his hands together. "Be back instantly with wine. Do you want a blanket or something?"

She shook her head. The shiver had not been from any external chill. Presently, with Carmen on the floor before the fire, and her in her chair, they sipped the pale sherry in a companionable silence.

Carmen broke it: "Let's play a game. Pretend you're suddenly supreme dictator with unlimited power and wealth, what would you do?"

"Dictator of what?"

"Everything, the entire earth."

"You mean God."

"Okay. You're God. What now?"

She laughed. Freshman games out of Philosophy 101. "Oh, I'd give everyone enough money to live on comfortably, and I'd put a whammy on all weapons, make them inoperative, and I'd cure the sick, heal the wounded. Little things like that."

He shook his head. "Specifically. And seriously." He looked up at her without a trace of a smile. "I mean if everyone had X dollars, then it would take XY dollars to buy limited things, and it would simply be a regression of the value of money, wouldn't it?"

"Okay, I'd redistribute the money and the goods so that everyone had an equal amount, and if that wasn't enough, I'd add to both until it was enough."

"How long before a handful of people would have enormous amounts again, and many people would be hungry again simply because human nature seems to drive some people to power through wealth."

She regarded him sourly. He was at an age when his idealism should make it seem quite simple to adjust the world equitably. She said, "God, with any sense at all, would wash Her hands of the whole thing and go somewhere else."

"But you, as God, would not be that sensible?"

"No. I'd try. I would think for a very long time about the real problems — overpopulation, for instance — and I'd try to find a way to help. But without any real hope of success."

He nodded, and a curious intensity seemed to leave him. She had not realized how tense he had become until he now relaxed again.

Very deliberately she said, "Of course, solving the population problems doesn't mean it would be a peaceful world. Sometimes I think history was invented simply to record war, and before records, there were oral traditions. Even when the world was uninhabited except for a few fertile valleys, they fought over those valleys. There will always be people who want what others have, who have a need to control others, who have a need for power. Population control won't change that."

"As God you could pick your population," Carmen said carelessly. "Select for nonaggressiveness."

"How? With what test? But, as God, I would know, wouldn't I?"

"There would be problems," he said, looking into the fire now. "That's why I started this game saying dictator; you said God. Where does assertiveness end and aggressiveness start? There are real problems."

She was tiring of the adolescent game that he wanted to treat too seriously. She finished her wine and went to the sideboard to refill her glass. There was a mirror over the cupboard. She stared at herself in dismay. Her hair was impossible, like dark dandelion fluff; her cheeks and nose were peeling; her lips were chapped. She thought with envy of Carmen's beautiful skin. At twenty you seemed immune to wind damage. Sunburn on Saturday became a lovely glow by Sunday. She thought of Werther's skin, also untouched by the elements, too tough to change anymore by now. Only she, in the middle, was ravaged looking. She hoped dinner would be early; she had to go back to her house, take a long soaking bath, cream her skin, then get out her checkbook and savings passbook and do some figuring. She could do the book somewhere else, but if Bobby didn't take it, would anyone else? She remembered her own doubts about a second one so closely following the first, and she was afraid of the question.

The real fear, she thought, was economic. Whoever controlled your economic life controlled you. Overnight she could become another nonperson to be manipulated along with the countless other statistics. Her dread was very real and pervasive, and not leavened at all by the thought that Hugh Lasater understood how to use this fear because he also harbored it. That simply increased his power because he too was driven by uncontrollable forces.

Carmen joined her at the sideboard, met her gaze in the mirror. "You said you would heal the sick, cure the wounded. What if you had a perfect immunology method? Would you give it to the drug manufacturers? The government?"

Slowly she shook her head, dragged back from the real to the surreal. "I don't know. Perfect? What does that mean?"

"Immune to disease, radiation, cellular breakdown, aging . . ."

She was watching the two faces in the mirror, hers with its

lines at her eyes, a deepening line down each side of her nose, the unmistakable signs of midlife accentuated by the windburn; his face was beautiful, like an idealized Greek statue, clear elastic skin, eyes so bright they seemed to be lighted from behind. She knew nothing changed in her expression, she was watching too closely to have missed a change, but inside her, ice formed and spread, and she was apart from that body, safely away from it. Is that what Werther had? she wanted to ask, wanted to scream. Is that why they wanted him so badly?

She started to move away and he put his hands on her shoulders, held her in place before the mirror. At his touch the ice shattered and she was yanked back from her safe distance. Startled, she met his gaze again.

"Would you?"

She shook her head. "I don't know. No one person could make such a decision. It's too soul killing." It came out as a whisper, almost too low to be audible.

He leaned over and kissed the top of her head. "I'd better see if Saul needs any help." He left her, shaken and defenseless. When she lifted her glass, her hand was trembling.

Saul? Saul Werther. He called him Saul so naturally and easily that it was evident that they were on first-name terms, had been for a long time. Had Saul Werther promised him that kind of immunity? Was that the bond? Slowly what little she had read of immunology came back to her, the problems, the reasons that, for example, there had not been a better flu vaccination developed. The viruses mutate, she thought, clearly, and although we are immune to one type, there are always dozens of new types. Each virus is different from others, each disease different, what works against one is ineffective against the rest. But Carmen believed. Saul Werther had convinced him, probably with no difficulty at all, considering his persuasiveness and his wide-ranging knowledge of what must seem like everything to someone as young and naive as Carmen was.

He was crazy then, with a paranoid delusional system that told him he could save the world from disease, if he chose to. He was God in his own eyes; Carmen his disciple.

She went to stand close to the fire, knowing that the warmth could not touch the chill that was in her.

She would leave very early the next day. There were other

eagles in other places — Florida, or upper New York, or Maine. And she would start filling applications for a job, dig out her old résumé, update it . . . If she stayed, Lasater would somehow find a way to use her to get inside this house, get to Saul Werther. And she knew that Saul and she were curiously allied in a way she could not at all understand. She could not be the one to betray him, no matter what he had done.

She hardly tasted dinner and when Saul expressed his concern, she said only that she was very tired. She found to her dismay that she was thinking of him as Saul, and now Carmen did not even pretend the master/servant roles any longer. Saul left his place at the table and came up behind her. She stiffened, caught Carmen's amused glance, and tried to relax again. Saul felt her shoulders, ran his hands up her neck.

"You're like a woman made of steel," he said, and began to massage her shoulders and neck. "Tension causes more fatigue than any muscular activity. Remember that blue float? Think of it bobbing up and down through the years. Nosed now and then by a dolphin, being avoided by a shark made wise by the traps of mankind. A white bird swoops low to investigate, then wheels away again. Rain pounding on it, currents dragging it this way and that. And bobbing along, bright in the sunlight, gleaming softly in moonlight, year after year . . . Ah, that's better." She opened her eyes wide. "Let's just have a bite of cheese and a sip of wine while Carmen clears the table, and then he'll take you home. You've had a long day."

He had relaxed her; his touch had been like magic, working out the stiffness, drawing out the unease that had come over her that night. His voice was the most soothing she had ever heard. Perhaps one day he would read aloud . . . She sipped her sweet wine and refused the cheese. He talked about the great vineyards of Europe.

"They know each vine the way a parent knows each child — every wart, every freckle, every nuance of temperament. And the vines live to be hundreds of years old . . ."

The flame was a transparent sheet of pale blue, like water flowing smoothly up and over the top of the log. Lyle looked through the flames; behind them was a pulsating red glow the entire length of the log. There was a knot, black against the sullen red. Her gaze followed the sheer blue flames upward, followed the red glow from side to side, and Saul's voice went on sonorously, easily . . .

"My dear, would you like to sleep in the spare room?"

She started. The fire was a bed of coals. She blinked, then looked away from the dying embers. At her elbow was her glass of wine, she could hear rain on the roof, nothing was changed. She did not feel as if she had been sleeping, but rather as if she had been far away, and only now had come back to this room.

"We have a room that no one ever uses," Saul said.

She shook her head and stood up. "I want to go now," she said carefully, and held the back of the chair until she knew her legs were steady. She looked at her watch. Two? Everything seemed distant, unimportant. She yearned to be in bed sleeping.

Carmen held her coat, then draped a raincoat over her. "I'll bring the car to the porch," he said. She heard the rain again, hard and pounding. She did not know if she swayed. Saul put his arm about her shoulders and held her firmly until the car arrived; she did not resist, but rather leaned against him a bit. She was having trouble keeping her eyes open. Then Saul was holding her by both shoulders, looking at her. He embraced her and kissed her cheek, then led her down the stairs and saw her into the car. He'll get awfully wet, she thought, and could not find the words to tell him to go back inside, or even to tell him goodnight.

"Good thing I know this driveway well," Carmen said cheerfully, and she looked. The rain was so hard on the windshield the wipers could not keep it cleared, and beyond the headlights a wall of fog moved with them. She closed her eyes again.

Then the cold air was on her face, and Carmen's hand was firm on her arm as he led her up the stairs to her house, and inside. "I'll pull those boots off for you," he said, and obediently she sat down and let him. He built a fire and brought in more wood, then stood over her. "You have to go to bed," he said gently. "You're really beat tonight, aren't you?"

She had closed her eyes again, she realized, and made an effort to keep them open, to stand up, to start walking toward the bedroom. She was surprised to find that her coat was off already, and the raincoat.

"Can you manage?" Carmen asked, standing in the bedroom doorway.

"Yes," she said, keeping her face averted so he could not see that her eyes were closing again.

"Okay. I'll look in on you in the morning. Goodnight, Lyle."

She got her sweater off, and the heavy wool slacks, but everything else was too much trouble. She rubbed her arm where Saul had given her the injection and remembered his words: "It may start to itch in a couple of hours, but it won't bother you." The itching stopped as she crawled into bed partially dressed; she fell asleep even before her head touched the pillow.

◘ 7 ◘

THE CABIN was dark when she came awake. She could not think where she was for several minutes. She was very thirsty, and so tired she felt she could not move the cover away from her in order to get up. Her head pounded; she had a temperature, she thought crossly. In the beginning, the first several times she had come home soaked and shaking with cold, she had been certain she would come down with a cold, or flu, or something, but she had managed to stay healthy. Now it was hitting. Sluggishly she dragged herself from bed, went to the bathroom, relieved herself, and only then turned on the light to look for aspirin. She took the bottle to the kitchen; it would burn her stomach if she took it without milk or something. But when she poured a little milk into a glass, she could not bear the sight of it, and she settled for water after all. It was six o'clock. Too early to get up, too dark . . .

The cabin was cold and damp. She remembered how she had been chilled the day before and thought, that was when it started. She should have recognized the signals, should not have spent the day on the beach in the wind . . . She had been walking back toward the bedroom, now she stopped. How had she got home?

There was no memory of coming home. She tried to remember the evening, and again there was nothing. They had gone to Saul's house, where she and Carmen had played a silly game, then dinner, then . . . Then nothing.

Like the night before, she thought distantly, the words spaced in time with the pounding of her head. Ah, she thought, that was it. And still distantly, she wondered why it was not frightening that she could not remember two evenings in a row. She knew she was not crazy, because being crazy was nothing like this. She could even say it now, when she had been crazy she had been frightened of the lapses, the gaps in her life. And suddenly she was frightened again, not of the loss of memory, but of her acceptance of it with such a calm detachment that she might have been thinking of a stranger. She turned abruptly away from the bedroom and sat down instead on a straight chair at the kitchen table.

What was happening to her? She forced herself to go over the previous day step by step. Carmen's hands on her shoulders, her realization that Saul was crazy, paranoid, and her own panicky decision to leave today. She nodded. Leave, now, immediately. But she had to wait for Carmen to come, she thought plaintively. Her hands tightened on the table, made fists. She saw herself walking toward Saul's open arms, felt the warmth of them about her, the comfort of resting her cheek on his shoulder . . . Unsteadily, she stood up and got another drink of water. Leave!

She sat down with the water, torn between two imperatives: she had to leave, and she had to wait for Carmen. If she stayed, she thought, sounding the words in her head, Lasater would use her somehow to get to Saul. Still, she sat unmoving, wishing Carmen would come now, take the decision away from her. She pulled an open notebook close and with block letters drawn shakily she wrote *Leave*. She nodded and pushed herself away from the table.

Packing was too hard; she decided not to take some of her things — the typewriter, some of the books, one of her suitcases. Dully she thought of the refrigerator, of food turning bad. She shoved things into a bag and carried it to the car and blinked at the trunk already full. She put the food on the floor of the back seat and decided she had enough. It was eight o'clock when she left the house and started down the driveway. At the bottom, a large blond man waved to her. She made the stop, prepared to turn, and rolled her window open a crack.

"Yes?"

"Lasater wants to see you. He's in a camper in the park." He went around the car, keeping his hand on the hood; at the passenger side, he opened the door and got in.

She looked at him, feeling stupid. Her door was locked, she had thought of it, but not that side. Slowly she pulled out onto the highway, climbed the hill, went down the other side thinking of nothing at all.

"There's the turnoff," the blond man said.

She turned and drove carefully down the steep gravel road to the campsite. She stopped when he told her to. They both got out and he motioned toward the motor home at the end of the campgrounds. She walked to it.

"Lyle, what an early bird! I thought it would be later than this. Come on in. I'm making breakfast, Mexican eggs. You want some?"

The interior was exactly like the ads she had seen in magazines. There was a tiny living room area with a narrow sofa and two swivel chairs. There was a counter separating that part from the even smaller kitchen, and beyond that another curtained-off part. All very neat.

"Why did you send that man after me?"

"Afraid you'd be up and out early, and I wanted to talk to you." He was dicing a red pepper. "Look, I can add another egg, no trouble at all. Pretty good dish."

She shook her head.

He reached below the counter and brought out a coffee cup. "At least coffee," he said, pouring. He brought her the cup and put it on a swing-out table by the side of the sofa. "Sit down, I'll be with you in a minute. You hung over?" His scrutiny was quick, but thorough. He grinned sympathetically. "Have you told them anything about me?"

"No. I'm sick, I'm going to buy juice and aspirin and go to bed."

He backed away. "Christ! What a lousy break! You okay? If you don't feel like driving to the village, I can send for stuff for you."

She shook her head again. "I'll go."

"Okay, but then in the sack, and stay until you're tiptop again, right? It's the rain. Jesus, I never saw so much rain. Has it ever stopped since you got here?"

He went on cheerfully as he added onions to the chili pepper, then a tomato. He tossed them all into a small pan and put it on one of the two burners of the stove. He poured himself more coffee as he stirred the sauce, and through it he kept talking.

"You know, it might be a good ploy, your getting sick now. You pile up in bed and he comes to visit, right? I mean, he digs you or would he have spent all day and most of the night with you? So he comes to visit and you ask him for a drink, a glass of water or juice, and later we come collect the glass, finis. Not bad actually."

Wearily she leaned her head back and closed her eyes. "You've been so smart," she said. "If I did what you asked and no more, I was safe enough. Hand over the prints, get my story on the eagles, forget the whole thing. If I poked around and learned anything more than that, you could always point to my medical record and say I'm just a nut."

"A plum," he said, correcting her. "You're a plum. I reached in and pulled out a real plum. You know there aren't any plums in plum pudding? Boy, was I ever disillusioned when I found that out." He had broken his eggs into a frying pan; he watched them closely, turned them and then flipped them onto a plate. He poured his sauce over them. "No tortillas," he said regretfully. "Toast just isn't the same, but them's the breaks." Toast popped up in the toaster and he buttered it quickly, then brought everything to the living area. He pulled out another table and put his breakfast down. "Look, are you sure you don't want something, toast, a plain egg?"

"No."

"Okay." He reached under the table and flipped something and extended another section. "Presto chango," he said. Then he pulled a briefcase toward him, rummaged in it, and brought out an envelope, which he put on the table. "While I eat, take a look at the stuff in there."

There were photographs. Lyle glanced through them and stopped when she came to one that had Saul Werther along with several other men, all looking ahead, as if they were part of an audience.

"Start with the top one," Hugh Lasater said, with his mouth full.

She looked at it more closely. It was an audience, mostly men, all with an attentive look. She studied it, searching for Saul, and finally found him, one tiny face among the others. Two other photographs were similar, different audiences, but with Saul among the others. There was a photograph of four men walking; one of them was Saul. And there were two blown-up pictures of sections of the larger audiences.

Lasater had finished eating by the time she pushed the photographs aside. "You recognize him without any trouble?"

"Of course."

"But in one his hair's almost white, and in another one it's dark brown. He has a mustache in one, didn't you notice it?"

"I assumed they're over a period of time. People change."

"Two years," Lasater said. He removed his plate and leaned back in his chair once more, holding coffee now. "One of those conferences was in Cold Spring Harbor, one's Vanderbilt, the last one's Cal Tech. He gets around to the scientific meetings. And at some of those conferences there were incidents. Each time, a young scientist either vanished or died mysteriously."

Lyle closed her eyes. Don't tell me, she wanted to plead, but no words came; she realized her head was pounding in time with the booming of the surf. The booms meant another storm was coming. When the waves changed from wind waves to the long swells that formed a thousand miles offshore, or at the distant Asian shores, and when the waves did not dash frantically at random intervals, but marched with a thunderous tread upon the land, there would be a gale or worse. Saul had told her about the difference, and her experience here had confirmed it, although she had not been aware of the difference before his mini-lecture.

"I'm leveling with you," Lasater said now. "I want to wrap this up and be done with it. You must want to be done with it too. Lyle, are you listening to me?"

"Yes. My eyes hurt, my head aches. I told you, I'm sick."

"Okay, okay. I'll make it short. Picture Berlin back in the thirties. You see *Cabaret?*" She shook her head slightly. "Oh. Well, Berlin's recovering from the worst economic slump in history, expanding in all directions under Hitler. At the university they're developing the first electron microscope. And at the university is Herr Professor Hermann Franck who is one of the pioneers in biochemistry. He's using the prototypes of the electron microscope fifteen years before anyone else has it. Right? Franck has a Jewish graduate student working under him and the work is frenzied because Franck is tired, he wants to quit, go back to his family estate and write his memoirs. Only he can't because the work they're doing is too important. He's on the verge of something as big in his field as Einstein's work was in his, maybe bigger."

"How do you know any of this?" Lyle asked.

"There were Gestapo stooges throughout the university. One of them tried to keep up with Franck and his work, made weekly reports that are mostly garbage because he wasn't being cut in on any of the real secret stuff. But enough's there to know. And, of course, Franck was publishing regularly. Then, something happened, and, I admit, this part gets shady. His grad student was beaten and left for dead by a youth gang. The professor applied for permission to take the body home for burial, and that's the last anyone knows of either of them. Obviously the kid didn't die. He survived, maybe killed the professor, maybe just hung around long enough and the old guy died of natural causes. He had a bum heart. Anyway, the student ended up with the papers, the notes on the work, everything. We know that because it all vanished. Eventually, when Franck didn't show up at work, the Gestapo got interested enough to make a search, and found nothing. The war thickened, things settled, and Franck was forgotten, another casualty. Then twenty years ago the Gestapo reports came to light and a mild flurry of activity began, to see if there was anything worth going after. Nothing. About twelve years ago a bright young scientist working on his thesis dragged out Franck's articles, and there was an explosion that hasn't stopped sending out ripples yet. Bigger than Einstein, they're saying now."

"What is it?"

"I don't know. Maybe three people do know. But for twelve

years we've been looking for that student, now an elderly gentleman, who makes it to various scientific conferences and kills young researchers. We want him, Lyle, in the worst way."

Lyle stood up. "It's the best story yet. They keep getting better."

"I know. I can't top this one, though. He's crazy, Lyle. Really crazy. His family was wiped out without a trace, it must have done something to him. Or the beating scrambled his brains. Whatever. But now he's crazy, he's systematically killing off anyone who comes near Franck's research. He's able to keep up with what's going on. He can pass at those conferences. Maybe some of the time he actually works in a university somewhere. But if we can get a set of prints, we'll know. The Gestapo had them on file; they fingered every Jew in the country. All we want to do is see if they match. Maybe they won't. We'll step out, go chase our tails somewhere else."

"And if they do match?"

"Honey, we'll be as gentle as a May shower. Somewhere there are a lot of notebooks, working notes, models, God knows what all. He can't keep all that junk in his head, and besides, he was just a student. Franck had been on it for years. It's on paper somewhere. We want him to lead us to it, and then he'll be picked up ever so carefully. There's a real fear that he'll commit suicide if he suspects we're anywhere near him, and he's too important to let that happen. He'll be better treated than the Pea Princess, believe me."

She went to the door. Her eyes were burning so much it hurt to keep them open; she was having trouble focusing. She still did not believe him, but she no longer knew which part of the story she could not accept. It was all too complicated and difficult. She wanted desperately to sleep.

Lasater moved to her side, his hand on the doorknob. "Honey, we're not the only ones looking for him. And we are probably the nicest ones. Science is pretty damned public, you know."

"Now you wave the Russian threat."

"And others," he said vaguely. "But also, there are pharmaceutical corporations that know no nationality. It's a real race and everyone in it is playing to win. Even if by default."

"What does that mean?"

"The ultimate sour grapes, Lyle. A really poor loser might decide if he can't have the prize neither can anyone else."

He opened the door. "Look, no rain. I must be in California. Go on, get your juice and aspirin, and then pile in the sack for a day or two. I'll be around; see you later."

He knew he had frightened her at last. It had taken the big guns, but there was a trick to knowing when to show strength and when to play it cozy. She was shaken. She had to have time now to let it sink in that her own position was not the safest possible. But she was a smart cookie, he thought with satisfaction, and it would sink in. She would get the point soon enough that this was too big for her to obstruct. The next time he saw her, she would ask what assurance she had that once done, she would be truly out of it, and he would have to reassure her, pour a little oil on her conscience.

Hugh Lasater was fifty, and, he admitted once in a while to himself, he was tired. Watching Lyle walk to her car, he thought of what it would be like to have a woman like her, to sit by a fire when the wind blew, play gin, read, listen to music, cuddle up in bed. There had been three women along the years whom he had tried that scenario with, and each time what he got was not exactly what he had been after. The women he liked to cuddle in bed were not the sort who played gin by the fire, and, he said to himself, vicy vercy. Lyle drove up the gravel trail to the highway and he motioned to Milt Follett to come back inside.

Not Lyle, or anyone like her, he decided emphatically. Too old, too dumpy. He hoped she had not spread flu germs around.

"Get up there," he told Follett, "keep an eye on her place. Werther's sure to pay a sick call, and when he leaves, the house is yours. She won't get in the way." He did not believe Follett would find the prints, either. In his mind was a scene where Taney handed them to him; he believed in that scene.

Follett scowled. "It's going to rain again."

"Take an umbrella. Rain's good cover. They'll be in a hurry to get inside, you won't have to stay so far back."

Follett cursed and, almost absently, Hugh Lasater slapped him. "Get your gear together. You'd better take some sandwiches, coffee. He might not show until after dark."

Follett's fists were as large as sacks of potatoes, and as knobby. "Relax," Hugh Lasater said. "Someone has to teach you manners." He began to gather the photographs, dismissing Milton Follett, who was, after all, no more than a two-legged dog, trained in obedience and certain indispensable tricks, but inclined to yap too much.

Two days, he thought cheerfully. After all those years, two more days was not much. He had been in the Company when Cushman first made the connection between Werther (or David Rechetnik) and Loren Oley's cancer research after Oley had vanished. Hugh Lasater had winkled out the details over a fourteen-month period, the Berlin connection, the old professor, everything he had told Lyle. Cushman had not then or ever grasped the implications and had shelved the investigation, but Lasater had stayed with it, working on it when he had time, keeping his own file. And four years ago Lasater had had enough to take his walk. He retired, pleading battle fatigue, nerves. He knew he had covered his traces so well that no one would ever be able to backtrack him. You're not going to write a book? they had asked, and he had laughed at the idea. A year later he had a new job, and was still on it. And in two days, he would know. But he already knew. He had known for over a year.

David Rechetnik, or Saul Werther, was smart, but not smart enough. He had left a trail, and if Lasater could follow it, so could others. Any spook in the business could stumble across the same opening information that he had found, could follow it to the same conclusions, and if there were official teams put on it — ours or Russian, or even the British, for Christ's sake — he knew they would muscle him out fast. He knew he had been right in not going to his own agency with it. They couldn't keep a secret from Monday breakfast to lunch time. And, he thought grimly, it would not do at all to let anyone even suspect there was a secret to keep. Not today. Not with fingers hovering over buttons constantly. No, he thought, let this come out exactly as aspirin had, neatly packaged, for sale to anyone with the right change, free market and all. No secrets. And soon, he added. It had to be soon. Too many people knew there was something now. He knew no one on God's little green earth who could keep his mouth shut, except himself.

He sat with his long legs stretched across the motor home, scowling at the carpet, while Follett grumbled as he began to put together sandwiches. Outside, the surf was booming like a cannon.

◻ 8 ◻

INSIDE LYLE'S head the surf was booming also. She flinched from time to time, and she was squinting against the light even though the sky was solidly overcast now. Her legs ached and her arms felt leaden. A gust of wind shook her car and she knew the rising wind would make the coast road hazardous to drive. It was not too bad where the hills were high on the west side of the road, but every gap, every low spot, every bridge, opened a wind channel, and it howled through, threatening to sweep anything on the road through with it. She came to the village and stopped at the supermarket. She had not had time to become very friendly with anyone in town, but they all accepted her by now with amiable good will. Most of the townspeople she dealt with seemed to know her name although she knew none of theirs. The woman at the checkout stand in the grocery nodded when Lyle entered.

"Morning. How're you, Mrs. Taney? That's a real storm blowing in this time. Got gale warnings up at Brookings already. We'll get it."

"Worse than last week's?"

"Last week?" The woman had to stop to think. "Oh, that wasn't much at all. This one's a Pacific gale. Better make sure you have kerosene for your lamp, and plenty of wood inside. Could lose the lights."

Lyle thanked her and moved down the aisle and began selecting her groceries. Juice, ginger ale. She remembered being sick as a little girl and her mother bringing her iced ginger ale with a bent straw. For a moment she was overcome with yearning for her mother's comforting presence. She saw straws and picked them up. Her pump was electric, she remembered, and picked up more juice. If the electric lines went down, she would have no water until they were restored. She knew she had to drink a lot; she was parched right now in fact. When she got to the checkout she was surprised by the amount and variety of potables she had picked up. Irritably she regarded them; she should put some of the stuff back, but it was too much effort and she paid for them and wheeled the cart outside to put her bag in the back seat. The wind was stronger, the gusts took her breath away. And the pounding of the surf was like a physical blow to her head again and again and again.

Before she started her engine, she found the aspirin bottle and slipped it inside her pocket where she could get it easily. She put a can of Coke on the seat next to her and then turned on the ignition.

This part of Salmon Key was on a bluff a hundred feet above sea level. On the streets running parallel to the coastline the wind blew fitfully, not too strong, but at each intersection and on the cross streets it was a steady forty miles an hour with gusts much stronger. Lyle went through an intersection, fought the steering wheel to keep her car in her lane, and then in the middle of the next block parked at the curb. She knew she could not drive up the coast against that wind.

She put her head down on the steering wheel and tried to think of someplace to go. The motel was closed for the season. She knew no one in town well enough to ask for a room for the night. Back to her house? She was afraid to go back. Saul would give her something to make her sleep again.

She jerked upright with the thought and knew it was right. He had given her something both nights. Why? She had no answer, only the question that kept slipping away as if she was not supposed to ask it, as if she had touched on a taboo that sent her mind skittering each time she came too close.

She remembered a gravel road that led from town up into the hills, following Salmon Creek to a picnic spot, going on upward past that. A logging road, dirt and rough, no doubt, but protected from the wind, and unused now since logging had stopped. She drove again, turned at the next corner and headed back toward Salmon Creek. It churned under the wind, whitecaps slapped against the boats at anchor at the docks. No one was in sight as she turned onto the gravel road, and within seconds she was out of town with only the trees on both sides of the road. At the picnic grounds she stopped to take aspirin and drink the Coke. She was very feverish, she knew. This had been a good idea, she decided, waiting for the aspirin to dull her headache and ease the aches in her arms and legs. She would rest until the storm passed — they never lasted more than a few hours — and by the time it was quiet again, probably after dark, she would go on, drive to Portland, return the car to the agency, get a flight back home.

She had no home, she remembered. She had leased her apartment. But there were people she could go to, she argued. Jackie, Chloe, Mildred and Jake . . . Neither Lasater nor Saul could find her here, and tomorrow she would be safe. The aspirin was not helping very much; reluctantly she turned the key and drove; the little park was too open, too accessible. Now the road deteriorated rapidly, from gravel to dirt, to little more than ruts. She should have stayed at the picnic area, she realized. No one would be there on a day like this, and she could not find a place to turn around, or to park, or . . . The road forked. Both sides began to climb steeply after this junction. Maybe she could turn around here. It took her a long time, and she knew she was scratching up the car, and scraping the bottom on rocks, but finally she had it pointing back down the dirt road and, exhausted, she turned the key again and leaned back with her eyes closed.

The wind was distant, high in the trees, hardly noticeable at ground level. She could not hear the surf, and that surprised her because her head was still pounding with the same rhythm and urgency as before, when she had thought the thunderous waves were causing her headache. The rain was starting finally, a pattering at first that eased up; soon it was falling harder. She had to get some things from the trunk. Warm clothes, her poncho, her afghan. It would get cold in the car. Still she sat quietly wishing she did not have to move again for a long time. The rain let up and now she forced herself out. She was appalled by the mess in the trunk. She had tossed stuff in randomly. Her camera case was not there, she realized, and remembered she had left it at Saul's house when they had gone down the beach. She had no further memory of it. She found a long coat, her poncho, boots, the afghan, notebooks. She knew she would not want anything to read; her eyes were bothering her too much. There was a fire banked just behind them.

She arranged the car, put down both front seats all the way, made sure her bag of groceries was within reach, and the can opener she kept in the glove compartment, and only then allowed herself to lie down and pull the afghan over her and finally close her eyes. The rain on the car roof was too loud, but presently she grew used to it and found it soothing. She slept.

Her sleep was fitful and restless, beset by dreams. When she wakened, she was very thirsty; her lips were parched, and her eyes felt swollen. Her headache had intensified and her body hurt all over. She swallowed more aspirin and drank orange juice with it. She slept and dreamed:

Saul was her lover and they ran down the beach like children, hand in hand, laughing, tumbling in the surf, which was as warm as blood. They started to make love in the gentle surf, and she woke up suddenly, aching with desire.

She should drink again, she thought, but it seemed too much effort; she was too tired. She was curled in a tight ball, chilled throughout, and burning with fever. She would die, she thought then, and they would find her here one day and wonder what had happened to her. She dreamed they were finding her, poking at her body with sticks because no one wanted to touch her, and she woke up again. This time she rolled until she could reach a can of juice and she drank it all, and only then remembered she should have taken aspirin. She pushed herself up enough to reach the bottle, and she opened a second large can of juice and took aspirin again. It was nearly dark, the rain was hard and steady. She could not tell if the wind was blowing.

She dreamed she was telling her mother she had to go to the bathroom and her mother said, Not now, dear, wait. She woke up squatting near the car; the shock of icy rain on her back, face, arms, thighs brought her out of delirium. She was shaking so hard she could hardly get the car door open again, and, inside, her hands seemed uncontrollable as she pulled on her clothes. She could not remember undressing. Her hair was wet, ice water ran down her back, down her face. She found a dishtowel she kept in the car to wipe the windshield with and she dried her hair with it as much as she could. It was too dark to see her watch. She was so cold that she turned on the car engine and let it run long enough for the heater to warm the car. Then she was so hot that she began to tear off her clothes again.

She heard Carmen's voice: "Don't be scared. I'll come get you and take you home. We'll take care of you." She looked for him, but he did not come. He lied, she thought dully. Just like Lasater. Saul and Carmen examined her carefully; they looked at her throat, her eyes, listened to her heart, took a blood sample, and took her blood pressure reading. She answered Saul's questions about her medical history, her parents, everything. It was reasonable and thorough, and he wrote everything down.

"I'm dying," she said, and he nodded.

She woke up. She remembered hanging the dishtowel outside the window to get it wet and cold. She dragged it inside and wrapped it around her head. She could hardly move now because of weakness and pain. It was not the flu after all, she thought distantly, as if diagnosing someone else. He had poisoned her with the injection she had watched him administer, she thought clearly. He was paranoid and he had known from the start that she was a spy. He told her so. He poisoned her and now she was dying from it. And they would find her body and prod it with sticks. She wept softly, then slept.

At noon the wind was rising enough to shake the motor home from time to time. The trees around the campsite bowed even lower, and the air tasted of salt. The tent in the campsite collapsed, started to fly away. The kid who had been camping out rolled it up and stuffed it in the trunk of his car, and then he joined Lasater who was standing at the railing of the park, overlooking the lagoon. The normally placid, protected waters were churning around and around; the wind-driven waves were meeting the outgoing tide in a free-for-all.

"Follett says something's wrong at Taney's house," the boy said, close to Lasater's ear.

"What?"

"Didn't say."

"Tell Turk to get his ass up there and find out."

The boy watched the water another second, then left, leaning against the wind. A few minutes later the rain started and Lasater went inside the motor home. Follett came in dripping a short time later.

"She never came back," he said, stripping off his wet clothes. "Werther's kid came over in the car at ten, carrying her camera gear. He went inside and came back out, still with the camera bag. He left. Been back twice on foot. Must wade the creek and come up the bank."

Lasater watched him with loathing. Follett's flesh shook when he moved; he had fatty flaps on his chest, like a woman who had been sucked dry.

"After he left the second time, I went to the house and looked around. She's flown. Half her stuff's still there, as if she wanted to fool you into thinking she'd be back. She left the refrigerator on, but she stripped it, and her toothpaste, deodorant, stuff like that, all gone."

Lasater could feel his fury grow and spread as if it were heartburn, and it scalded him just as heartburn did. He was getting his ulcer back, he thought, enraged. She had sat there looking stupid, pretending she was sick, and all the time she had her car packed, her plans to skip out all made, everything go. And they were back at the starting post.

Wordlessly, he got out a map and looked at the roads, the distances. She could be halfway to Portland by now. And he did not have a man in Portland. Or, if she was heading south, she would be in the Siskiyous approaching the California border.

"Okay, so we change plans," he said brusquely. "Take me up to her place and then you get down to the village and ask around, find out who saw her, which way she was going. Come back up to her place. And for God's sake, keep your mouth closed until we have a new play to run with. Let's go."

She had taken out maybe a third of the stuff she had brought in, he guessed, judging from the condition of the living room, where there were still books, papers, and even mail. She had not bothered to open many of the letters. He did so and scanned them quickly. Nothing. He went through her drawers, and the darkroom, where there were many prints of the coast, trees, hills, and an empty nest. Nothing. She had started to make notes in a new large notebook, nothing. His search was very methodical and, when he finished, everything was as she had left it, and everything had been examined. Nothing.

He built a fire in the stove and made coffee. She had cleaned the refrigerator but had not taken the coffee or sugar, or anything from the shelves. It looked to him as if she had left in a dead run. Why? Something had scared her out of here, what? Not his doing; she was already running by the time he had talked to her that morning. Werther? He heard his teeth grinding together and made himself stop. His dentist had warned him that unless he quit doing that he would be in dentures within a few years. He even did it in his sleep, he thought disgustedly. The thought of wearing dentures made him uneasy and irritable. It made him want to work his dentist over.

While he sat facing the door waiting for Follett to come back, he prepared his story. By the time the soft tapping on the door stirred him, he had made a phone call, and he had the new play ready.

Carmen stood with the wind whipping his hair into his face. "Is Mrs. Taney here yet?" he asked, and the wind swept his words away.

Lasater stepped back and motioned him inside. "What? Are we going to have a hurricane or something?" He slammed the door as soon as Carmen was inside. "My God! It must be a hurricane!"

"I don't think it's that bad. Is Mrs. Taney back?"

"Oh, you're a friend of hers? Do you know where she is?"

Carmen shook his head. "Who are you?"

"Oh. But we do take turns, you understand. I'm Richard Vos, assistant editor at Rushman Publications. Your turn."

"Carmen Magone, just a friend. I got worried that she's out in this weather. She's sick with flu or something."

"When did you see her? Today?"

"Last night. How'd you get here?"

"I was just going to ask you that. I didn't see a car out there."

"I walked over from next door. You walk in from New York?"

Lasater didn't like him, too young, too flip, too bright-eyed. Mostly, too young. He had found his dislike of young men increasing exponentially during the last few years, and while he was prepared intellectually to admit it was jealousy, that did not prevent the feeling nor did it help once he recognized his antipathy had been roused yet again.

"I'm with a friend," he said. "Milt Follett, you ever see him play? We're doing his book on college football. He's gone to the village to buy some things. We thought Lyle would be here, she said she would be here. I brought her contracts to her." He indicated his briefcase which he had brought in with him. Aggrievedly he went on, "I could have mailed them, but she said she'd be here, and Bobby, her editor, said it would be nice to visit and see how it's coming, since I had to be in Portland anyway to see why Follett's stalled. We'll end up with a ghostwriter," he confided. "I could have mailed them," he said again then. "You say you saw her last night? Did she say anything about going somewhere for a few days? Maybe she went somewhere to wait out the storm. Maybe she's scared of storms."

Carmen shrugged. "She didn't say, but she seemed pretty sick, running a fever. I've got to go. If she comes in will you ask her to give us a call?"

"Camping out with a buddy?"

"Not exactly. See you later, Mr. Vos." Carmen had not moved more than a few inches inside the door, and now he slipped out before Lasater could ask anything else.

That was a real bust, he admitted to himself. Briefly he had considered sapping the kid and giving the old man a call, tell him the punk fell and broke his leg, wait for him to drive over to pick him up and then grab him. How easy it could be, he mused. Grab him, make him tell us where the paperwork is, be done with it. He took a deep breath and went back to his seat on the couch. Maybe later it would come to that, but not yet. Taney would stay out a day or two, simmer down, but she would come back for her stuff. Someone like her wouldn't abandon a thousand-dollar camera. He'd twist her arm just a little and get what he needed that way. No suspicions, no fuss. And then, he thought coldly, Mrs. Taney, you and I have a little party coming up, just the two of us. First work, then play, right?

Besides, he added to himself, the old man made a habit of killing off kids Carmen's age or a little older. No way could he believe Werther would lift a hand for this one. He made a bet with himself that Follett would suggest they grab the kid and use him for bait.

All afternoon Carmen was out in the white Volvo during the height of the storm. There was a report that he had shown up at the park twenty miles down the road. He had checked it out, then had left, heading south. An hour later he had driven past again. He had checked out the Lagoon camp, and had gone north from there. Looking for Taney, Lasater knew. Why? It had to be something that had happened at their house. He was convinced the old man had said or done something that had scared her off. At dark the Volvo made its way back up the steep driveway next door, and stayed put the rest of the night. Early the next morning Carmen was at it again. The storm had blown itself out overnight.

At eleven Lasater could stand it no longer and he called Werther's house. After six rings the old man answered, and Lasater released the breath he had been holding. Belatedly, it had occurred to him to wonder if Werther might sneak out in the trunk of the Volvo. He told his story about being an assistant to Lyle's New York editor, expressed his concern about her, suggested calling the police.

"I have done so," Werther said. "They obviously were not very impressed. You however have a vested interest in her, and you had an appointment with her that she missed. They would have to pay more attention if you voiced your fears."

Lasater had no intention of calling the police, and he was mildly surprised that Werther had been willing to bring them in, if he had. Hugh Lasater seldom expected the truth from anyone. Truth, he was convinced, was of such a nebulous nature that no one should expect it more than once or twice within a lifetime. You have to ferret out facts, data, scraps of information wherever you can find them and arrange them in a pattern that seems to make sense, always knowing that tomorrow you may have to rearrange the same bits and pieces to make a different pattern. That was sufficient, that was truth, always relative, always changeable, always manipulable.

Late in the afternoon the sun broke through the clouds and the air was spring-warm and fresh. The sea had turned a deep unwrinkled blue; it rose and fell slightly like a blanket over the chest of a sleeping woman moved by gentle breathing. Sunset was breathtakingly beautiful without a color left out. Carmen returned home an hour after sunset. He was alone in his Volvo. He looked exhausted, the report said, and mud was so high on the car that he must have been up and down logging roads all day.

At dark they all settled in to wait yet another day. Lasater felt he was caught up in a preordained configuration like the constellations of the zodiac, where each star is going at its own rate of speed in its own direction as a result of actions started long ago, which today resulted in this particular arrangement of parts. Although their motion might be imperceptible, they were all on the move; some of the stars were as close as they would ever get to one another and their destiny now was to separate, draw farther and farther apart. Others, he knew, were on a collision course that was equally predetermined and unavoidable.

He was nervous, and was keeping in very close contact with the watchers up and down the coast road. He had a man in Portland now, and another one on I-5. If anyone moved, he would be ready, and eventually someone had to move. Until then he had to wait. He had ordered Follett out to the motor home when he felt he would have to kill him if he remained in sight another minute, yawning, scratching, foot-tapping, too dumb to read, too restless to sit still. He wanted to go over and peek inside Werther's house, see what they were up to, and he knew there was no way. Heavy drapes, window shades; they were well hidden.

By late afternoon the next day fog moved in after a morning brilliant with sunshine. Carmen had gone out at dawn, and was back by two, and Lasater began pulling his watchers closer to the driveway. Fog was the most treacherous enemy of a surveillance job. The white car could move through it like a ghost, appearing to a watcher to be no more than a thicker drift, if it was spotted at all. The walkie-talkie unit remained silent through the long afternoon; no one was moving yet.

That afternoon Lasater felt like a chrysallis tightly wrapped in a white cocoon. The way the fog pressed on the windows gave him the illusion that the windows were giving, bowing inward slightly but inexorably. He half expected to see tendrils of fog forced through small entrances here and there, writhing like snakes as they squeezed in, then flowing down to the floor where they would spread out like wide, shallow rivers, join, become a solid white layer, and then begin to rise.

He got out the book on hawks, which he had started then put aside. He did not like books on natural history, could not understand people who became rapturous over animals or scenery. From time to time he looked up swiftly from the book as if only by catching it unawares would he be able to detect the fog if it did start to penetrate the house.

He came to a chapter that dealt with Sir John Hawkwood, a fourteenth-century mercenary, and his interest quickened. Here was a man he could understand thoroughly. With no nonsense about loyalty to a state or church or any abstract principle, he had gone about his business of hiring himself out to the highest bidder, had done the job contracted for, then gone on to the next without looking back. He had used the weaknesses of others against them and in the end had been rich and honored. Taney was sharp, Lasater thought then; she had made her point that Hawkwood and those like him somehow had been bypassed by one aspect of the evolutionary growth of consciousness. They had not achieved the level of conscience that would necessarily act as a rein on their desires. Unlike the hawk, also without mercy, they were creatures whose needs were not immediate and inseparable from survival. Forever barred from the garden where the innocents still dwelled, and stalled on the ladder of evolution, they existed apart; symbol making, dissembling, unrecognized before they acted and often after they acted, they were capable of incalculable evil.

Lasater snapped the book shut. She was going too far, talking as if those people had some kind of deficiency like a diabetic. And she contradicted herself, he thought angrily, first talking about all the stuff hawks grabbed for lunch — baby birds, rabbits, chicks, whatever they could lift — and then saying they could do no wrong. If he took something, she would be on his case fast. He despised people who were that unaware of their own double standards.

"Taney," he muttered, "deserves whatever she gets."

◻ ¶ ◻

SUNSHINE ON her face awakened Lyle. She stirred, turned her head fretfully, and slowly drifted to full consciousness. Almost resentfully she pulled the afghan over her face and tried to go back to sleep, but she was fully awake. She did not move again for several minutes. She had not expected to wake up. She remembered snatches of consciousness, pain, fever, thirst, and she remembered that she had gone through the stages she had read about. She had felt self-pity, then anger, fury actually that this was happening to her, alone in the wilderness. That had passed and she had felt only resignation, and finally anticipation. She had read about those stages preceding death, and when she realized she was looking forward to the end, she had thought with a start: it's true then. And now she was awake.

Her fever was gone, or at least way down, and she felt only a terrible weakness and thirst. Her mouth was parched, her throat felt raw, her lips were cracked. She raised herself to her elbow and looked for something to drink and saw a can of orange juice; she had not been able to open it the last time she had been awake. She reached for it and pulled it close to her but was too tired to find the opener and finish the task. She rested until her thirst drove her to renewed effort and this time she found the bottle opener and punctured the can with it only to find she could not lift it to her mouth. Straws were scattered over the car; she groped for one and finally got it in the can and sipped the drink. She rested, drank again, then once more. By then she could pull herself up to a sitting position. Even propped up against the door, she found sitting too strenuous, and lay down again. She dozed, not for long; the sun was still on her when she opened her eyes the next time.

For the next several hours she sipped juice, dozed, sat up for seconds at a time, then minutes. She tried to remember what she had done through her ordeal, tried to remember her dreams. In one of them Lasater's face had grown so large it took up her entire field of vision; it had said, "Are you going to do it?" When the mouth opened, it became a terrible black pit.

"No."

"Honey, why can't you lie just a little?"

"Why can't you not lie just a little?"

"You make categorical statements and then feel obligated to live up to them. Now I have to get you out of here so I can bring in someone else." He shot her, and while he was dragging her down the beach for the tide to take, he kept complaining, "You're nothing but a headache, you know? What would it have cost you?"

"Stop," she said then. He released her and she stood up laughing.

He stared at her aghast, then furiously stalked away.

She thought of the dream and could make no sense of it. It was either straightforward and meant exactly what it said, or it was so deep it eluded her. What would it have cost? she thought. She was not certain. Maybe she would have done a good thing even, but it was dirty; she felt certain of that, although she would have been unable to defend it if it were ever proven that Saul was a killer, or a smuggler, or whatever else they might claim.

She remembered a silver rain when all the fir trees had been transformed into Christmas trees heavily decorated with tinsel. She had been delighted with it, and if she had been able to get up and go out into it, she would have done so. That must have been when she was at her most feverish, her most delirious, she decided.

In a dream she had agonized over having to choose between Saul and Carmen, and they had waited patiently while she vacillated. She smiled; the rest of the dream was gone, forgotten, and probably it was just as well. Resting now she thought of the meaning of that dream: although she was almost ashamed of her admission, she was attracted to both of them. It was because they both accepted her unquestioningly, with approval, and either they were blind to her flaws, or thought them so unimportant that they actually became insignificant. She could not remember being treated exactly like this before. When she had been younger there had been the standard boyfriends, a proposal or two before she and Gregory had decided to make their arrangement permanent. All that, she thought decisively, had been biological, a burning in the groin, an itch between her legs, nothing more. Even at the height of passion, she had always known that Gregory was fantasizing someone else, someone made up of bits and pieces of movie stars and pictures in magazines. She never had talked about this with anyone because she had accepted it the way she accepted hunger and thirst and growing old, everything that was part of being human. But Saul and Carmen had not looked at her as if they were comparing her to an ideal who existed only in their heads. They had looked at her, had seen her as she was, and had accepted her. And she loved them both for it.

They were not afraid, she thought; everyone else she knew was afraid, at least most of the time. She remembered telling Saul she had been afraid all her life without ever knowing of what or why. Gregory was afraid. Mike's death had terrified him, as it had terrified her. She, blaming herself, had lived in dread of the day he would also blame her, because that would have justified her guilt. He must have felt the same way, she realized, and felt a rush of sympathy for him that she had not known before. He had needed to run all the way across the country, just as she had needed to run to the woods, to the hills.

She thought of Hugh Lasater, whose fear made him try to manipulate reality by manipulating truth, but the reality was always there, just out of sight, out of hearing, with its infinite terror.

Thinking about Hugh Lasater, she sat up again, this time without the accompanying dizziness she had felt before. She knew she needed food, her weakness was at least partly attributable to no food for . . . How long? It had not occurred to her to wonder until now. She tried the radio, nothing but static up here in the hills. She began to think of bread in milk, and chicken broth steaming hot and fragrant. She settled for an overripe banana and ate almost half of it before she was too tired to bother with any more. She dozed, wakened, tried another banana, and later in the afternoon decided she had to try to get to the creek for water. She had stale bread, and wanted only some water to soften it in.

She was sticky from spilled juice, she felt grimier than she had been since childhood. The creek was no more than fifteen feet from her car but she had to stop to rest twice before she reached it. The dishtowel she had been using to cool herself with was muddy, filthy; she could imagine what her face looked like. The water was shockingly cold; she held the towel in it until some of the dirt was washed away, wrung it out slightly and washed her face and neck. She was seized with a chill then. Shaking so hard that she spilled almost as much water as she had been able to get in the juice can, she started back to the car, thinking of the heater, of the afghan, of going back to sleep wrapped snugly in her poncho, covered from toe to head, sleeping deeply without dreams . . . And she knew she could not do that, not now. It was time to go home.

The heater took a long time to warm the car. She sat huddled in the afghan until then, leaning against the door, her eyes closed. She was afraid to lie down for fear she would fall asleep. She kept seeing her own bed, her covers, sheets, a hot bath, something hot to drink, coffee. She wanted to be home before dark, and she knew it would take her a long time to get there.

She ate a few bites of bread softened in water and marveled at how hungry she was and how little she could eat at any one time. Two bites of this, three of that. She imagined her body as a giant sponge, absorbing water, juice, whatever she could pour into it, sucking it up greedily, dividing it fairly among her parched tissues. Her tongue felt more normal, and her throat hardly hurt now; she imagined her blood as sluggish as molasses from the refrigerator, demanding more and more of the fluids, stirring, starting to flow again, scolding . . .

She smiled at her nonsense and turned the key, and this time she started down the dirt road. Within ten minutes she had to stop. Her arms were quivering with fatigue; her feet were leaden. And when Hugh Lasater turned up with more threats, more demands, she thought, with her head resting on the steering wheel, she would tell him to get out and, if he did not go, she would call the police and complain.

And she would call Saul and tell him a man was asking strange questions about him. No more than that. If he knew he was guilty of something, it would be enough. And if he was guilty of murder, she asked herself, was she willing to be his accomplice? She couldn't judge him, she knew, and she turned the key and started her lurching drive down the hill, down into fog.

She could remember nothing of this road, which was so steep and curvy it seemed now a miracle that she had driven up it. It twisted and turned and plummeted down, faithfully following the white water creek. As she went down, the fog thickened until by the time she knew she had come far enough to have reached the picnic area, she could see no farther than a few feet in any direction. She knew she had missed the park when her wheels began to throw gravel. She stopped many times, sometimes turning off the motor, sometimes leaving it on while she rested.

Then, with her front wheels almost on the coast highway, she rested for the last time. She would not dare stop again on the highway. She closed her eyes visualizing the rest of her route. The steep climb straight up, over the crest, down again, straight all the way to the lagoon, then the sharp upward curve around the far side of the lagoon, down to the bridge and her own drive. She could leave the car in the driveway and walk the rest of the way. Not soon, but eventually. Reluctantly she started the last leg of her journey.

One more day, Lasater told himself, he'd give her one more day to show, and if she didn't . . . He had no other plan and his mind remained stubbornly blank when he tried to formulate one. He was certain she would be back before his self-imposed deadline.

He should have used a professional, he thought suddenly, as if stricken with terrible hindsight. If this fizzled, it would be used against him that he had gone with an amateur when there were people available who could have done the job the first week. He worried it the way a cat worries a mouse, playing it this way and that, looking at the possibilities, and then he left it, just as the well-fed cat leaves the corpse behind. He did not believe Werther would have let any professional inside his house. He had not stayed loose and on the prowl all these years, first eluding the Nazis, and then customs, whatever had come along, by being stupid. He had accepted Taney because she was an amateur, and Taney had to deliver. Lasater still held the image of Taney handing over the evidence he needed. It was a strong image, strong enough to keep him immobile in her house while he waited for her to return.

It was nearly five when he heard the car in the driveway. A minute passed, another, and finally he could wait no longer; he stamped out into the fog to see why she was stalling. He yanked open her car door to find her slumped forward against the steering wheel. He thought she was out, but at the sound of the door opening she stirred and raised her head. She looked like hell. He had not taken it seriously that she might be really sick; he had been convinced that she had run because her nerve had failed. But she was sick all right.

"Lyle, baby, you look like death warmed over. Come on, let's get you inside." He helped her out, then steadied her as she walked to the house. "Jesus, you had us all worried. Carmen's been all over the hills looking for you, they called the cops even." They had entered the house by then and he deposited her on the couch. "What can I get you? Are you okay sitting up like that?"

"Just get out," she said. Her voice was hoarse as if she had a sore throat. "I won't do anything for you. I don't care what you threaten. Get out."

"Okay, okay. I'll give Werther a call. I told him I would when you showed up. He's been worried." She started to get up and he pushed her back. She was too weak to resist his shove, which actually had been quite gentle. For the first time he wondered if she was going to get well, if she had pneumonia or something.

Carmen answered the first ring. "Mrs. Taney's back," Lasater said. "She's really sick, she might even be dying. I think she should be taken to a hospital, except there's no way you could get there through that fog. Is there a doctor anywhere nearby?" He knew there was no doctor closer than twenty-six miles. Carmen said he would tell Mr. Werther and hung up. "Do that, kiddo," Lasater murmured. He turned again to Lyle, who had her head back, her eyes closed. "Listen, sweetie, they think I'm Richard Vos, a New York editor. I told them I had your contracts for you. They don't need to know more than that. Got it?"

Her nod was almost imperceptible.

"Okay. He'll probably send the kid over. When he gets here, I'm leaving. I'll be back at the park by the lagoon. You just get some rest now, take it easy for a couple of days. I'll see you later in the week."

Again she moved her head slightly. "I won't help you," she said.

"Okay, just don't worry about it for now. Get well first. And, Lyle, don't tell them anything. You're up to your pink little ears in this and it's classified. You blab, and, honey, they can put you away for a long time."

She started to take off her coat, and when he touched her in order to help, she flinched involuntarily. He shrugged and moved away again. Her eyes were sunken, her face haggard, but her windburn was clearing up. She was pale as a corpse. "Honey, you look a hundred years old," he said softly. "I wouldn't lie down and stay still very long if I were you. Someone might want to shovel you under." She opened her eyes and for a moment he was startled. He had not noticed how very green they were before. Or now they looked greener against her pale skin. There was hatred in her gaze; when a woman is on the downhill slide of thirty-five, she doesn't want to be told she looks like hell, he thought maliciously. He regretted his own impulse to make her open her eyes and acknowledge his presence; now she looked more alive. Coolly he said, "I'm leaving your contracts on the table. I think he's coming. Remember, I'm Richard Vos."

He had heard steps on the porch, but no automobile noises in the driveway. It was the kid, come over to check first. He nodded, it was as he had expected. He opened the door and admitted Carmen who was carrying a paper sack.

"Mrs. Taney, how are you?" Carmen hurried to her and took her hand in both of his, studying her face. Lasater noticed that his fingers went to her pulse. Medical school dropout? Paramedic? He made a mental note to check it out.

"Don't try to talk," Carmen said, rising then. "I brought some soup. I'll just heat it up for you. Have you eaten anything at all since you left?"

"A little," she whispered in her hoarse voice.

"Soup is what you need," Carmen said and went to the kitchen where he shrugged off his coat and tossed it over a chair, and then rummaged for a pan.

"If you think you can manage," Lasater said, "I'll be going. I'm susceptible to viruses and bacteria and things like that. Get a sore throat if anyone within a mile coughs, you know. I tried to get a doctor, but there isn't any in Salmon Key. I'll be going back to the Lagoon Park." He was keeping his distance from Lyle, watching her as if afraid she might sneeze in his direction without warning. He snatched up his coat and tossed it over his shoulders and opened the door. "If you need me, you know. But I can't do anything. I don't know a thing about how to care for sick people."

Inside the motor home he snapped to Follett, "Let's go. Back to the park."

"What the hell's going on?"

"Never mind. We're leaving. At the first turn, I'm going to stop and you get out, go back up here and keep an eye on things. Werther's got to come over. The kid will either call him or go collect him when he thinks the coast is clear. She's really sick."

He drove slowly, unable to see more than two feet ahead through the fog. Grumbling, Follett left the motor home when he stopped, and Lasater continued down to the highway. Visibility was so poor it would take him nearly an hour to get back to the park. If Taney could drive in it in her shape, he thought, so could he. He reached the bottom of the drive and stopped, trying to remember if the road had the white line on the side all the way, or only on curves, trying to remember if the road curved between here and the bridge.

"This is silly," Lyle said, as Carmen held out a spoonful of the clear, strong broth he had brought from the other house. "I can feed myself."

"I know," he said, smiling. "Open up. This is fun."

"Carmen, wait a second. I have to tell you something. That

man who was here, he's an agent of some kind. He's after Saul. You have to warn him."

"We already know," Carmen said. "Open up, you're almost done."

She swallowed, then shook her head when he offered another spoonful. "You know?"

"Not who he's working for. But it's been pretty obvious that there are people watching us."

Lyle felt childishly disappointed, as if she had run a mile to warn of robbers only to find them already safely locked up.

Carmen looked at his watch, then said, "Now a hot bath for you, and then bed. Hold up your foot."

He pulled her boots off, as he had done another night, she remembered. She had forgotten that night. Again it alarmed her that she was not more fearful of the lapse, not at all fearful about it, in fact. He met her gaze and his face was somber.

"You'll gradually remember it all now. By morning when you wake up, it will all be there waiting for you to examine. You're not afraid?"

She shook her head.

"Good. I'll go fix the bath for you."

A few minutes later, at her bedroom door, he said, "Yell when you get in bed. I'll tuck you in." His grin was back; he looked like a precocious child enjoying enormously this reversal of roles.

She didn't dare remain in the tub more than a few minutes; she had become so relaxed that she feared falling asleep and sinking forever under the water. Regretfully she got out, toweled herself, rubbed her hair briskly, and pulled on her gown. She was as eager now to be in bed as she had been to be in the tub. When she called Carmen, her eyes were too heavy to keep them open. She was in a time-distorting presleep state that made it seem to take him a very long time to get to the bed, but when he was there, his voice close to her, she was startled that he had arrived so quickly.

"You're going to sleep like a baby," he murmured, and touched her shoulder lightly, drew the cover up closer to her neck. "You won't hear anything at all until morning. I'll be here tonight, no one will come in to bother you. Goodnight, Lyle." He kissed her forehead. She slept.

Driving the motor home at any time was difficult for Lasater, who had never driven anything like it before this trip. He had trouble getting used to the rearview mirrors, which more often than not seemed focused on the sides of the monster itself instead of the road. And he did not like the feel of it on the highway; it was too high, the weight was in the wrong place, it felt skittery if there was a glaze of ice or a slick of water on the road, and that night fog was freezing to form black ice. He feared black ice more than an ice storm, because it was invisible; it formed in one place but not another that was equally exposed. The road surface of the bridge was already covered, and he skidded alarmingly. He shifted gears and slowed down even more, wondering if he would be able to pull the grade up to the top of the hill between here and the lagoon.

He had passed Werther's driveway and was starting up the hill, when he heard a car engine roaring somewhere in the fog. His first thought was that it was an idiot speeding on the coast road, driving blind. Then he heard a crash, and he knew someone had gone off the cliffs behind him. He yanked on the brake and got out, ran back on the white line at the edge of the road.

"Turk?" he called. "What the hell's going on?"

"Mr. Lasater? Where are you?"

The fog scrambled directional signals; it was impossible to say where any sound originated. Only the surf remained constant, and it was everywhere.

"Hey!" Turk yelled then. "Stop! Where you think you're going?"

"Get out of the way! I'm going down to find him." Carmen's voice.

Lasater crossed the road; he could hear scuffling sounds now, then a sharp exclamation followed by harsh cursing.

"Turk, what's happening?" he called again.

"The old guy came down like a bat outta hell, picking up speed all the way, didn't even try to stop, but straight through and over the cliff. The kid's just gone down the trail. Must have radar."

"Call Follett. Tell him to meet you at Werther's house and give it a good dusting. Give me your flashlight. I'm going down there."

Turk began to signal to Milton Follett, then said softly, "Jesus H. Christ! Look!"

Up the hillside the fog was lighted from within as if by volcanic fires. There was a glow in the form of a mammoth aureole.

"That bastard! That goddamned fucking bastard," Lasater muttered. "Get up there with Follett, see if anything's left." He snatched the flashlight from Turk and looked for the trail down to the beach.

▣ 10 ▣

By MIDNIGHT the fire had burned itself out; the woods had not ignited; they were too wet and the moist fog had acted as a damper. The house had burned thoroughly, down to the foundation stones. Carmen sat huddled in a blanket near the stove in Lyle's house, his clothes drying on chairs. Lasater sat on the couch staring moodily at the exhausted boy, who had tried to find the car for over an hour until, retching and gagging, he had staggered from the pounding surf into Lasater's arms. The police had come and gone; they would be back at daybreak to look for the car and the body. Accidental death, they said.

Except, Lasater thought coldly, no one was dead yet. He did not believe Werther had been in the car when it went over the cliff, no matter what Turk thought he saw. Werther had to be somewhere nearby, freezing his balls off in the woods, waiting for the coast to clear enough to show up here at this house. Taney wasn't out of it yet. Werther must be planning to use her to get him out of here.

Lasater slept on the couch that night; Carmen rolled up in the blanket and slept on the floor. At dawn he was up cleaning Taney's car with Lasater watching every movement, thinking she was more of a pig than he had realized. Carmen made coffee then, and presently said he was going shopping and would be happy to drop Lasater off at the park. When they went out, the trunk lid was still raised, airing out, and the back doors were open. Lasater felt a cold fury when the thought came to him that the boy was playing games with him, demonstrating that he was not hauling Werther out of the woods that morning.

Lyle awakened slowly, first semi-aware that she was in her own bed again, that she was warm and dry and comfortable, and hungry; and slowly she began to remember the two evenings she had spent at Saul's house. She sat upright and pulled the blanket around her.

All those questions! He had examined her as thoroughly as any medical doctor had ever done. And she had permitted it! She closed her eyes hard, remembering. He had said she was to feel no fear or embarrassment, and she had felt neither; it had seemed the most natural thing in the world. She was startled by the memory of telling him all about Lasater, her involvement with him. Saul had known since that first night, and still had treated her with kindness and even love. The second night swam up in her consciousness and she shook her head almost in disbelief. He had injected her with something, and the rest of the night he had monitored her closely, her temperature, her pulse, her heart . . . She looked at her finger; he had taken a blood sample. Except for the physical examination, which had taken place in the bedroom, Carmen had watched it all, had participated.

As she remembered both evenings, snatches of conversations came back to her; they had talked seriously of so many things. She had been lucid, not doped or hypnotized, or unnatural in any way that she could recall now. But she had allowed it all to happen, and then she had forgotten, and had accepted not remembering. He had told her about that part of it: a drug in the sweet wine, suggestion. He had even said that if she truly objected to anything, she would refuse the suggestion. And she had refused nothing. Except, she amended, she had left the next morning although he had told her to wait for Carmen.

Slowly she got up and went to the bathroom. As she showered, more and more of that last evening came back to her. Just before telling her to wake up he had asked if she wanted to sleep there, in his house, and she had said no. She remembered thinking at the time that there was something she had to do the next morning, something she would not be able to do from his house. She had already made up her mind to leave so that Lasater could not use her to get to Saul. And she had to be home in order to carry out her intention. If he had asked even one question about her reasons, she would have told him, she knew, but he had not asked. He had suggested that she wait for Carmen to come for her.

It was nine o'clock when she finished with her shower, dressed, and was ready to face Carmen. She was still weak, but she felt now that it was due to hunger, not illness. The house was empty. Coffee was on the hot plate. She poured herself a cup of it and sat down to read a note from Carmen on the table. He had gone shopping for breakfast. Back soon.

She was still sipping the strong coffee when he returned. He looked her over swiftly. "I'd say the patient is recovering," he announced. "What is prescribed for this morning is one of the biggest steaks you've ever tackled. Bet you finish it all."

"I've never had steak for breakfast in my life. Toast sounds like plenty." She wanted to challenge him, demand an explanation, but she was too hungry. After breakfast she would have her confrontation with Saul, not with Carmen, who was simply a tool.

"Wait and see." He was unloading grocery bags and putting things away. When he unwrapped the steak, she almost laughed. Big enough for a party. While the steak was broiling, he opened a package of frozen peaches and sliced a banana into a bowl with them. She eyed it hungrily. He laughed and moved it out of reach. "Dessert," he said.

Then he brought two plates out of the oven where they had been warming, and they ate.

Lyle was on her second cup of coffee when Lasater arrived. He scowled at the table. "Surprised you can eat on a morning like this."

"What does that mean?" Lyle asked. She had a dim memory that he was pretending to be someone from her publisher's office, and Carmen was pretending to believe that.

"They're searching up and down the beach for Werther's body," he said bluntly. "No luck so far."

She dropped her cup; it hit the saucer and toppled over, spilling coffee on the table. She turned to Carmen, who nodded.

"He had an accident last night. He drove his car over the cliff."

Lyle did not move. She was trying to remove herself so far that she could see the house, the cliffs, the road, beach, forests, everything as she had seen it all in a dream once. So far back that nothing could touch her ever again. Faintly she could hear Lasater talking about a blood-stained car, one shoe, the wool-knit, navy blue cap that Saul always wore. The distance seemed even greater when Lasater said something about leaving that afternoon. She was brought back when Carmen covered her hand with his.

"He's gone, Lyle. Are you okay?"

She nodded. He began to wipe up the spilled coffee.

"Why didn't you tell me?"

"You had to eat something. I knew you wouldn't afterward."

"What happened? Was it something I did?"

"No. There was a fire at the house and he went out in the car and the car went over the cliff. That's all they know about it."

"Is he really leaving?"

"I don't know. Maybe."

She nodded. They needed the body to make their identification. She started to speak again, but Carmen put his finger on her lips, silencing her.

Late in the afternoon she felt so restless that she could no longer stand the house and the waiting for something, anything, to happen.

"Let's go for a short walk," Carmen said. "Are you up to it?"

She said yes. All day she had felt stronger and stronger until by now she felt almost normal. Her recovery was proceeding as rapidly as the illness had done. Carmen drove to the beach they had walked on before; he went closer to the black rocks to park this time.

Today the sky was gray and low, pressing on the tops of the coast range mountains, making the world seem very small, confined to this winter beach. The water was a shade darker gray, undulating with long swells, breaking up into white water where the wind waves rushed to shore. They walked slowly, not speaking.

That was where they had investigated the tide pools, exclaiming over the multicolored life forms there, the starfish, urchins, crabs . . . And over there she had found the blue float after its journey of many decades. And there they had eaten their lunch, and Saul had put the Styrofoam cup in his pocket to throw away later. And Saul had talked about the way the ocean savaged the winter beach when so few people were around to witness its maniacal fury.

"It seems lonesome," she had said, looking both ways on the deserted beach.

"It has presentiment of endings now," Saul had said. "Endings of life, of pleasure, of laughter in the sand. The winter beach is lonesome, but it fights back. Each grain of sand wrested from it is fought for, yielded finally, but never easily. And in the summer, very peacefully it all comes back, scoured clean by the mother ocean. But in the winter, that's always forgotten."

Gray, black, white; the winter beach was a charcoal drawing today, chiaroscuro colors that reflected her guilt, Lyle thought suddenly. And her guilt lay over every corner of her soul, every phase of her life. Her child, her ruined marriage, her failure as a teacher, her loss of faith both religious and secular . . . Her helplessness even. Had she told Saul why she had lost faith in history as it was taught? She could not remember. She hoped she had.

One day it had occurred to her that every great change brought about historically had been the result of a very few people, men usually, who were driven by the basest impulses: greed, the urge to ever more power, vengeance . . . The great majority of people had always been content to work their land, to mold their pots, weave cloth, do the life-sustaining things that were also soul fulfilling; and the great majority of the people had always been manipulable by those few, ten percent or less, whose needs were so far removed from simple survival and personal salvation.

That day she had realized that she was living during one of those turning points of history, and like countless millions before her, she was doing nothing, could do nothing. Prometheus brought fire and civilization, she had jotted in her notebook that day. The new Prometheuses bring another kind of fire and threaten to put us all back in the caves, those of us who survive for a short time. Who could control them, the politicians, the scientists, the military? Day by day they drew closer to unleashing that new fire, now by inches, now by giant steps, but always closer. Trained to see the patterns, educated to see the recurring patterns through the ages, she had seen this pattern emerging, and she had withdrawn, helpless. The marches, the demonstrations, the petitions, the letters to congressmen, the president, none of it caused a missed step, none of it caused even a hesitation as inch by inch, giant step by giant step the world advanced toward that new fire, drawn along by a minority in power who could see no other way. She had lost faith.

Saul had understood that, even if she had not explained. He had been interested in the other people, the ones with great ideas, the ones who created beauty, the ones who had tried to comprehend the mysteries.

Saul had been her natural ally, she thought dully, and by silence and inaction she had failed him, she had betrayed him; she had allowed herself to be used by Lasater, who was a member of that minority.

And that was how they always succeeded, she went on, taking it to its conclusion, allowing herself no excuse, no possibility of deliverance from guilt. True in the large political arena, it was also true in the private, personal confrontations. They found people who were too weak to resist, who were too afraid, too apathetic, too ignorant of their methods, and they wielded them like swords to strike down or capture the opposition. She had recognized Lasater immediately, had known his goals were not hers, were not even human, and she had done nothing. She had tried to ignore evil, deny its ability to influence her, and now Saul was dead and she would always know that she might have saved him if she had spoken early, before the trap was too tight, before Lasater and the blond man came. Just a few words in the beginning might have been enough. She had done nothing.

And if Saul had been crazy, if he had killed people? She could not resolve the confusion in her mind about him, about how she had responded to him, about the grief and sense of loss she now suffered.

"You're crying," Carmen said, his hand on her arm.

She bowed her head and wept, and he held her for a long time, until finally she tried to free herself. "I'm sorry," she said. "It's so pointless, isn't it? I didn't even know him. And he must have been very sick, he must have suffered terribly. No one like that can go around killing people and not suffer. He almost killed me. I know he almost killed me and yet, I can't help it, I'm crying for a madman who would have been put away if he hadn't killed himself, and I know he wanted it this way . . ." There was no way out of the contradictions and finally she stopped. When she looked at Carmen's face, she realized he was laughing silently.

Stiffly she drew away and started to walk toward the car. "You can't deny that he tried to kill me and almost succeeded. That injection of his, you were there, you know about it."

"It was a gamble," Carmen said, still smiling slightly. "But you were dying anyway."

"That's a lie. There wasn't a thing wrong with me before that shot. I had a life expectancy of at least thirty years."

"Exactly," Carmen said. "This walk has probably been too much for you so soon after your illness. Let's go home and have dinner."

She opened her mouth to respond, then clamped it shut again and got inside the car where she sat staring out the window all the way home. He was as crazy as Saul, she reminded herself.

□ ‖ □

LYLE SAW A speck in the distance and knew the eagle was coming home finally. Every day there had been fresh evidence of the arrival of at least one of the pair, and now it was coming. She watched the speck gain definition, become separate parts. A wing dipped and the bird made a great sweeping curve, and she could see the tail feathers spread like a fan, rippling now and then as it made adjustments in its flight. She could see the white head, gleaming in the sun; it was looking at something below, turning its head slightly; it abandoned whatever had attracted it and looked ahead again. She was watching it through the view finder of her camera, snapping pictures as it came nearer. It cupped its wings, its feet reached out before it, and then it was on the spur, settling its wings down along its sides, stretching its neck. She snapped a few more shots of it as it preened, and then she sat back with her camera at her side and simply watched it. If the eagle was aware of her presence, it gave no indication of it. She was certain those sharp eyes had studied her blind, that they had seen her that day. There was a touch of majesty in its indifference to her.

Throughout the afternoon the eagle toiled at refurbishing the nest. It brought long strands of seaweed, and mosses, and sticks up to four feet long to expand the sides, and it worked the materials into place with an intentness and fastidiousness that was awesome.

Under the tree was a circle of litter; the eagle had picked out materials that had been good enough last year, but no longer pleased it. Old moss, old fern fronds, sticks. With an almost reckless abandon it tossed them over the side. When the light began to fade, Lyle picked her way back down the hillside, around the ruins of Saul's house, through the creek and to her own house, where Carmen was waiting for her.

She had not asked Carmen to stay, but neither had she asked him to leave; it was as if they both accepted that he would remain with her for now. The matter had come up only indirectly when she had said she couldn't pay him, and he had shrugged. For eight days he had been with her in the same relationship apparently that he had had with Saul. He did the shopping, a little cleaning, cooking; he prowled the beaches and brought home clams or scallops or crabs, sometimes a fish. Best of all they talked for hours in the evenings, never about Saul, or Carmen's past, but of history, current affairs, art, music . . . Lyle knew that one day he would get restless and drift on, but she refused to think about it and the hollow in her life that would result.

When she entered the house that day, the odors of food

cooking and wood smoke and the elusive scent of another person greeted her. She felt nearly overcome by contentment.

"Carmen! He's home. He's beautiful! A wing span over eight feet. All day he's been fixing up the nest, getting ready for his lady love to join him. Tomorrow you have to come up with me and see for yourself." She was pulling off her outer wear as she talked, unable to restrain the excitement she seemed filled to overflowing with. "I can't wait to see the pictures."

She stopped at the look on Carmen's face, a look of such tenderness and love it made her knees weak.

"I'll come up tomorrow. Maybe I can help you in the darkroom after dinner."

She nodded. And still they looked at one another and she wondered when she had stopped seeing him as a boy, when he had stopped looking at her as if she were untouchable.

Then she said, "I'm filthy. I'd better get washed up and change these muddy clothes." She fled. She was afraid he was laughing at her confusion.

They had dinner and worked in the darkroom for two hours. She felt like purring over the proof sheets; at least half a dozen of the pictures would go in, maybe more. Throughout the evening she avoided his gaze, and spoke only of eagles, her day in the blind, the dinner itself. She began to make notes to go with the pictures, and found herself writing a poem instead. When she finished, she felt almost exalted.

"May I read it?" Carmen asked.

She handed it to him silently.

He read it twice, then said, "I like it very much. It would make a good introduction to the book. I didn't know you wrote poetry."

"I don't. I mean I haven't before, not since college days." She took the sheet of paper back and reread her poem.

> The dead tree flies an eagle on the wind,
> Then steadily reels it in,
> Dip, sway, soar, rise,
> All the time closer.
> To the left, to the right,
> Now too low, now too high,

But closer.
From nothing, to a speck
That could be a cloud,
To a being coming home,
It takes shape:
Sun on snow, the head,
Great wings without a waver,
White fan as graceful
And delicate as a black one
In a pale practiced hand.
From the tree's highest crotch,
From a nest of branches, sticks, twigs, moss,
Elaborate skyscraper room,
A silent summons was sent.
Now the dead tree reels the eagle home.

Abruptly she stood up. "I guess I'd better get to bed. I want to be up there early. I expect the other one will come in tomorrow or the next day."

In a scruffy camper in Lagoon Park Hugh Lasater played the tape over again, listening to their voices intently, following them through dinner, into the darkroom where their voices were almost too low to catch, back to the living room. He wished one of them had read the poem aloud. He heard their goodnights, her door closing, Carmen's movements in the living room for another fifteen minutes; then the long silence of the night started. He turned off the tape player. Something, he kept thinking. There was something he should be catching. He rewound it and started over.

What he did not hear, because the device was activated by sounds and this was done in silence, was the opening of Lyle's door at one-thirty. She stepped into the living room to look at Carmen sleeping on the couch, and when she saw him instead at the window that overlooked the sea, she did not retreat. Instead, after a slight hesitation, he came to her, barefoot, visible in the red glow from the glass door of the wood stove. He reached out his hand and she, after a slight hesitation, took it, and together they went back to her bedroom and softly closed the door.

Hugh Lasater listened again, and in the middle of the tape, he suddenly slapped the tabletop hard, waking up Milton Follett on the bunk bed.

"Son of a bitch!" Lasater said. "The camera bag. Where was it when the house burned down?"

Follett regarded him with hatred, rolled over and went back to sleep.

Lasater had not been asking him; he already knew about the camera bag. Follett was good at certain jobs; he could watch and report movements down to a casual scratching of the head. And Follett had said that Carmen showed up with the bag at Taney's house when she was gone, and he had left with it. He had not been seen with it again. So Werther considerately put it on a stump out of danger before he set the house afire?

Lasater mused about the boy for a long time that night. He knew photography enough to help Taney in the darkroom. He remembered that sure way he had taken her pulse when she returned from her little jaunt. They had only his word that he had been hired by Werther in Los Angeles; if that was true, what had made him jump into that crazy surf in an effort to find the old man? No one risked death for someone he had known only a couple of months, and that surf was a killer. Someone had to make sure that the car door had not jammed shut, Lasater said to himself. That would have screwed it up royally, if there had been no way Werther could have been thrown out. They had waited for the right kind of night with a pea-soup fog for their little charade; maybe the kid even had a rope guide to take him to where he had figured the car would land. No one paid much attention to him; he was always on the beach prowling around.

Lasater knew his foremost problem now was to convince Mr. Forbisher that his theory was right, that Werther had not been in that car, and that the boy would lead them back to him sooner or later. Turk was convinced that he had seen Werther go over the cliff; Follett believed him, but Follett would have bought anything to get him off this job. He hated the rain and wind and cold weather, and he hated the isolation here. He wanted a woman. When they got back to civilization, Follett would vanish for a day or two. There would then be a news item about a woman's body being found . . . It was one of those things with Follett, a little weakness of his. Lasater could sympathize with his frustration even while his own frustration mounted to a dangerous level. Even Lasater had to admit that he no longer believed Werther was hiding out in the woods now. Not for eight days. In another day, August Ranier would show up, listen to the arguments for continuing the hunt, make his evaluation, report to Forbisher by phone, and then render the decision. Lasater's mouth tightened as he repeated the phrases to himself, all so legal sounding, so proper and genteel.

He was certain they would not continue to pay the small army Lasater had brought to the coast to watch the old man and the kid. Maybe one operator, or two at the most. They might go for that. He would bring in someone who could get in close to Carmen, and stay close to him. A girl, he thought then, remembering Carmen's body as he had stripped in Taney's house. Even blue with cold and shaking almost uncontrollably, he had been good-looking, so young and unmarked it had been like a stab to Lasater. Hell, he thought, the kid was human, he must be almost as horny by now as Follett. If he could produce a girl who looked even younger, who looked hurt and vulnerable, who asked for nothing and apparently expected nothing, a runaway with a car of her own, a little money, Carmen would figure he could use her to get him to where he had to go. And where he had to go, Lasater had convinced himself, was home to Saul Werther.

"Look," Lyle said softly. "She's pretending she hates it. That's stuff he just brought in yesterday." The female eagle was discarding seaweed vigorously; the male sat on a nearby tree watching her.

Carmen laughed. There was mist beyond the blind; it was too fine and too gentle to call rain, it was rather as if a cloud were being lowered very slowly to earth. Carmen had joined Lyle only minutes earlier; there were mist beads on his hair.

She had been afraid the morning might be awkward, but he had been up when she awakened, and when she had gone into the living room he had kissed her gently on the nose and had continued to make breakfast.

The female eagle reared up and half opened her wings threateningly when the male approached the nest. He veered away and returned to his perch. "All in the genes," Carmen said in a hushed voice. "She's doing what nature programmed her to do."

Why this pretense of free will? Lyle wondered. She knew the female might pretend to become too disgusted with the nest, with the male; she might pretend to leave, might even go through some motions of starting a new nest. And in the end they would mate here and the fledglings would hatch out and learn to fly from that dead spur.

She found herself wondering about her own attempts to escape Lasater's plans, to free herself from the burden of betraying Saul, her own mock flight to freedom. From any distance at all, it now seemed as programmed as the eagles' behavior, at least her actions and Lasater's. Only Saul and Carmen had been unpredictable. Suddenly she felt that they had been from the start as alien to her as the eagles were, as strange and unknowable. And it had not mattered, she thought, and did not matter now.

"Why are you smiling like that?" Carmen asked.

"I was thinking that you and Saul came to Earth from a distant planet, that you're aliens. They won't find his body because he changed himself at the last moment into a great snowy owl and sailed away in the fog. He could come back as a butterfly, or an eagle, or whatever he chooses."

"I hope Lasater doesn't start believing that," Carmen said, laughing. "He might get the Marines out."

"Oh, no. He thinks that Saul was a Jewish student in Hitler's Germany and that he discovered something tremendous . . ."

She stopped at the change that came over Carmen's features. He leaned toward her and suddenly there was nothing boyish about him, nothing soft or tender.

"Tell me what he said."

"That last morning he stopped me as I was leaving, when I was ill . . ." She told him all of it. He did not move, but she felt more alone than she had felt in her life, as if a barrier that could never be scaled had come up between them.

"It's true, isn't it?" she whispered.

"Essentially. Some details are wrong. David's two younger brothers died from Tay-Sachs disease when they were children, and it nearly killed his mother. David and his older brother Daniel swore they would find a cure for it. But Daniel just couldn't make it in school. He dropped out, David went on. The professor was already into genetic research, and he allowed David to pursue his own studies because he saw that the two would come together at a later date. When the two lines did converge they realized they had something they had not counted on. The professor was terrified that the German government would get it, he was vehemently anti-Fascist, and of course there was the danger that David would be picked up and forced to work in a government lab somewhere. So they kept it very secret, kept the papers on the farm the professor's family had owned for two centuries. David's brother knew what he was doing. When David was called up for registration, fingerprinting, the works, Daniel went. No one noticed. All those Jew boys looked alike, after all. So David never was on file actually. David's parents and Daniel were hauled away one day. He found out — they always found out rather quickly — and he returned to the laboratory that night to destroy certain cultures. A Hitler Youth gang caught him there carrying a culture dish across the laboratory. The culture had to be maintained at blood heat or it perished. All he had planned to do actually was to put it in the refrigerator, because there was a danger of incriminating the professor if he actually destroyed anything in a way that could be proven. When the gang burst in on him, he dropped the dish. They threw him down on the mess and rubbed his face in it. Glass, culture, dirt . . . Then they took him outside the building and beat him to a pulp, and they dragged him back to the professor's house, and left him on the steps." He paused. "The rest of it is pretty much as Lasater suggested, except that the professor wasn't dead. They escaped with the paperwork."

"If his fingerprints aren't on file, why did it matter if Lasater got a set? It would have ended there when they didn't match up."

"David's prints aren't in anyone's file," he said slowly, gazing at the eagles' nest. "But the professor's are. We simply couldn't be certain they wouldn't be available for comparison."

"You're saying that Saul is that professor. What about David?" Her voice sounded harsh and unfamiliar to her; she had to make a great effort to speak at all. She was caught up in a battle against disbelief and despair: Carmen was mad, as mad as Saul had been.

"You know I'm David," he said gently, as if only now becoming aware of her distress. "Don't look so scared. You really did know already. Watch the eagles this afternoon. I'm going down to the beach. See you for dinner." He leaned forward and kissed her lips lightly, and then was gone.

Dry eyed, she stared at the eagles' nest. Crazy. Paranoid delusions. It had to be that. Gradually she found that she was accepting that he was mad and that she didn't care, it didn't matter. He had to be insane, or she had to accept something that had kept him twenty for all those years, that had stopped Saul at sixty-four and held him there. Something that had made them both immortal. And she could not accept immortality.

The female eagle returned with fresh seaweed to replace that which she had discarded; her token resistance was ended. The male followed with a long scrap of white material he had found somewhere. Together they rearranged the interior of their nest.

The sun came out and steam rose throughout the forest; the air was heavy with spring fragrances and fertile earth and unnamable sea smells.

And still Lyle sat staring, not taking pictures, trying to think of nothing at all. She would not think about tomorrow or the next day. She would do her job and if Carmen stayed, she would love him; when he left, she would miss him. Each day was its own beginning and ending. That was enough.

But she knew it was not enough. Carmen had pointed out the listening device on the underside of the table in her house. Lasater was still out there, listening, spying. Maybe he thought Carmen would lead him to the papers he so desperately wanted. Maybe Carmen could go to them. And, she thought suddenly, she was still here for Lasater to use. He had put her here, he thought of her as his instrument, his property to use when he got ready, to discard afterward, and so far she had not worked for him. The next time he might use her without trying to force cooperation, without her awareness or consent. When he started moving pieces again, he would turn to her and make use of her, she felt certain. Like the winter beach, she felt buffeted by forces she could not comprehend or thwart or dodge, and like the winter beach, she felt a presentiment of endings, a loss of laughter in the sand.

◙ 12 ◙

AUGUST RANIER had come and gone and Lasater had been stripped of his army with a single word spoken very quietly. "Do I continue?" he had asked.

"No."

Ranier had handed Milton Follett and Lasater their termination checks — they had been hired as consultants — and he had left in his dawn gray Seville.

"Let's get out of here," Follett said.

"Aren't you willing to wait to pick up your bug up in the house?"

"Yeah. I'm driving the camper up there. That little baby cost me sixty-three bucks. Let's go."

"Milt, hold it a minute. Listen, I know that old man's alive and well somewhere and the kid's going home to him one of these days. I know it just like I know the back of my hand. Now that Forbisher's out of it, we could double the price when we get the stuff. You and I, Milt, just the two of us. A million, two million . . ."

Milt turned the key and jerked the camper away from its parking spot. He did not even bother to look at Lasater.

"Milt!" Lasater said softly. "Remember Karen?"

The camper shuddered to a stop and Milton Follett started up from behind the driver's seat. His hands were clenched.

"Would you like another Karen?" Lasater asked, whispering the words.

Follett was pale and his fists opened, the fingers spread wide, then clenched again. "What do you mean?"

"I'll let you have Taney."

Follett sat down on the bunk bed. "Tell me," he said.

"What if the cops find her messed up, dead, her money, jewelry, car, all gone? What do you suppose they'll think, especially since the old guy disappeared so mysteriously such a short time ago? They'll wonder why a good-looking kid like Carmen was hanging around an old dame like her. But you can have her first, as long as you want, whatever you want."

"Why?"

"I want that kid to run home to papa. He'll run when he finds her. He'll know they'll be after him, he's not a dope. He'll run and we'll be there. Who's the best team in the business, Milt? Not Turk and that bunch of amateurs. You think there's any way in the world the kid can shake us? I think he'll take us home with him."

"When?"

"We need a car. One of us has to go up to Coos Bay and get a car, and then we're all set."

"You," Follett said. "Too many people recognize me. You paying?"

"Yep. All the way. I pick up all expenses."

Milton Follett continued to study the idea. Lasater could tell when he stopped considering it and let his mind drift to Lyle Taney; a film of perspiration put a shine on his forehead.

Outside, the rain started again. It was like a drumbeat on the metal roof.

Lasater was not even certain he had heard a knock on the door until he opened it to see Lyle Taney there with rain running off her. She was dressed in her down jacket and jeans, boots; her hood was pulled low on her forehead. She looked like a commercial for a hikers' club. He grinned at her and stepped aside to allow her to enter. She pushed the hood back and stood dripping on the rug.

"My God," Lasater said. "You look great! I've never seen you look better!" Her lips were soft without any trace of chapping now; her eyes were clear and bright, as green as seawater; her face glowed, the windburn totally gone. She had swept Follett with one quick glance, and now was looking at Lasater steadily.

"I think the lady wants to talk to me in private," he said to Follett.

"Raining too hard," Follett said, not shifting his gaze from Lyle Taney.

"What can I do?" Lasater asked helplessly. "He's bigger than both of us. You want a cup of coffee? Let's get that jacket off, dry out a little." He made no motion, but continued to study her, the changes in her. Always before she had kept herself way back where she thought she was safe, but now she was right out front, not hiding at all. Her eyes blazed at him, straight on. Then he thought, She's sleeping with the kid! He was fascinated and disgusted by the idea.

"Why are you still here?" she asked. "What else do you want? You drove Saul Werther to his death. What more can you do?"

"He isn't dead, Lyle. Let's not pretend. Werther, the kid, you, me, we're all in this together. We've come too far to try to kid each other."

"I'm warning you," she said, "if you don't get out of here and leave Carmen alone, and leave me alone, I'm going to call the sheriff's office and the nearest FBI office and anyone else I can think of and make a loud noise about an ex-agent and an ex-football player who keep threatening and harassing me."

"Baby, I'm on their side. National security takes precedence over local affairs every time."

"You're a liar, Mr. Lasater. I intend to make those calls if you don't get out of here and leave us alone."

Lasater laughed and reached past her to lean against the door. "Honey, what makes you think you'll be going anywhere to do any complaining?"

She did not move. "I asked everyone in the park which camper you and the football player were in," she said evenly. "Two tents, a motor home, two campers, and a trailer. Some of the boys thought it was neat to be camping out next to Milton Follett. They might even ask for an autograph."

Follett made a sound deep in his chest, a grunt, or a groan.

Lyle continued to watch Lasater. "Just so there wouldn't be any excuse to delay," she said, "I brought you this." She took her hand from her pocket and tossed the bug onto the bunk bed.

"She's lying," Lasater said to Follett then. "She doesn't want cops asking that kid questions any more than we do."

"Let her go," Follett said. He had stopped watching her and now was looking at Lasater murderously. "She's been using my name around here. Let her go."

He was infuriated because the plum had been yanked out of reach, Lasater knew. There would be no way of getting him to cooperate again soon if she walked out the door. "Let's take off, go down the beach a ways and decide how to handle this."

"You'll have to move my car," Lyle said. "It's blocking you. One of you will have to go out and move it, and some of the people I talked to will be curious enough to be watching." Now she looked at Follett, as if she knew he was the one to work on. "I left a note for Carmen, telling him I was coming here. If he comes down, and he will, and finds all of us gone, he'll call the police fast."

"He put you up to this, didn't he?" Lasater demanded.

"You win because no one really opposes you," she said, and there was a new intensity in her voice. "I tried to close my eyes to what you were, what you were doing, trying to make me do. But I'm not afraid anymore, Mr. Lasater."

She was telling the truth; she was not afraid. He knew it, and he realized that Milton Follett knew it. For a moment the tableau held. Then, as if from a great distance, Lasater heard himself mutter, "Oh, my God!" and suddenly he knew what it was the old man had found. "It wasn't a cancer cure, was it?" he whispered. Wildly he turned from her toward Follett. "I know what it was! Look at her!"

Follett was moving the few steps that separated him from the other two. Savagely he jerked Lasater away from the door. "Get the hell out of here," he said to Lyle.

She left. She had not yet reached her car door when the camper shook as if a heavy weight had been slammed against the side of it. She did not look back, but got inside her car and put the key in the ignition.

She started the car, left the camping area, climbed the steep gravel driveway.

He used it on me, she thought clearly, and it seemed as if the rain had come inside the car, was blurring her vision. She saw Carmen on the road and stopped for him. He examined her face quickly.

"You could have been hurt!"

"But not killed?"

For a moment he was silent. She started the car again and drove south, toward the beach where they had walked with Saul.

"You could be killed," he said then. "But you could be hurt and hurt and hurt for a long time first."

She nodded. "Why did you do it to me?"

"We need help. We have to stay together in case one of us gets hurt. The other has to take care of him. No hospitals. No doctors. There are a few others, but they all have work to do, and some of us have to be able to travel here and there."

"To attend conferences, see who is getting too close."

"Yes. Lyle, who would you hand it over to? Our government? A church leader? Who should be given it? A billion Chinese? Two and a half billion Asians? Four and a half billion of all of us? A scientific elite? The military? Who, Lyle?"

She shook her head. "You're as bad as Lasater. Judge, jury, executioner."

"We know we are," he said very quietly.

She thought of the immensity of the sadness she had detected in Saul.

"Four people so far have followed that line of research," he said. "One of them was already spending his Nobel Prize money. I killed him and buried him."

They had reached the wide beach. Today the water was almost black under the low clouds and pounding rain. It was low tide, the waves were feeble. Lyle parked and they sat staring out at the endless sea. She thought of the story of the fisherman and his three wishes. This was her third trip to this winter beach. I wish . . . I wish . . . There was nothing to follow the words. Golden wings, she thought. She could wish for golden wings. Why me? she had wanted to demand of Lasater. Why me?

The windows were fogging up. "Let's walk," he said. They

pulled up their hoods, left the car, walked in the rain to the edge of the water.

"I don't want it," she said. "I didn't ask for it. You didn't ask me if I agreed."

"I know. If you had wanted it, we wouldn't have chosen you."

"You can't make that decision for the rest of humanity. No one can make such a decision for everyone."

"I know. We can't, but we have to, because if we don't someone else will. Who? That night, in Germany, Saul took me to his country house to bury me. When I didn't die immediately, he almost killed me himself because he knew that the Nazis would use me for forced labor, or in an experiment, or kill me outright, or something. He was opposed to the Nazis, but he didn't leave the country as many other scientists did. Instead he immersed himself in work, tried to pretend he didn't know what was happening all around him. There was a lot of that going on. He'd had a heart attack a year or two before. He really thought he'd be out of all of it very soon. But I didn't die. I started to run a fever, like yours, and after a couple of days, the fever subsided, and my cuts started to heal. He had wanted to kill me not only because he knew what the government would do, but because he could see that I'd be disfigured, maybe lose sight in one eye. My recovery was complete," he said simply.

Lyle stood with her hands thrust deep into her pockets, her shoulders hunched, although she was not really cold. As he spoke, she saw the incident again, saw the beaten, bleeding boy.

"We talked about it, and talked," he went on. "We had to get out of the country, not let our work end up in Hitler's hands. Think what it would have meant to him if he had been able to immunize his troops. We had no idea yet of the limitations of the stuff. It just seemed that it would cure anything, wounds, disease, whatever. And we knew that we didn't dare let Hitler get it. But Saul couldn't have left with me. He couldn't have walked all night, hidden wherever he could find shelter, go without food, be out in the winter cold. He was old and he was sick. Thinking about how I had been inoculated decided it for us. The serum entered through cuts and scratches, broken skin was all it needed. We became blood brothers. There wasn't any more of the serum and he didn't dare go back to the lab, put in months refining more of it. Any day his heart might have given out. We didn't know that it could kill half of those who tried it, either. We might not have gone through with it if we had known. I think we became really frightened when it took with him and we realized how easily it could spread. Transfusions, sexual contact, anything that allowed lymph secretions to enter another human body would do it. We began having nightmares about it, afraid we might spread it unwittingly, unknowingly. We got to Switzerland and hid there for the duration of the war. *Lebensraum*. In Germany, in Japan, that's what they said the war was all about. Living space. And we thought we had a secret that would make everyone immortal. We visualized the population doubling, doubling again and again, and everyone living on and on until they all died of starvation."

"But you said it kills half of those who use it. It almost killed me."

"We found out later. We had both been lucky. The next two people weren't." He started to walk and she fell into step by him. The waves hissed at their feet, made patterns in the dark, wet sand.

"We had taken money out, jewels, we had enough to set up a small lab and we went to work. We happened to come across a scientist from Poland. He and his family had fled the terror, and he was the only survivor. We took him in, included him, and he died." He stopped and looked out at the gray ocean. "The other one was my fault. A girl. A refugee, alone, without money, without papers, friends. She . . . I fell in love with her. She died."

Love me and die, she thought bleakly. She remembered the look on Follett's face back in the camper. She had recognized that look, cruelly possessive, hungry. Sexual contact. And the Folletts and the Lasaters would be the ones to get it. The others might all die, but not the Folletts and the Lasaters of the world. Although Lasater knew, it did not matter. No one believed him, and soon he would grow old and die. She gazed at the sea, wishing for a sign, for a rainbow, a streak of gold at the horizon, anything. There was only the gray water rising and falling in slow swells, and the steady rain.

"We watched it all. The Holocaust, the V-Two attacks on England, the fire bombings, the start of nuclear warfare. It ended and we knew we needed a bigger, better-equipped laboratory. We had made no progress at all. We came to the United States, the only civilized place, it seemed, that hadn't been devastated, where we could get supplies, a building, whatever we needed. And the madness went on — the cold war, the McCarthy years, the buildup of nuclear arsenals. The Soviet satellite states. Korea and Vietnam. It was all going to happen again. War was inevitable again, and what we were going through was no more than a pause, a time for regrouping, for rearming. It was like the inter-stadial of the glacial period we're in. We think the ice ages are over, but the records show that this is a pause among many pauses, a retreat of the ice for a period that is an eye blink, geologically speaking. The ice will come back. War will come back. And it gets worse each time, as if each time it's a new dress rehearsal for the final war. We think, all of us, that the next war will be the final one. And the serum we discovered could be the trigger to start that war."

A harbor seal barked and was answered by another and both became silent. A sea gull screeched once, wheeled away. "Just the two of you," Lyle said in a low voice, "deciding the fate of the entire world?"

"For almost twenty years, just the two of us. Think, Lyle. We believed then that a woman would live on and on, as we seemed capable of doing. Her childbearing years stretching out indefinitely, and her children's and their children's, procreating, limitless babies, limitless new adults to procreate. The population explosion is real now, but it isn't the fertility of the human race that has made the world crowded today. It's altering the death rate. Every time we increase the life span, every time we invent a new device to save those who would have died without it, every time we find new ways to purify water, dispose of wastes . . . These are the things that have given us the population explosion. But it's a feeble explosion compared with what we could have handed out, or so we thought."

"You learned something new," she said dully. "What else?"

"In the fifties we began to recruit others. And we found out the real limitations of the serum. Sexual contact with a woman inoculates her, immunizes her, or kills her. And if she's immunized, there is no pregnancy. It's a total immunological system."

They both stopped. "But then . . ."

He shook his head. "We thought so at first. There were six of us. We wanted to run in the streets, celebrate, have a party . . . Publish. We were drunk with excitement. When we sobered up, we knew this was even worse. Half the people dead, the survivors all sterile. A static world, a dying world with no hope."

She remembered what he had said to her earlier: "You could be killed." Of course — accidents, murders, suicides. God, yes, suicides! A long, slow death of the human species.

"There has to be an answer to that problem," she said at last. "If enough people work on it, with government support, a big project . . ."

He was shaking his head. "We thought of that, too. We've recruited some of the best biologists in the world. We've got one of the best laboratories in the world. And we're all as motivated as human beings can get, believe me. We've been searching for even a clue about this part of it for thirty years, following every lead, searching the literature for something we might have missed." His voice was flat, without hope. "We haven't dared reveal the secret. What if there really isn't an answer? Sometimes there aren't any."

Living like pariahs all those years, she thought, walking, seeing the lace edges of waves crumple, fade, vanish. Pariahs, outcasts. Turning others into pariahs, or killing them. Turning her into a pariah.

"Why did you do it to me? I can't help you. I don't know anything about science. What do you expect of me?"

She realized with surprise that they were approaching the car again. She did not know when they had retraced their steps.

"First write your eagle book. We'll stay here and go on just as we've been doing. You'll become rich and reclusive. Saul and I were both happy to meet you because of your book. Others will be happy to meet you, too. They'll be attracted by the same things that attracted us: your honesty and courage, your compassion, understanding, your gentleness and your strength. You'll travel around the world, taking pictures, talking to people, moving on. And now and then you'll meet someone who would work out. We need others, Lyle. We need help in finding them, and recruiting them, and we need someone who can help them accept what it means. No friends beyond our own group, no lovers, no children . . ."

Friends, lovers, children, all the relationships that made them human, those were the things they would be told they would have to give up.

"Others for what purpose? To do what?"

"At first we thought no one could ever have it, no one at all. It doesn't change you. You don't gain wisdom, or courage, or anything else. You just keep living, exactly the way you are. But we've decided that if the world could change, if enough people could change . . . I don't know if it will work. Sometimes I know it can't. But we have to try. We can't keep waiting for answers we may never find. We have to try something else. A few people here and there, people like you who don't want power or glory, who don't want to drive others to do their bidding. Unwilling recruits every one, the most reluctant elite the world has ever seen. Lyle, if we don't try to do something, this world is going to blow itself to hell. You know that. You ran away from it once."

"And you've dragged me back into it."

"Yes."

They reached the car; she walked to the driver's side and opened the door, looked at him over the top of the car. "What if I said no? What if I run away again?"

"You won't."

She felt a flash of anger that they had taken her so much for granted, that they were so certain of her. She looked past him at the ocean. It was starting to get dark; the clouds pressed closer to the sea, as if waiting for darkness to hide their possession of it. Lyle got in the car and turned on the ignition. Carmen sat watching her, waiting.

"Why are you here, at this place?"

There was a long pause before he answered. "Sometimes we have to go somewhere far away from people, where there are things that haven't changed much, where no one talks to us very much. There are a few mountains, places in the desert, upper Maine, here. We need a place where we can just live without having to think for a while."

Lyle nodded. When the pain gets too great to bear, you try to escape, she thought — the bottle, pills, sex; and when none of them gives more than a momentary surcease, you go to the woods, or to the winter beach.

"Saul is well, then. It was a trick to get him out of here."

"Yes. We waited until we knew you had made it. If you had died, it would have been much the same plan. I would have hung around for a day or two, then drifted on."

How casually he said it, if she had died. She turned on the windshield wipers.

"I kept waiting for you to remember everything," Carmen said, still watching her. "Tomorrow I'll send a message to the *Times* personal column to let him know you're okay, you're one of us."

Now she shifted gears and started to back up. "I know what the message should say. 'Blue float is safely ashore.' "

"Welcome home," Carmen said in his most gentle voice.

She thought of the eagles, beyond good and evil, the winter beach entering a transition now, going into spring, and then summer when the ocean would bring back the scrubbed sand, make amends. All ordered, necessary, unavoidable. She started the drive home.

◻ **13** ◻

A PHRASE KEPT repeating in Lyle's mind: the glow of the beech, the flame of the maple. The cemetery, outside Lancaster, Pennsylvania, ended at a wide, brown field, and bordering that were woods with beeches and maples turning color. This part of the cemetery, the new part, held no mausoleums, no tall columns decorated with sweet angels; here the headstones were low, simple. The path was gravel, stark white against the grass that showed no sign of the drought that had devastated the fields beyond. She could hear the grating of her feet on the stones, keeping time to the phrase: the glow of the beech, the flame of the maple. By a student perhaps. Something she had come across in one of the student magazines or newspapers. The cemetery would soon be out of space, what would they do then? It worried her that she did not know what they would do when they used up the available space. She was slowing; as soon as the realization came to her, she walked faster.

"Do you want to stop to buy flowers?" Carmen had asked.

"No. I just go there and look, sit down for a minute or two, think . . ."

No flowers. No ritual to appease her conscience. She regretted that rituals had fused with orthodoxy, with dogma, with rigidity. But was this annual visit a ritual in itself? A set way of behaving, go there and look, sit down for a minute or two, think, remember . . . She had reached the Taney plot. She paused and read the first headstone, as she always did: Louise Weber Taney . . . Gregory's mother.

Louise Taney had climbed a ladder to pick cherries from their back-yard tree; the ladder had slipped, she had fallen. Gregory had arrived home from school, assumed his mother had gone out somewhere, and had left again to play ball. His father had found her when he got home from work. She had died at midnight. First Gregory's mother, then his son. If only he had done something. Always that same desolate cry, if only I had known, if only I had done something.

She moved past the grave and stopped at the next one. It was indistinguishable from the others, the grass the same, the neat little headstone of red schist, more tan than red, no matter what they called it. The day of his birth had been so hot, over a hundred, stifling, with dead air and the oppressive feeling of a thunderstorm that had not yet shaped itself, but hovered just out of consciousness. Strange how she could remember with such clarity the ride to the hospital that day, how frightened Gregory had been, afraid to drive fast, afraid not to.

She stood at the graveside for a moment, then walked a few feet away and sat on the grass, looking toward the woods across the field, seeing the baby, the boy, seeing the past that remained undimmed. When she began to see the beeches and the maples once more, she stood up, feeling as if she had been gone a long time to a very distant place. She whispered goodbye to her son, and turned to retrace her way.

"Hello, Lyle." Gregory stood in the shadow of a pine tree.

She stopped. "Hello, Gregory." The only surprise was that she felt so little.

"Do you come here every year?"

"Yes."

"I saw you in town, driving through. I thought you must be coming up here. It's good to see you."

She started to move again; as she drew closer to him she could see how he had aged, how tired he was. He always had looked older than his years, but it was a shock to see him now like an old man, like his father.

"Congratulations on your book. I meant to write to you, say that."

"Thanks."

When she reached him, he turned to walk by her side. The path was so narrow that their arms brushed lightly.

"You look wonderful," he said.

"And you look terrible. What's wrong?"

"Not much. Just everything. Dad's dying. That's why I'm back here. I'm separated from my wife. The world opened up a crack and I blundered into it." His jaw was clenched in the way she remembered.

"I'm sorry about your father. Is it his heart?"

"Another attack last week. Intensive care, but the doctor says he won't make it."

Cry, she thought at him fiercely. Weep, scream, show something! "I'm sorry about your marriage," she said.

"Don't be. It was pretty bad from day one."

His arm brushed hers, and he stopped walking, caught her wrist. "Lyle, when I saw you in town all I could think of was to find you, talk to you again. Can we go somewhere to have coffee, a drink?"

She shook her head. "I'm sorry. It wouldn't help." He had the look she remembered too well, vulnerable, somehow hurt, somehow betrayed that his body demanded a reaffirmation of life at a time when his brain was numbed; it was the look of desperate need.

"Help me," he said harshly, as if he resented the thought, resented the need.

"Not me. Someone, but not me."

"You! We never should have drifted apart! I always loved you."

"Don't do this! Just don't do this," she said in a low voice. "It's over and done with. We have different lives now."

"Just for one evening, one night. Please, Lyle. Can't you give me that much?"

She started to walk, he remained unmoving.

"Lyle, I'm really scared. I need you so much. Just one night let me hold you, someone warm and alive. Just one night. If you ever cared for me at all, please, just one night!"

She ran.

Carmen drove, she gazed out the window at the Pennsylvania landscape, static, yet moving inexorably from summer to fall.

"Are you all right now?" Carmen asked.

"Yes."

"Can you talk about it?"

He had asked nothing when she had run to the car, crying for him to take her away from there. Her eyes hurt from weeping, and she wanted a drink of water. "Gregory was there," she said finally. "It was bad. He . . . he wanted to go to bed with me."

Carmen let out a long breath. "I'm sorry."

"He doesn't really want me, not me, Lyle. He wants the past, back where we were before everything went to hell for us. That's what he wanted for just a few hours. Something no one else can give him, no one but me. And I couldn't."

"No, you couldn't. No one can give the past to anyone else."

"You don't understand," she said wearily.

Carmen reached for her hand and held it. "I understand exactly, Lyle."

Looking at him, she knew that he did. She thought of the high north country of Maine where they went occasionally, the Oregon coast, the desert . . . Sometimes when it gets too bad, you have to go away from people, she thought, and knew with a pang what that meant. Carmen's face was set in a way that made him strange, like a child wearing an old man's face. She lifted his hand and kissed it; for a long time neither spoke as he drove northward toward the mountains.

Everything had gone as Carmen had said it should. They had stayed at the coast; she had written her book, all she could do away from a good library; then they had moved into a New York apartment, where she had finished the work. To her question about when would she visit Saul, he had answered that first they had to establish her lifestyle. Five months had passed, long enough to show that she was a well-off middle-aged woman with a live-in young assistant. If anyone had been watching her during that time, that was all that could have been learned.

"He's really dead, isn't he?" she had asked one night.

Carmen looked up in puzzlement. "Who?"

"Saul. Just tell me if he's dead."

"No, of course not."

"Then why can't I go see him? I have to talk to him."

"Soon."

October had come and her annual visit to her son's graveside.

"Let's take some time, go through the Pocono Mountains. The foliage will be beautiful this time of year," Carmen had said.

This was part of their plan, too, she thought. Now she would start traveling, establish that she would come and go freely so that when they needed her to go somewhere for them, it would not appear unusual to anyone who might notice.

The countryside flowed by: brown fields, flaming sumac, scarlet maples, yellow poplars. Most of the barns had hex signs on them, all slightly different, all maintained with fresh paint, clearly delineated. The land became hillier and they were in the Delaware River district. Carmen stopped at the water gap, the passage through the mountains the river had made for itself, and they walked to the summit to look out over the farms, the lovely river. Everywhere there were the signs of an early autumn.

"It's because of the drought," Lyle said, when they started to drive again. "A drought brings fall, as if the trees have decided they might as well go dormant until spring."

"I always liked autumn better than any other season," Carmen said. "I'm glad we're back east for it."

"I am too. Where are we going now?"

"A place called Hawley, in the Poconos. Not in Hawley, actually, but near it. There's a pharmaceutical company up there — "

"Saul!"

He turned to grin at her, nodded.

"Why didn't you tell me?"

"I thought it would be better to tell you after you stopped at the cemetery. Maybe that was wrong."

She shook her head. "No. I'm glad." She knew that if he looked at her now, he would see her cheeks flushed, see the excitement she could not hide. And yet, and yet . . . She glanced at him, away. How many times had she played through this scenario where she had to tell him that it was Saul she loved? Sometimes she played it through to an end, other times she faltered, or she denied it . . . There were many variations, all difficult, impossible even.

"The place we're going is actually a private residence with a laboratory, the production plant and main lab are near Philadelphia."

"What's the company name?"

"M and S Pharmaceuticals."

Lyle exclaimed in disbelief, "But that's a real company! I use their stuff. My doctor used to prescribe some of their sleeping pills."

He laughed. "It's real. We pay taxes and everything. And we do real research."

"You too?"

"Most of the time."

"This must have been a hard year for you then."

"Sabbatical. I was due time off."

She turned her gaze to the countryside again, trying to assimilate this new information. A real company, real drugs, real identities. "How old is the company?"

"Twenty-five years now. Saul — Dr. Hermann Franck, that is — is also Clive Markham, the M part, and I'm Joseph Steilburg, Jr., the S!"

"Do other people work there?"

"You mean outsiders? No, not at Hawley. Right now there are four researchers, you'll meet them. Others come and go. They are mostly outsiders at the main lab."

"How many altogether?" She heard sharpness in her voice. He looked at her. "What is it? What did I say?"

"How many insiders? And are they all scientists?"

"Oh. I see. You're the first nonscientist. There are a couple dozen, twenty-six actually, altogether, and you make twenty-seven."

"Maybe I can keep their computers oiled, or sharpen their pencils for them now and then."

"Lyle, if we hadn't wanted you, needed you, we wouldn't have included you. We do need you."

"So you keep telling me. How many women are there?"

"You're the eighth."

"Do you draw lots for them?"

Carmen snorted with laughter and did not answer.

She had not asked questions before, had been reluctant to talk about any of it when Carmen brought it up. For hours at a time she had managed not to think of a group at all. A small band of lonely men, she had thought once, frustrated in their work, frustrated sexually, forced to maintain isolation from other human contact, how had they survived? She had endured celibacy for several years, but that was different. She had been dead emotionally. She had shied away from the answer she found in her mind. They had endured the same way prisoners do, the same way men at sea for long periods had endured through the centuries, the same way human beings always find to endure. Anyone who could not tolerate celibacy found sexual relief with other human beings, she had concluded, and had thought of it no more. Carmen never had spoken of any women in the group, but she must have known there were some. How else could they have tested the theory that no pregnancy could take place? She had known, had put it out of her mind so thoroughly that it had become almost a taboo, something that was no longer forbidden because it had dropped totally from consciousness.

In her mind the configuration had been with herself between Carmen and Saul; no other pattern would form now. She had been like a child, she realized, refusing to think of something in the hope that it would go away. If she did not think about it today, maybe she would not have to tomorrow and the next day.

After a few minutes of silence, Carmen said, "Let me tell you about the building. It's rather pretty. Used to be a mill, abandoned years ago, but the water wheel is still there. We generate our own electricity with it. The building is made of stone, as if they meant it to last for all eternity, and the water is so pure, so cold all summer you can't even wade in it without having your feet go numb. A few hundred feet down from the building there's a waterfall with a drop of seventy-five feet. That's the background noise. We set up a bird refuge years ago; people come from all over to bird watch, take photographs. You'll like it."

"You let other people in?"

"Sure. We have regular maintenance people, a little parking area for the tourists, picnic tables. They don't get inside the main house, of course."

"And the maintenance people . . . ?"

He answered slowly, "They're all local people, outsiders."

And from time to time you have to get away, go to Maine, or to the Oregon coast, or a desert somewhere . . . She sighed. "Is Saul going to tell me what I'm supposed to do now?"

"I think so. Remember, I haven't seen him either for a long time. And talked to him only briefly a few times. I know as little about this meeting as you."

It was dark by the time they arrived at the company house. When Lyle got out of the car she heard the waterfall like a noisy grumble in the distance. Then Saul was hurrying to her, his arms out, and the waterfall entered her, thundered inside her head.

"Lyle, my dear! My dearest Lyle!" He held her tightly against his chest and rubbed his cheek on her hair. "Welcome home, Lyle. Welcome home."

Several other people had come out, were helping Carmen with the bags, embracing him.

"Let's get inside," Saul said. "Introductions, hot coffee, a drink, a hot bath, food, whatever you want. Inside, come on now."

There was a woman's soft laughter at his peremptory tone, and a deep chuckle from a man; as a group, they all moved up the walk and into the building. Saul kept his arm about Lyle's shoulders.

They entered an anteroom with a desk and a few chairs, passed through it into a wide corridor. At first Lyle felt self-conscious with Saul's arm around her, but Carmen was being held by the woman and one of the men, and she had the feeling that touching, hugging, open displays of love, friendship, whatever it was, was the norm here. The corridor was paneled in pale golden wood; there were silk prayer rugs on both sides, and a plush red Persian carpet on the floor. At the end of the corridor there was a circular room, or continuation of the corridor, with a center post that was eight feet or more in diameter; it had a circular staircase leading to the upper floor. Here there were many large potted plants, some nearly full sized trees, all lush and healthy looking.

"I'll show you around properly tomorrow," Saul said. "Surprisingly big, isn't it? They used to drive their wagons right inside the building to unload the corn, wheat, whatever they wanted ground. We had to do some extensive remodeling, of course, but as soon as we saw this place we knew it was just what we wanted."

He guided her through another doorway into a very large room with several groupings of comfortable chairs and a pair of matching couches at right angles to a mammoth fireplace. It was a green and brown room with touches of brilliant red in cushions, picked up in a bowl of chrysanthemums. There were modern paintings here — Kandinsky, Miro . . . One entire wall was made up of windows.

"It's rather pretty in daylight," Saul said.

"It's beautiful right now," Lyle protested. It was beautiful, but more, it was comfortable, with books on tables, magazines here and there, a bowl of nuts with some shells in an amber dish . . .

"Now, let's see, where will we start? Dora Lewis, Lyle Taney."

"Hello, Lyle," Dora said, moving in to shake her hand. Dora

was tall and very slender, almost thin. She had the same look of good health that Saul and Carmen had, that Lyle herself now had. And she had the same hint of underlying sadness. Dora was very young, she thought, then corrected herself. There was no way of telling how old she really was. She was striking, but not pretty; her eyes were a bit too deep-set, her nose a bit too prominent, her mouth a little too large. When she smiled, Lyle forgot her instant assessment. Her smile was lovely.

She met the others: Hilary Nast, whose accent betrayed his British origins, portly, middle-aged, ruddy complexion with startlingly blue eyes. Steve Trumbull, as young as Carmen, but heavier, with broad shoulders, big hands, and very thick and long red-brown hair. His eyebrows were like woolly bear caterpillars; she bit her cheek to suppress the giggle that followed the thought. The last one was McDermott Evans, Mutt, Saul said gravely. She knew why: his brown eyes were very large and soulful. He was suntanned a deep mahogany color, his hair was wiry and almost kinky curly.

"Do you play bridge?" he asked, still holding her hand.

"Yes."

"Well?"

"Not very, I'm afraid."

He let out a whoop of pleasure. "Wonderful! Confidentially, two of the people present in this room at this very moment are nothing less than card sharks. They must never be allowed to play partners. Now if one of them has you, and I have the other one, we may be able to get a decent game."

Dora threw a pillow at him, and Saul took Lyle's hand and steered her to a buffet table. "We didn't know if you'd stop to eat a full meal, or just snack along the way. Anyway, we're prepared. It wasn't easy to keep Steve from gobbling it all up while we waited, I want you to know."

There were chafing dishes with hot roast beef, mushrooms simmering in a wine sauce, an icy, crisp salad, and tiny pickled carrots. Steve filled a plate alongside Lyle and Carmen.

"Lesson I learned real young," he said cheerfully. "Eat when food's available or you might not eat at all."

Their talk was good-natured, bantering, a little teasing. Anyone looking at them would think what a nice group of people, how pleasant and civilized they all were. Lyle wondered if they fought, if they became angry with each other, jealous of each other. Did they become too depressed to stay and work? She knew the answer to that one. Saul and Carmen had left for almost a year. She tried to imagine how the others would pair up to go away for a few months, a year, two years. They never went alone. Carmen had said they did not dare go out too far alone. What if one of them got hit by a car, was taken to a hospital? "What would show?" she had demanded. "How are we different?" He had hesitated, then said, "If you're really battered and start to heal all by yourself, they might notice. If they give you an anesthetic and it doesn't take, they might notice. Sleeping pills, drugs, they won't work for you anymore, Lyle. Yesterday you scratched your leg, where's the scratch now?" It was gone, no scratch lasted more than a few hours. Her face never got windburned anymore. Her lips did not chap.

We're not quite human any longer, she thought suddenly. None of us here is really quite human. She had sensed a difference in Saul at her first meeting with him, and a bit later she had known that Carmen shared it, even though she had had no idea then what the *it* represented. They all looked radiantly healthy, and tonight the gaiety was unfeigned, was deeply felt, she was certain, but it was the kind of gaiety that comes with a programmed holiday, and when the holiday ends, the gaiety departs with it. Underlying the holiday spirit that Carmen's return had generated, there was a bitter sadness, the same relentless sadness she had detected in Saul. The same despair. They were like prisoners in a common room celebrating Christmas, knowing that as soon as curfew comes, they would once more be prisoners. It made them look haunted in a curious way.

Carmen was in a deep discussion with Dora and Hilary, a technical discussion that Lyle had not tried to follow. Steve was eating cookies. Mutt had gone to the window and was standing with his back to the room. He beckoned to Lyle.

"Look, two does and a buck. They come every night."

The deer were across the stream, just visible in the light from the building. The buck finished drinking, raised his head. For a moment his eyes glowed orange, he looked downstream and the light was gone. The does drank and they all walked away sedately.

"Hasn't anyone ever taught them about guns?"

"This is a refuge, forty thousand acres. Even so, they'll vanish during hunting season," Saul said. He stood up and held out his hand for Lyle. "Would you like to see your room now? You've had a long day."

She glanced at Carmen in confusion. He blew her a kiss.

"Goodnight, Lyle. See you in the morning." He returned to his conversation with Dora and Hilary.

Everyone was saying goodnight, sleep well, see you in the morning, and she walked from the room with her hand in Saul's.

◻ **14** ◻

"I'M AFRAID your room isn't quite as large as some of them in this part of the building. There are bigger ones in the new addition. If you want to move tomorrow . . ." He led her back the way they had entered the building, stopped at the first door in the main corridor. "Here we are."

The room was spacious, with a sitting area curtained off from the bed. There were easy chairs, tables, a coffee table with a bowl of fruit, and there was a wide window that overlooked the stream. Her suitcase was on the floor by the bed.

"It's a lovely room," she said faintly.

"Your bath is through that door," he said pointing. "Are you very tired? Can we sit and talk for a few minutes?"

They went to the chairs, which were in shadows. Light from the bedside lamp was filtered through the curtains. Lyle stood looking out over the water, aware that Saul was watching her.

"You were very upset when you found out, weren't you?"

She moistened her lips. "Yes. Did you think I wouldn't be?"

"I knew you would be. I'm only sorry I wasn't there. Are you still unhappy?"

She turned to face him. "Yes. You didn't ask me. You didn't warn me. You just went ahead and did it. What I might have wanted never came into it. I feel . . . used. Lasater used me. You used me. It's degrading."

"I'm sorry," he said. "Please sit down." She sank down into a soft chair and he sat opposite her, across the coffee table. "Have you remembered that night yet? Remembered it all?"

"Yes. You examined me, took my medical history, gave me an injection . . ."

"That was the second night. Have you remembered anything of the first night?"

Her lips had gone dry again. She felt strange, disconnected, apart from herself. She closed her eyes, and saw the fire in the hearth, heard the rain beating on the roof, saw Carmen on the floor, Saul in the chair opposite, speaking.

"Do you believe that we all have a duty to humankind?"

"Yes, but it's too hard to know what it is."

"If you could perform such a duty, at great personal cost, do you think you would?"

"I don't know. I think I would, but what does that mean? I think I would be generous, and kind, and good, but I'm not always, not even very often."

"I'm going to tell you a story, Lyle, and then I'll ask you a question. I'll ask you to decide."

Her eyes jerked open. "You told me that night! Before you included me!"

"Yes, Lyle. You decided that night."

"But I was hypnotized!"

"No. I hypnotized you before that and then woke you up. When we talked you were perfectly normal. Later I hypnotized you again and told you to forget the conversation until you were ready to deal with it. I don't know why you didn't remember it before now."

She remembered her disbelief, then confusion, and finally acceptance of what they had told her.

"It should be a wonderful, joyful gift!" she had cried. "Not a burden laden with guilt."

"Half the people who try to use it die," Saul had answered soberly. "Those who can use it successfully are sterile. That is not a gift we can give to the world, not yet."

And then she had forgotten it all. Why? She looked at Saul who was watching her quietly. When she was with him she believed that she might have a role to play, she might be able to do something for the world, she was not simply another failure. But only with him. As soon as they were parted, she knew herself again. "Most people who are basically decent really want to serve their fellow human beings," she had said that night. "I'm no exception. Only there's usually no way we can find to do it. March in demonstrations. Donate to causes. Serve on committees. And all the time feel futile, feel that we're spinning our wheels, accomplishing nothing. I want to help you, if I can." And then she had forgotten it again. She was such a glib backslider.

Saul stood up and came to her, holding out both hands.

She shook her head. "I have to tell you about Carmen and me."

"I know about you and Carmen. Come, Lyle, I want very much to make love to you, if you'll have me."

She reached out and he took her hands and drew her up from the chair. They stood apart and she knew he was waiting for her decision.

"I love you," she said faintly. "I've loved you from the start. Even when I thought you hadn't been fair."

"We've had to wait an awfully long time. I've envisioned this night many, many times during these past months." He stroked her hair gently, then traced her eyebrow with one finger. "You are so lovely."

She awakened alone and could not stop smiling. Supporting herself on one elbow she looked at the pillow where his head had rested all night. Several times she had come awake and had reached out to touch him, just to make certain.

"Good morning," he called from somewhere not in her room.

There was another door that she had not noticed last night. Now she got up and looked inside the other room; it was his study. He was near the window, rising from a deep leather chair. He crossed the room quickly, his smile wide and infectious.

"I left the door open so I could hear you when you began to move. Did you sleep well? Are you hungry?"

"Yes, yes. Good morning." He kissed her and she left to shower. When she came back, he had coffee and toast waiting, an orange peeled.

"This is why I wanted you in the little room," he said. "Next door to me. What I thought we would do first is go inspect the geese. They began arriving two days ago. Did you hear them last night?"

She shook her head.

"And then we'll look at the waterfall, there's a nice path we can take on the other side. I want to show you our refuge. The colors are magnificent right now. Nothing as wild as the Oregon coast was, but still nice in its own way. I think you'll like it."

"How long can I stay here?"

He poured more coffee for both of them before answering. "A week, maybe a bit more."

"When can I come back?"

"Next month."

She put down her toast and pushed her plate away. "Isn't there any way I can work here, stay with you?"

"I'm looking for a property to buy, somewhere not far from here. It will be yours, in your name, your retreat. I have two that I want you to inspect this week. Then I can be your house guest."

"I'll take one! The first one I see! I don't care what it is."

He laughed. "No you won't. This is a lifetime investment. You want a house with suitable facilities for a darkroom, for guests, something you'll be comfortable in."

She laughed too then. "I'll find something fast. I promise."

The days were golden, one after another. Each day Saul kept her out for hours to look at geese, to admire the waterfall, to walk in the woods where the leaves were knee deep. She talked with the other scientists from time to time and came to like them all. She got to know the housekeeper, Mrs. Lanier, and her grown daughter, Alice, who was retarded. Saul took her to inspect the two properties that he had mentioned.

The first house they looked at was a derelict, vacant for six years, mistreated for many years before that. They did not even bother to go inside. The second one was too small, a two-bedroom A-frame summer house.

"Why do I have to have a big house?" she asked, back in his study afterward. A freezing mist was painting everything beyond the window with fairy silver. Lyle was on a pillow on the floor, her head on his knees; he was stroking her hair.

"Where were you during the Cuban missile crisis?" he asked.

She glanced at him in surprise. "I was a student."

A rueful smile crossed his face. "I keep forgetting. Of course you were. We were here, Carmen, I, a few others. For several days it appeared that the war we all dreaded was in the making. And we had not done anything to plan for it, nothing. When the crisis passed, we did begin to make plans. We were all still certain we could find answers to the two major questions about the serum, why it kills so many, and how to achieve pregnancy. Just a few more years, we all thought. That's all we needed, just a few more years. But what if another crisis developed? What if the next one was not averted? We had to have something planned just in case. And we needed more help. Our group was too small. So many died," he said softly. His hand tightened on her hair, then he resumed stroking. "We built up our staff gradually over a long period, and we were as far as ever from our answers. Two years ago we decided to expand again, this time to bring in people who aren't scientists, but are clear-sighted, intelligent, knowledgeable about the world. People like you. You're the first one we've found. Carmen and I both knew at once that you would fit in, that you would be a valuable asset. If you can help us find others, help them go through the period of adjustment . . . You'll need a large house for that."

The period of adjustment, she thought and nodded. "What do you want with your larger community when you get it?"

"We need to make decisions. What if we finally have to admit there are no solutions to the problems with the serum? Will we abandon it utterly? Will we break up our group and go back among the public at large, start spreading it through human contacts? Go to the government, start a massive project? Publish? If we decide none of those will be appropriate, will we then try to infiltrate governments? Try to perfect the institutions, the people? Each of these is a possibility. Each has been discussed for many hours, and we have no final decisions about any of them. We decided to postpone all decisions until we had found a few other people to bring in, people not from science, but from the humanities, from history, literature, the arts, maybe psychology . . ."

She was shaking her head. "What you'll get is a mess."

Now he laughed. "We talked about that, too. Lyle, I can't tell you how happy I am that you're here. That first night when you came to the house on the cliff you talked about the Titans, Prometheus and his brother Epimetheus, and I could hardly contain my happiness. I doubt that a single one of our brilliant scientists here even knows that Prometheus had a brother, much less what his name was. You made me realize how desperately lonely I had become, and become used to being."

Later, reading in the living room, she remembered that she had meant to return to what he had said about making plans following the Cuban crisis. There would be time, she thought, and looked up as Dora joined her.

"Find a house?" Dora asked, sprawling ungracefully on the couch.

"No. The search is on though."

"I hope it's soon. It'll be nice to have someplace close by where we can go when the pressure here gets too high."

Lyle felt a mild surprise that Dora should have mentioned what she herself had not detected. They appeared loose, easy, comfortable with each other. But there had to be times when they snapped at each other, times when the sight of one of the others would drive any one of them out of the house, away altogether.

"How long have you been here?"

"This time? About sixteen months now."

"Working on the serum all the time?"

"No way. None of us could take that. We get an idea, run it into the ground and then work on something else until there's a new idea. We've come up with some pretty nifty things for the company over the years. Whenever we get a new idea about the serum, we drop everything and go back to it. I stayed with it for seven years once before it nose-dived." She looked disgusted.

"How were you brought into the group?" Lyle asked, and quickly added, "I hope you don't mind my questions. It sounds like prying, doesn't it?"

Dora laughed and waved her hand, as if clearing the air of the objections. She had been one of those child prodigies, she said, with heavy self-mockery. In college by fourteen, a doctorate by twenty-one. "The great white hope of the University of Wisconsin," she said, laughing. When she was twenty-four, she had read a paper at an international symposium of biologists in Denmark; she had met Carmen, and through him Saul, under different names, of course.

"They told me where my work would lead, and I didn't believe them. They showed me proof, their notes, diagrams, figures. It was all there. And the conclusions were obvious. If I continued with the work, at the university, others would be involved, they would know. At that point I was pretty much alone and the implications certainly were not apparent. But there aren't any secrets in a university laboratory. The funding comes from the government, work has to be approved, reports written, verified, approved. When I published, others would be free to replicate my work, carry it on even if I dropped out. I had to leave it, Saul told me quite firmly. The only way I could continue that line was by joining the group here, and I could work for the rest of my life on whatever I chose in complete freedom, privacy, with more than adequate funding. Only I would never publish or be famous." She laughed quietly. "That's what he said to me, I could work the rest of my life on whatever I chose."

She seemed to be looking back into the past with a glint of amusement now as she continued.

"I didn't know what to do. I was twenty-four! What did I know? I screamed and had a tantrum and called them names! As a child prodigy I had been allowed to use language. I had been allowed to do anything I damn well pleased. Everyone was scared to death of me because I was so bright."

"Did they tell you about the sterility? About the mortality rate? I mean, before they gave it to you."

"Oh yes. Everything. They talked to my brain and my answer came from my guts."

"But you agreed."

"The next day. That night I cried and screamed at them for hours, then I did a flip-flop and became all cerebral on them. I went over the work again, point by point, pretended not to believe their conclusions. They knew I was lying. The funny thing is that from the start I knew they both loved me. You don't know what that means to the kind of kid I was. Precocious, funny-looking all my life, afraid of boys, more afraid of men when I grew up. No friends. No social life at all. Hated my family, my pretty sister, handsome dumb brother. I lived in a vacuum. Just me and work. Anyway, they looked through what other people saw and they found something different and showed that they approved of it. I don't know why or how, I don't even know what I mean by that, but it's true."

"I know it is," Lyle said. "That's how it was with me. They loved me, accepted me just the way I was. It was the first time that had happened to me, too."

"Well, that was in nineteen sixty-eight. I pretended illness and left the conference, went with them, and later resigned from my position, claimed bad health, a breakdown. No one doubted it. Too busy saying 'I told you she was crazy.' I'm not officially dead, not like some of them around here, but I'm officially through, a has-been."

The morning before Lyle and Carmen were to leave, Saul got a phone call from Seymour Oliver. Lyle was with him.

"You probably don't know of him," Saul said, after hanging up, staring out the window at the stream. "He's the head of the biology department at Harvard. One of us. He thinks the Russians have discovered the serum."

Watching his face, Lyle felt a chill that raised goosebumps on her arms. She never had seen him like this, distant, hard, cold, ruthless even. For a long time he continued to stare out the window. Then he sighed and looked at her. "My dear, can you occupy yourself today? I'm afraid Carmen and I have a lot of work to take care of."

She nodded. He already was lifting the house phone to call Carmen when she left him. In her room she sat before her own window and tried to think what it would mean if the Russians really did have the serum. A new phase, she thought. Something was ending, something else beginning.

That afternoon, too restless to stay inside, she took her camera and tripod to the pond half a mile from the house, and for hours she photographed the geese. There were about a hundred of them by now. Adjacent to the pond was a field with standing millet, food for them, for the deer, for field mice, whatever came along for a free meal. The sun went behind the hill and the air became cold fast. Reluctantly she returned to the residence.

No one was in the living room, or in the room they called the nursery, where there was a pool table, a television, the card table, another table with a chessboard inlaid with mother-of-pearl and black marble. She wandered around the circular corridor and then went up the steps to the second floor. Dora and Mutt were at the far end of the laboratory talking in low voices. There were stone-topped benches and work tables, refrigerators, sinks, burners, shelves of glassware that Lyle could not identify, and several desks. Across the hall from the lab there were two offices, both with the doors standing open.

In the first one there were two desks, a couch, two leather chairs, files, and a library of reference books. The second office had a computer that had made her catch her breath when she first saw it. In here there was a printer, a very large screen, the terminal keyboard, and again, files. No one was in either office.

She went downstairs. This was what she had feared; they all had skills, things they could do, work they wanted to do. She was like a third elbow. She caught a glimpse of Alice Lanier, but that young woman smiled and fled, as she always did. She had said no more than a dozen words in Lyle's presence. Lyle continued to her own room.

Had they discussed this possibility also? It was bound to happen eventually, if not now, that the Russians, or the Chinese, or some other group would find the secret, a group they could not monitor, could not restrict, could not recruit. She remembered the hard, set mask that had come over Saul's face and she knew they had discussed this, had planned for it somehow, and she shivered hard.

Unaccountably, her thoughts turned to the geese stuffing themselves on the millet, preparing for the next leg of their long flight. Responding to signals they could not perceive, they left their nesting grounds, their feeding grounds, and started the hazardous journey to a place many of them had never even seen. Oblivious of the hunters, the traps, the destruction of their resting places where ponds had been filled in, houses built, roads built, they carried out the imperative of their genes. It mattered little that many of them would not arrive, the species was preserving itself the only way it could.

What if the Russians did have it? she thought then. What would that mean? Troubled, and suddenly afraid, she sat down to consider what it might mean to them here at the residence, to the rest of the world.

□ **15** □

SEYMOUR OLIVER and Daniel Malone arrived at ten that night. Lyle had read many of Daniel Malone's science articles in the *New York Times* and the *New Yorker*. Seymour Oliver was white-haired, benign-looking, with pink cheeks and pale blue eyes. Daniel Malone was almost preternaturally tall and thin, like a latter day Ichabod Crane, gangly, awkward in his movements, so slow speaking that she expected him to stammer at any moment.

Lyle had known that someone would accompany Oliver, and after a momentary feeling of surprise to find that it was someone as famous as Malone, she thought, how appropriate. He could go places where none of the others would be admitted. He traveled throughout the world. His credentials were very good; he had been a physicist or something like that. She caught Carmen's gaze and shrugged. If the president or the chief of staff or a senator arrived, she would accept that, too.

As soon as everyone had been introduced and they were all comfortable, Seymour Oliver spoke.

"Let me fill you in on background," he said. "Four years ago the International Biology Congress was held at Vienna. At that time I met a number of Russian scientists, including Boris Lepov, whose paper was disturbingly close. I found the opportunity to talk to him before we adjourned. We agreed that there are some things in science that should never be controlled by any government. It was oblique, of course, but I thought at the time and think now we both understood exactly what was being said. We talked a little about the feasibility of forming an international group of people dedicated to the principle of keeping some discoveries out of the hands of governments. Again, I am convinced our understanding was mutual. I told him that if ever he, or any of his people, wanted help of any kind, to please write to me directly and include the phrase 'we would appreciate your personal assistance' and finish the sentence any way that would be appropriate. This morning I received such a letter from Boris Lepov."

There was a long silence that Hilary Nast finally broke. "Do you think he wants you to help him get out?"

"Not him. He was scheduled to read a paper at the Congress in Amsterdam at the end of the month. He has withdrawn his own paper and presence. One of his assistants, Yuri Korolenko, will appear instead. Lepov has asked for our assistance for Korolenko."

"Have you met him?" Carmen asked.

He shook his head.

"I have," Malone said in his halting manner. "When I was in Moscow three years ago I met Lepov and his assistants, five in all. Yuri Korolenko and his wife, Fanya Shchastny, both worked with him at that time."

"It could be meaningless," Steve Trumbull said. "Political. It could be unrelated."

"The paper submitted for Yuri Korolenko to read is titled: 'Spontaneous Mutations as a Result of Specific Variations in the Gaseous Elements.' "

Lyle looked from one to another of them, and when no one spoke she said, "I don't understand the significance of that."

"It's five-year-old work," Saul said. "Not even Lepov's work."

Lyle sighed in exasperation. "If you all know that, won't it seem suspicious to other people for them to change it at this late date? What was the title of Lepov's paper?"

"He hadn't submitted it yet. Sometimes it works that way," Seymour Oliver said. "I'm on the committee, you see. If Lepov said he would appear and read a paper, I'd know it was going to be important enough to allot him program time, and I would hope to get the paper in enough time to have it translated, distributed, and so on. The fact that they have submitted this title tells me that nothing of any consequence is to be presented by them. They'll probably tie this work in with their space program and no one will give it another thought. But when I talked with Lepov we both agreed that the really important work was going on here on Earth, not in space. I read the title as a message, as much as the key phrase is."

Lyle sat back and for the next half-hour listened to them discuss it, arguing for and against the idea that Lepov wanted them to get his assistant out of Russia. She was startled when Saul looked at her and said, "Lyle, exactly what would it mean if Russia had this secret?"

"Why me?" she asked. "You all know more about this than I do."

"Not more about history, about the odds of one action as opposed to another. What do you think it would mean?"

She thought for a moment about the notes she had made that afternoon. Then she asked Seymour Oliver, "Has there been another international meeting since the one when you talked to Lepov?"

"No. About every four years more or less is common."

"Then I would assume that in the intervening four years they came up with the same method you have. And if they did, I would assume that their government knows about it. Depending on when that happened, probably the government has already started testing it on human subjects — prisoners no doubt. That's what this government would do. And the scientific team more than likely is under some kind of restraint if not actually in prison." She paused, thinking. "They'll want to find out exactly the same things you do: why the fifty-percent mortality rate, and how to predict it; and why the sterility and how to overcome it. If they have the answer to either question, or both, they will start using it on their top leaders, military personnel, key industrial figures, and so on, in something like that order. And they will probably start thinking seriously of launching a first-strike attack as soon as they know their people are protected from radiation, and before the other side has a chance to develop it for themselves. I also think," she said deliberately, "that this is the scenario that either side will follow if that side believes it alone possesses the secret."

"Why?" Saul asked quietly. "It isn't a new weapon system."

"But it is. Civil defense is also a weapon in the war that's going on now. And this can be seen as a civil defense system that is invulnerable to attack with the weapons that are set to be fired. Radiation no longer will be a necessary deterrent to war. If A and B are at parity more or less and either side develops a new system that cannot be equaled instantly, that could be the trigger. We have to leak secrets, and so do they. We are afraid not to. Because paranoia is so rampant, either side will have to assume the other is learning of this secret, and will be tempted to strike before the other gains access and deploys the new system also, or else fear being hit before they can deploy it fully themselves. They call it a preemptive defensive strike," she finished bitterly. "Why are you doing this? You must have gone over it again and again."

Saul nodded. "We have. I hoped you would see something different. There was the possibility that our own thinking had become paranoid."

"Remember how the flu and meningitis spread around the world in nineteen eighteen?" Dora said. "This will spread even faster. The world will go screw crazy!"

"That's why I think there would be very little time between using it and striking," Lyle said. "Assuming the Russians have solved the problems with the serum, they will feel most vulnerable during the time it takes to start using it and before it spreads around the world. They know, just as we do, that a small group like this one, dedicated and committed, can contain it, but not the military, not the party functionaries, whoever else they select to receive it. Its only real value as a weapon lies in their being the only ones who have it when radiation covers the world, otherwise it's simply parity all over again on a higher level. We have to keep in mind that our military and theirs are equally crazy. To talk about a preemptive defensive strike is insane and yet both sides do it. They could see this as the deciding factor, just as our government could see it that way, and they could be planning to distribute it and strike very quickly afterward."

"That's where we kept ending up no matter where we began," Malone said, studying her with interest. "But we've lived with the problem for a number of years."

"And I've read history for a number of years. There's nothing in all the history I've ever studied to make me believe this crop of political leaders is any different from the others that have gone into the history books starting more than four thousand years ago. Smith and Jones have fought over that shrinking water hole from the dawn of civilization."

"You said we leak secrets," Mutt Evans said thoughtfully. "Of course we do, they do. We're scared to death they may think we have the edge, and so are they. But what if this leaked? There could be a new Manhattan Project–type research group set up with orders to discover the secret overnight. It can be found, you know. Dan found it, others can."

Malone said to Lyle, "I caught on to their little secret. Lost my greatest book, I'm afraid. They drafted me." His voice was rueful. "But that's right, it is out there to be found. It's just that no one really believes in it."

"Hugh Lasater does," Lyle said.

"And no one believed him," Carmen said.

"Not then. But if they suspect there's anything to it, if they suspect the Russians have it . . . They'll believe him enough to follow up on what he told them," Lyle said with certainty.

We should have killed him, she thought, and felt a deep chill at the ease with which the thought formed, wrapped itself in words. She looked at the others, Saul with his eyes that had gone so hard and cold; Carmen intent, frowning in concentration; Mutt, Dora, Steve, all thoughtful, all capable of killing. Hilary Nast could do it without a qualm, coolly, neatly, expeditiously, and then go back to his newspaper or novel without another thought of the deed. And Daniel Malone? Could he? Could Oliver? Judges and juries, all of them. Deciding the fate of the world. She closed her eyes hard. They were keeping the world safe for death.

"To get back to the question," Oliver said then, "I'm afraid a leak is the last thing we want right now. There's the time element," he said apologetically to Mutt. "If they've had it a number of years or even months, they've had time to start producing it, if that's their plan, if they've decided it's safe enough to use. They'll be watching so closely there's not a chance of duplicating that kind of work without their catching on to it. I'd say every biologist in the country must be under surveillance at this point, if that's what they're up to. Any sudden activity in that area might be the signal for them to make their move."

"And if this government finds out and realizes that they're that far ahead, possibly ready to start mass distribution, *that* could be the opening move," Malone added.

"We have to know," Carmen said suddenly. "What are we going to do about Yuri Korolenko?"

"What does he look like?" Saul asked Malone.

He gazed at the ceiling thinking. "About five ten, slender, almost delicate looking. Dark brown, rather thin hair, sallow complexion, brown eyes. Twenty-five to thirty, I'd say."

"Why would they send him, a nobody?" Dora asked.

"Oh, I expect because they think he'll go back. He and his wife were newly-weds when I met them."

"Why let anyone go to the meeting?" Lyle asked. "You'd think if they really had it, the government would forbid any of them to go anywhere."

"It would look too suspicious for no one to show up from that team. They are the foremost biologists in Russia. It might make other people go back through their past papers to see what they were onto."

"We don't know for certain that he'll want to leave," Saul said then. "Maybe he just wants to talk to Oliver, tell him what they're doing, ask his advice. We don't know. But if he does want to leave, we have to have a plan. Any ideas?"

"Wouldn't they turn to the CIA for something like that?" Lyle said. "You certainly don't have the manpower for such a maneuver."

"Remember, they may want to keep it out of the government's hands," Saul said. "They may have the same scenarios in mind that you outlined for us. If this government knows what they have, it could be disastrous."

"We'd have to do it before the conference gets started," Carmen said thoughtfully. "Away from the conference center. It'll be swarming with CIA, KGB, God knows who all."

"He'll be watched closely, at the center or away from it."

"Franz can help. That makes three of you who will be there," Carmen went on. He looked at Malone. "You could be interviewing Franz while on a sightseeing tour. Franz already asked Yuri to go along, so he's there, too. You probably would be a little annoyed that Franz is making it a party, taking Oliver along, taking Yuri. Anyone else going to be there?"

Oliver nodded. "Luis Betancourt."

"He's part of the group too. That's enough. You go to Anne Frank's refuge, take a ride on the canal, end up at the Van Gogh Museum and that's where we make the switch."

"What do you mean?" Lyle asked sharply. "Who? What switch?"

"Didn't you hear the description he gave? He described me to a T."

"*No!*" She looked from Carmen to Saul. He was nodding slowly. "You can't let him do it! It won't work! They'll just end up with Carmen and their own man!"

No one paid any attention. Each of them seemed to be considering the plan, each of them willing to risk him. She stood up and went to the buffet where the coffee was on a heating unit. Her hands shook when she poured it. Capable of killing, capable of losing Carmen. Inhuman, all of them.

She stood with her back to them, not listening to their talk any longer. They were trying to come up with a workable plan to get Carmen out. What if this Russian scientist told them his group really had it? What would they do? What could they do? She remembered her notes, her conclusions, and asked herself if she believed them, and had to answer yes. Either government was capable of starting the next war over a misunderstanding, over a series of incidents that might escalate, over a third country, over a secret as world-changing as this one was. And the next war was destined to be a war of extinction — except for anyone immune to radiation, she corrected herself. Even they, though, even they would be doomed, eventually, when the food ran out, when a poisoned earth could no longer support crops, when the animals and birds died. They had to know that, the governments had to know that. They knew it now, and pretended it was not true. They acted as if they believed their own statements that a nuclear war could be won; if either side had immunity from radiation, that side would certainly believe the war could be won. Did they have it? Did the Russians have it? They had to find out, she admitted to herself. They had to know.

She stared at the coffee cup that she had put down when her hand shook too hard to hold it steady, and now she lifted it again, and returned to her chair. Her hands were no longer trembling. She had stepped back, had become an observer, very distant from everyone in the room.

". . . pass as a waiter. Your Dutch is still fluent, isn't it?"

"Sure. And be sure a bike is waiting for me to use. That sounds pretty good."

Pedal away from all the spies in Europe on a bicycle, Lyle thought in disbelief. She shook her head slightly. "I'll have to bring Yuri Korolenko home. Do I bring him straight back here, or to my apartment?"

Carmen looked at her sharply, but again Saul was nodding.

□ **16** □

HUGH LASATER never slept past six o'clock. He had tried blackout shades, and plugged in a white-noise machine, but it made no difference. Six in the morning and there he was back in the world, no matter what time he had gone to bed the night before, no matter how many nights in a row he had stayed up late. This morning he looked at the woman on the other side of the bed with dislike. At six in the morning none of them looked good. Suddenly he realized that he should not be able to see her and could only because the bedroom door was ajar, the light on in the hallway.

Noiselessly he slid out of bed and removed a .38 from the nightstand drawer. He did not bother with his robe or slippers. Let the dude see him naked, he'd never tell what he saw, he thought grimly, and went to the door, keeping flat against the wall. No one was in the hallway. He listened. The kitchen. Water running!

Now he went back for his robe and slippers. He put the gun in his pocket, keeping his hand on it, and went out into the hallway, down the length of it to the kitchen, listened. Making coffee! He pushed the door with his foot.

"Morning, Hugh." A man standing at the sink, running water into the coffeepot, turned and grinned at him. "Don't shoot."

"Alex, what the hell are you doing in here? How'd you get in?"

Alex Radek, he thought coldly, could get in wherever he chose. Whenever he chose. They had worked together often enough for him to know locks did not exist for Alex.

"Now, Hugh, that'd be telling. You always liked it pretty strong, didn't you? We both will need it strong this morning."

"What do you want?"

"Just some talk for openers, but not until the lady friend is gone."

Hugh turned and went back to the bedroom, shook Marcie awake. "Up and at 'em, tiger," he said. "Business. Come on, time to be up and out."

"My God! It's the middle of the night! What's wrong, honey?"

"Told you, business. Five minutes, sweetie. Give you five minutes."

She was groaning as she staggered toward the bathroom. He went back to the kitchen. "She's on her way."

Alex shook his head admiringly. "You can really pick them. Toss her out at six in the morning and she doesn't even holler. I couldn't get away with that. I didn't even dare wake up Lori." She was his wife.

When Marcie was dressed, Lasater hurried her to the door. "Don't I even get a cup of coffee?"

"All-night place half a block away, sweetie. Call you later."

Her look was venomous. "Don't bother."

He closed and locked the door after her, and went back to the kitchen where Alex was pouring coffee for them both.

"Okay, give."

Alex Radek was forty-seven. He had served in the Navy, then Naval Intelligence, and finally CIA, where he still worked. Lasater had known him for at least twenty years, and it didn't mean a damn thing, he thought, watching Alex. On either side, he added.

"They want you in Virginia," Alex said. "You think you have it rough, this early-morning stuff. They called me at five. It's the difference in time, you know. They never remember that three-hour difference. Rawleigh was bright and cheerful, already had his shower, his breakfast, shaved. Called from home. Would have been better if he'd waited to get to the office, at least. Would have given me another hour of sleep. We have a plane to catch at eight-twenty. Drink up."

Lasater grinned and sat down at the kitchen table, sipped his coffee. "Hot. There's just one little hitch, Alex, old pal. I don't work there anymore, remember? They can call you and tell you to get your ass to Virginia, but not me. Not anymore."

"Maybe they want you to come back, after all."

"Nope. Tried that back in April. No dice."

Alex sat down and leaned back. "It's like old times, isn't it, Hugh? You and me sparring when we both know exactly what we'll be doing at eight-twenty."

"Rawleigh say what he wants?"

"You know better than that. Does he ever say more than six words at a time on a long-distance call? Rawleigh the miser, remember?" He glanced at his watch, then said, "Almost forgot. Stopped for some Danish on the way over. Don't like to fly on an empty stomach." He went to the counter and picked up a paper bag, brought it to the table, and sat down again.

Lasater helped himself. The rolls were still warm. Again Alex looked at his watch. The phone rang and Alex nodded in satisfaction. "Right on the button," he said. "It's for you. Rawleigh."

Lasater pushed his chair back, reached up, and took the wall phone. "Yes?"

"I was hasty last April," Rawleigh said, sounding just as he always had, like a prissy schoolteacher. "I want to talk to you about that material you have. We may want to purchase some of it. Alex will bring you to the farm." He hung up.

"Bastard!" Lasater snapped and replaced the phone.

Alex grinned in commiseration. "Don't forget to pack some warm clothes. It's already getting cold back east."

Flying across the country, Lasater tried to fix a scenario that would play. Rawleigh had turned him down flat in April, not interested in anything Lasater had dug up about anybody.

"It's our budget cuts," he had said. "Can't do anything with the money they're giving us this year. Sorry."

Lasater no longer wanted them to take him back. Now he

wanted cash for what he had. Cash deposited in a Zurich bank, with a secret number and everything. But how little could he tell and still have a product they would buy? He would not tell them about Taney, he had decided already. Probably not about Carmen. Just the old man. He'd give them the old man, let them play games with him. He had confidence that Werther would not be found, not after being on the run for all those years. He had tricks he hadn't even thought of pulling out of the hat yet, he was certain. Crafty old bastard. They could chase their tails for a long time looking for him, and he, Lasater, with money to back him, would get on with it. How much should he ask for, how much should he settle for? That was the hard part. Rawleigh talked like a man with his mouth full of marshmallows, but he was shrewd, and he was miserly.

In April Lasater had asked to be taken back, had told enough of what he knew to tantalize them, and they had treated him as if he had lice. Now they could screw, he thought coldly. Demand half a million, and accept half of it. No less. He closed his eyes and napped until they were ready to land at Dulles.

Grover Rawleigh liked to tell people that he was a simple farmer; his family had been farmers back four hundred years or more. The real satisfactions came from growing things in the good land, the good earth. His farm had been in the family for six generations, his father born in the upstairs bedroom, his grandfather before him born in the same room, laid out in the living room when he died . . . He entertained congressmen, visiting dignitaries, the president even, not this particular one, but others before him, and no doubt there would be others after him that would make their way to his farm. Hollywell, it was called. Everyone who worked on it, the house staff down to the stable hands, were all ex-spies.

Lasater and Alex were greeted by Aunt Jane, the housekeeper, who had appeared one day without a past, or a past known only to Rawleigh. She was forty-five, handsome, and had an accent that might have been Slavic. *He* was due at nine or a little after, she said, serving them roast chicken and mashed potatoes in the kitchen. Home-grown chicken, garden potatoes.

"You'll have the same room as usual," she told Alex. "And I'll show you yours as soon as you finish eating," she added to Lasater. "You two boys are the only guests we have right now. Do you want apple pie for dessert?"

Grover Rawleigh liked simple food, good country food.

It was after ten when Rawleigh sent for Lasater. Rawleigh was sixty years old, six feet five, just starting to show a paunch, deeply sunburned, with pale brown hair that was thick and lustrous. All those home-grown turnip greens, Lasater thought sourly, greeting him.

"Hugh, you look fit. Keeping busy? Alex, you've had a busy day, why don't you turn in?"

Alex waved at them and vanished, closing the library door after him. The books in the library were all leather-bound, behind glass doors.

"Sit down, Hugh. That's a comfortable chair. My father had it made. He was a big man, bigger than I am. Needed specially made furniture."

Lasater sat down and waited. Rawleigh chose an even larger leather chair and grunted when he sprawled out in it. "Getting old," he said. "Too much running around, too much traffic, can't take it anymore." He stretched out his legs, reached high with both hands to stretch his arms, then relaxed. "Well, Hugh, you gave us a little problem last spring. Did you bring your material with you?"

Lasater shook his head. "I don't keep stuff like that in the house. And there wasn't any time for a side trip."

"Too bad. Should have thought of that. Oh well. Tell me about it again, just to make sure I haven't forgotten anything."

"Business first," Lasater said pleasantly. "I made an offer and you turned it down. Your turn."

Rawleigh laughed. "Pissed you, didn't I? Can't blame you. You wouldn't believe the budget they expect us to operate with! It's incredible! We can offer you an independent contractor's stipend, the usual thing. Can't hire anyone full-time, just can't do it."

"How much?"

"Ten thousand."

Lasater stood up. "I've had a busy day, too, come to think of it. Maybe I should turn in."

"If it's good, I can go to twenty-five, but that's it, Hugh. Believe me, if the money was there, I wouldn't hesitate, but . . ."

"Oh, I believe you," Lasater said. "Really. But I'm not in a hurry. I've been sitting on this stuff for a long time, it's not going anywhere. Things will get better. Light at the end of the tunnel, all that stuff. I believe in it. Things will pick up again."

"Hugh, not too fast. Whatever happened to Milt Follett?"

"You've got me. What?"

"The LA police department's asking questions still, I understand. You ever tell them you were with him just before he disappeared?"

"Did he disappear? I hadn't heard."

"Yes, right after you abandoned the siege of Mrs. Taney and her assistant. Never did show up again."

Lasater waited.

"Did you report that little transaction to IRS, Hugh? The cashier's check, or was it more than one?"

He sat down again, waiting, watching.

"You can have twenty-five thousand, although it's going to mess up our cash flow, you understand. If what you have is good enough to warrant it."

The next day when Lasater woke up it was nine o'clock, East Coast time. He grinned. The only way to beat the six-in-the-morning routine was to go east. When he got down to the kitchen for breakfast, Aunt Jane told him that Mr. Rawleigh was at work, and Mr. Alex had left very early. He could ride one of the horses, or take a walk, or read, whatever he wanted that day. Mr. Rawleigh would join him for dinner.

Hugh Lasater detested horses, except at races, where, he had to admit, they looked damned good running their hearts out.

"Pretty dreary out there," he said glancing out the window. Everything that wasn't growing was painted white, fences, barns, sheds, the stable. The trees were bare but no leaves were on the ground. It was a *neat* farm, also an isolated one, miles from anything.

"You should have been here last week before the leaves were

knocked off. It was so gaudy, like a postcard. Then we had a rainstorm, and that was the end of them."

He wandered around the house after breakfast, almost decided to take a walk, and thought better of it. He did not mind walking when he had to get somewhere, but to walk for the sake of moving his feet and legs never struck him as necessary. There was a smaller library off the one that obviously was for show. The smaller one had books that people actually read: paperback mysteries, half a dozen biographies, even Taney's book about hawks. He looked at it thoughtfully; a page was dog-eared two thirds of the way through. He sat down and picked up a mystery and opened it, and thought about last night.

He did not know how much Rawleigh believed. He had told him the same story he had told Taney, had drawn the same conclusion that Werther was the kid from Germany, getting old, and very crazy now. A man with a secret cure for cancer. That was the sticking point. Now when he said it, when he considered it, he wondered why anyone had ever bought it. Why he had bought it. It was so patently ridiculous. Say Rawleigh did not believe it, then why was he sending Alex back to California to get the evidence Lasater had stashed away? Why was he shelling out twenty-five thousand dollars? His mouth tightened when he thought of the amount. It would be enough, he had decided last night. That and his own money, and Milt's money. It would be enough.

But they were holding out on him. Something had made Rawleigh hot for him now after all this time. Something had made him dig around to find a lever to use if Lasater came on stubborn. Something was going on and no one was going to tell him shit about it. He turned a page, just in case anyone was watching, give him something to report. Subject sat in red upholstered chair for two hours and turned pages now and then.

It was fair that they were holding out on him, he thought, and flipped several pages, as if bored with the story. Tit for tat, that was fair enough.

"Hugh, it really isn't sporting to charge us for the tip that you got from our own files," Rawleigh chided that night.

"I reported to Cushman. He said to forget it, not interested."

"Yes, Cushman. Too bad he's dead now. He'd see the error of his ways, I'm afraid."

"Yeah, too bad."

"It certainly does appear circumstantial, doesn't it? There he is time and again at the scene of the crime, you might say."

He looked through the pictures once more, sighing. "You're certain he didn't die in that car crash?"

"It was the oldest trick in the book. A real setup. They waited for the foggiest night of the year to pull it, burned down the house and everything, just like from a script."

"But your erstwhile, ah, employers believed he died."

"What do they know? Naive, all of them."

"Yes, of course. Now tell me again about Mrs. Taney, and the young man, Carmen? Is that a man's name?"

"Damned if I know. Look, why again? We've been over it three times. You know everything I do. I'm a good agent, I don't forget details and plug them in later. Let's get some sleep."

"You say she cried, carried on when she found out that the old man was presumed dead? Was it an act?"

"No. She's a schoolteacher, not an actress. She turned white as a ghost, dropped her cup. I thought she might pass out. I told you she'd been sick, good and sick. Nearly died. It was a shock to her."

"Strange, isn't it, how she formed such an attachment to him in such a short time. She's a mature, intelligent woman, educated, experienced. I wonder how that happened. I mean, if your neighbor dies a violent death, you're shocked, but you don't act personally grieved, now do you? Most people, I mean."

"I told you I think it's because she was still weak and sick. She wasn't normal yet. It hit her harder than it would have if she'd been well."

"Yes, you did say that. And then the young man stayed on with her. Isn't that strange?"

"I don't know. She liked him, they were sleeping together. Maybe he thought she was a soft touch."

"Yes. Opportunistic young people like that don't really care much about appearances, do they? Are they still together?"

"I told you that, too. I don't know. I paid the grocery store clerk to tell me when they left the area. It was in July. I lost them after that."

"Of course. It's good that you didn't hang around and keep them under surveillance, after all, now isn't it? All those months! You say she came to you and threatened to call the local police, the FBI, news media, and so on if you didn't leave her alone. That suggests that she still believed Werther was dead, that there was nothing for her to hide, doesn't it? Was she sincere?"

"Milt thought so. So did I. We pulled out." He looked at his watch and yawned.

"Hugh, I don't understand. West Coast time it's only eleven. I thought you were a night person."

"It must be the country air. Look, let's knock it off. You pay me, and I go to bed, and tomorrow I go home. Okay?"

"Oh dear, I'm afraid I did forget a detail. We'll want you to stay on the East Coast for just a few days, to identify someone for us next Tuesday. Can we help you get a hotel room in New York?"

"You paying expenses?"

"Of course."

"I'll get a room. Who is it?"

Rawleigh smiled gently. "We'll want you to tell us that."

Lasater stood up. "You want me to call, give you my address, room number, all that?"

"Yes. Just tell anyone who answers the phone. Aunt Jane, probably. Alex will be in touch on Tuesday morning. Be certain to keep the day free."

"You bet." He paused as Rawleigh picked up the pictures once more. "You were going to pay me my independent contractor's stipend, remember?"

"Sorry. Let's see." He reached inside his desk drawer and pulled out a large manila envelope. "Twenty thousand now, and Alex will pay the other five on Tuesday. Is that agreeable with you?"

"You know damn well it's not!"

"Of course, I know," Rawleigh admitted with a sigh. "It's just that we're so used to doing business this way, it's hard to break the habit. I'm afraid I didn't bring more than twenty thousand out with me." He pushed the envelope across the desk. "An assortment of used bills, nothing over one hundred. It'll take you a while to count it, I'm afraid." He began to examine the pictures.

◙ **17** ◙

TUESDAY WAS a mystery to him. He knew about the international conference coming up in Amsterdam, due to start Tuesday evening with opening ceremonies, a cocktail hour, whatever they did to break the ice. But Tuesday in New York? Taney and the kid, maybe. That shouldn't be a deal for them. They knew as well as he did that they were still living together in a posh New York apartment. Or they could know it if they were interested.

He flew to JFK, made a phone call there, took a limo to Manhattan, and checked in at the Victory, where they found a room for him when he produced a twenty.

Later he walked the few blocks to Fiftieth, turned left and went another half block. The street was packed curb to curb with traffic; the sidewalk packed with transients, down and outers, call girls, pimps, spaced-out cases, nuts, all pushing, all in a hurry. It was ugly and it stank. He found the address he sought and looked at the building with disgust. It was crumbling, the sidewalk before it was broken, the curb worn down to nothing. This was why he had moved to the West Coast; New York was on the skids, no doubt about it.

He paused before the jewelry in the window of the ground-floor shop, but he knew no one was following him. Not yet. After today he would not come here this directly, but for a short while it was safe enough. He left the shop window and entered the building through the business door into a dusty short foyer with a ten-watt bulb over an elevator door. There was a directory that he ignored. When the elevator wheezed to a stop and the door opened, two young men in jeans and leather jackets got out talking Arabic or something. He stepped in and pushed eleven, praying the elevator would make it.

Herb Balinski was a licensed private investigator; his sign on the door admitted it in chipped and fading letters. He had been trained in the FBI but had run afoul of Hoover himself over, it was rumored, his fondness for adolescent boys. Balinski never said. His office had good upholstered furniture, good paintings on the walls, and he was dressed conservatively in a three-piece suit as if due to make a presentation to the chairman of the board at any minute.

His polished desk was bare, except for a white ornate telephone, but his secretary's desk had the usual clutter of in and out baskets, typewriter, a couple of notebooks.

"Lasater, good to see you. You get a room at the Victory? Settled in okay?"

"Yeah, it's okay. Thanks for the tip."

Lasater had known him for eight, ten years. Balinski was good, he delivered, but he never looked as if he knew his way around the block. He looked dumb. Big open face, blond hair, an ingratiating smile.

"Well, as you see, I let my secretary go early, while I stayed put this afternoon, waiting for you. Didn't know you were east again."

"I'm not. Short visit. Too damn cold here, and too ugly."

"It's what you get used to. I can't take those waving palm trees myself. What can I do for you? You said on the phone you wanted me personally. That was a nice thing to say, but I have several top-notch people working for me these days. Business is pretty good."

Lasater had called him from the airport, and he was getting the impression now that Balinski no longer worked cheap. He sighed. "There's a woman, Lyle Taney, and a kid she's living with I want watched." He wrote her name and Carmen's, and their address in his notebook, tore the page out, and handed it to Balinski.

"How close?"

"Real close. I have a feeling that she's going to bolt and run in the next few days and I want to know where to. That's all. We'll play it by ear."

Balinski pursed his lips. "Close means three people around the clock. Doesn't come easy, Lasater. You know? My people like to eat too well. Not like the old days, not anymore."

Lasater sighed again. "When she runs, I don't want it to be one of your people who follows her. I want it to be you."

"That's real flattering, you know. Okay. Five grand in advance, and we'll see how long that lasts at five hundred a day."

They settled the details, Lasater counted out five thousand dollars in cash, got a receipt, and then said, "I'll call you every day. If you want me, leave a message about insurance. I'll call back."

For the first time Balinski looked interested.

Lasater called the farm and talked briefly with Aunt Jane. He went to a movie, had dinner at a delicatessen, and finally at eleven returned to his hotel. There was a message from an insurance agent waiting for him.

He got Balinski at home.

"You're off the hook with your money for a while," Balinski said. "The woman and the kid are out of the country. In Europe somewhere. Won't be home until Tuesday."

"Jesus Christ!" he muttered. "Okay. I'll see you on Monday. Not at the office. I'll call."

Europe! The Netherlands, he thought coldly. Amsterdam. And that son of a bitch Rawleigh knew it. Something had happened recently, since they left, and now all at once he wanted a look at the kid. It had to be that. Her picture was on her book, had been in the papers; she was too easy, but the kid . . . That's who they wanted him to finger for them. Carmen. When they returned on Tuesday. But why Tuesday? The conference started Tuesday night and they'd be home by then. Unless they were delayed? Something would come up to keep them for another day or two? Must be.

He left the pay phone, took the elevator to the twenty-third floor to his room, and there sat at the open window looking at the lights, the traffic far below, too distant for the noise to intrude enough to interrupt his thoughts. He should have asked Balinski how long they had been gone, he thought, but decided it didn't really matter. Not long, or that faggot editor would have told him. He thought briefly of the people he had manipulated in order to get to Taney in the first place: her department head, the magazine editor, the book editor, the clerk at the grocery store . . . Everyone had had a handle he had found, everyone had a soft spot for him to poke. They all delivered. And then Taney had balked at playing. He could almost admire her for not caving in, almost.

So she was in Werther's camp now, taking orders from him, doing his dirty work, although she had looked at him, Lasater, like some kind of lowlife because of the job he had tried to do. And what difference did it make in the long run, who had the secret? They were the selfish ones, the Fascists, trying to keep it to themselves, even killing to keep it. His people would have made a buck with it, sure, but they would have made it available for a price, and there wasn't any price too high. Not any.

His room was stifling, the way New York rooms were summer and winter. It did no good to turn the heat down; the controls accomplished nothing. He opened the window wider. Wasteful. No wonder his room cost eighty-five a night.

When he finally went to bed and closed his eyes, he saw Taney walking toward him, handing something to him. The same image he had carried from the beginning, the image of Taney coming through finally. And she would, he said softly to himself. She would.

◙ **18** ◙

LONDON HAD BEEN rainy, cold, gloomy, and exciting down to their last day. They had met her editor near Fitzroy Square and, after lunch, she and Carmen had walked through the neighborhood, stopping to point now and then: "Look, Virginia Woolf lived there!" and again, "H. G. Wells!"

It was strange to walk the same streets that Virginia Woolf had walked, to see the same houses, the same park, the same trees even. Had Mr. Wells paused here for a carriage, at a corner where a kiosk now sold newspapers, flowers, cigarettes, and candy? Had he walked through that small park deep in thought about his Martian invaders? Deep in thought about his men in the moon? Had Virginia Woolf looked at the trees across from her house only to see the lighthouse that beckoned, ever beckoned? Listening to the wind through the window had she heard the mysterious rhythms of the waves?

They had viewed the crown jewels, had visited the Tower of London, the majestic buildings that contain the Houses of Parliament, and they seemed contrived now that she had seen the house where Virginia Woolf had lived and thought and written, the house where H. G. Wells had dreamed his fantastic stories. Money could buy a magnificent building, could buy gems of inestimable value, but no money could buy one exquisite phrase of an inspired writer, she thought. No money could order the sensibilities of a Woolf, the linkages of a mind like that of H. G. Wells, who combined and recombined the familiar to invent the new and wondrous.

Dreamily she permitted Carmen to guide her to the bus stand, and dreamily she boarded it when it came, and took an upper-level seat. Neither spoke now. The London skyline was another of those things that could never be ordered, planned, bought. Against the chimney pots, here a gargoyle, there a lion rearing like a horse. There a pair of angels . . .

The bus filled as they drew nearer Piccadilly, but suddenly it swayed to a too-fast halt in the middle of a block.

"All out! Out here now!" the conducter began to call.

"Why? What happened?" Lyle asked, bewildered.

"Riots in Piccadilly," someone muttered as the upper-level passengers began to leave their seats, file down the narrow, curving steps.

When Lyle got to the front of the bus, she could see through the wide windows a mass of people a few blocks ahead, but not until they were on the sidewalks could she hear the dull roar that surged, ebbed, surged.

"Come on!" Carmen said, clasping her arm, nearly dragging her in the opposite direction. A few blocks later they were able to find a taxi that took them to their hotel.

"If I were you, being Americans, I mean, I think I would

stay inside this evening," the driver said kindly. "By tomorrow it will be quiet again, I'm sure."

They watched the riot on television in their room. It had started in Covent Garden, a rally against American rearmament, but had erupted explosively until it had filled Piccadilly Circus, where cars were overturned, buses set afire, store windows smashed. Late that night there were still fires smoldering in a cold drizzle that held the smoke low, made the area look like a scene from Dante.

They went to Sloane Square to a pub for a light supper and even here where they had had meals nearly every day since their arrival, they were met with hostile looks and open snubs. They ate quickly and went back to their room.

The next morning they flew to Paris.

When you're playing a role, Carmen had said, you have to be it every minute of the day and night. No lapses. They played it well, she thought, watching him the day they arrived in Paris.

He carried her camera gear and hung back a step or two at the hotel desk, probably flirted with the young woman who was at work there. Her gaze kept drifting to him as Lyle signed the register.

He had been like this when she first met him, she remembered. She had believed then that he was Saul's handyman or something. Not subservient, but neither was he an equal, that was apparent in his every movement, his every look. When she walked to the elevator, he was slightly behind her. Lyle glanced back at the reception desk and caught an amused look on the face of the clerk. It was clear what she thought, at any rate.

They had a two-room suite, and if the rooms had been joined to make one, it would have been considered small by American hotel standards. A porter followed them into the room and put down the bags.

"No!" Lyle said sharply. She walked out stiffly, back to the elevator, not looking to see if Carmen or the porter followed. She returned to the desk and made a scene with the receptionist. She had reserved bigger rooms, she insisted, a suite of large rooms. It was robbery to charge a fortune for broom closets.

"But, madam," the woman said in flawless English, "we have no other suites."

"Then we will go elsewhere." She glanced at her watch. "I have an interview in one half hour. I have no time now to inspect other rooms. Carmen, take care of it." She swept from the lobby. End act one, she thought, and wondered if they had noticed the shaking of her hands, believed it was from anger.

She returned three hours later, tired, from a magazine interview, a session with a fussy photographer who spoke no English but smiled a lot, and from a difficult television interview. She had not expected that one. Her publisher had arranged it, had been jubilant that he could work her in on such short notice.

At first she did not recognize Carmen when he crossed the lobby to join her near the entrance to the hotel. On this trip he was wearing a wig that was exactly what his own hair would be like if he ever allowed it to grow too long: thick black curls like a bush. And now he was wearing a pale gray cowboy hat with a spray of feathers, and a red and gold band.

"Where on earth did that come from?"

"Shop around the corner. Isn't it neat! They love cowboys here."

"It's ridiculous. Did you change our rooms?"

"Yes, ma'am. A really nice suite overlooking the garden in back. You'll like them."

"Tomorrow we have a luncheon with my editor and his publicity people. And on Friday there is another luncheon. We'll have Thursday and Saturday free." Still talking, she entered the elevator and waited for him to press the button for their floor.

As soon as they were moving, she slumped against the wall, and looked at him miserably. He winked.

"When I was a little girl, eight or nine," Lyle said, looking at the stained-glass windows in Notre Dame, "my father brought me here, and I burst out crying. I never did understand why exactly."

"Not even now?"

"Not exactly. I think I was simply overwhelmed by it all."

She turned from the *Rose Ouest* and glanced back through the cathedral. People were everywhere, walking up and down the aisles, looking at the engravings, the candleholders, all the magnificent art that adorned the walls, every niche. Off to one side there was a mass being said, the faithful on their knees, oblivious of the tourists coming and going. Somewhere in a clump of people a loud German woman was talking, talking.

Out there, among the tourists, the faithful, was there someone watching her and Carmen, noting their actions, where they went, whom they saw, what they did, how they treated each other? She said abruptly, "Let's get out of here." Carmen looked like an ugly American in his grotesque cowboy hat, carrying her camera everywhere they went, ogling the women. She looked like a rich bitch with a pet on an invisible leash.

The next day they went to the Jeu de Paume. The Louvre would take a full week, she had said, choosing the smaller museum.

"Besides," she said, standing below Monet's water lilies, "this is what I wanted to see again." She had had a fantasy once in which she had glided in and out among the lilies, never touching them, but feeling them with some other sense that she could not locate. She could not recall what form she had had in the fantasy; no form, probably, just a spirit weaving in and out of the flowers. She backed far enough away so that she no longer could see the brush strokes, and for an instant she almost achieved the same feeling she had had that other time. The moment passed and she was outside looking at them again. She wished she could talk to Carmen about the feeling, what it meant to her to be able to slip inside the painting even for an instant. She felt tears form and turned away, not wanting to see anything else now.

Their last real talk had been on the day they had left Pennsylvania when they had walked to the pond.

"Why did you volunteer?" he had asked.

"Not because I think it will work. I don't. But it has a slightly better chance this way than any other."

"Is that all?"

"No. I want to be with you as long as possible. I'm afraid for you, afraid I'll never see you again."

"I'll be back within a week of your return," he said.

She had stared at the pond, at the geese floating easily in the cold water that looked like liquid steel, hardly rippling it with their movements. He touched her shoulder and when she turned toward him, he took her into his arms and kissed her. She wept.

"I think I must be crazy," she had said. "I love you. I love him, too. I don't want you to go. I don't want to lose you."

"I'll be back," he had said again. "I don't want to lose you either, Lyle. I'll be back."

In the car returning to New York, he had outlined their plan for the trip, had gone over the details thoroughly, and they had not talked of anything else. And then they had stepped into their roles for the next act, and they would not leave them until they met again at the laboratory, if they met at the laboratory.

She left the museum, trusting him to follow. A fine mist was settling on the pavement, on their clothes when they walked toward the corner to hail a taxi.

That night they had dinner in a small restaurant not far from their hotel. "Our last night in Paris," Carmen said. "Let's hit a night spot or two."

At the next table several Englishmen were talking in loud voices, complaining about the sandwiches in Paris. "Thick pieces of bread with a crust no one could bite, no one. And buried somewhere a transparent piece of ham, if you can find it. I told them, more ham, and cheese for God's sake, enough to see without a post mortem. I told them."

Lyle looked at them with distaste, then glanced at Carmen. "I'd rather not. I'm a bit tired."

"You've been tired ever since we got here!"

The Englishmen stopped talking, watched them with interest.

"That's not true. But tonight I'm tired. I've had an exhausting week with interviews, luncheons, too much sightseeing. It was your idea to walk for miles today."

"I may never get to Paris again. I want to see some nightlife!"

"I don't."

"And it's your money, isn't that the rest of it? Isn't that the next line? You bought me and paid my way, I'm to behave myself, right? Wrong! I'm going out tonight!"

He stood up, picked up the cowboy hat and jammed it onto his bush of curls and stalked from the restaurant. Lyle signaled to the hovering waiter for the check. She could feel her cheeks burn as she began to count the unfamiliar money. Finally she pushed too much across the table, gathered her purse and coat, and walked out, looking straight ahead. At the door Carmen fell into step a few feet behind her, and they returned to the hotel not speaking, not looking at each other. When she entered the elevator, he remained in the lobby, his hands jammed into his pockets, scowling.

The next morning when she paid their hotel bill, she was cool and distant with him, treated him exactly the same way she treated the porter who carried their bags out to a waiting taxi. She did not speak to either of them.

At the airport she checked them both in, then left him to change the remaining French money for Dutch guilders, again without speaking. It was as if he had become a necessary shadow, a robot that carried her camera bag, nothing more than that.

In Amsterdam at the hotel she changed their room reservation. "I'm sorry," she told the man at the desk, "there's been a mistake. We need two rooms, obviously."

"But, madam, your wire, here it is, it says a large room."

"Two."

She got the large room overlooking the canal, and Carmen was to be put in a back room that the manager moaned over as inadequate, but all they had. If only he had known . . . It was fine, Lyle said, cutting him short.

"As soon as you're settled," she said to Carmen, looking past him at the wall, "I want to take the boat ride, and walk over to to Dam Square to see the Royal Palace." She did not wait for a reply, but went to the staircase and up the one flight to her room.

It was comfortable, with antiques; the view was lovely even if the canal looked frigid, and the naked trees were all shivering in a steady wind that had come straight down from the North Pole.

Lyle had a heavy, fur-lined raincoat, and Carmen wore a shapeless black mackintosh that came down to his calves. There was a light, icy rain, the wind was piercing. They walked the three blocks to Dam Square, but they took a taxi to the boat loading area several blocks beyond. There were few people out that Sunday afternoon. Last week there had been demonstrations, but now it was quiet. When they looked at the glassed-in launch with its few passengers, they changed their minds and walked to a sandwich shop instead.

"The idea," Carmen had said, "is to let anyone who might be watching see that we're together, what we're wearing, see that we're not speaking, hardly even bothering with each other by now. That's going to be important, our attitudes toward each other."

The sandwiches were delicious, inches high with delectable ham, topped with cheese, the crusty rolls meltingly soft inside, liberally slathered with butter that made Lyle close her eyes with pleasure. Why weren't they all obese, she wondered, glancing at the other people in the warm, cheerful shop. She did not let her gaze falter as she recognized a man near the door, ordering something. She had seen him at the airport, buying a newspaper. It had to be coincidence, she told herself, it was too clumsy otherwise. Even she would not let herself be seen twice if she were following someone. Unless they wanted her to know, wanted her and Carmen aware that they were being watched, that they would not be able to get away with anything.

"Are you finished?" she asked sharply then. "It's stifling in here."

The man's order had not arrived yet. Would he leave? Would he remain there, prove her wrong? Carmen picked up the camera bag and they walked out. The wind-driven mist was sharp and penetrating; she pulled her coat tightly around her, glanced both ways down the street for a taxi.

"We'll have to go to the taxi rack at the corner," Carmen said, starting to walk ahead of her.

She caught up with him, keeping her head ducked against the wind.

"Don't look back," Carmen said in a low voice. "He's there."

They got a taxi at the corner and returned to the hotel and did not leave again that day. There was a small restaurant off the lobby where they ate Indonesian food for dinner, and then went to their rooms.

Lyle sat at her window looking at the canal with the play of lights on it for hours that night. Here the streets were too narrow for more than one car at a time, and sometimes the cars were lined up from corner to corner waiting for someone to park, or leave a parking space. One day they would close in their canals in the name of progress, she thought, trying to follow a ripple of light from its source to its demise. That would be the end of Amsterdam. Maybe they would reject the notion when it was seriously suggested. She almost wished they had taken the boat trip, even though the glass had been fogged, visibility terrible. To glide over the canals would be nice. Too bad they were not yet frozen, or did they still let them freeze solid? Stories of Hans Brinker and his magic skates stirred in her mind. To skate the canals would be lovely.

Van Gogh had walked these narrow streets. Rembrandt. Just a few blocks away was the house where the child Anne Frank had been hidden for two years, had left a childhood hardly even lived, had become an adolescent, and then had died. Had been killed. Intrigues, deaths, wars, always they intruded on the beautiful, the peaceful, the human.

Where would a watcher post himself out there? In one of the parked cars? Shivering, wishing he were in a warm bed, wishing someone else had drawn this assignment.

One more full day to get through, meet her Dutch editor, see the cover art he had commissioned for her book, meet the artist, have dinner with them, pretend Carmen was invisible . . .

She closed her eyes, wishing they had had this one last night together, wishing they were back in New York, back on the Oregon coast, anywhere but here.

When this was over, she would leave them both, she decided. She had to leave them both. All the others acted as if they were on an ocean cruise, loving each other, leaving each other, but she could not live that way, not with the confusion that made her thoughts spin and curl around themselves and refuse to come to an end that she could accept. She would walk away from them, until, perhaps in some future, she had found a way out of her dilemma and could return easily, as easily as the others did.

Out there in the cold rain someone was watching, someone who believed that she and Carmen had come here to murder a scientist. And in other circumstances, another time, that was what they might have to do. Cold-bloodedly, mercilessly, as deliberately as the Nazis had taken the girl Anne Frank out of her refuge and killed her. Where was the difference? Saul could make it sound reasonable, plausible, acceptable. Carmen could also. But here in the dark, staring at the canal, knowing someone was watching and waiting for murder, she knew she could not accept it. As soon as she knew Carmen was safe, if he ever would be safe again, she would leave them both, leave them to their deaths, their intrigues.

The pain she felt already at the thought of leaving them both was intense and real, and again she wished Carmen was with her, in this room, in that bed that she was so reluctant to get into. He would understand that she was afraid, she admitted then. His danger was greater than hers, but she could be caught, seized, imprisoned, interrogated . . . Now that she had shaped her fear with words, she started to shiver. If she had to be caught, please, she thought at the silent canal, don't let it be the Russians. She was most afraid of them. But it would be bad, she knew, if any secret agency caught her or Carmen. They all had learned from the same teachers, used the same great weapon of terror against their victims. Her shivering increased until she was forced to crawl into the bed, under the down comforter, where she huddled staring at the ceiling until a pale light filtered through the curtains.

◙ 19 ◙

Monday was as bad as Lyle had anticipated. She met people she could not remember an hour later, pretended interest she did not feel, ate food she could not taste, and when night came and she was alone in her room, she stared again at the canal until the lights across it went out one by one, and until she started to shiver violently and was forced into bed, where she could not sleep.

Tuesday morning they ate a leisurely breakfast and then went to the reception desk together.

"We're checking out," Lyle said to the clerk on duty. "Is it possible to hire a taxi for the entire morning? We have a plane to catch and have to be at the airport by one, but I want to see your museums before we leave."

"Indeed it is possible," the clerk assured her. "When will you want the car?"

"Half an hour. That should give me time to finish my packing and settle our bill, I think."

It was nearly eleven when they reached the Rijksmuseum, and it was raining again. They left their suitcases in the taxi and Carmen carried the camera bag over his shoulder. Inside, he had to check it, as they had known he would. They went straight to the painting *The Night Watch*.

Lyle caught her breath sharply. She had only seen this one in copies that she realized had all been bad. The flesh in the painting was alive, glowing; the clothes were fabric, woolens so real she felt that if she were to touch them her hand would sink into the material. Each face was expressive, with living lights behind the eyes . . . She did not know how long she had been standing there; she had entered the painting, just as she had entered the water lilies painting before. She had been there, had seen those people, had felt them, had known them. She had seen them with Rembrandt's eyes, sensed them with his senses . . .

"We have to leave," Carmen said, pulling her arm.

She blinked dazedly and followed him to the check stand where he retrieved the camera bag. They left the museum, and, she felt, entered a world confounded by time. Slowly she shook off the disorientation. This is what linked all people, she wanted to say, in spite of time and space; this joined them in a timelessness, a spacelessness, in a collective mind that transcended all boundaries. This is what endured forever and ever, as long as the painting was preserved, as long as the written word endured. Sappho's few words, Plato's, Homer's . . . The works of a great artist entered that other kind of reality, the words of a great poet lived there; this is what human history is all about, our efforts to transcend our limitations, our petty wars, our fears. We build cathedrals, paint pictures, write our poetry, our music, all in the same effort to transcend ourselves. They fill the history books with trash about conquests, wars, treaties, and they are transitory. The human spirit sails high above them, yearning for that other reality, finding it in moments through great art . . .

The taxi had stopped again, this time at the Van Gogh Museum. The driver looked at his watch and said, "If you have to be at the airport by one, we should be on our way there in half an hour. It is not much time for a museum."

It was raining somewhat harder now; they ran to the entrance, Carmen's hat pulled low, Lyle's hood down to her eyes. Again Carmen had to check the camera bag. They wandered through the lower level for a few minutes, then went upstairs to the van Gogh collection that started with his early, more conventional work and progressed to his last paintings where the brush strokes were inches long and, at close range, the paintings merely blobs of color. Backing away from them, Lyle could almost see the colors merge, blend, magically fuse to make coherent houses, trees, flowers. At what point did the change occur? One moment there was the incoherence, the work of a madman, and then it was orderly, sublime. She could not find the one point where the change happened.

"I'm going to the john," Carmen said at her shoulder.

She froze. Now it would begin. "Give me the check for the camera," she said, amazed that her voice worked. "It's nearly time to go. I'll get the bag."

He handed her the check and walked away, the ugly American in his wet cowboy hat, his shapeless raincoat. She forced herself to turn again to the painting, but she no longer could see it.

Wait one minute, then go down to get the camera.

Halfway down the stairs she saw the group of men heading for the lavatory. There was Seymour Oliver, talking, joking with a strange man; there was Daniel Malone talking more earnestly with someone else, including now and then in his comments the young Russian who kept his head lowered. Two of the men had heavy coats. The other three, including the Russian, wore raincoats. She had gone down steadily; when she reached the ground level she no longer could see the Russian. Two of the other men were taller, broader than he was; only from the higher vantage point of the stairs had it been possible for her to pick him out. From up there the plan suddenly had become ridiculous, doomed. No one would be fooled.

The men disappeared into the lavatory and she went to the check stand for the camera, took it to the outside door to wait. She looked out through the rain for their taxi. The driver waved urgently to her, pointing to his watch. She nodded and looked back inside impatiently.

It was going wrong, she thought in despair. Something had happened; they both had been caught in the restroom . . . Then she saw the cowboy hat and the black raincoat, and she opened the door, held out the camera bag for him to take. As soon as his hand took the strap, she ran ahead of him to the taxi, did not look back. The driver had got out, was holding the door open. She hurried to get in, the Russian right behind her.

"We must hurry, madam. I was afraid half an hour was not enough time . . ." The driver closed the door, rushed to get in behind the wheel.

"Now we can go," Lyle said. "There surely isn't much traffic at this time of day?"

"No. We will make it. Don't worry."

He turned on the windshield wipers, and they moved away from the museum, away from the other taxis, the other waiting cars. Lyle did not dare look at the man beside her. She kept her gaze out her side window. The driver had accepted him. No one in the museum had looked at them suspiciously, she was certain. She did not look behind to see if anyone was following. Someone would be, of course, someone who did not believe they intended to fly out of Holland this afternoon without even attempting to kill a scientist, or kidnap one. Her hands were clenched; slowly she relaxed her fingers. They were very stiff.

The landscape spread out flat, was lost in rain and clouds in the distance; the canals were like gray ribbons holding the sodden fields in place. Traffic was light; the driver concentrated on the road that held a skim of water; now and then he muttered about the windshield wipers. They were hardly able to keep the rain off enough for visibility.

"There it is," he said finally, nodding off toward their right. "Not quite one right now. You have plenty of time."

It was nearly ten minutes before they came to a stop. The

driver found someone to help with their suitcases, and wished them a pleasant trip when Lyle paid him and tipped him generously.

Again she did not look directly at the man with her, but went ahead, following the porter to the check-in counter where there was a line. Near the head of the line was Hilary Nast. He was dressed in a heavy tweed overcoat and was chewing reflectively on a pencil stub. When he got to the ticket agent, he said in a voice that carried to the end of the line, "I say, you don't think our flight will be delayed because of the weather, now do you?"

He was assured that there would be no delay, his bags were checked through, and he sauntered off a few feet, stopped suddenly, and drew a folded newspaper from his pocket. He looked at it intently, filled in a section of a crossword puzzle, and walked on. In front of Lyle a man and woman watched him, smiling.

"The English are crazy," the woman said. The man nodded.

Was the watcher still there? Still watching? Would he board with them, sit in the first-class section with them, go to New York with them? Lyle's fingers were clenched again; she felt as if a heavy weight were on her chest restricting her breathing. They should have warned her about the fear, prepared her for this, rehearsed her. At the counter, she pushed her ticket across silently, watched her companion load the suitcases onto the scale, and saw that his hands were trembling. At once she felt removed from the scene, distant from him, from the line, the man behind the counter, as if she were watching everything from a safe place.

"Nonsmoking," she said calmly, almost coldly. "Will there be time for a coffee before we depart?" She picked up the tickets he was returning to her. Her fingers were quite steady.

"Yes, madam. There is a first-class waiting room where they serve coffee, wines, cocktails, whatever you wish."

He directed her, then looked past her at the next person, and she walked away with her companion a step behind her, carrying the camera bag, the cowboy hat low on his head, the shapeless coat hiding his body.

"I would like a cup of coffee," she said, hoping to ease his tension, hoping the trembling of his fingers would not yet betray them both. "You must want something also. It's been a long time since breakfast. Of course, we'll have dinner on the plane, but that will be quite a while . . ."

In the waiting room, seated in comfortable chairs with a tiny table between them, their coffee in delft cups, Lyle looked directly at Yuri Korolenko for the first time, and she could not conceal her start of recognition. He seemed to glow with good health, as Carmen did, and Saul, and as she did also. She averted her gaze, but not before he acknowledged her recognition with a very slight nod. When he picked up his coffee, his hands were no longer trembling.

Their flight was announced and the first-class passengers were escorted aboard before anyone else. Yuri took a window seat, let the back down all the way and stretched out, the cowboy hat over his face. The steward smiled at Lyle. "If he falls asleep before takeoff, will you see that he is upright, please?"

She nodded. "Yes. We're both very tired. He'll probably sleep all the way." The steward took her coat to hang up, offered to take Yuri's. "Perhaps later. We were chilled by the rain."

Three seats in front of her, Hilary Nast was settling himself. Other people on both sides were arranging their carryon bags, finding books, surrendering coats and hats to the steward . . .

Which one, she wondered. Which one would watch her every movement, Yuri's movements, ready to pounce if either of them made a mistake? She leaned back and closed her eyes. It was futile to guess. A spy who looked like a spy would be a failure.

As soon as the plane was off the ground and the FASTEN SEAT-BELTS sign had been turned off, she went to the lavatory, locked the door, and leaned against it taking deep breaths. They had done it! Now she felt weak, faint almost, and, curiously, she wanted to weep. She found herself wishing that alcohol still had an effect on her; she wanted to drink a very large brandy, to get lightheaded from it, to celebrate the success of her part of the plan. She looked at herself in the mirror, clear skin, clear eyes, unlined face, a youthful woman going into middle age, who had given up drinking. She sighed. She would settle for a very good wine, glass after glass of it all the way home, and let them wonder how she had managed to build up such a tolerance.

And, she knew, she would try to follow the thread of tortuous reasoning that now presented itself. She had recognized Yuri exactly the way Lasater had recognized her on the Oregon coast. It was unmistakable — the glow of health, the clear eyes, the lovely smooth skin . . . Soviet science, like all Soviet institutions, was closely supervised by the government, and that meant the serum was controlled by the Soviet Union. How to use it would be a state decision, a political decision. They must have felt secure in their belief that no one had penetrated the secret, that no one even suspected there was a secret. Their first thought now would be that the CIA was involved, that the United States government had learned about the serum, or had learned enough to seize the scientist. No doubt they would also assume that he would tell everything eventually. She found herself going over the scenarios they had talked about that last night in Pennsylvania and she knew that all at once the world had become an extremely dangerous place for every living creature, more so than at any previous time in its history.

◘ 20 ◘

RIGHT UP TO the time that Alex Radek collected him to go to Kennedy, Lasater believed that their jaunt would be cancelled. Lyle Taney would come down sick, he had reasoned, or the kid would, or they would be delayed and miss their flight, or something. They were not likely to leave Amsterdam before the biologists even got started on their meeting, he was certain. He was surprised when Alex entered the coffee shop promptly at one.

To his relief they took a cab out to the airport. That made him believe that Rawleigh had been leveling with him, that they only wanted an identification; they did not want to pick up anyone. He knew this routine. He would make the identification; someone would be around with a camera taking pictures, and they would all fade away, job done. Then they would run the pictures through and come up with zilch.

The driver talked about the damn Puerto Ricans, damn voodoo economics, damn kids standing on bridges throwing rocks at cars passing below. Alex blew his nose a lot and ate throat lozenges and talked about the damn cold weather when he could get in a word. Lasater felt no urge to say anything. He hoped he would not catch a cold from Alex; he did not even want to breathe the same air Alex was breathing.

They entered the terminal and Alex looked about discontentedly. "God, I hate airports. I remember how I used to love them, all of them, no matter how ratty. Flying was still exciting."

"Yeah, back when the dinosaurs roamed. I know."

"You too?" Alex glanced at him and sighed. "I guess we're both getting on, a little long in the tooth. Takes a hell of a lot more than a plane in the sky to fire us up these days. Sad, ain't it?"

"If I had a violin, I'd play. Honest. You going to tell me anything yet?"

"Soon. Let's go look at the board."

The terminal was as crowded as usual. People were sleeping sprawled out on the floor, in chairs. Little children were running, laughing, screaming. Teenagers were trying to look bored. Young couples looked forlorn, or elated, or stoned, or all three. Nothing was out of the ordinary. Lasater did not spot Herb Balinski, and had not expected to. He did not know Balinski's associate, did not even try to find him in the crowd, nor did he try to find Alex Radek's camera man. Let them do their thing, he thought, following Alex to the arrivals and departures board. He did spot the plane from Amsterdam: three-ten, on time.

"Nearly half an hour to wait," Alex said. "You want a beer, or something? Let's go to the bar and I'll fill you in."

Lasater shrugged. He drank very little; ulcers ten years ago had put him on the wagon for over a year and afterward he had not found it necessary to pick up old habits.

The bar was dark and there were empty tables although men were standing hip to hip at the bar itself. "What do you want?" Alex asked. "I'll get it. Never get waited on over here." Lasater told him a beer and watched him ease his way between two men at the bar. He came back with the beer and a screwdriver for himself. "For the orange juice," he said.

They drank in silence until Lasater said, "You were going to tell me a story, remember?"

"Yeah. It's your girlfriend, Taney, and lover boy. We want to know if she's still playing house with the same kid who was on the coast."

"You couldn't just wait outside their house, apartment, whatever? Had to drag me down here for this?"

"They've been on this trip for a couple of weeks," Alex said in a tone that was almost conciliatory. "They'll get home and go inside and maybe not come out again for days, tired of traveling, tired of restaurants. You know how that goes. It seemed easier this way."

"Yeah, yeah. When do they come in?"

"Oh, I thought you saw on the board."

"Pal, you haven't even told me where they're coming from," Lasater said. It *was* like old times, he thought, sparring with Alex. He had been right about that. Testing each other, always testing, that's how it had been with them.

"Right. Amsterdam. Due in at ten after three. Our man in Amsterdam sees them off. We see them in. It's a miracle, isn't it? They leave Amsterdam at two and get in at three."

Lasater looked at his watch. "Christ! They'll be an hour in customs. You want another one of those? I'm getting another beer."

At four they made their way to the corridor where international travelers entered the terminal. There was a mob there.

"This is the pits," Lasater said with disgust. "I can't get close enough for her to get a glimpse of me. What am I supposed to do, turn on my x-ray vision and look through the jerks?"

"Take it easy," Alex said, but he looked worried now. "Come on, if we stay back near the wall, she'll go past and you'll get a look at her and the kid, right? That's all we want. No chat or renewing old acquaintances, anything like that. Just a good look at the kid."

People were coming through the corridor, being met, hugging, kissing, vanishing with their loved ones, or their creditors, or whoever it was who met planes.

The crowd did not thin out; if anything it seemed to increase moment by moment. Suddenly a shrill voice cried: "There she is! She's coming!" Now the crowd surged forward, and Lasater saw that the parcels many of the people had been holding were being unwrapped, bags opened, satchels unstrapped; they were carrying Lyle Taney's book on hawks. A goddam fan club, he thought savagely.

"What the hell . . . ?" Alex muttered.

"Yeah, you and your bright idea, get them before they lock themselves away . . ."

He saw her then and instantly she was surrounded by a couple dozen fans thrusting books at her for her autograph, all talking, pushing, shutting her up in a people wall. Briefly he had seen a cowboy hat, curly hair sticking out, but too briefly. A tall, broad man in a tweed coat, enveloped in the mob, was in the way. His voice carried over the others.

"Oh, I say, are you a cinema star? If only I had known on the flight! Dear me, don't push, please, you'll crush her . . ."

The mob surged past, headed toward the door where the sign said TAXIS, the tweed man talking all the way, completely blocking the view of Lyle and the boy in the cowboy hat.

"Shit!" Alex said.

"That says it. I'm going home. You have something for me, right?"

"Yeah. I'll call the farm and be in touch with you in a couple of days. You hanging around?"

"Do I have a choice?"

"Hugh! What a thing to say. Here you are, the envelope. I hope you don't want to count it in here."

"I'll trust you for it, until I get to my hotel room anyway. You going back to town now?"

"Might as well. Can you wait just a minute? I want to speak to someone first."

"I'll be at the door over there. You paying the taxi back?"

"Yeah. What a bust. And me with a sore throat and a cold. Shit!" He looked at Lasater hopefully. "Did you see enough to say one way or the other?"

"Are you kidding?"

"Yeah. Goddam!"

Lasater waited while Alex went to find his camera man, who could not have had any better luck than they had. No way could anyone have got a picture of them. A perfect setup, he thought suddenly, right down to the dude in the tweed coat, surrounding the kid. Why him? What was so special about Carmen all at once? He never had tried to keep a low profile before. Why start now? Suddenly he started to laugh. They had pulled it off! Hot damn! That wasn't Carmen; he must still be back in Amsterdam, or in a rowboat heading for England, or in a wet suit swimming one of the canals. They had lifted someone and brought him home in Carmen's place!

Alex returned and looked at him sourly.

"Foiled by the Bird Watchers of America," Lasater said, still laughing.

He nodded toward a small group of young women who had been in the mob around Taney. One was showing her autographed book to the others. "She'll actually come out and talk to us," she was saying. "And bring the pictures they couldn't use in the book! Wasn't she wonderful!"

Lasater glanced at Alex, who seemed to qualify for sick leave, and he started to laugh again. "Wonderful!" he said. "She was just too wonderful!"

"Just shut up, will you?"

"Ninety-eighth and Riverside Drive," Lyle said. She leaned back in the taxi and closed her eyes. Beside her Yuri Korolenko was taking deep breaths.

"You someone famous or something?" the driver asked.

"Not at all. I just wrote a book about birds and they liked it."

"Yeah, you never know what'll turn people on. I thought I saw you on Carson's show few weeks ago. Some homecoming."

"Overwhelming," she admitted.

"Picked up Bette Davis once, just like I picked you up now. Kept wondering where I'd seen her, you know? Never expected to have *her* in my hack . . ."

He talked about the famous people he had driven, and Lyle slowly relaxed. Yuri's breathing returned to normal. He began to stare out the window intently. The driver talked on and on.

"Worst possible time of day, you know? Look at them cars! Lined up five miles already!"

The traffic increased until they were barely moving; the trip to Manhattan took over two hours, and then they were at the corner near where her car was parked.

Don't go near your apartment. Get your car and head for the Tappan Zee. Traffic will be bad, but that can't be helped.

She waited until the taxi was lost in the swarm of cars, and then crossed the street with Yuri. They carried the suitcases halfway down the block where she said, "Wait here until I get the car. Do you understand me?"

"Yes," he said.

"You speak English?"

"Very little, and bad." His accent was thick.

"I'll try to be fast," she said, "but it will take a few minutes."

He nodded and she hurried to the attendant of the garage. It took them ten minutes to move enough cars to get to hers and then bring it to her with brakes squealing at every turn on the ramp.

Finally, they were in the stream of traffic heading for the Tappan Zee Bridge.

"I think I am afraid before," Yuri said, sitting straight upright, his hands balled on his thighs. "But I am wrong. Now I am afraid. And in taxi I am afraid very much."

"I don't blame you," she muttered, gripping the wheel hard. "I hate this kind of driving. It scares me too."

"I wish you don't tell me this," he said. "For you who are so brave to say this makes me close my eyes."

She glanced at him and he managed a weak smile, but he obviously was frightened by the traffic. "It's all right," she said. "Really, we're all used to this. I don't like it, but I'm used to it."

They crossed the wide bridge and headed north on Interstate 87. The traffic thinned out now as car after car overtook them and passed. Lyle held a steady fifty-five miles an hour. No ticket, no trouble, just a steady drive to the next turnoff. She was getting very tired. There was a tightness in her shoulders, and she was hungry now. It had been hours since they had eaten on the plane. Too much excitement, too much tension, always made her hungry. Yuri had hardly touched his food; he must be even hungrier than she. She turned on the radio and switched the stations hunting for news, and realized she was trying to find out if Carmen had made his escape, if Yuri's disappearance had made the evening news.

At last she found a news station and they listened intently. War in South America, as usual. Talk about the new Congress. They had held an election without her. A new biological control for the Med fly. A kidnapping in Rome, and one in San Salvador. Blizzard in Wisconsin. Russians blame CIA for the disappearance of brilliant young scientist . . .

". . . Yuri Korolenko, one of the Russian scientists at the International Biology Congress in Amsterdam vanished without a trace from the hotel where the conference was being staged late this evening. The American government has denied any knowledge of the incident."

"It worked!" Yuri said in astonishment.

"It worked," Lyle repeated, wondering where Carmen was, how he was. "Do you want to keep listening?"

"Please," he said, gazing at the radio with rapt attention. He listened to it all up to the sports news, and then leaned back.

Lyle was watching the highway signs now. Her turnoff onto 17 was coming up soon. One mile. She eased up on the accelerator, made the turn, and drove more slowly. It was not very far to Monroe, where they would stop. The headlights behind her could be Hilary, or police, or CIA, or anyone. They did not get any closer, and, watching them in the rearview mirror, she realized that they had been there for a long time, exactly that far away. Other cars had come between them and had passed her, but one pair of lights had remained, never wavering.

Hilary, she prayed. Please let it be Hilary.

She reached out and turned off the radio. "I have to tell you the next part of the plan," she said. "We'll stop soon at a roadhouse, a restaurant. Friends will meet us there. You will go with one of them who will take you the rest of the way. Do you understand?"

"Yes. But you? What do you do now?"

"I'll come along with someone else a little later. That's not important. We have to be certain no one follows you."

"Yes, is important. I have many thank yous to give to you. Is important."

"We'll meet again very soon, Yuri. I promise you. Then we'll talk, if you like."

"Yes. I like."

She slowed to forty-five; the lights behind her maintained the same distance. Another car sped around her follower, accelerated and passed her; its taillights dwindled to nothing very quickly. She neared the turn and visualized the streets leading to the restaurant. She and Carmen had driven to it, had looked at the parking lot together, had checked the hours. She made her turn, made another sharper right turn and cut off her headlights for the next two blocks; she went through an alley to the roadhouse and pulled into the parking lot from the back.

The Volvo was there! It had not been Hilary following, after all. Even before she got her door open, Hilary appeared at it. "Quickly," he said. "Yuri, come, get on the back seat and lie down. Hurry!"

The Volvo door opened, Yuri darted toward it and flung himself inside, vanished down onto the seat. The door closed. Hilary said to Lyle, "Go inside and order for two as if he's still with you. Come out in half an hour."

She hurried inside the restaurant. The door was closing behind her when another car pulled into the lot. She found a booth and sat down facing the door. When the waitress came, she said, "Two coffees, please. My husband is fixing something on the car. We'll both have roast beef sandwiches."

A young black man entered, glanced down the length of the restaurant on his way to the restroom. He could not tell if anyone was across the booth from her, she knew; the backs were too high. He reappeared in seconds and stood at the bar, not ostensibly looking her way, but including her in his range of vision. He watched the waitress deliver two cups of coffee to the booth. He was still there ten minutes later when the sandwiches were ready.

"He's taking his time out there," the waitress said. "The sandwich's going to get cold."

"I know. He won't mind."

"Won't even notice, if he's like most of them." She went away.

The black man was eating pie, drinking coffee. Lyle picked up her sandwich, then began to eat it hungrily. It was good, hot, with a spicy mustard. She drank her coffee, then the other cupful, and it was nearly time to go outside again. The waitress came back shaking her head.

"I'll take it out to him," Lyle said, getting out her wallet. The waitress left, came back with a white paper bag, and took the money and the bill. When Lyle left, carrying the bag, she did not look at the black man.

Hilary was at the wheel of her car. She got in the passenger side, locked the door.

"Now we lose them," Hilary said happily. "I was afraid they would catch on and go after Steve, but they didn't. You've been splendid, Lyle, really splendid!"

He pulled out of the parking lot and drove to 17 again. "Ah, there they are, faithful dogs." He hummed as he drove. The countryside was very dark, deserted looking. "What we will do," Hilary said a little later, "is turn onto Interstate 84 and make them think we have some serious traveling to do tonight. Won't be long now. I may accelerate sharply, Lyle dear, so do brace yourself, won't you?"

The turn was very sharp. He made no signal, hardly slowed for it, and they screeched on the ramp terrifyingly. As soon as the car was straightened out on the interstate, he accelerated and passed two other cars that were cruising more sedately; then he turned off his lights, hit the brakes, and they were turning again, leaving the interstate, heading back to 17. Now he stopped and waited. Two cars passed, a third, another one. He began to hum again, and put the car into first, started to drive.

"I do believe we've lost them," he said, after a few miles. "Now we can go home. I say, is that a sandwich you've brought me?"

Lasater had been waiting in Herb Balinski's office for hours. Balinski's secretary was sleeping on a couch, snoring gently. She was heavy-breasted, blonde, and could even type. He had seen her typing a long time ago, hours ago. A natural blonde, with pale blue eyes, fair skin, she had a twangy Kansas accent.

She was meant to reassure clients; Balinski had no use for her. "You going to wait all night?" she had asked earlier.

"If I have to."

"Okay by me, but I'm getting some sleep. See you in the morning, honey." And just like that she had stretched out on the couch, closed her eyes and started to snore. For this he was paying her overtime, he thought bitterly, glaring at her.

She hardly even twitched when the phone rang finally at fifteen minutes after twelve.

"Yes!"

"Listen, I'm afraid we lost them."

"Where the hell are you?"

"Monroe, New York."

"Just tell me for Christ's sake!"

"Yeah, I'm trying. It was sledding on a twelve-foot snowpack all the way to Monroe. She was driving nice and slow, not paying any attention to anything but the road in front of her. A real Sunday driver. Then she pulled a fast one in Monroe, doused her lights, did the back alleys, and ended up at a restaurant. She was just going inside when we pulled up. My associate went in and I checked the car, made sure no one was hiding in it, you know? Anyway, my associate spotted her, and thought the guy was with her in the booth. He would've had to go look in directly to tell otherwise, you know? High back, dim light. Anyway, he thought the guy was there. I stayed outside. A white Volvo pulled out right after we got there, but what the hell? Duck soup up to then, we weren't expecting anything fancy. Then that English guy from the airport comes from nowhere and gets in her car, and a minute later she comes out alone, gets in and they take off. He knows a trick or two and lost us on Interstate Eighty-four. Probably pulled off at Seventeen and doubled back, but no way to be sure. We cruised around some looking for them, no dice."

Lasater stared at the blonde malevolently, wishing she would choke on the next snore. He remembered the white Volvo, the one Werther had run off the cliff in Oregon. It made him feel weird — Werther raised from the dead, the car reassembled.

"Hugh, you there?"

"You son of a bitch, where'd you think I'd be? What else?"

"Not much. But if it helps, the Volvo that pulled out had a

Pennsylvania license. It was out of sight before we got more than that."

"You know how fucking big Pennsylvania is?" He smashed the phone down and stalked from the office, slammed the door as hard as he could. "Wake up, you bitch!"

◻ **21** ◻

"SOMEONE FOLLOWED ME to Monroe," Lyle told Saul before he had time to embrace her.

He swept her into his arms and kissed her, cutting off her words. When he released her, he said, "You were wonderful all the way. Come inside where it's warm. Everyone wants to congratulate you."

"Have you heard from Carmen yet?"

"We don't expect to until he's in Canada. Don't worry about him. He's too wily to be caught."

The night was clear and still, very cold, nearly down to zero. Saul hurried her into the house. Hilary had already entered the living room; the others rushed to her as soon as she appeared in the doorway.

"Here she is, the hero of the day," Hilary called out; he was warming himself at the fire.

There were hugs and kisses, as if she had been part of them for years and they seriously had worried about her. Yuri was standing near the fire also, smiling at her. He had taken off the wig; his own hair was brown and straight, cut short.

"A hot drink first, and then talk. We would not allow Yuri to say much of anything until you two got here." Saul made two Irish coffees and handed one to Lyle, one to Hilary, and then sat down on a couch near the fire. The others arranged themselves; Steve and Dora chose cushions on the floor, Mutt sat next to Saul, and Lyle and Yuri sat opposite on the other couch. Hilary dragged another chair close to the group. The room glowed; Lyle realized it was because the gold drapes on the wall of windows were drawn.

"Actually," Hilary said, "Dr. Korolenko and I haven't really met even though we do keep bumping into each other. Hilary Nast," he added.

They shook hands and Yuri turned to Lyle. "We have not met too."

She felt her cheeks go hot. "Good heavens! I never did tell you who I am. Lyle Taney. I'm sorry."

He kissed her hand and sat down once more. "She is very brave woman. Very smart and brave."

Saul nodded. "I know. She doesn't know it yet, but we all do."

Lyle looked at the whipped cream on her Irish coffee and waited for them to change the subject. Brave? She had been baby-sat all the way, with Carmen or Hilary or someone always within reach. Even so, she had been terrified. Smart? She had led someone almost all the way to the door. She looked at Saul when he spoke again.

He was being very courteous, radiating warmth and charm, and more, friendliness. He looked at the young Russian as if he had known him for a long time, and liked him very much. There was compassion in his look, perhaps even pity.

"Are you too tired tonight, Yuri, to tell us about your group? If so we can put it off until tomorrow. There really isn't any rush."

"Now," Yuri said quickly. "Is all right to speak French? I speak too bad English, have to stop to think too much."

His teacher, the director of the biology department in the University of Leningrad, he said in rapid and perfect French, was Boris Lepov, a genius. He had been studying molecular biology for many years, even before Watson and Crick made their fantastic discovery of the structure of DNA. Dr. Lepov had been pleased with their announcement because he had been certain it would stimulate other scientists to look into the matter of the ability of the cells on some occasions to heal themselves quickly, almost as quickly as they were damaged. He had been dismayed by the start-and-stop progress in an area first broached fifty years ago. Boris Lepov had studied the articles written in the thirties by a German biologist, Hermann Franck, he went on, and stopped in confusion when Hilary laughed softly.

"Meet Herr Doktor Professor Franck," Hilary said, pointing at Saul.

Yuri leaped to his feet. "You? Is true?"

Saul nodded. "Boris Lepov came across my old articles? How curious. I didn't know they were extant anywhere."

"Yes, we have your articles! If only Boris could be here instead of me! He would be happy! He said you made the same discovery of the DNA structure, twenty years earlier!"

"Not quite, but close. But go on, please."

Yuri sat down once more, but he kept his gaze on Saul; his attitude had changed, as if now he knew he was addressing an angel, or a god, perhaps.

Seven years ago Boris Lepov had discovered that the tissue samples they were using in their lab had been contaminated with the curiously long-lived HeLa strain of uterine tissues that had traveled around the world masquerading as everything from brain tissue to epidermis tissue. The samples were good for nothing, had to be discarded, the laboratories decontaminated. But then he began to wonder why those tissues had the ability to contaminate everything in the same building with them, in the same city even, it seemed. Why did they keep on living?

Hilary explained it to Lyle the next day. In 1951, a woman named Helen Lane (hence HeLa) had donated her body to science when she knew she was dying of uterine cancer, and after her death, the uterine tissue had been kept alive for experimentation. If even one cell of that tissue found its way to samples of any other tissues, it overwhelmed them; the HeLa cells divided, multiplied, overcame everything else until the entire sample was HeLa, the original completely gone. Quite a few years later it was learned that most tissues from a number of laboratories that supplied others throughout the world had been contaminated with the HeLa cells, had become HeLa tissues, no matter how they had started. The life work of many scientists had to be done over, was being done over even now, because the findings suddenly had been invalidated.

"That's the very line I was following at Stanford," Steve said. "I'll be damned! I wonder how many others are poking into those tissues with this in mind."

"Too many, no doubt," Hilary said. He looked at Yuri. "Boris

Lepov found what he was looking for and didn't publish a word of it."

"We were forbidden," Yuri said simply. Although Steve and Hilary had lapsed into English, his response was in fluent French. "When I went to work for Boris Lepov, six years ago, he was already well into the research. I became one of his assistants; during my first year with him, it became clear. He found what he was looking for."

"Not DNA," Saul said quietly.

"No, not that. RNA, ribonucleic acid, the messenger of the gods."

Saul glanced at Lyle who was following the conversation with little comprehension. She met his gaze and shrugged helplessly. "Bear with us," he said, then turned again to Yuri. "And you found that although you could isolate the factor, you could not test it on living organisms, only on tissues. Is that correct?"

"Exactly so. It does not work with animals, not even chimps."

Hilary laughed. "Ninety-nine percent is too far away," he said to Lyle. "Chimps share ninety-nine percent of the same chromosomes as humans. That one percent is a terribly big gap, though."

"Yes. Too much difference. We had to test it on a human. Boris wanted it to be himself, and we panicked, all of us. We would not permit it. Instead we drew lots. There were eleven of us then. We did not allow him to gamble with us. One of the women was our first test subject. She became very ill and nearly died, but then recovered completely. This was four years ago. Boris went to the conference knowing what he had discovered, but not enough about it yet to dream of publishing, even if it had been permitted. But he was frightened. The paper he read was sufficient for anyone who knew enough to guess the significance. Your professor Mr. Oliver guessed and that was when he told Boris to get in touch with him if he wanted help. Boris was even more frightened at the thought that the Americans had the same secret. Only very slowly did he come to believe that your government did not have it, that it was in the hands of a small group of people who were keeping it a secret."

"Were you testing it yet?"

"Not yet. The woman was being observed very closely, of

course. Gradually the extent of her immunity became evident, and also, she infected her lover, and he became like her." He was looking at Saul fixedly, speaking to him as if the others were not in the room.

"Then we knew we could not contain it. There were eleven of us in the laboratory, working on this research. Some of them were party members; there were also administration people, supervisors; few of the others knew exactly what it meant, but we all did, all eleven of us. We were all treated early. Five of our team died. Some of the others used it, many of them died. And the government took it over." He became silent.

Mutt Evans got up and put another log on the fire. Dora went to the buffet and poured herself more coffee, no one spoke.

"When the government took control," Yuri went on, "they isolated all of us, the scientists, the secretaries, the administration, the supervisors, everyone who possibly could have had any contact with it, their wives and husbands and lovers. But some of the officials used it. Would they report themselves, lock themselves up? I think not. They began to test in a massive way, with prisoners. That was when we discovered that no woman who survived the treatment became pregnant."

"Oh damn!" Hilary said. "The same stone walls! We hoped you would have something different to tell us."

Yuri nodded. "Yes, I understand. We too were dismayed for three years. Then we learned that my wife, the first one of us to be given the serum and survive, she was pregnant. There is an answer to that problem. Within a week to ten days she will bear our child."

"That's why they sent you," Steve said softly, with great sympathy. "Those bastards! Is she all right?" Again he spoke in English and Yuri answered in French.

"Perfect. And the baby, a boy, is also perfect. They did an amniocentesis. He is one of us, naturally."

"Do you know why she was able to become pregnant? Are there others?" Saul asked.

"Fanya, when she was only a girl of thirteen, became enchanted with mysticism. She became a follower of yoga, and she became an adept over the years. She never gave it up, not even when her university studies became difficult and demanding and there was little time. She learned to control her autonomic system, control pain, do all the things an adept is able to do. We think she controlled her own immunological response to the sperm."

"I'll be damned," Dora said in awe. "*Are* there any others?"

"Two others have become pregnant. However, there are very few adepts who are young women."

Dora began to laugh. She put her head down on her knees and laughed until her voice became faint. "God, it's finally happened! It's in the hands of the women! Finally!"

"It's in the hands of the Soviet government," Mutt said bluntly.

"For now. As Yuri said, it can't be contained. Not forever. All girls, all women can be trained to meditate. With biofeedback methods anyone can be taught!"

"I'm really more concerned with the near future than with forever," Mutt said. "What's going to happen over there?"

"They are still testing with prisoners, trying to find why it kills so many. We are housed in a prison, something like a prison. No one tells us the plans, but we think they will start a massive inoculation this year, this winter, and call it flu shots or something of that sort."

Saul closed his eyes, frowning, as if in great pain.

"Dear God!" Lyle whispered. "They wouldn't do that to their own citizens! Half of them will die!"

"They know that," Yuri said. "But the half who do not die will be protected from radiation. They will start with the Politburo, officials, party members, the army . . ."

Mutt was staring at him fixedly. "How many of the original survivors knew about Seymour Oliver's offer to help Boris Lepov?"

Yuri nodded at him, as if had been thinking the same thing. "Four besides Boris. One of them is too political, a party member. One is crazy. We didn't tell them our plan. If the government had chosen Ilya to attend the conference, we would have had to kill him. One of the four had to come, had to speak with you. It had to be Fanya or me."

"But the others will tell eventually. One of them will," Mutt said, still looking hard at Yuri.

"Of course. Perhaps even Fanya. There is the baby, a tool they can use against her very soon."

Mutt stood up. "I'll go call Seymour, tell him his brother is dying, he has to come home on the first flight."

Saul nodded. "They will assume he's with the CIA, and in turn the CIA will become interested in him. I'm afraid his career has just come to an end. A pity. He liked his work."

Yuri looked strained and tired now. "For us too the careers are over. Already the government has taken the laboratories, moved them, moved all of us to this secret place where we were not allowed to leave, to make phone calls, send out uncensored mail. Now the others will be locked up, away from the work. There are many new people in the laboratories, none of the old will be there again."

"Oh, damn!" Hilary said then. "It's two in the morning, and I must say I feel as if I've had a rather full day. Yuri, let me show you to your room. There's an assortment of clothes, I just hope something in there will fit you all right. Let's do totter off to bed."

Lyle had not admitted how tired she was until she let herself relax in a hot bath. The tensions melted, flowed away, dissolved in the fragrant water, scented with a mixture that Saul had given her, herbs, flowers, seeds that he had collected, dried, ground, blended. Everything had changed, she reflected, lying back. What about her plans to walk away from it all? What about the confusion she still felt about Saul and Carmen? Neither seemed very important any longer. Everything had changed. She could smell wood sorrel, and a hint of the spiciness of carnations, and something else too elusive to identify. The water was silky, spring water, incredibly pure and soft. Billows of suds had filled the tub enclosure the first time she had washed her hair with this good water. She wanted to think of Yuri and the new problems he had given them, the new worries, but her mind kept skittering away, locking onto things of no consequence like the softness of the water, the fragrance of the sachet . . .

Resolutely she got out of the tub and dried herself, put on her robe, and went to the study door. She could hear nothing from the other side, but she knew he was not yet asleep. He would be sitting in his deep chair by the window in the dark study, looking out over the silvery world that was so quiet and cold that night.

She tapped on the door softly before she opened it enough to see in. He was at the window, as she had known he would be.

She went to him and put a pillow on the floor, sat down on it and rested her cheek on his leg.

"Listen," he said in a near whisper.

She could hear it now, distant honking of geese.

"They've had their rest, now they're on their way again," he said, still speaking very low. "How I envy them. No hard choices to make. Just listen to the blood, or the nerves, or the sound of moonlight on cold waters, or a strange god we can't even conceive of, and obey. That's an enviable freedom."

She shook her head. "No. Freedom is knowing you have to choose and being able to do it."

"What a rationalist," he said with a touch of laughter in his voice.

"Whoever followed me must have been waiting at the airport," she said. "I can't imagine anyone would have been keeping a parking garage under surveillance."

"I think you're right."

"Yes. And that means they knew when I would be back, the flight number, time, everything. Do you know who it could have been?"

"I don't think so."

"Me neither. Anyway, if I go back to New York, I'll have to remain there. I can't risk coming here again. Next time they might be more clever, and they surely would be more careful."

"I don't want you to be exposed, as you would be in New York," he said. "And we can't spare Carmen now."

"I know. Or I could run somewhere and hole up, hide. There are a lot of cities to hide in."

This time he did laugh. "And you know so much about how to hide!"

"I know. I'm an amateur, but I probably would learn very fast."

"Yes, no doubt. But there's another choice, isn't there?"

"Yes. I could simply stay here."

She became silent, looking out the window at the gleaming water, the still woods beyond. "Does the brook freeze in the middle of the winter?"

"Not all the way. The waterfall becomes very lovely with ice sculptures that no artist would ever attempt."

"Do you ice-skate? The pond must be wonderful."

"I used to, many years ago. My wife and I used to go out to a pond behind our house and skate there. She was a very good skater; I'm mediocre at best."

"I didn't know you had been married."

"No, I suppose not. I was thinking of her earlier, before you came in. She died when she was forty. A senseless, pointless death, useless death. There were skirmishes between the Communists and Fascists, sometimes they turned into outright war on a limited scale. Germany could have gone in either direction, I think. It just took someone with enough power, enough charisma to say this way. You know about the bad times in the late twenties, early thirties; you had them in the States here, but not as bad as we did. We, my family, were not hurt too much; we did not go hungry, or have to beg or steal. There was land, and a house that was like a miniature castle, four hundred years old, with turrets, gray stonework . . . There were fields of wheat turning golden in the fall, livestock . . . We were living well even if our money was worthless. There were no debts to pay off, just taxes, and we managed. Then, in the village near us, between our property and Berlin, there was a skirmish. Fifty men fought for causes none of them could explain. She had taken a wagonload of wheat, apples, eggs . . . I don't know what all she had gathered together. She was delivering it herself to the village church, for distribution, when the fighting started. Someone shot her."

Lyle pressed her face hard against his leg.

"Even the village is gone," he said. "It's become a suburb of Berlin. And my house is a historical landmark of some kind. They permit tourists to wander through to see how life used to be."

"That was a long time ago," Lyle said gently.

"Yes. A long time. Only sometimes it seems such a recent past. Listening to the geese brought it to mind, I guess. We used to sit on cold nights like this and listen to the geese fly overhead. We never could see them, just hear them."

"Your house, the turrets, that's where the logo came from that you use for the company name?" The M of M and S Pharmaceuticals was ornate, with two turrets, or crowns, on the points. The S looked like a winding path leading away from massive doors.

"I know I should have resisted, but I liked it. I liked the old house very much."

"I think seeing Yuri, knowing he has left his wife and unborn child behind has made you go back," Lyle said. "Everything is changed now, isn't it?"

"I'm afraid so."

"May I stay here with you?"

"Are you sure you want to?"

"Yes. But will you please never ask me to kill anyone?"

Saul's hand on her hair, the warmth of his body, the distant geese saying their farewells, the brilliant moon-lighted, crystalline world where only the brook moved, was all dreamlike, almost surreal. Her question could have been asked only in such a surreal setting; his answer, when it came, could not have been said anywhere else, under any other conditions.

"So much death," he said in a voice so low she could hardly hear it. "So much dying. Senseless deaths, brutal deaths. If I could go back to that night when Carmen lay close to death, would I do the same thing? I don't know any longer. I filled a syringe with a lethal dose of morphine. I held it against his skin, and I withdrew it. How different it would all be now. How different. I wept over him as a father weeps over a dying son, bitter tears, filled with rage and despair and helplessness. As I had wept over my wife. Over so many others. And now . . . I can promise nothing, my dear." His hand had stopped moving over her hair. She covered it with her own hand. "Lyle, I would not keep you here. You know that. You are free, not a prisoner."

"You've made plans for something like this, haven't you?" she asked, not moving, her hand still on his.

"Yes. We have always known that one side must not have it exclusively. Boris Lepov and Yuri understand this also, that's why Yuri risked everything to come here. Their government has had this for years without divulging anything. Now that the pregnancy problem seems to be solved, they probably will start administering it, and if they do, we must also."

She shut her eyes so hard they hurt. So much death, she thought, hearing his words once more in her head. So much dying.

"Let's go to bed now," he said gently. "Not to make love. Not tonight. Let me hold you. You are so tired."

She was. Two sleepless nights, the long exhausting day. Certain she would not be able to sleep, she fell asleep in his arms, listening to the voices of the geese. Later, when she woke up before the morning light, he was not beside her and she knew he had stayed only long enough to comfort her, to permit her to sleep. The geese were still crying their farewells in the cold distance.

▣ **22** ▣

"YOU READ THE story?" Rawleigh asked, tossing a newspaper across his desk to Lasater.

"What story's that?"

"About the scientist who vanished at the Amsterdam meeting."

"I saw it."

Rawleigh sighed and leaned back in his chair. It had high, carved posts supporting a leather backrest. His great-granddaddy had made it, no doubt, Lasater thought bitterly.

"Look," he said. "I'm getting fed up with Alex popping in and telling me I have to take a trip. I'm not on the payroll, remember?"

"I do regret all this, Hugh. Really. It's a damn nuisance to all of us, believe me."

When he had gone down to the coffee shop at ten, Alex had been there, finishing his own breakfast.

"Milking time on the farm," he had said pleasantly.

"So what is it this time?" Lasater was seated across the desk from Rawleigh, but his chair was not comfortable, did not have a leather back, and he was tired. He had been up nearly all night.

"It's that damn conference in Amsterdam. And your friend Taney and her child lover."

This time Lasater sighed. "I hope Alex told you all about the airport mob. No way could I get a glimpse of the kid."

Rawleigh waved it away. "We'll catch up with him sooner or later. They didn't go back to the apartment, you know."

"I didn't know," Lasater said evenly.

"Oh, right. You see, we're all in a bit of a dither today. The Russians seem to really believe we have their man. He's like the man who walked around the horse. You know that one, Hugh?" When Lasater shook his head, he went on, "It's a famous disappearance. This chap gets out of his carriage and just walks around the horse, or horses, I forget if it was one or two . . . Anyway, he walks around them, and is never seen again. Ever."

"They never used to have horses in Amsterdam."

"Not just like it, but enough, is what I meant," Rawleigh said with a touch of impatience. "Don't be difficult, Hugh. It's been a really bad morning. I think I have a headache coming along. Let's see, where was I? Oh, yes. The young Russian. He left a group of people, to wash his hands, or whatever, and was never seen again. That's what I meant."

Lasater listened with interest. The paper had given no details, only that he was gone. He still did not know how Taney and Carmen had pulled it off.

"That's not quite the same thing," he objected, when Rawleigh seemed to want him to say something. "A conference hotel is full of people, mostly men. He got lost in the crowd."

"I suppose. But who helped him? He never had been out of Russia before. He speaks very little English, some German, very good French, and positively no Dutch. I think even the Dutch will have to give it up soon, don't you? I mean only eight million people speak the language! And they all speak English. They could do worse than simply adopt English as their national language."

Lasater sighed again, louder, and looked at his watch.

"Sorry. But you see the problem. He had to have help. No

money, Russian clothes, no language except French that was passable, besides his own Russian, I mean. Where could he have gone? And really the big one, why? Who would want to take a Russian scientist, not even a physicist, you understand, but a biologist? We didn't lay a hand on him. The English? Why? And how? He walked into a restroom and never came out. People saw him walk in. Good people, honest people, people with no reason for lying about it. I mean not just Americans. If they had just been Americans, God help us all! But they weren't. There was a German, a Cuban, a Peruvian . . . I don't understand it, Hugh, and that's God's truth."

"Well, I sure wish I could help, Mr. Rawleigh," Lasater said.

"Now, Hugh, don't get sarcastic."

"He had to have made contacts earlier in the day," Lasater said, going along with it since Rawleigh seemed to want to play the inane gambit to some sort of finish.

"That's what we thought. We've been checking. He spent the day in the company of a group of biologists, and the writer Daniel Malone. They went sightseeing."

"Well, there you have it. He goes out in a crowd, slips off for a few minutes, and returns with no one ever the wiser."

"I'm afraid not. It was a group of five. They were together all the time."

"Then there has to be a conspiracy."

Rawleigh shifted in his chair, making it creak. He laughed, but not a very good laugh, and Lasater felt chilled throughout.

"Well, that one's not your problem, is it, Hugh? And not ours, either, since we never laid a hand on him. What I'd really like to ask you to do is go through some more pictures for us."

"He won't be there," Lasater said in resignation. The game was over. Who scored? He did not know.

"I suppose not," Rawleigh said broodingly. "There aren't many, though. One other thing, before you leave again, would you mind just running through the other disappearances once more? I asked Edgar Bushnell to come over and take it down, if you don't mind."

"I do mind, Rawleigh. You know damn well how Edgar operates. In real time, minute for minute, that's how. He wants you to remember one hour out of your life and it takes him days to get to it, get through it. No dice. You've got what I found out, all hearsay. I wasn't investigating, had no standing, asked no questions. Go ask the local cops, or the FBI. Either one can tell you more than I can."

"What is it? More money? We probably could scrape together a few more thousand, but not much more than that. It has to come out of petty cash as it is."

Hugh Lasater had seen too many people in trouble not to recognize the symptoms, even if Rawleigh was one of the higher echelon untouchables in the CIA. He had stood up, but now he sat down again, looking intently at Rawleigh. "I'll be damned," he said softly. "Well now, I'll just be damned! I do believe you're flying solo, Mr. Rawleigh. Why are you having Alex, a West Coast kid if there ever was one, hanging out here back east? Why are you seeing me here at the farm instead of the office? Why petty cash? You could have covered the airport like a blanket if you'd wanted to, but you didn't. Why not?"

"If I were you, Hugh, I'd be very careful," Rawleigh said, without a trace of the southern gentleman in his voice.

"Oh sure. And if I were you, Rawleigh, I'd be very polite. I seem to have something you want. Why not just come right out and say what it is and be done with it. Not money," he added. "Just an exchange of ideas. A frank discussion. Isn't that how the TV people put it when both sides are out in the open, each hoping the other will drop dead before dinner?"

"Hugh, do you think I'm not being open with you? What have I left out?"

"Where was the KGB spook when the scientist took a piss?"

"Didn't I mention them? Two of them. They'd been with him all day, through the museums, watching the group eat *rijsttafel*, back to the hotel. They saw him go into the washroom. I expect they're feeling rather chagrined right now."

"Two on one? Really?"

"You know, we should have talked you out of leaving us. We really should have. You pick up on the right things each and every time. Two of them. He must have been important to them."

"Then why'd they let him go in the first place?"

"He's the least important member of the team and he has a

pregnant wife. Someone had to show. I guess they thought he was the likeliest to return." He spread his hands helplessly. "I don't know why they do anything. They seldom say. Now, Hugh, I've been frank. Just look at the pictures, and go over the other disappearing acts again, with Edgar listening. Not his usual session, I promise you. I want to be there, and I certainly couldn't stand to watch him nibble away like he does."

Lasater shrugged. "Why not? It's all in my report."

It took six hours; Alex joined them, Rawleigh sat in, and Edgar led Lasater through each disappearance he had mentioned in his notes. Who, where, under what circumstances, how the investigation had proceeded. He was thorough, but obviously not happy with being limited in time. He was a small mouselike man with a thin mustache, pale, lank hair that fell over his forehead repeatedly. Absently he brushed it upward, it fell again, over and over. Also he put his glasses on when he read or wrote anything, and took them off when he listened. By the end of the first hour Lasater wanted to kill him.

There was nothing helpful, as he had known from the start. Each case was different. One man had walked away from a Mexico City restaurant and was never seen again. Another had gone to bed at midnight in Paris, and vanished. Another had left for the airport in San Francisco to meet colleagues from Harvard, and failed to show up. And so on. There were scant details about any of them, but no one had been watching any of them. They had had it easy. The Russian was different.

The pictures proved hopeless also. Twenty men, young, dark-haired, not Carmen.

Aunt Jane served them dinner, pork chops, mashed potatoes, green beans — good wholesome American food, Rawleigh said with satisfaction. Edgar was sent to bed early, and Alex and Rawleigh remained with Lasater.

"When you went to the drug companies for backing, what did you tell them?" Rawleigh asked.

"What I told you. I thought the old man had a cancer cure."

"But they saw the published articles, the papers that had been read at conferences, all that. What did they say about it?"

"Not a damn thing."

"They didn't believe in the cancer cure, though, did they?"

"I told you, they didn't say. I thought they did."

"Yes. Well, I doubt it."

"Take the stuff to Lawrence Truly and ask what he thinks," Lasater said. Lawrence Truly was their man; he was also a very good biologist, one of the experts they relied on for germ warfare advice.

"He's on sabbatical," Rawleigh said. "And Hanford Wilkes is out of reach, making a tour, or something." He was the other biologist who could be trusted.

Lasater considered this, his eyes narrowed, alert now to a difference in the air, a difference in the way Rawleigh was watching him, the way Alex was watching both of them. Now it was coming, he thought coolly, and waited for it, whatever it was.

"Strange that they both should be gone, isn't it? Not even a forwarding address," Rawleigh said.

"Off in Afghanistan or somewhere checking out germ warfare," he suggested.

"Yes, probably that's it. Hugh, the files on those disappearances are gone. What do you think of that?"

"Gone, or reclassified?"

"Well, reclassified, actually. I can't see them. I don't know anyone who can."

"You mean the local police files too?"

"Everything."

Lasater stood up. Very carefully he said, "I don't think I want to know anything else about any of this, Mr. Rawleigh. If you don't mind, I think it's past my bedtime."

Alex laughed, a sharp barking noise that turned into a cough.

Rawleigh looked at him morosely. "And he's coming down with a bad cold." He stood up also. "Yes, it is late. I'm sorry to keep you at it so long. I just have the feeling that you have something that hasn't come out yet. You know the feeling? Intuition, of course, nothing to back it up. Probably you don't even know what it is yourself."

Lasater almost felt pity for him. He was getting old, this was his life, and suddenly he had had the rug pulled out from under him. He didn't know how, or why, only that it was very big, likely the biggest thing to come his way, and he was being cut out. Also, Lasater thought, Rawleigh knew he was holding out something; he could not have a suspicion of what it was, just something. And he was afraid.

Rawleigh went to the door with him. "Look, I hate to ask, but could you hang around on the East Coast for the next week or so? I know you and Alex love California, but if something comes along that I want to talk to you about, it does make it easier if you're handy."

"I can't afford to live in a hotel, or even a Manhattan apartment," Lasater said. "And I hate Washington."

"Yes, of course. I understand. New York's where the action is. Isn't that what they say? Can't see it myself, but I do understand how others feel. We'll pick up the tab. One thousand a week living expenses? Surely that would cover it."

"Two grand comes closer."

Rawleigh shut his eyes hard and nodded. "Agreed. It won't be for long. A week, ten days, probably not more than that. As soon as Taney and her lover show up, Alex will be in touch again. Sooner if anything else comes up that we should discuss. All right?"

"Whatever you say."

Lasater was awake for a long time that night. What did Rawleigh want from him? What did he expect to get? Why had he told him as much as he had? He worried each question over and over, poking at it, posing it differently, feeding it answer after answer, each one more unsatisfying than the last. Suppose, he mused, Rawleigh had figured out that he, Lasater, was still on this case, on his own now, without any client. Suppose he expected Lasater to find Taney, the old man, Carmen, and the Russian scientist, just to make it a jolly foursome. That meant that he would be having Lasater followed, his phone tapped, the works. Crude. Too crude? He was not certain it could be too crude for Rawleigh. The real reason he did not like it was that it made Rawleigh think that he, Lasater, was a dummy, and he did not believe Rawleigh thought that. But what then? To identify Carmen when he surfaced again? Probably no one else could, but that seemed too little a payoff for the cash Rawleigh was shelling out. Because he had linked the various disappearances? Now that the files were closed, no one else could make the connections he had made. No one besides Rawleigh and his few trusted people knew the connections had been made already by someone on the outside of the agency. He felt a prickling on his arms, scalp, down his back at that thought. He remembered the way Rawleigh had reacted when he had suggested a conspiracy among the group of scientists who had been with the Russian in Amsterdam. He cursed under his breath. Of course Rawleigh believed that. It had to have been a conspiracy, but Holy Mother of God, he breathed, what exactly did that mean?

He backed up. Rawleigh believed the group in the hotel had been in on it, not the group out touring all day. Lasater knew better. Carmen and the Russian had switched places early enough for the Russian to fly home with Taney, and they had left Amsterdam at two. All day Carmen had pretended to be the Russian and no one had caught on, not the KGB anyway, following at a distance, watching outside the restaurant where the group gorged on *rijsttafel*, probably never closer than fifty yards. Heavy coats, the group being careful to keep Carmen shielded, it could have worked. All of them had to have been in on it. Then back to the hotel where Carmen vanished into the john. Probably put on an apron, took off a wig, or added one, and carried trays of food right in front of the KGB, jibbering away in Dutch. Who had been in that group? Rawleigh had said simply a group of biologists, and a writer, Daniel Malone, five in all. Daniel Malone! Rawleigh would not have given away a name if he believed that was the group of conspirators. He thought the conspiracy was during the vanishing act later, at the hotel. But the Russian had been halfway to the States by then. Daniel Malone! One of them? He had to be. Who else would risk his neck in a crazy scheme to help a defecting scientist? And Daniel Malone, he thought with satisfaction, could be reached, could be contacted. Rawleigh had given him a piece after all.

Daniel Malone and four others, he thought with a chill. An international group? It had to be. Some of the people who had vanished over the years had been French, there had been two Englishmen, an East Indian . . . For a long time he had thought each and every one of them had been killed. He had been wrong. How big was the group?

This was what Rawleigh had come up with, he realized, and this was why he was frightened. Someone had gone over his head to reclassify the files he wanted, no one was telling him anything, he suspected that something bigger than a cancer cure was at stake, and an international conspiracy was afoot. No wonder he looked bewildered and no wonder he wanted Hugh Lasater at hand to talk to from time to time.

He realized too that his own safety now depended upon Rawleigh's cupidity, his ambition, his fury at being excluded from something as big as this was turning into. Just keep the lid on, he thought, beaming the message to another bedroom where Rawleigh was more than likely also awake, staring at the ceiling. Keep wondering how the Russian managed to vanish from the hotel, he thought at Rawleigh. As long as he concentrated on that, Taney was relatively safe, she was still his to find.

The fact that Carmen had pulled the vanishing act under the noses of the KGB and a dozen other witnesses did not surprise him, or even interest him very much, except as a technical maneuver. Carmen and Saul Werther, he thought darkly, had been around long enough to learn a lot of useful tricks. No doubt they could teach the best agent a thing or two.

Finally he turned his thoughts to his own plans for the next few days. Herb Balinski, in spite of himself, had told him several useful things. One was that the man who had driven Taney away, and lost the following car, had been the same man who had hovered around her and her companion at the airport, the Englishman. It had all fallen into a neat pattern with that bit of information. But Balinski had had more. Taney had known the town where she had met the Englishman. She had been able to drive to the restaurant through alleyways, with her lights off. That was a good bit. The Englishman had known the area also, enough to know exactly where the turnoff from the interstate highway was, just four miles from where he had entered. And the other car had had Pennsylvania license plates.

It was not a lot, but it was something, and it was more than anyone else had. And he knew about Daniel Malone, he thought, and now he yawned. Surprisingly the day had turned out all right after such a lousy start. Not bad at all. He yawned again, turned to his side and fell asleep.

◙ 23 ◙

YURI AND LYLE stood at the pond regarding the ice. It was frozen across, but how deep? That was the question they had come to answer.

"Do you have a way to tell?" she asked. "My father used to go out on a pond near our house carrying a light hammer and a stake. As long as he could still drive the stake through the ice, he kept us all off it. We used to hold our breath waiting for the day he couldn't get the stake in; then he stamped on it, and finally jumped up and down. Of course, we already had skates on."

Yuri laughed. "Is good way." He looked at her anxiously and corrected himself. "A good way." He tentatively stepped onto the ice. "How we find out," he said. He put his other foot out and stood there for a moment, listening. He took a step, listened again. Then he stepped off. "Not yet."

"What did you hear?"

"I don't know exactly. Water? A cracking noise? Is not clear, but something. Soon."

They walked back to the big building companionably. He was practicing his English with her; for technical discussions with the other scientists, he still preferred French. He talked about his wife, about his childhood growing up in a small village, working on a collective farm. His mother had lived in Paris for over ten years, had spoken French at home, taught it in secondary school. He had met his wife at the University of Stalingrad. Although he did not say so, it was evident that he was homesick already, that he desperately missed his wife, that he was worried about her, the repercussions she might suffer because of him.

"Are you political?" Lyle asked. It was a gray, still day with a threat of snow in the air, and it was very cold.

He shook his head. "I did good work in mathematics and in science, that is all. Later there was no time."

"You left out languages," Lyle reminded him.

"Yes. Language, and mythology. I read mythology very much."

"You covered more ground than I ever did. I never could grasp math, and science seemed too . . . finished. Or something. If they already had the answers, why should I interest myself in it? That was my attitude."

"Covered more ground? What does this mean?"

"You learned things in many different areas. You did not limit yourself to your own field."

"Yes. But no political courses, except what was required. What do you mean when you say science seems finished? I do not understand this."

"Oh. I know that I was mistaken, but when I was still in school they seemed to teach science as if they had solved all the problems. They understood physics, and they understood the Darwinian theory, and astronomy and chemistry, and everything. I thought from what they said that great scientists had discovered all the secrets, that from now on it was just a matter of applied science turning the discoveries into the appropriate technologies. Do you understand what I mean?"

"Yes. But it is wrong."

"I know that now. But because I believed it at the time, I didn't bother with science. I think a lot of people are like me in that."

"In Russia all students study science and math. It is required. All mothers can boast that their daughters married engineers, or are engineers themselves. Do you know this passage: 'And God shall wipe away all tears from their eyes, and there shall be no more death, neither sorrow, nor crying, neither shall there be any more pain; for the former things are passed away'?"

"It's from the Bible."

"Yes. Boris Lepov told us that. We memorized it because we were afraid of what we had done, what we were continuing to do. We were afraid of what our government would do, what your government would do. Knowing science cannot protect anyone from the consequences of great discoveries. I say to Fanya I wish I still worked on farm, still drove tractor, mowed hay. Fanya say to me this passage from Bible, and she say to me: 'Former things will pass away and world will be open now for all things. There will be time to mow hay, and do science, and learn scuba diving, and study brain, and learn everything. Everything!' " He laughed self-deprecatingly. "Not that I can do so many things, but some people will do all. There will be time to learn science and mathematics and politics and history and poetry . . ."

They were walking on the gravel driveway that led to the building hidden by firs and spruces and rhododendrons. Only the little drive hinted that something was there, something not seen. Lyle looked back at the pond, the driveway that wound out to the road, barred now with a chain, closed for the season. A new world, she thought. They were entering a new world where time was no longer the limiting factor. It seemed to her that the world she examined was different, more fragile perhaps, and the responsibility for the earth belonged to those who used it, not their descendants. No longer could the living claim there was not enough time to undo what their carelessness did. There was time to plant a tree and watch it grow to maturity, time to rake its leaves, pluck its fruits, time to watch it become gnarled and tired . . . Time to study, to learn, time to explore the world below, the universe above . . . Time enough, or no time at all.

Yuri touched her arm. "You are troubled. Is it political?"

"Time enough," she said. "Or no time for anything except annihilation. Those are the alternatives now."

"Yes. We know this also. For all my life there has always been the threat of war, and your life also. So many brave people go die for what? Ideas. Idea of religion, or idea of politics, or economics. They think perhaps life is so short, causes are important enough to die for. But now, if annihilation does not come, if war does not come first, and people know life is not so short, will they die for ideas? I think they will not. There will be time to try ideas first, test ideas, no reason to fight and die for them."

"If war doesn't come too soon," she said and he nodded. "Let's go inside. I'm getting chilled." Soon it would be dark; nights came early and stayed long at this time of year. They were all terribly frightened that war would break out first, she knew, and knew that was the reason for the chill that had seized her. Smith and Jones, she thought, and now Jones was erecting a new shield, immunity from radiation poisoning. Would he shoot before Smith could do the same? Would Smith shoot before Jones had it fully in place? If Smith and Jones were sane, the question would never even arise, but over the years, she thought bleakly, Smith and Jones had both become terrifyingly insane.

Lasater stopped in a diner in Stroudsburg, Pennsylvania. He had covered the town thoroughly, up and down every street, up into the hills around the town, nothing. For the first time he began to believe his plan was foolish. He was not even sure what he was looking for. A sign. What kind of sign? He did not know. He would spot the white Volvo with the Pennsylvania license if he saw it, and he would spot Taney's black Renault if he came across it, but neither situation seemed as likely now as it had when he left New York earlier. After studying the map of this section of Pennsylvania he had been certain no one could hide here. If they had wanted to go to Philadelphia, they would have flown, he had reasoned. If they had wanted Scranton, or Pittsburgh, same thing, airplane. They had chosen to drive, had been met by someone who knew Monroe, New York. Taney knew Monroe. That meant they were not heading for anywhere too far from the New York border; he had been certain yesterday, the night before, and this morning. Now, in a steamy diner that smelled of doughnuts and bacon, he no longer felt so certain.

He drank coffee and went over his own reasoning. Not Stroudsburg, he had decided. Interstate 80 came straight to it from New York City. They would not have kept so far north if they had wanted this dump. He had decided to use this place as the outside boundary of the area he would drive through, search, look for a sign in. He felt reassured now; if they had wanted to rendezvous outside Stroudsburg, they would have chosen one of the little towns across the river in New Jersey, not Monroe, New York.

It was going to get dark soon. He would get a motel, find a decent restaurant, turn in, and start his search first thing in the morning. All he needed was a sign. He could not anticipate what the sign would be, but he knew he would recognize it when he saw it. A feeling he had, like Rawleigh's feeling that he was holding out. Intuition, that was it. He was following his intuition. Rawleigh would be pleased to know that.

"Let me tell you," Seymour Oliver said to Lyle. He had rejoined them that evening. "We spotted you instantly in the museum, of course. We were all a bit nervous, but you were so poised, so calm that it made me, for one, feel like a schoolboy. Anyway, we worked on Carmen and Yuri as fast as we could to make the transformation, while Franz stood at the door, holding it closed just in case. Full house, he was going to sing out, if he had to. He didn't." He was grinning broadly as he retold the adventure. "After the museum, always keeping Carmen covered as best we could, we went to a restaurant, and took as long as possible. More wine, more coffee, more everything! We waddled out, believe me. Carmen had on a janitorial outfit under that awful raincoat, of course, so it was nothing at all for him to get into a disguise. All he had to do was take off the raincoat, take off the wig, and he was a simple janitor mopping the men's lavatory. He stuffed the raincoat and cap down in the mop bucket — one of those great tubs on wheels with a roller mechanism on top. And he flushed the wig down a toilet. When someone asked him if he'd seen a man enter, he answered in Dutch, then in good, but accented, English. No one gave him another look."

"But how did he plan to get out of Holland?" Lyle asked, unable to laugh with the others.

"Train to Rotterdam, boat to England. He was going to play the part all the way, even waiting for a standby flight to save money."

"And the bicycle? He said he wanted a bicycle."

"To ride to the train station," Seymour said, as if she should have known that. "All the Dutch workers ride bikes everywhere."

She leaned back on the couch and took a deep breath. It sounded so simple, but she knew from her own escapade that it had been difficult, terrifying, and very dangerous.

"Of course, when they exhaust the possibilities of vanishing from the men's room, they will start to backtrack," Mutt said, his face furrowed in thought. "The Holmes method will assert itself eventually. I think everyone with Yuri and Carmen that day should run to cover."

"Dan will balk," Steve said.

"I sent a message out today," Saul said quietly. "I didn't tell anyone that we have to move now, but I warned them that it may happen very soon. Dan will go along."

There was a long silence in the living room. Lyle finally broke it. "Is anyone going to tell me what that means?"

"Yes, of course," Saul said. "We've known for a long time that the day might come when we would have to disperse the serum ourselves. We have several different plans for doing that. But first, before any plan is initiated, our people around the world have to be warned to take cover, to get ready. The fact that someone followed you makes me think that it is time now for them all to take the first step. The next step will wait for Carmen's return. Meanwhile, Seymour and Mutt will start for California tomorrow, and Dora will return to the Philadelphia plant and resume her job there."

"Have you decided to try the lotion?" Dora asked.

"Yes. We have to know. I gave a sample to Alice this afternoon."

Lyle turned away from him, tried not to react; she felt frozen. Alice Lanier, the thirty-year-old retarded daughter of the housekeeper, worked hard and cheerfully all day, dusting, mopping, changing linens, doing laundry . . . She never spoke, but always smiled at anyone she came across, and then fled. Poor Alice, she kept thinking, poor Alice. If she survived, doomed to clean after others forever? Or would her damaged brain be mended, as Saul's heart had been? If she died, killed by something she could not have understood, she would be the first totally innocent victim . . . She got up, walked to the window to look for the deer that still came for a drink every night, looked beyond the room, out to a clean world, a world of ice and stillness, a world waiting, holding its breath, waiting.

She sat in her dark room gazing out the window at the rushing brook. It was snowing lightly. Not a serious snow, but a forerunner of what the winter would be like here in the Pocono Mountains in a few weeks. She had left the door open to the study; Saul and the others were still talking in the living room. Their talk concerned the details of distribution, if the lotion they were testing on Alice worked. A simple lotion, mineral oil, perfumes, cocoa butter, emulsifiers, a solvent that would carry it all through the skin to the lymphatic system, and a minute quantity of a new, nameless substance, a messenger of the gods. She remembered the phrase Yuri had used: messenger of the gods.

She thought again of the Bible quotation: ". . . and there shall be no more death, neither sorrow, nor crying, neither shall there be any more pain; for the former things are passed away."

But there would be pain and sorrow, suffering as there never had been on earth. The lamentations would echo and re-echo. Families sundered. Mother from child, lover from loved one, brother from sister . . .

Saul had told her they would make an effort to see the president, to try to persuade him that the Russians did not pose a threat by having it if the United States began a mass distribution immediately, if they made it available worldwide. He had said it and neither of them had believed the effort was worth making, but it had to be tried. And it could not be tried until they had the samples ready, until they had literature ready, directions for isolating the serum, directions for the care of the ill, information about what it was, how it was transmitted . . . The biggest fear was that the United States government would find out the Russians had it before the samples could be readied. Time, it circled around itself, came to a dead end, or it extended into an indefinite future, and no one could say for certain which was the correct perspective of it.

She thought of Alice. None of them had any doubt that it would work. Had there been enough time for her to start feeling headaches, start shivering with fever chills, start dreaming fever dreams? What did a woman like Alice dream?

Less than fifty miles away Hugh Lasater was watching his television, unaware that it had started to snow. On one of the beds was an open map; he had gone over his route with a yellow highlighter. He should be able to cover it all in a single day, he felt reasonably certain, but if it took more, he would put in the time. He hoped Alex did not call while he was out of New York. No point in alarming Rawleigh any more than he had done to himself. He watched the television with the sound turned too low to catch, the picture too fuzzy to try to follow; it was company, no more than that. He went over one more time the final conversation he had had with Rawleigh that morning at breakfast. It had been a puzzling talk, disturbing, and snatches of it that had come back to him off and on during the day now flooded back, as if it were a conversation he had to report to someone, remembered with clear details, down to the hesitations, the nuances.

"Hugh, try some of the ham. Finest damn smoked ham in the world. Virginia ham."

He already had eggs and homemade sausage on his plate, two biscuits, honey on the side, raspberry jam, sweet butter, churned every Tuesday . . .

Aunt Jane glanced over the table, then left. Alex was ignoring food, trying to drown himself in orange juice. His eyes were red, his nose red and runny; he looked miserable.

Rawleigh ate heartily, jam on one biscuit, honey on another, ham and sausages . . . He looked at Hugh and shook his head. "Nobody eats right anymore, you know that? All those health faddists have people afraid of good food. Look at me, do I look like a man dying of high blood pressure or too much cholesterol?" He laughed and cut his ham. "People believe too easily these days. Whatever comes along, they believe."

Alex sneezed. Rawleigh said emphatically, "I haven't had a cold in fifteen years, maybe more. Good food, that's what keeps a man healthy." He poured more coffee for them all. "Hugh, there's one other little thing I wanted to bring up last night, but we all got too busy and I forgot. You know how the department always braces when there's a change of administration? Remember? I've been with the department for twenty-two years, and it's always been like that, always will be. Nothing really changes, but still, we're ready for it if it should ever happen. You know?"

Lasater nodded. He knew.

"A new man comes in at the top, new names on a few doors,

memos fly, meetings are held, and then things settle down and the old experienced hands run things just as they always have. It has to be like that, you know? It really does have to be like that."

Lasater waited, done with eating, done with drinking coffee, wanting only to be on his way, out to Pennsylvania, to get on with it.

"We see a Republican president after working under the Democrats for years, and we think, this time things will really change, a clean sweep, out with the old, in with the new. We are braced, but it doesn't work out like that. Then a Democrat returns to power and it's the same kind of trepidation. Back and forth, nothing really changes, not at the level where things really get done. Only the names on the doors change, the top half-dozen people who come and go, glory in power for a few years, feel in on the secrets of government, go back home and itch to write books about what they've learned. You know how that goes. You remember all that."

He made the same point a few more times before he was willing to leave it. Alex yawned and sneezed.

"But we never expect things to change much after an administration has been in as long as this one has."

Lasater was careful not to glance at Alex, to avoid Rawleigh's gaze. He studied the way his remaining egg yolk ran, how it edged around the sausage grease . . .

"You remember Carl Ely, don't you? Best damn Soviet man that ever worked."

"I remember Ely."

"Yes. Funny how you brought up Lawrence Truly last night, made me think of Ely. I wanted him for a little matter and he's out of touch. Nothing in the files, nothing anywhere, just out of touch."

"Truly, Wilkes, and Ely? That's a curious combination," Lasater muttered. "Are there more?"

"As a matter of fact, several more. Most of the team that worked out of Denver a few years back when there was that ridiculous sheep death panic. Remember? Nerve gas escaped, something like that. They put every biologist they could find to work on that one. I keep wondering," Rawleigh went on, offhandedly. "You know, you can't help wondering in this business. You begin to make connections without noticing. But I wonder. What if Ely had found out something important? He reports back to Lightfoot, you know. And then he vanishes. Nothing in the files. Lightfoot reports to Scanlon, one of the new people, and Lightfoot is off on a year's R and R all at once. Curious, that's the word for it."

"Do they know you're poking your nose into any of this?" Lasater heard the harshness in his voice but did not try to soften it even a little.

"Hugh! I have my own show to run, keeps me plenty busy, too busy to mind anyone else's business, I can assure you."

"But you do have to wonder," Lasater said.

"Exactly. Scanlon, Ballinger, that whole crowd, they sometimes worry me. They don't know how the game is played, you see. They don't understand the balancing act we've come to accept and even anticipate. They tend to link communism with Satanism, or something like that, and they are too frightened to trust with important decisions. Frightened men are likely to become very dangerous men. You understand what I'm saying?"

"How much of this did you know back in April when I came to you?" Lasater asked coldly. "You had your chance then to get a hand in."

"I knew some of it," Rawleigh admitted. "Not enough. And I couldn't quite believe that whatever file I wanted was unavailable. I thought it was a temporary matter. But, Hugh, if I had known, I still would have turned you down. No matter what you have, no matter how much you know, or suspect, I would turn you down. I would not like to think that you suddenly had found a tremendous need for a year's sabbatical, or rest and recreation out of touch with anyone who ever knew you. If you returned to the payroll, and if I had to report your fantastic story, why . . . Who knows? Your file could even vanish overnight."

On the television a man had broken into an apartment and was shooting everyone in it. It took them a long time to realize that he was slaughtering them all.

Rawleigh was frightened. With cause. It was scary to think of the new people and the president getting together and discussing how to handle immortality. If the Russians had it and Truly and Wilkes could not come up with it, then obviously the government would have to stop the Russians before they had a chance to use it on their people in any significant way.

Lasater realized that the screen was gray and wavery and did not know how long the movie had been over, how long he had sat looking at the blank screen.

If the government decided they had to stop the Russians before they could use the stuff, he had concluded, all hell was going to break out, and soon. Better no one should have it than for the satanic powers to have it alone. Better to take your chances with a preemptive nuclear war, which they maintained was winnable, than to risk having them bomb the hell out of this country after they had spread the stuff around over there.

He thought of the dogged insistence of the government spokesmen that a war was winnable, in spite of the protests overseas, in spite of the protests in this country, in spite of the articles, the books, the television specials, in spite of everything to the contrary. The statements had become more persuasive, more widespread, more insidious, more sloganlike during the past year, during the period that they had had Wilkes and Truly and Ely and others stuck away somewhere looking for something.

And if the new Manhattan Project, Son of Manhattan Project, he thought darkly, came up with the secret, what then? Would they see that the balance had been restored, equilibrium again achieved? Slowly he shook his head. The Russians had had it too long. They could have been using it for years, depending on when they got started. Rawleigh was right about the new people, he went on, in that they seemed genuinely to believe their own rhetoric. They believed that the Russians were satanic, that the world was engaged in the opening moves of the final war between good and evil. They would assume now that the Russians would strike just as soon as enough of their own people were protected. They still believed that we blew it with the bomb, that we had the chance of a lifetime to dominate the entire world, make it safe for capitalism, apple pie, and Christianity, and we were too chicken to take the advantage that was clearly ours. They would assume now that the Russians had that kind of advantage, and, being satanic, they would not be chicken. They would use the advantage. They would strike, knock down the opposition, and go on from there.

And our good old boys, he thought then, certain of all this, would be compelled, justified even, in hitting back first.

But did they know what it was they were looking for? That was the tough one. Did Truly and Wilkes have enough to go on to find it? He stared straight ahead and knew he would have to find out. But first he would find Taney.

The agency had come to it from the Russian angle and had no reason to link Taney and her gang with any of it. Only Rawleigh had that connection and he was not telling anyone anything. He was thoroughly frightened; he knew the ones calling the play were dangerous men even if he did not know what it was they had, or were looking for. He had told Lasater enough for him to plow through this, to come up with the conclusions he obviously had made also. Lasater knew that Rawleigh was smart, but not how smart. He could not decide if Rawleigh had given him what he had with the idea in mind that Lasater would find Taney for him, haul her in, let him in on the secret. Or had he counted on his going away to mull it over, and coming back frightened, eager to divulge everything? Or had it all been a lie? Maybe they had a dozen people on him, watching his movements, wiring his rooms, tapping phones . . .

He shook his head. He knew no one had followed him that day. And tomorrow he would spend as many hours as it took searching for the sign he knew was out there waiting for him. Taney was near, the old man not far from her, probably, and Carmen on his way back to them both, he felt certain. Like old times, he sighed, and turned off the television, glanced again at the open map, and then went to bed.

▣ 24 ▣

THEY ALL prepared their own breakfasts and ate in the kitchen, or the dining room, or even in the laboratories upstairs. Mrs. Lanier and Alice arrived daily at noon and made lunch for one o'clock, and dinner for seven. This morning Lyle sat in the kitchen alone sipping coffee, not hungry, thinking about Alice, waiting for the phone to ring.

Yuri and Mutt entered, nodded to her, but did not interrupt their conversation.

"Scientists don't want to rule the world," Yuri was saying firmly. "Scientists want to do science. Painters want to paint. Doctors want to heal. Dancers to dance. Only a few people want to run the world and they must be prevented from doing it ever again."

"How the hell will you make other people take on the problems of government?" Mutt demanded. He foraged for eggs and bacon in the refrigerator. Yuri poured two cups of coffee, took one to the table where Lyle was sitting.

"You make them, that's all," he said.

"Christ! Make them! What, with guns held to their heads?"

"No! Never again! Obligations, duties, respect . . . Why do men volunteer to save flooded peoples? Climb mountains to save someone unable to save himself? Put out dangerous fires? People do things they don't want to do all the time, this would be another such thing."

"Maybe. Maybe."

"People don't do it now because they don't think they have enough time. Their careers, their families, everything they love will be gone too soon, no time for other things. When they have time . . . You make them."

They had leaped ahead, to afterward, Lyle thought, twisting her empty cup around and around, envying them the ability to do that. They were creating utopia out of the chaos that would envelop the world, and she was fixated on the creation of the chaos. Once, she had been able to look ahead, see herself ten years in the future, fifteen years, all the way to the end, but now her gaze could not penetrate the rest of any single day; tomorrow was too uncertain to consider, next week a fairy tale, next month a nightmare . . .

The phone rang and all three stopped, watching it on the wall, not moving, hardly breathing. Saul would take all incoming calls today, he had said. They waited. On the third ring it stopped. It was nine-fifteen.

Five minutes later Saul came into the kitchen. No conversation had been resumed, although Mutt had turned to the task of frying bacon and scrambling eggs. Yuri had sat staring out the window, as had Lyle.

"Mrs. Lanier won't be coming in today," Saul said quietly. "Her daughter is ill with a high fever." He turned and walked out again.

Yuri took a deep breath. The smell of burning bacon began to fill the room; Lyle got up and left the kitchen.

Lasater had seen a lot of summer camps, boy scout camps, school camps, lodges, summer homes, most of them closed up for the winter. There were hunting camps just opening, and signs directing him to ski areas, open starting December 1, if weather permitted. Did they all make snow? Surely there would not be enough snow in a couple of weeks. The light flurry of the night before had vanished soon after daylight; he saw traces in sheltered spots here and there. He had driven a scenic route, and the business route, and dirt roads. He had seen townships so small that it appeared any group of three buildings could qualify for a name just as long as there was a gas station and space for a mail drop. He had seen enough waterfalls and rustic, quaint bridges and sparkling brooks to last him a lifetime, two lifetimes. He had driven half a dozen dirt roads that he had had to back out of when he reached a chain with the now familiar sign: CLOSED FOR THE SEASON. Summer playground for New York City, winter playground for the same, and right now was in between time. No one was playing, no one was out at all, except high school kids who drove like truckers on bennies.

He had seen deer, too, and he did not like that. Some of them were grazing along with cattle in one field, passing. Several

had been on the side of the road, dead. He had heard about
deer at twilight, after dark, the worst menace there was in this
part of the country. Three different people had told him that
today and he believed them. At twilight he would pack it in,
he had decided, get a motel room in Milford, or Matamoras,
and study the map a little more.

Highway 6 wound upward out of the Delaware valley, blacktop
here and wide enough to pass, but there was no one else on
it. The traffic was on the interstate a few miles back. He would
go to Hawley, twenty-five miles up the road, turn around there
and go back to Milford for the night and consider his next move.
If Hawley was anything like Dingman's Ferry, or any of the other
little towns he had passed, it would take no more than a minute
or two to check it out. Why people lived in places like this was
a mystery to him. Nothing here but trees and deer, nothing to
do but get in the car and go for a drive, no one but hicks.
When the summer people were around it must be okay, lively.
Probably some gambling if you knew where to look for it,
parties . . .

Saul and Lyle walked by the pond late that afternoon. "Carmen
may arrive tonight," he said. "I hope so."

"So do I!"

He stopped. "Are you still confused?"

"Of course. I don't see how a woman can love two men equally
and not be confused."

He laughed and started to walk again. "Look, the ice is nearly
white all the way across. It's thickening fast."

"I have to have something to do," Lyle said. "Everyone else
is off at work on various things, but I have nothing. I've been
thinking about it. I should write the history of this group, yours
and Carmen's, Dora's, Steve's, everyone's. It should be preserved, in case . . . It should be preserved."

"I agree. You remember that idea I was working on back in
Oregon? It's been a project of mine for many years, but I always
get sidetracked from it. I am seriously interested in writing a
thorough study of the idea of immortality through the ages. I
have reams of notes; my problem is too many reams of notes.

If you're at all interested in including any of that material, it's yours."

"It should be included. Why don't you mind that I sleep with Carmen, that I love him?"

"Maybe because I've had more time to think about it than you've had. I don't believe love is something that comes in discrete packages that can't be divided, that it can be used up, like a battery that steadily grows weaker until it is exhausted. You would think nothing of it if for so many years you loved one man, and then stopped loving him and started to love another. Sequential love is all right, but simultaneous love is a sign of moral turpitude, isn't that what bothers you?"

"You know it is. And don't laugh at me again."

He was gazing thoughtfully at the ice. "I never thought of it before, but can you use *turpitude* without *moral*? I never saw it used alone, did you?"

She sighed. "You never really tell me anything, do you? I ask a question, raise a doubt that's bothering me, and you manage to sidestep it and make me find my way every time." They walked on silently for a minute and she said, "I envy Mutt and Yuri. They seem able to put things out of mind, just go on to the next stage."

"Remember that Yuri has lived with the testing for a long time. And he knows that his government plans to disperse it. It isn't a new idea for him to adapt to. He's forcing Mutt not to dwell on the near future since it can't be avoided."

They were almost directly across the pond from the building now. Soon it would be dark. Soon Carmen would be home.

Lasater drove very slowly, studying driveways, dirt roads that left the highway, planning a more thorough investigation of the area on the following day. He passed a bird sanctuary with the usual CLOSED sign and drove on, then suddenly braked, and belatedly looked in the rearview mirror to make certain he would not be clipped from behind. Nothing was in sight. He backed up and pulled off the road at the sign. There was a chain across the gravel driveway. It was locked with a padlock. From here he could see the driveway wind and lose itself among the trees.

Nothing was different from the many other closed camps, parks, lodges he had already seen that day, but something had caught his eye as he drove past. Now he studied the wooden sign that was on a stout post. Bird sanctuary, with the dates it was open — April through October, like most places around here, eight in the morning until dusk, day use only. Welcome. He gnawed his lip, staring at the sign. An insignia of some sort in the lower lefthand corner, M and S, done in fancy letters. The M had turrets on the tops, the S looked like a path, or a river . . . He had seen that logo somewhere, he felt certain, but where? M and S. The M looked like a castle almost. He knew he had seen that same design . . .

Alex sneezing, Alex popping another throat lozenge . . . Closing the small box . . . He blinked and suddenly felt almost faint. The drug company! He had found them! There was no doubt, no uncertainty. He had found them! It almost frightened him that he had been looking for a sign, that was how he had thought of it from the start. Looking for a sign.

Slowly he took out the keys, left the car, locked it up, and then stepped over the chain, started to walk on the gravel driveway. He felt as if he were dreaming. He remembered his heavy coat only when he began to feel chilled, but he did not go back for it. He came to a fork; one side had the sanctuary sign, the other a no admittance sign. Everything was very still, no breeze stirred, nothing moved, and he heard faint voices off to his right. He went that way, walking on the side of the drive, ready to step into the underbrush if he had to. Then he was at the end of the drive; before him was a pond, a field beyond that, and coming around the pond, walking toward him were Lyle Taney and Saul Werther, arm in arm.

He wished he had brought a gun with him, something. What if Werther had a bodyguard with a gun? What if he carried one himself? What if Taney had taken up weapons? He almost smiled at that thought, but he did not move out from under the trees yet. He could hear the sound of her voice, but not the words.

"I can't imagine why I'm so excited at the thought of ice skates," she said. "It's so silly. I skated in high school and through college, but not since then. Yet, I can hardly wait for the skates to get here."

"Maybe you've grown so used to activities that you are finding this sedentary life a strain," he suggested.

"Maybe. For years all I did was walk to my car and back, and pace a little before my classes. And then I hit Oregon. Up and down mountains like a goat. And, of course, in New York you walk all the time . . ." She stopped, staring, her fingers digging into Saul's arm.

"You!"

"Hello, Lyle. You look absolutely smashing! And Mr. Werther, your recovery is complete, I see." He stood near the trees, his hands in his pockets, smiling at them.

"What do you want now?" Lyle cried. "How did you get here?"

"Carmen get back from Amsterdam all right?" he asked. Neither of them moved. "I didn't blow the whistle on you and the Russky at the airport, Lyle. I could have, and there were CIA swarming everywhere, but I didn't. It's only a matter of time until they begin checking on the other passengers, the English gentleman, for instance. One thing will lead to another . . ."

"What do you want?" Saul asked calmly.

"In. That simple. I just want in."

Saul shook his head.

"I know. I know. But, you see, I can help you, and you're going to need help. Have you got a pencil, pen? Something to write on? I have a number for you to call when it's time to shuffle and redeal."

Lyle was staring at him incredulously. Saul shook his head again. "I don't have anything to write with."

"I'll do it." He fished a pen from his pocket, and his notebook, wrote down Herb Balinski's number, and put the paper on the ground, weighted it with a stone. "I'm calling the shots now, Professor Hermann Franck. This mess is going to blow up right in your face. It's out of control, getting awfully near critical mass. Three things can happen. They can find you and haul you and your friends away for a vacation. They can find the formula and use the stuff themselves. They can push the panic button. I'm in a position to keep an eye on what they're up to. I can get word to you, and at that time I want in. Understand? I want in!"

"How will you get a message to me?"

"You'll get a phone call and one hour later, exactly one hour later you call that number. Is that a good number out on the sign?"

Saul nodded.

"Be seeing you, Lyle, Professor. Take care of yourselves."

He turned and strode away quickly, was lost to sight within seconds.

"He's lying! Can't we stop him before he gets away?"

Saul walked slowly toward the paper Lasater had left on the ground. Lyle followed.

"You can't trust him! He's treacherous! I don't believe anything he says. I don't think he can tell the truth."

"I know, but . . ." He stopped, listening. They could hear a car engine start, then the squeal of tires, the roar of acceleration, and finally nothing.

Lyle drew a long breath. He was gone. They had simply let him go. She watched Saul retrieve the telephone number, glance at it, place it in his pocket. Silently they started back toward the building. They could not have stopped him, she knew. They might have thrown rocks at him, or raced him to his car, but they would not have caught up, they had been too distant. She looked at the ground as they walked, despising herself for leading him here, for not being smart enough, aware enough to know he had been following. She had brought him to Saul and Carmen, had nearly worked with him once, had put the only two men she had ever loved in danger because she had been weak and foolish, and now she had done it again.

At the door Saul stopped and touched her cheek gently. "He would have found us sooner or later," he said. "He's so afraid, you know. Nothing would have stopped his finding us eventually. Now's the best time, after all, because already we have started to move. Don't blame yourself so much, my dear. Please." He looked at the driveway thoughtfully. "He's a rather extraordinary man. He leaped to the correct conclusion back on the coast, identified me, found us here. I don't believe there was a thing you could have done to prevent any of it. He's really a remarkable man."

"And a dangerous man."

"Undoubtedly. But he may be useful to us, after all. If he is in a position to learn something he can use for barter, that could be very important."

25

CARMEN ARRIVED at ten that night. He was dirty and hungry; he had hitched a ride from Scranton with a trucker, and they had had engine trouble.

"How on earth did you get to Scranton?" Lyle asked.

"Actually I hitched from Canada, and I was sort of compelled to go where my various rides would take me, as long as it was in the right direction. I figured Scranton was as far west as I wanted to get."

They were in the kitchen where Saul was broiling a steak for him, and Lyle was making a salad. He looked wonderful, even if he was grimy and thinner than she remembered. Yuri was beaming as if his own brother had appeared. The two had embraced each other like old friends. Steve had a wide grin that he was not even trying to control, and she knew her happiness at his return was just as open as everyone else's. How strange, she thought, tossing the salad, that she never had been part of a group in her life, never had had this kind of love for others who were not related, never had felt so uninhibited about displaying her love for others. She had been the first one to reach him, to hold and kiss him. She found herself wishing that Dora had not had to leave before now, and she felt her confusion rush back over her.

While Carmen ate, Saul gave him all the current news. He ended up saying, "Of course, Lasater saw the crest, my little display of childish egocentricity, and he put two and two together without any difficulty. A drug company, two initials, the two of us." He turned to Lyle. "He warned me years ago that it was a mistake to use that logo; I refused to pay heed. I liked it."

"It took both of us," Lyle said. "I led him here, you invited him in. Two of us."

He came to her and kissed her lightly. "This man is in desperate need of a bath and clean clothes. Why don't you go tell each other your adventures while Steve and Yuri and I plot. I'm afraid I'm going to have to send him and Steve away in a few hours."

So soon? But, of course. Lasater knew where they were; Carmen had to be safeguarded, the plans had to go forward. She looked from Saul to Carmen, back, and then nodded. She reached for Carmen's hand, and they left the other three in the kitchen, went down the long corridor to his room and closed the door softly.

"I'm too dirty to touch you," he said. "I'm so proud of you, Lyle. I love you very much. I was so afraid for you."

"I was the one who was afraid, for you. It was so dangerous." She remembered how beautiful she had thought him when they first met. "You are beautiful," she said faintly. "As dirty as you are, you are still beautiful."

Now he laughed and took her into his arms. "You've stolen my lines, witch. For that you get greasy and smelly and wet, just like me." He pulled her along with him to the bathroom and they undressed each other and got under the shower together laughing.

For a long time they debated if Yuri should go with Carmen and Steve, until he settled it himself.

"I stay here," he said firmly, looking at Saul, "with you. I know no manufacture processes, have too bad English . . ." He switched to French. "I would be a burden for them, someone to look out for. Here, I can try to think how we can get samples into Russia, into Poland, Hungary. It is not enough to tell the world how to do it if in some countries it is not allowed, the process is controlled by the state. There must be a way. If there is, we two will think of it, will think how to implement it. This I can do without burdening others. If they come here and catch me, I say I kidnapped Lyle with a gun, forced her to bring me with her, that I have held you both captive for all the time I have been here. They may think I am crazy, but —" he finished in English "— what the hell?" His thick accent made it sound even more incongruous.

They all laughed; as soon as it was quiet again, Lyle said, "Why don't we just close this place down and go somewhere else? You must know dozens of safer places than this."

"You forget Lasater," Saul said. "If he can find out anything that he thinks we'll value, he'll tell us. He's desperately afraid."

"You can't trust him! You can't believe anything he says. I don't think he can help himself, he has to lie."

"I know. But if there's even a slight chance that he can tell us anything useful, I have to accept the risks. You don't, obviously. You could go with them, even be of help to them."

"You know I won't. I'm going to write a history book, remember?"

At two in the morning Carmen and Steve left. No one said where they were going. From now on, the less any one of them knew about the activities and whereabouts of the others, the safer they would all be. Only Saul and Carmen knew all the details of the plan that had evolved over the years.

Lyle knew there were drug manufacturing companies in the country that were already at work packaging the samples containing the serum, samples of after-shave lotion, hand lotion, bath soap. She did not know how many plants there were, or what their names were; she knew that Saul and Carmen had bought them over the years. And she knew the Philadelphia plant would not be involved in producing the samples, even though it was geared for the work; now that Saul's identity had been discovered, that plant was suspect. They regretted not being able to use it because of its capacity for turning out a sample a second, but it was not worth the risk. She knew there were plants in foreign countries, but not which countries, or how many plants.

Yuri insisted on cleaning up the kitchen, and refused Lyle's halfhearted offer to help. She sat before the fire with Saul and felt the emptiness of the big building, like a resort hotel after all the seasonal guests are gone.

"You should go away now," Saul said after a lengthy silence. "It will be hard to participate, to know what is happening. It will be very hard, Lyle. It isn't fair to let you get involved. You haven't had all the years we've had to think it through and accept it. It will be very hard."

She nodded. "On all of us."

The next day she learned how hard it would be. Mrs. Lanier called to tell them that her daughter had died.

"She's going to her sister in Georgia for the winter," Saul said, facing the window, away from Lyle and Yuri. "Alice was her only reason for staying here, she was frightened by travel, frightened by strangers . . ."

Yuri murmured something in Russian, turned, and left the room. Lyle went to stand by Saul at the window. Snow was falling in large drifting flakes that settled gently on the shrubbery, the trees, everything. She saw through the snow, back to the cemetery outside Lancaster, the small, neat headstone of red schist, the field and woods . . . They were running out of space at the cemetery, and what would they do then?

Lyle studied the frozen waterfall. Where the flow of water was greater, ice masses had built up like chalcedony in a thunderegg, rounded, gleaming, with deep blue shadows captured inside. Where the water flow was less, where it seeped, grotesque shapes were forming, some jutting straight outward, some curved and recurved, flower shapes, alien flowers. An ice shelf was trying to grow from side to side of the stream, but always it fell before the linkage could be made; each successive start thickened the ice, the shelf was a foot thick at the banks of the stream, and the strata were clearly defined, narrowing to nothing finally. The edges farthest from the banks were as thin and delicate as the finest crystal goblet. The sunlight sparkled on them.

The brook never had frozen completely since Saul had been here, he had told her. It was spring fed, and the shallow water flowed too fast. Below the waterfall it was too deep to freeze solid. There was a cover of ice and snow on the brook, hiding it, making it treacherous. Under the insulation, secretively, it raced to the waterfall, rushed to create ice sculptures.

The sun held no heat, radiated no warmth. Now that the weather had cleared it was even colder than it had been during the three days of falling snow.

She had not planned to come so far, had not dressed warmly enough to stay out more than a few minutes. She walked back in the trail she had made through the snow, picked up her bucket of birdseed, and went inside. They were feeding cardinals and juncoes, and sparrows, the ever-present sparrows; last night she had heard the plaintive call of an owl, the first time she had heard one. And there were grosbeaks that came at dusk every day. It was good that they had an abundant store of seed; it was going to be a long winter for the birds.

Life had settled very quickly into a routine that burdened no one, left out no one. Yuri had attempted to take over all household chores, and together Lyle and Saul had forbidden him to do their share. For hours Yuri and Saul played chess, using it as a focus, she felt, for their attention, because at any point in the games, one or the other of them might suddenly make a suggestion about getting samples inside one of the Soviet states, and the game was forgotten until they talked it out thoroughly. They had come up with no idea that they both agreed would work.

She was writing the history, as she had promised, using the word processor in the upstairs office. Her material was scattered, not organized in any coherent form yet. As she thought of bits of dialogues she had overheard, or participated in, she included them.

Yuri: "I read that after the Black Death in Europe, the terrible plague years, there was abundance such as the world had never seen before. Is true?"

Lyle: "Yes. There are theories that it led to the renaissance in art, commerce, exploration, everything. For at least a generation, people had their basic needs and a surplus without having to work from sunlight to dark. In many places we think the mortality rate could have exceeded fifty percent. Then, of course, the population pressures caught up with them again and it was a scramble to find another piece of arable ground, another method of preserving foods, shipping them . . ."

"This time it will be different," Yuri said matter-of-factly.

"Women will learn the meditation techniques necessary to control their immunological systems," Lyle agreed. "It will take time. Is it true everyone can learn to do this?"

"Oh yes. Already people are learning to control their blood pressure, to lower it when it rises. They are learning to control their sugar metabolism, no longer needing daily insulin injections. They can control other organs, other systems. They will learn this one also. A few years. It will not take very long when the necessity is understood. And the world will have time to plan, to think. The women will control it. It will become a strange, perhaps wonderful, world, when the first period has ended."

Lyle reread those words on her video display screen and then touched the print button. A strange world. Perhaps a wonderful world. She wanted to weep. If only they could just *be* there, not have to get there. Resolutely she continued to work.

She left the office door open, and they left the door open to the lab in an effort to dispel the feeling of desolation the big building had acquired. They all shoveled snow, and they all used the tractor with the snow blade and worked at keeping the drive open to the highway. Saul was firm about that; it had to be kept clear at all times.

He was in touch with others of the group daily through his computer hookup; they were busy, working long hours, shipping samples here and there, getting ready for distribution. Dan Malone had finished several papers, one instructing scientists in the methods of isolating the RNA factor, ways of storing it, using it. One paper he had worked on even harder, he said, was for nonscientists, trying to explain what the factor was, how it worked, to reassure people that pregnancy could be achieved. He had done articles for newspapers, television, radio, and the popular magazines, each slightly different from the others, written for each particular audience. The final one would be for the science journals; he was not finished with that one yet. As he completed them, he transmitted copies through the computer for Saul's approval, editorial changes, whatever he felt he should contribute. Lyle put them through the printer, stuffed them into envelopes, affixed address labels on some, typed some, wrote out some, stamped and boxed them. Ready.

Somewhere else Dan Malone was doing the same thing, duplicating her work. Perhaps even a third person was also preparing copies, she did not ask.

Dan Malone had not returned to New York. Balinski could find no trace of him anywhere he tried. Lasater chewed a fingernail, caught himself doing it, and spat it out in disgust. He had not bitten his nails since what, thirteen, fourteen? His old man had painted them red and promised to do it again every time he found them chewed up.

He had not thought of his father or mother for a long time. They were both alive, in a retirement community in Florida, playing golf, fishing, sunning themselves, drinking gin and tonic all day.

"Think of all the money you're saving," Balinski had said. "You want them watched, and they're already out of sight. Costs nothing to watch someone you can't even see. You got another one for me?"

"Not now. Maybe later. I'll have to find someone who's on a cruise first."

"Yeah, another grand saved. See you later."

He had to find out the names of the others who had made the museum circuit with the Russian in Amsterdam. Five of them altogether, Rawleigh had said. Dan Malone had dropped out of sight. Seymour Oliver was gone. Two to go. He knew where the Russian had gone. He'd have to go to the farm, he thought angrily. Rawleigh had not sent for him, might never send for him, just one day tell him the spigot had been turned off, no more dough coming through. Get lost. He would have to give him something. Not Taney. She was his.

He had to have something to trade, he knew. And right now he had nothing that Werther didn't already know, or suspect. He began to feel panicky again and he forced himself to go back over his reasoning. Werther would stay put, hoping to learn something from Lasater that was worth a dose of his magic elixir. Rawleigh would turn to Lasater again, hoping for an inside track also. Werther believed he had an in with the agency, and Rawleigh believed he was onto Taney and Werther, or something equally important. He was not certain what it was that Rawleigh expected of him at this point. The only thing he felt certain about was that if Rawleigh found the hideout first, or if the agency found it, he was out on his ass. But he had done the right thing, he reassured himself once more; he had found them, made his offer and left, before they could consider shooting him, having him run off the road, anything dirty like that. He knew they would be capable of any dirty trick that occurred to them; he had been lucky in making his pitch and hightailing it away from them. They must be as worried now as he was, wondering what the others were up to, how close they were, when the knock on the door would come.

He knew that other people were moving, doing things, only he was at a standstill, and it was lousing up his eating and sleeping. He had thought Rawleigh would want him before now, had been certain of it. It had been ten days since he had located Taney and the old man. Ten fucking days! He saw them again coming around the pond arm in arm. And, by God, she had looked smashing. Not a day over thirty-seven, he added derisively. Any woman over thirty was too far gone to suit him. Any woman. Even if she did look as good as Taney, with her cheeks fired up by the cold, her curly hair blowing around her face like a kid's.

Again he thought of his parents, arm in arm on a beach. They liked to walk on the beach every evening. He thought of them as they had been fourteen years ago, the last time he had seen them, the time his father had called him dirty, filthy, underhanded, cheating, lying, reprehensible . . . The list had gone on. All good clean words, all razor sharp, not a one had missed or failed to cut deeply.

"I thought you were the patriot," he had answered. "I'm in the service of the country."

"You're a spy. You can't be a spy and keep your hands clean. No one can. Your country! You're doing it because it's a game with you, a dangerous game, exciting, makes you feel superior. Do you think I don't know you?"

"Old man, you don't know nothing! Nothing!"

"Thank God, I don't know what you know! Thank God!"

And he had left, just like that. No goodbyes, no last-minute kisses, nothing. Fourteen years. Suddenly he realized that they weren't the way he had seen them then. They were old. They could even be dead. Who would have told him? The state would have notified him, he thought quickly. One of them could have died, but not both. The state would have told him. He did not try to understand the relief that rushed through him.

He had paced his hotel room for nearly an hour. It was cold and gray outside, with too many people everywhere, too many crazies, nowhere to go and not be surrounded by them. He had come to hate New York. They had warned him at the desk about the gangs of teenagers who picked out victims randomly, pursued them, and beat the shit out of them, money or no money. There wasn't enough money in the world to buy them off, it was the beating up they were after, the act of beating someone. He had almost hoped someone would try to mug him, pull a knife, a gun, anything. Nothing had happened yet. But he did not like the noise of the streets, or the smell of exhaust mixed with dirt and the acrid cold air.

He had gone to movies, to shows, and even had walked quickly through the Metropolitan Museum. He had had women, had played cards and won, had done everything he wanted to do in the city for the rest of his life. Now he wanted action, any action.

Two more days, and if Rawleigh did not get in touch, he would make the call himself. The next morning when he went down to the coffee shop and saw Alex, he could have hugged him.

"Milking time," Alex said cheerfully.

"Your cold all gone?"

"Yep. Fit as a fiddle again. But I'll tell you in strict confidence, I think the East Coast is the pits. I even lived here for a couple of years, and now . . . The pits."

"Too bad. It's the first vacation I've had in ten years. Real vacation, nothing to do except play."

"Rub it in, pal. You going to eat, or leave?"

"When's the flight?"

"Noon."

"I'll eat."

Rawleigh was not in a good mood. He mentioned he was burning apple wood, that was why the house smelled so good, but he did not really boast about it, or repeat it more than a couple of times. He led Alex and Lasater to the small study and closed the door firmly, then stood with his hands behind his back at the window. "Snow again before night. Won't last, never does here, but still, it's a mess. Can't keep denying it, those damn weathermen, it is changing. Anyone who's lived here more than a year or two knows it, why don't they?"

He wheeled about and said brusquely, "Hugh, this affair is too important for you to try to play it alone. I want you to come clean with me."

"I know. You think I have something I'm not telling."

"Yes. That's exactly what I think. Alex, get those pictures."

Alex left the room and returned quickly carrying an artist's portfolio.

"Stand them up against the bookcase," Rawleigh directed, watching Lasater.

They were the pictures of Saul taken at various conferences, the same pictures Lasater had shown Lyle nearly a year ago, but now Saul's face was blown up to sixteen by twenty size.

"Examine them closely," Rawleigh said, scowling at the pictures.

Lasater examined them and found nothing he had not seen before.

"Taken over a ten-year period? Isn't that what you told me?"

"About that."

"Look at his face! Makeup, hair color, all that can do wonders, but it can't really age a man, can it? Look at the lines around his eyes, just look at them. They're exactly the same in every picture! Exactly the same!"

Lasater kept his face turned toward the pictures, cursing silently.

"You know what causes wrinkles, Hugh? I asked an expert. What he said was mainly solar radiation; it dries out the skin, makes it lose elasticity. Exposure to the elements does it, not aging in itself. Radiation. He's discovered an immunity to radiation! That's why Scanlon had the Russian grabbed in Amsterdam! They think the Russians have it already."

Weakly Lasater sat down and pretended to continue to study the pictures. Too close. It was far too close, but not a home run yet.

"You think Scanlon has the Russian?"

"What else? Who else could have pulled it off like that? Not in the hotel, in the restaurant! And that means everyone in that little party was mixed up in it. Malone, Oliver, Franz Leiberman, Luis Betancourt, every one of them! Working for Scanlon, all of them!"

Rawleigh leaned forward and jabbed toward Lasater with his forefinger. "They've all vanished. Every man jack of them! Like Ely and Lightfoot, Wilkes and Truly. Gone, every one. Nothing in the files, no forwarding addresses, just gone!"

Rawleigh had opened the door a crack and glimpsed an international conspiracy, and promptly had slammed the door on it. It was easier for him to suspect the people he knew, the methods he knew, than to accept that a group of amateurs could be operating, and doing it better than his own people. Accordingly, he had to believe they were all part and parcel of an inner circle at the CIA. Let him, Lasater thought, and frowned as if trying to follow Rawleigh's reasoning.

"You could be right," he said finally. "But where do I fit in? What do you want from me?"

"I don't want you to vanish out from under us, Hugh, my boy. That's what I don't want. I want you to know everything I've been able to learn, Hugh. Everything. Soon after the first of the year this government is going to start a mass inoculation. Remember the swine flu shots a few years ago? The fiasco, the lawsuits that followed? This time it's to be a secret. They don't want a public outcry again. The first round will go to a very select group. The Joint Chiefs, the Cabinet, certain members of Congress, the president and vice president, the armed forces, or part of them . . . All very secret, discreet. There won't be time for a second round."

"And you're not on that list."

"That's right. I'm not. You're not. Alex, Aunt Jane. Most people aren't on that list, Hugh. Hardly anyone you know is on that list."

"If they've got something like that, why not just hand it out wholesale, to everyone?"

"There's not enough time. And there would be a leak. It would be disastrous if the Russians knew we have it, too. If they get a couple thousand doses of whatever the damn stuff is, they'll be lucky. But the word is that in a few weeks, they'll be ready to start giving it out. And the Russians have had it a couple of years! You know what that means? God knows how many of their people are protected already. The way our side figures it, our only chance now is a very massive and secret launch with everything we have. As soon as enough of them have the goddam stuff!" He took a deep breath. "They're praying that they'll have time for that much, because the idiots know that the Russians plan exactly the same thing. Hugh, if both sides are that sure the other is planning the first strike, one of them's going to do it, and it won't make very much difference which one it is. Not to you, not to me, not to most people."

"That's crazy," Lasater said, but he knew they would do it. Rawleigh knew they would do it.

"Crazy. Exactly. What do you think I've been telling you about this bunch of new people? They're amateurs, and they're crazy. Push the button, that's their solution to everything, always has been. But they'll be protected before it starts."

"Christ! Look, if I can remember anything at all, I'll let you in on it, but it's a blank up here." He touched his head. "I think I've given you everything I ever had. I never put the pieces together in this way, I have to think about it. Give me a few days."

"Take as many days as you want, Hugh. Just keep in mind that the new year starts in Washington with shots for certain people and not others. I'm sure your imagination will carry it on from there."

"Keep it in mind. Right. As if I could forget." He stood up. "I've got to go walk and think."

"No way, Hugh. I can't risk you out there. Think of Dan Malone, gone. Or Seymour Oliver, gone. Ely, Lightfoot, all of them. Everyone who's been near this is gone. I want you safe, Hugh. You're safe here on the farm. No one suspects that I have even a finger in this. I don't know anywhere else you could be as safe as you are right here."

◪ 26 ◪

LYLE HAD SET up a darkroom in the laundry, and for weeks before Christmas she worked on presents for Yuri and Saul. For Yuri she did a group of portraits of Saul, and for Saul she worked on finishing a study of the waterfall, the frozen sculpture. Day after day she was disappointed in her results and doggedly went back to photograph again, from another angle, from another perspective.

They exchanged presents on Christmas Eve. Yuri had carved an elongated, stylized bird for her; it was poised for flight, and very lovely. Saul gave her a necklace with a cluster of garnets around a pearl. It had been his mother's. Yuri was moved to weeping when she gave him his present, and Saul looked at the pictures of ice for so long that at first she feared he did not like them, or see them as she did, but then he sighed and kissed her.

"I'm afraid you're really an artist, not a historian, or writer, or anything of the sort."

"And why is it so sad if I'm an artist?" she demanded, again studying her pictures. They had not worked as well as she had hoped, but they did capture the waiting feeling, the time-frozen feeling that she had been after.

"Because you're probably destined to starve in a garret."

"It's same in Russia," Yuri said gravely. "Unless you are honored by state, it is best not to be artist. Except in spare time."

The clock above the mantel chimed midnight softly.

"Merry Christmas, my dears," Saul said.

They raised their glasses in a toast of champagne.

"If you can't come up with a workable plan to get the samples inside Russia and the Soviet states," Lyle said later, "what you can do is have ready a broadcast in the different languages telling the people that the government has it, where the plants are, who developed it and so on. Would the people demand it then? Would they demonstrate the way they do here?"

Yuri laughed derisively. "For longevity or even immortality? I think they might demonstrate. But government probably would deny it, call it American ploy to disrupt society. Who knows if anyone would believe?"

"The scientists would," Lyle said. "If you gave the particulars, they would believe, and they would try to isolate it to see for themselves, surely. They wouldn't believe a government statement to the contrary. And if your government does start using it and the death rate continues, it would be hard to hide, wouldn't it?"

"Government is able to hide many things in closed society," Yuri said somberly. "You don't understand how closed society functions, I'm afraid."

"I think I do, but usually most people are able to say that whatever is happening doesn't have anything to do with them. They can't do anything about foreign policy, or trade problems, or allocation problems, and they deny their responsibility about all of it, because it's too complex. But think how fads sweep the world, even your world. People are determined to hear the same music, read some of the same books, eat the same kinds of food, wear jeans . . . Many governments try to keep out the American influence, but to what avail? Can they really keep them out?"

He was gazing at her thoughtfully.

"Besides," Lyle went on, "if your government believed it's being distributed widely, among civilians as well as armed forces, as it will be, they will want to hand it out, won't they? Once it's known they possess it, once it's known that others are getting it, they would have to yield to the pressure."

Every day Lasater walked around the farm; every day he had company, sometimes at a slight distance, sometimes by his side. Alex hated his walks. The others who kept an eye on him were the regular employees of the farm, a stablehand, a groundskeeper, Aunt Jane, others whose functions he did not know. They would shoot if he tried to get away, Alex had warned the first day, and he believed that. He had eyed Aunt Jane, then had given up the idea of trying to get anywhere near her. She might shoot even if he did not try to get away.

He had written a letter to Balinski, and carried it with him all the time, stamped, ready to go. Down the road there were several mailboxes, rural delivery, but he never had a chance to get near them. The nearest town was fifteen miles away.

Two weeks before Christmas he wandered into the kitchen where Aunt Jane was at the table addressing cards, jotting a note in some, just signing others, consulting an address book, preoccupied by the ritual.

"I'm not allowed calls," Lasater said morosely. "First Christmas in years I won't be calling my parents. They're getting on, expect things like that, you know? Seventy-eight, seventy-six, they get set in their ways."

Aunt Jane made a noise and went on writing her note.

"Maybe I could send them a card, no message or anything, just my signature. Wouldn't be the same, but . . . Could I have one of your cards to send them?"

She seemed annoyed with his interruption. "Help yourself. I'll have to look it over."

"Sure, sure. I know that." He sat down and began to sort through the cards, examining the pictures, the verses. They were all sickly sentimental, and expensive, with gilt and silver and red plush, cute angels and reindeer.

"Pretty neat," he said, picking up one then another. Finally he stood up, holding one. "Address is in my room. Be right back."

He walked out studying the card, and in his room he looked at an envelope he had pocketed, addressed in her heavy, bold script. Also he had a spare envelope. When he readdressed Balinski's letter it would have taken an expert to tell that Aunt Jane had not written it. He addressed his parents' card, and returned to the kitchen with all three envelopes. He did not try to replace her card yet, or to slip Balinski's into the stack. One thing at a time, he told himself, handing over the legitimate one. She looked at it carefully, sealed it herself, added it to the pile. He went to the sink for water.

"Mind if I put on some coffee?"

"You drink too much coffee."

"Yeah, I guess so, but still, it helps me think."

He splashed water around on the shiny-clean counter, and spilled a few beans on the just-as-shiny-clean floor, and whistled as he waited for the automatic machine to grind the coffee, then brew it. When it was done, he spilled a little as he filled his cup. He stepped in the spilled coffee and left prints.

"Want some?"

"No. I never drink coffee after four in the afternoon. You shouldn't either."

"Yeah, yeah." He went to the windows near the table and stood sipping his coffee. She was methodical. She wrote her notes, read them over, put the cards into the envelopes, sealed and stamped them, one by one. The stack must have had thirty-five cards or more. She had maybe a dozen to go. He sipped coffee and waited.

It was getting dark already. Everything outside was mushy and gray, sodden. It was lonely as hell out here in the country; he could not fathom why anyone stayed, no matter what Rawleigh was willing to pay. Maybe he had something on each and every one of them; that would account for it.

One of the workers came in with a load of firewood in a leather carrier. Aunt Jane looked at him sharply. "Did you take off your boots?" He was in his socks, his boots left out on the back porch. Aunt Jane saw the coffee on her floor, the footprints in it, through it, tracking it nearly to the window.

"Damn you, Lasater! Look at that mess you made!" She jumped up and went to the other side of the kitchen and cursed when she stepped on a coffee bean, crushed it.

The worker grinned at Lasater and hurried on through with his wood, heading for the living room where he would make a fire before Rawleigh arrived, have the house fragrant with apple smoke for him. Lasater moved closer to the table shaking his head over the mess he had made.

"I didn't even notice," he said. "Sorry. Want me to clean it up? Where's a broom and dustpan?"

"Just stay out of it! Don't set a foot in it again!" She went to the utility room and returned with the broom, dustpan, a mop, and a pail.

Lasater sauntered to the hall door and stood watching her. "Guess I'm just in the way here." He was carrying his empty cup. When she glared at him, he reached out and put it on the table, as if he was afraid to move into the room again. Then he left, the two cards safely buried in the stack she had finished with. Now, if only she did not go through them one more time, if she did not notice a strange name among them, if she mailed them promptly, if the post office actually delivered them, if Balinski opened his and read it, if he believed Lasater would pay him for going to an obscure village in Virginia and holing up for an indeterminate time . . . He took a deep breath. It was a try. The first step of what he knew would be his only attempt to get the hell out of here.

At dinner that night Rawleigh said, "Aunt Jane tells me you sent your parents a card. Where are they?"

"Down in Fort Myers, Florida. Why?"

"You had to go upstairs to get the address. I'm surprised you don't know it."

Lasater shrugged.

"Where's your address book?"

"On the bureau. What are you getting at, Rawleigh?"

"You just never struck me as much of a family man. Go get the address book, Alex."

Lasater glowered at him and drank his wine. Alex went out and came back quickly and handed the black book to Rawleigh who leafed through it, stopped when he came to the address. Lasater had written it in that day. A post office number. It was a good address, as was the telephone number. He hoped Rawleigh would tell Alex to call it just to make sure. Instead, Rawleigh turned pages, stopped now and then, remarked: "Janet. Marcie. Liz. Betty."

Betty was his code name for Balinski. Soon he would get to Tess, Taney's code. He was glad he had not added an area code to any of the phone numbers. Let him think they were New York, or LA.

Rawleigh tossed the address book down and picked up his fork, resumed eating, dismissing the incident. After Aunt Jane had served cherry pie and coffee, Rawleigh said, "Tomorrow Edgar's coming to spend a little time with you. I want everything, from the beginning."

"You've got everything," Lasater snapped. "I won't play with Edgar. He drives me crazy."

"You don't have a choice, I'm afraid," Rawleigh said. "Time's running out, Hugh. Cooperate, or we use some harsher methods. If you've told us everything, you have nothing to worry about. If you've forgotten anything, Edgar may help you remember. I've seen a lot of his debriefings come up with useful stuff that had been forgotten, sometimes for years."

Lasater tossed down his napkin and stalked from the room, went up to his bedroom and paced angrily. Rawleigh had been right about one thing, time was running out. How long until the damn letter got delivered? Five days? Maybe. He had said he would meet Balinski the day after Christmas, but now he did not know if he could stand this that long. That night he got his first ulcer attack. Two hours after dinner he pounded at Rawleigh's door and told him he was sick, Aunt Jane's food was getting to him. He knew all about ulcer attacks, knew exactly what symptoms to complain about, what would relieve them. Aunt Jane was furious with him.

Edgar was concentrating on Taney, everything he could dredge up about her, every minute he had spent with her, how she had looked at the airport coming home. Had he seen the man with her, could it have been Carmen, or someone else? Would Carmen's hair be that long, that curly, enough to stick out from under a cowboy hat? On and on and on. He became ill rather quickly and they had to stop.

Rawleigh, damn him, he thought, again in his room. If he was onto Taney, that must mean he no longer believed the CIA had snatched the Russian, and he had ruled out the restaurant as a possible place for the switch. If he had backtracked that much, the others must have also. Once they got their collective noses on Taney's scent, they would run her down. It was too easy to make the connection, if that's what they were looking for.

He knew Rawleigh, his kind, too well to believe he was acting out of anything more noble than self-preservation, as he was doing himself. If Rawleigh could deliver Taney, Werther, Carmen, the Russian in any combination, they would have to deal him in, that was how his mind worked. In his situation, Lasater would be acting the same way. But he did not believe they would deal in anyone at this point. They might put Rawleigh away for safekeeping, and all others connected with him, but they would not include him. They were playing too close for that; this crew was taking care of its own, preparing for the worst. He thought Rawleigh was an idiot for pretending to trust them with his catch, if he made a catch. They had dealt him out, they were not likely to deal him back in, no matter what he came up with. He'd wake up behind a locked door, if he woke up at all. And Lasater would not be at his side, no matter what.

They found that Lasater could work with Edgar no more than an hour or two a day. He was too ill to continue after that. Almost every night he had an acute attack, usually one and a half hours after dinner, sometimes during the night. Ten days after his first attack he vomited blood.

"I need a doctor," he said weakly. "X-rays. That's what they do. They x-ray the stomach. Rawleigh, I could bleed to death without a doctor."

Rawleigh nodded, almost as if he wished he would do just that. "I consulted a doctor a few days ago. What we're doing is what he recommends — diet, rest, no coffee, no alcohol, bland foods . . ."

"Sometimes that's not enough. I know, Rawleigh. I've been here before, remember? It's killing me."

"He said if the medicine didn't help, he would give you something else. They have all kinds of new medications these days for ulcers, Hugh. We'll get the other prescription filled for you."

Lasater spent Christmas Eve in his room, too sick, he said, to join the festivities. He was starving, he thought darkly. He had forced himself to stay out of the kitchen, not to snitch at night, to keep the hell away from the goodies that Aunt Jane had spread around the house this week — cookies, fruit, nuts, candies. He had not gone outside since his first attack; he was pale, thin, as well he should be, since he was starving to death.

He passed Christmas day in bed. When anyone came in to see him, he drew up his legs in pain and moaned. Rawleigh sat by the bed and watched him for a minute or two.

"If you're shamming us, Hugh, I'll skin you for it. You hear me? Tomorrow I'm having Alex take you to town for x-rays. The doctor agrees that you need them. Hugh, if this is an act,

I'll have your head, but first we'll empty it of everything you ever put in it. You hear what I'm telling you?"

He dressed carefully the next morning, feeling shaky and nervous now that it was act two. He was careful not to have anything suspicious on him, no knives, no lead weights, no rocks . . . When Alex searched him at the front door, he carefully did not smile. He knew the routine as well as they did. A follow-up car, he was thinking, when Rawleigh said:

"Teddy and Ray will be right behind you all the way in, all the way back. Don't try anything fancy, Hugh. Don't let's have any more trouble than we already have. Seven or eight days, Hugh, will you keep that in mind? That's all the time we have left."

"Sure," he said. "I know."

It was very cold outside; he started to shiver when the wind hit him. It looked good, he thought, made it all more authentic. Poor sick, weak Hugh shivering in the cold, shivering from weakness . . . He was so hungry he wanted to cry.

"The story," Alex said, driving, "is that you're a house guest from New York. Rawleigh has agreed to take care of your bill, so there shouldn't be any questions about insurance, stuff like that. If you have to sign a release, your name is Tony Mudd."

"You're kidding."

"Nope, that's it. They're expecting a Mr. Mudd at eleven." He was being careful, watchful, but he had accepted that Lasater really was sick, that was apparent. When he turned too sharply, he murmured, "Sorry. Does motion bother it?"

"Yeah. Everything bothers me."

Alex slowed down a little.

"Even if I had something, what would Rawleigh do with it?" Lasater asked. "It's crazy. What could he do except take it in and make them add his name to that list? Where does that leave you?"

"Right at his side," Alex said cheerfully. "We go together. And you do have it, Hugh. We agree about that. You give and we all three go."

"You just wish I had something for you. You've got nothing

to bargain with. It's wishful thinking." He leaned back and closed his eyes, visualizing the town, where the motel was, where the clinic was. He did not know where the clinic was. "If this is a quack doctor, he doesn't touch me," he muttered. "And he sure to God doesn't cut."

"Hugh! Really! Would we trust you to a quack? He's Rawleigh's own doctor, runs this little clinic out in the boonies two days a week, cuts in Roanoke at a real hospital. Don't worry about him."

They crossed the highway where there were two motels; three blocks down they slowed, turned into the clinic parking lot. When they left the car, Lasater saw the follow-up car with the two farm workers in it. He staggered and leaned against the hood for support, taking in the layout of the clinic, parking lot, street, then walked up the steps and into the anteroom.

"Mr. Mudd? Dr. Casterman is expecting you. This way, please." The nurse was competent, efficient, in her forties. She took his arm and started to lead him past the reception desk.

"I'll come too," Alex said, following.

"You wait out here," she said without glancing at him. "We'll take good care of him. Have a seat, please."

"Mr. Rawleigh asked me to stay with him," Alex insisted.

"Will you please take a seat! Mr. Rawleigh knows Dr. Casterman will take care of his friend. Only patients are allowed in the examination rooms."

"After the examination, when the doctor is explaining what's wrong, maybe he could join us then?" Lasater said.

"Of course, if you wish him to. This way." She led him through a doorway, turned left into a hall lined with open doors to tiny cubicles. "We don't usually open until one," she said. "But Mr. Rawleigh asked Dr. Casterman if he could see you early, before anyone else arrives. Have you had this much pain very long?"

There were no windows in the cubicles. A back door? He hoped so, otherwise he would have to face the goons in front of the building, and he was not ready for that, not today.

"Over a week," he said. "Could I use the bathroom before the doctor sees me?"

"Of course. Back down the hall, first door on the right. I'll be in room number three. That's where the doctor will examine you."

No window in the bathroom. He left quietly and went down the corridor away from the examination rooms. There was the x-ray room, no window. Next to it was a small empty office, and across from it the doctor's office, the door slightly ajar. He glimpsed a man in a white coat at the desk, and tiptoed past. The last door opened out onto the back of the parking lot, which was empty. Satisfied, he went back up the corridor to room three.

"Good, there you are. If you'll just take off your outer coat, I'll weigh you and take your temperature and then let you get undressed for the . . . What are you doing?"

He had glanced around the room quickly. There was a tiny sink, with several towels on a rack near it. Before the nurse could say anything else, he clipped her once on her neck and caught her as she fell. As gently as he could, he bound her wrists and ankles, hesitated over taping her mouth, and settled for one of the towels instead. He liked the way she had put Alex in his place.

He went to the doctor's office and entered. Dr. Casterman rose from behind his desk and came around it, his hand out-stretched. "Mr. Mudd? How do . . ."

Lasater hit him before he realized it was happening, and he fell heavily. Lasater used the doctor's belt and tie to bind him, and he taped his mouth. Any doctor who would treat Rawleigh deserved it.

There was a window in the office. He looked out and stepped away instantly. The follow-up car was there. Alex must have sent them around. He cursed briefly. He looked around the office for a weapon, anything, and his gaze stopped on bookends on the desk. Onyx, in the shape of whales. He lifted one, hefted it once or twice and decided it would do, had to do. Now what? He stopped and thought, then took off his overcoat and jumbled it on one arm and hand, the one holding the bookend. He pulled his tie off, stuffed it in his pocket, pulled his shirt tail half out, as if he had dressed hurriedly, and then strode down the hall to the door to the waiting room.

He opened the door, nearly doubled over, one hand clutching

his stomach, the other under his coat. "Told you," he mumbled. "Told you no quack can touch me . . ."

"What the hell?" Alex said. "He's not . . ." He came to Lasater who was reeling, nearly falling, and reached for him. Lasater brought out the hand clutching the bookend and smashed it against his head, right behind his ear. He was breathing heavily by the time he had dragged Alex to one of the cubicles and taped his wrists, ankles, and mouth. "Sorry, old pal," he muttered, and went out and closed the door. He arranged his clothes, put on his coat and walked out the front door, walked to the motel, and asked for Herb Balinski.

"North," he snapped to Balinski when they were in his car. "And the first hamburger place you see, stop and get me half a dozen, and a malted. Then back to New York. As fast as you can get there."

◻ 27 ◻

HE HAD SIX HUNDRED dollars, more or less, on him, the rest was in the hotel safe. Rawleigh had sent Alex back to check him out, bring his clothes to the farm; no one had asked about the money and he had not volunteered. But the hotel was not a good place to go to now. There really was no good place, he added to himself.

"You don't look too hot," Balinski said when Lasater was finishing the hamburgers.

"Yeah. I've been sick."

The car swerved slightly, straightened out again. "You haven't had the flu, have you?"

"No, why?"

"You hear any of those rumors going around? About this new kind of flu? It's in Washington, maybe in Europe. No one's saying much about it officially, but it's a killer, from the rumors. Don't want any part of it."

"Rumors," Lasater muttered.

"Yeah, but this time it's a little different. We had this job last week, tailing a woman up in New York from Washington, can't mention names, you understand, but there she was having herself a little holiday fling while hubby's on the job in the higher circles, paying to have her watched, phone tagged, the works. One of the calls was from her housekeeper, dragging her back because her husband was sick as hell with flu. Not a word about it in the paper, and with him being who he is, you'd think there would be something at least. Could have died by now for all I know. The housekeeper was scared, and so was she. Didn't even want to go near the town for fear she'd get it. That's not your garden variety rumor, Lasater, you have to admit that."

He shrugged. There was always a new killer flu in the works. He remembered Rawleigh's mention of the fear of swine flu a few years back, and there was Hong Kong flu, Asian flu . . . The list went on and on. All the more reason for them to start the bogus flu shots the next week or so. He stopped listening.

He had to have a car, with snow tires, or studded tires, or something. He wished he had his maps, but was glad that he had gotten rid of them before Alex cleaned out his room. Good training, get rid of everything that might lead someone to where you didn't want him to go. But he might need a map. He had gone out on the route Taney had taken, but there were other ways, shorter ways. He needed some clothes, a toothbrush, razor . . . Most of all he needed to ditch Balinski as soon as they hit the city.

Balinski turned on the radio and Lasater turned it off again. "If you don't mind," he muttered. "Still headachy, can't stand the noise." No way did he want Balinski to get word of a crazed drug addict who had mugged a doctor and nurse for dope. That was the story they would put out, he felt certain. A good enough story, enough to keep the doctor and nurse quiet without telling anyone anything real. Eventually they would get around to the motels and they would find Balinski. Hours? A couple of days? He did not care now. As long as he got to the city, got to a car rental agency, he did not care about Balinski, who had been around long enough to know how to cover his own ass. He owed Lasater nothing, and would throw him overboard without a blink when they got to him, but what could he tell? Damn all. Nothing that Rawleigh did not already have, or almost have. And by then he would have got to the little hideout in the mountains; they would all be gone somewhere else.

It sounded okay to him, but he was worried. Things were happening that he could not control, could not anticipate, plan for. He wanted it over, his part done with. He wanted away from all of them, Taney, Werther, Rawleigh, all of them.

They had just cleared Washington when he realized that he had been a fool. He really had been weakened by his ten-day fast. What if Rawleigh's people got to the motel sooner rather than later? They would find out the car make, model, year, license, everything right there on the registration card. Any second a siren could sound . . .

"Take the next turnoff and head back into Washington," he said curtly.

"What now?"

"I have to do something in the city, that's all."

"Jesus, Lasater, make up your mind. You know it's going to snow before evening? I don't want to be dragging my ass through snow all night."

"You drop me in Washington and take off," he said. "You got any of that deposit left?" He had paid a grand in advance, just in case he needed someone at a funny time.

"Damn little. Today will just about eat it up."

"Okay, okay. We're square as of right now. Just turn around and head back to Washington, anywhere downtown."

He would rent a car, get a map, and get off the damn interstate, and then pay a call on Taney and her pals. He would go by way of Philadelphia where he knew a place to buy a gun.

Midmorning Christmas day Carmen called. Dan Malone had been picked up, everything in his house confiscated.

"Carmen, are you all right? Are you secure?" Saul asked.

"For the moment. But I'm clearing out. Call me after seven in the morning Wednesday. From a safe phone. I can't get to the computer terminal any longer. I go to Seymour now, all right?"

"Yes. Seymour has to try. Get out now. Take care."

He hung up and frowned at the phone for a long time. Lyle watched him, waiting. "The government has seized Dan," he said finally. "Carmen and Seymour are both in Washington. Carmen will try to get to Steve in California. We'll have to distribute our information from this end, after all, I'm afraid."

Lyle moistened her lips. "Can they make him tell them anything?"

"Yes. They can always make people talk if they have time enough," Yuri answered brusquely.

Saul shook his head. "We just don't know. We have to assume he'll talk finally. You always assume that much."

"How will Seymour try to get in to see the president?" Lyle asked.

"They went to Harvard together, they've been friends for many years. I have to stay here, Lyle, and wait for whatever develops, but you can still leave. You and Yuri . . ."

"He'll believe Seymour! He has to believe him! I'm sticking, Saul!"

He rubbed his eyes. "For now we have to wait. Carmen will get in touch with Seymour, tell him it's time, and then we have to wait for twenty-four hours. We have to give them time to consider our plan."

Yuri nodded. "You can trust them not to talk for twenty-four hours, for a week perhaps, but after that every hour is suspect."

"The problem," Saul said, "is that now they know what our plans are. They know what Dan had, the information he was going to mail out. Perhaps they will assume that was all of it, perhaps not. And we have to assume that they have linked Dan to your disappearance, Yuri, and that means they could have backtracked all the way to Lyle. If that man Lasater could find us here, so can they. He may even lead them to us."

"I should take all that stuff and go somewhere else with it," Lyle said.

He shook his head. "You daren't. With this snow we may lose our telephone. You can't put anything in the mail until we're certain the president isn't going to act. We won't know for another twenty-four hours. We have to sit here and wait and watch the television for an announcement. If we haven't heard by seven tomorrow evening, we'll assume the worst."

Their lights would not go out since they generated their own power, but the phone . . . Lyle had not thought of it before. Of course, here in the country in a snow area it must happen often. She was glad they had had their Christmas celebration the night before.

"If Seymour can't persuade the president to make an announcement about the serum," she said, not believing that was possible, "we'll know by tomorrow evening. Then, why can't the three of us leave? You won't have to stay here. What's the point?"

"He'll tell them everything except where we are. But I don't think that will be a problem very long for them. They'll come sooner or later. If it's right away, they had better find me here, and Yuri. They'll think they have the ringleaders, and perhaps give you time to mail the envelopes. If I'm gone, they may put up roadblocks everywhere instantly. You have to remain free through the night and morning, no matter what. You must call Carmen! He'll wait for that call, thinking, if it's delayed, that we're dealing with the government. Stay out of their hands, Lyle, until you have made the call, until you know the envelopes have been delivered. Stay out of their hands altogether, if you can, but do whatever you have to at least that long." He was studying her as he spoke.

It was strange, she thought, how she could look at them, including herself, as if she were high above them all. They had not taken off their boots and now the snow had melted, leaving puddles here and there on the kitchen floor. Her own face looked frozen, although she was not cold, was sweating in fact, dressed as she was in a heavy jacket and snow pants, heavy boots. You really won't have to do it, that other self seemed to say without words, without a voice. Something would happen, she thought, something that would make it no longer necessary. Something. At the last minute. No one can make such a decision and stay human. Something would happen. Something, at the last minute.

The day stretched out interminably. The snow piled up under the windows, crept over the sills. They took turns working with the tractor to clear the driveway, keep it clear enough for a car to leave. It seemed hopeless. By dark fourteen inches of new snow had fallen and another foot was forecast for the night and early morning.

Nothing of any consequence was on the late news, and during the night the telephone lines went down. At times throughout the night Lyle could hear the road maintenance people trying to keep Highway 6 open. She kept closing her eyes, willing herself to sleep but finally admitted that it was futile and left the bed.

"Lyle?"

"I'm sorry. Did I wake you up?"

"No. Are you all right?"

"Restless. I'll read for a while." But she could not read. She turned on the television, switched stations from movie to movie to talk show to. . . She did not even know what she was seeing and turned it off again, and went to stand before the window to watch the snow.

She was not thinking, not wishing, not anything, she realized later. Just watching the snow, her mind not functioning at all. She found that she was weeping and did not try to stop. When Saul came to her even later and led her back to bed gently, she did not resist and finally fell asleep with his arms about her.

In the morning when they went out to start work on the driveway again, they saw that the road crews had failed; the highway was impassable.

The world was a wonderland that morning: the spruce branches touched the ground under their sparkling white mantle; the hedges had vanished under mounds of glistening snow; the brook was buried. It was there, running, hidden away, pursuing its own destiny that would carry its water finally to the sea, take the sea a message from the mountains of Pennsylvania.

How different this storm had been from the Pacific gales of a year ago, how silent, how deceptively beautiful the world it had created, how cruel to the wildlife that had to forage for seeds, roots, anything edible . . . Lyle filled the birdfeeders before she took off her heavy outer wear. It was bitterly cold outside although now the sun was shining.

They all had hot chocolate while the radio played in the background. They would keep it on all day, in case there should be word of an announcement. The storm had swept into upper

New York State, was creating blizzard conditions there; a new snowstorm was predicted for tomorrow in Pennsylvania. The road crews finally had been able to open Highway 6, but they were advising everyone to stay home.

"I'll finish the driveway," Saul was saying over the radio background noise. "You and Yuri should load up the van, have it ready to move as soon as you can get out, if you have to go. And put in extra blankets, and a sleeping bag, just in case you get stranded somewhere. You must be prepared to stay warm. Take the thermos of coffee. Maybe the camp stove would be better, and soup. I'm really concerned about letting you go out at all, my dear."

"You're coming on like a Jewish mother."

He laughed. "So I am. Well, back to work. Don't either of you stay out too long in the cold . . ." He caught himself, laughed again, and pulled on his coat and gloves, left them.

Rawleigh hung up the telephone and stared murderously at Teddy and Ray. No cars had been reported stolen that day, no hitchhiker had been noticed. No one had seen anything.

"You sat on your thumbs and let him beat up Alex, a doctor, and a nurse. It didn't even occur to either of you that an hour and a half was too long for a simple examination. You gave him an hour and a half head start. He could be in New York by now. Get out of here!"

As soon as they were out, he dialed again, this time to his superior. "Mr. Scanlon, please, this is Rawleigh. I have to talk to him immediately."

He listened, protested, listened, and hung up. Mr. Scanlon would return his call. He was still sitting there a few minutes later when his phone rang, the sheriff's department on the line.

"We just got a call from a private investigator in New York," the sheriff said. "Heard the news release. Says he's clean, but he picked up a man at the motel in town today, different name, but still, it could be . . ."

This time when Rawleigh hung up, he did not waste any time; he called his office, told his secretary whom to have waiting for him, gathered up what material he thought he might need, and left his house, not even telling Aunt Jane where he was going or when he would be back.

A line of traffic snaked up the valley by the side of the Delaware River with enough room on the road for two cars to pass in opposite directions only if they were moving very slowly, very carefully. Trucks were not permitted on the highways yet, not until more snow had been removed. Lasater inched along, cursing now and then, but absently, not with any enthusiasm. There had been a news item about the mugging at the doctor's office; they were looking for him, for Tony Mudd anyway. The doctor and nurse were okay, but Alex was hospitalized with a possible skull fracture. His condition was called guarded.

Since it was already on the air, Balinski probably had heard it too. He would have hightailed it to the cops, come out smelling like roses. The cops would have called Rawleigh by now, keeping him informed, and if Rawleigh got his hands on Balinski . . . He would know everything Lasater had found out. Taney, Werther, the Russian, the Monroe connection . . . Rawleigh could add just as well as Lasater could, and he would have access to computers with lists of drug companies and their locations. It was enough, Lasater knew, for him to take to Scanlon, get himself back in the game.

He had not counted on being this long, had not counted on snow up to his eyebrows, had not counted on being paced by a state trooper through the boondocks of Pennsylvania. If one driver had a flat, or ran out of gas, or lost courage, everyone had to stop and wait for a truck to make it through the line, tow out the stalled car, and then they would creep forward again. It would slow *them* down just as much, he kept telling himself. They did not have a magic wand; they could not make the snow vanish. But his fear was deep and the chill he felt was not caused by the weather.

Lyle and Yuri put snow tires on the van and carried out the boxes of envelopes to be mailed. She kept thinking that at any time the radio would interrupt the music and someone would say the president had an announcement to make . . .

He had to believe Seymour, she told herself firmly, positioning boxes, tucking a sleeping bag and blanket near the front seat where they would be available easily. He would trust Seymour, his old friend, a knowledgeable scientist, a responsible teacher, in touch with other responsible scientists all over the world. Seymour would make him understand that since one of the terrible drawbacks had been removed, they had to give it out, let people choose. The president would have to believe him. No doubt they would call in their own scientists who would confirm what Seymour said . . . And the president would go on television, radio, make a world-shaking announcement, offer this gift to the entire world . . . The Russians would have to do the same thing. They would explain the risk, no one would be allowed to choose for anyone else, each individual would be responsible for accepting or not. But available to everyone who chose to take that risk. A new world tomorrow . . . He had to believe. She kept coming back to that until it set up a rhythm in her head, until it lost all meaning.

It was dark when they finished with the van, and the driveway was cleared, the mountain of snow at the road entrance removed. If the road crews came back, they might pile it up again, and if that happened, one of them would go out and clear it again.

No one spoke as Yuri prepared their dinner. They were in the kitchen watching the evening news, silent. Weather stories predominated. And war stories. War in the Middle East, war in the south Atlantic, war in the Far East. Toward the end of the broadcast there was an item about influenza in Russia, a particularly virulent strain, it was said, that was killing many people.

"They have started," Yuri said soberly. "It is started." His face looked pinched, he was pale.

Saul nodded. He turned the volume down, but left the set turned on. He looked at Lyle. "First we eat."

Although she tried to eat, she could taste nothing, forgot to take one bite after another, and found herself staring at the food on her plate with no recognition. She had not believed it would happen, that they would be forced to go through with it. She had not allowed herself to believe it. Something would happen. Something. She remembered her plea to Saul: "Promise you won't ask me to kill anyone." And he had refused to make that promise. Not any*one*, but thousands, hundreds of thousands, millions.

She watched Saul incuriously when he got up to make sandwiches with thick fillings of ham and cheese.

"We'll erase all signs of your presence here for the past months, try to convince them you have been somewhere else, if they come. They must not even suspect that you have duplicate mailings. We can't have them looking for you on the roads. Take any route that's open, Lyle. Forget the plans, head south out of the snow zone. And tomorrow morning at ten call here. If the lines are still down, or if I don't answer, hang up and call Carmen, tell him to go ahead. You have to do that, Lyle. No one is going to move until there is a signal from here. Carmen won't know if we're secure or not and he won't call long distance for fear of being traced. He has to be free to contact everyone else. You'll be the link; we can't get in touch with anyone else with the phone lines down."

Slowly she found herself concentrating on his words even though they had been through it all before. He was speaking calmly, matter-of-factly, reviewing everything, giving her time to accept that it was going to happen.

"If I answer and don't mention . . . what, Lyle? What should our signal be that I have been forced to answer the telephone? Or that it is I on the phone, not an imposter."

"Welcome, chaos," she said. "If you don't say welcome, chaos, I'll know, and hang up."

He nodded.

"If the lines are still down, if I can't get through to you?"

"Call Carmen. He'll have to decide alone. It's all we can do."

She felt numb. When she dressed again in her heavy coat, boots, gloves, she moved like an automaton. The outside air made her blink, she had forgotten how cold it was. Saul put a package inside the van on the passenger seat, then held her tightly.

"Be careful, Lyle. I love you very, very much."

Then Yuri kissed her and she got behind the wheel, locked the doors, and turned on the ignition, eased out of the garage. She had one more chance to look at them, to look at Saul, his face like marble; she made the turn onto the driveway. She drove slowly and carefully on the winding driveway out to the road, where she had to stop and wait for a motorist to let her take a place in the line of traffic that was following a snow plow to the cloverleaf of the interstate, twenty-five miles away. The plow was widening the lane, going ten miles an hour.

Halfway down the hill she saw helicopters that followed the road in the opposite direction. Checking traffic? Police? Government agents? There was no way to know.

Lasater listened to the radio as he drove, stopping and starting automatically in the jerky traffic. Nothing but weather stories and static was on the air. Bored, he turned it off; more bored, he turned it on again, over and over.

He heard the helicopters before he saw them. They swept up the hill, hovered, then descended. And when they had gone, he found himself looking at the approaching traffic dully; he had lost after all. Then he saw her, Taney, pass by so slowly that walking would have been faster. The other line was like his, stopping, starting, creeping when it did move. He spotted a partially cleared driveway ahead, drew abreast of it and twisted the wheel hard, rammed into the snow and became stuck. He jumped from his car, started to run after her in between the two lines of traffic. Horns blared, cars stopped in his line, some of them skidding, and he ran.

When the other line stopped, he caught up to her van and pounded on the window. He averted his head so she could not see him fully; when she rolled down the window, he reached in, unlocked the door and yanked it open.

"Slide over, baby. Move!"

She looked past him, looked behind the van.

"You don't want cops any more than I do, Lyle, honey. But that's what you'll get if you make a scene. Now move over!"

She moved over to the passenger seat, staring ahead. He got in behind the wheel, slammed the door and locked it, and edged forward with the traffic that had started to roll again.

□ **28** □

AFTER TALKING to Herb Balinski, Rawleigh had turned him over to Edgar Bushnell for further questioning. Half an hour later he had demanded to see Scanlon. It had been a shock to Rawleigh to realize that his superiors in the agency had not kidnapped the Russian. With over twenty years of agency training in his past, nothing of this feeling had shown, he knew, but during the few seconds that he had to assimilate the information, he had leaped to the only other possible conclusion: there really was an international conspiracy, and the group that had gone sightseeing in Amsterdam was made up of its members. The man who had come home with the Taney woman had been the Russian. That was what Lasater had been holding out.

He now studied Lee Scanlon thoughtfully. How much did he know? Scanlon was military in appearance, had been a light colonel or something in Vietnam, and had no government experience behind him. He had come out of a business school, had done some research for the president-elect, and had been rewarded handsomely. In his fifties, handsome, smooth, he was so erect that he made Rawleigh feel tired with his own effort to keep his developing paunch sucked in. They were in Scanlon's office, richly decorated with sleek Danish furniture, and American Indian rugs.

"You have some pieces of a great puzzle," Rawleigh said, "and I have other pieces. Neither of us can finish without the other. I think it's time to talk."

"And I told you we're not interested in the Russian. The British probably picked him up for something they have going."

Rawleigh shook his head. "What if I told you I know about

an American-led group that has both the Russian and the solution to radiation sickness?"

Scanlon leaned forward, both hands flat on his desk. *"What do you know?"*

Now Rawleigh sat down. He had not been invited to before. He had been told he could have one minute, no more than that, Scanlon was busy today, would be busy tomorrow, next week . . .

"Ely learned that the Russians have come up with a new health treatment," he said slowly, watching Scanlon. Business school had not taught him how to hide. He went on. "You put a team of scientists on it, not really believing, but not daring not to follow it up. The Russians pulled their heavy gun out of the conference in Amsterdam and sent a relatively unknown member of their team instead. He vanished. Not from the hotel, but from a sightseeing tour earlier." Scanlon twitched and tried to cover it with a cough. "The other four in the group were all in on it. Dan Malone, Seymour Oliver, Luis Betancourt, Franz Leiberman. But I know who brought him home, and I know approximately where he is now. Or at least where he was taken."

Scanlon nodded, almost in relief; he took a deep breath. "You're right, Rawleigh. I said you should be included from the start. Old experienced hand like you, we should have let you in on what was happening. But, goddam it, no one believed there was anything in it, not for months, almost a year! Where is the Russian? Who got him out?"

Rawleigh shook his head soberly. "Not so fast, Mr. Scanlon. I've given you a lot. It's your turn."

"Of course. Of course. Ely got wind of it a little over a year ago. They had moved the team of scientists down to a prison complex on the Gulf of Taganrog, twelve, fifteen miles south of Rostov. And half the team had died. That was what alerted him. Then prisoners began to die, a lot of them, but others didn't die. And they didn't get sick again, ever. He flew home with it and we called in Lawrence Truly and Hanford Wilkes for a conference. They went back through the papers the Russian scientist has published in the past dozen years, and when they put it all together, they came up with an immunological system that seems impervious to everything. Everything!"

Rawleigh was rigid now, while Scanlon was talking eagerly, as if he had been corked so long he could not contain the flow once it started.

"We really thought the British were onto it," he said. "We thought they got the Russian, and only gradually realized they were completely in the dark, not a suspicion of anything at all. We ruled out the hotel, too, of course. No way could he have vanished there. And we ended up with the same group you did. But they were all out of sight by then. Every last man of that group, gone. Fortunately Malone was one of them, and he's been under a rather loose surveillance for years, ever since he wrote those articles about nerve gas, and Agent Orange even before that. You know him, negative, all the way, every time he does an article about the military, the government, any authority at all, it's always negative. Anyway, we staked out the places where he showed up now and then, and he did indeed appear."

Rawleigh felt a great heaviness pressing on him. If they had Malone, they would not need him, what little he had left. He remained impassive, listening.

"They have it, all right," Scanlon said darkly. "And they're terrorists, murderers! They plan to hand it out! Do you have any idea what the death rate is for it? Half! They're willing to kill millions of people! Terrorists, conspirators, collaborators, anarchists, satanists, communists . . . I can't tell you how I feel about them! They're guilty of treason, every last one of them! They'll hang. One by one, they'll hang!"

"But you don't have them yet," Rawleigh murmured. Of course, he thought, Malone would not talk, not this soon anyway.

"No! We'll get them, naturally, but not soon enough. We have to stop them before they hand out so much as a sample! And they're ready. Malone had tons of material ready to mail out. Radio, television, magazines, newspapers, universities . . . They're ready to move and we have to stop them!"

"It's just a matter of time before Malone talks," Rawleigh said when Scanlon finally stopped.

"And we don't have time! They've issued an ultimatum! They're giving the president orders! They plan to start distribution if the president doesn't make a public announcement telling the world what has been discovered, promising distribution to everyone who chooses to take the chance on it!"

Rawleigh tried to make sense of it. Why would they do it now, when they had not given it out before? They had the Russian; they knew whatever the Russian knew, and that had to mean the Russians were using it, or planned to use it soon. The flu epidemic? Of course, the flu epidemic. Fifty-percent mortality!

"What was the time limit for the ultimatum?" he asked briskly.

"Right away. Oliver came to the president himself, told him they were going to move in twenty-four hours if the announcement is not made."

Would that be so bad? Hand it out to the world, let the pieces fall? He thought suddenly of the secretary of defense who had died, whose death had not yet been made public. Flu?

"Have you had a treatment yet, Mr. Scanlon?"

"Don't you understand? Half of those who try it die! Half! A couple of our own people have died. We aren't going to use it again until we find out why and fix it. And we're not going to let the Russians keep on handing it out either!"

"Today the president is going away for a vacation. And the vice president is out of town, Congress adjourned . . . When, Mr. Scanlon? When are you going away for a short vacation?"

Scanlon looked gray and haggard. "Tomorrow. I'm leaving in the morning."

"We don't have much time, do we? You were right about that. If they plan distribution, they have the means to make the stuff. A pharmaceutical company, chemical plant, something of the sort."

"Yes, yes! We're looking into them right now."

"But in the right place? Let me tell you where I think we should be looking." Concisely and thoroughly he reported everything that Lasater had told him, everything that the private detective, Balinski, had told Lasater.

Two hours later they decided that the firm M and S Pharmaceuticals was the company they were after. Because of the recent blizzard in the area, they chose to use helicopters to pay a call on Mr. Markham. Grover Rawleigh elected to go along with the fourteen men who would make up the party.

Rawleigh sipped coffee and watched the old man. It had been almost too easy, dropping out of the sky, walking into this place that could have been a fortress. Markham, Werther, whatever he called himself, and the Russian had been in the kitchen finishing dinner; now the three of them were in the living room while the place was being searched. But no one else was here, obviously. Just as obviously it was headquarters of their group.

"It's over," Rawleigh said. "Your friends have told us everything, you might as well confirm it and save us all a lot of trouble."

"Am I under arrest? Are you taking us away in your helicopters? I should turn some things off if that is the case."

"Soon," Rawleigh said. "There's no rush any longer. Our agents are picking up your people around the country at the moment. Mr. Oliver was very helpful."

Now Werther/Markham smiled at him, and he had the feeling that the man was laughing inside. He knew Oliver would say nothing that had not been long planned. Rawleigh finished the coffee and waited for the search to be concluded, waited for Doerring to report. They would find nothing, he was certain. No trace of anyone else, nothing incriminating, nothing to haul back as evidence.

"How long have the phones been out?" Rawleigh asked.

"Since the storm hit, I imagine. I really don't know. I haven't been trying to call, you see."

"Probably they'll be back in service soon now. The roads are passable, crews are out working. I have to admire those men working out in such weather. I'm surprised that you stay up here through the winter."

Someone would call, Rawleigh reasoned. They had to get a signal to him, or he had to get one out to them. For all they knew Oliver was still waiting to see the president. None of his people could know the house was occupied; someone would call. They all waited for Doerring to report.

This would be as good a place as any to wait it out, he decided.

Plenty of hills between here and New York City, no targets nearby, plenty of food in the freezer. He would send back one of the helicopters, most of the men, and he would wait it out with Markham/Werther, wait for the call, wait for whatever came next. His gaze was bleak as he stared at the fire. Whoever launched first would win, he knew. But he also knew that there would be retaliatory strikes. The only question was how many and how big? That was the question no one could answer. He hoped the strike was so massive that no Russian would be left with a finger to push down on a button.

Doerring finally reported in, and Rawleigh left Rusty Wagner with the two men in the living room.

"There's a fancy computer hookup in an office on the second floor. And I don't think the woman's been gone very long. Her bed's stripped, but the sheets are still in the washer in the laundry room. No papers of any account, but it will take time to go through everything. We need a computer man here."

"Are we in radio touch?"

"Yes, it's hooked up now with the scrambler."

"I'll talk to Scanlon."

By the time he finished the conversation with his chief it was close to midnight, and he was tired. His bedtime was usually earlier than this.

"Dr. Korolenko, we are sending you to Washington to talk to our people there. The helicopter will be leaving in a few minutes. You'd better dress warmly."

Neither the Russian nor the old man spoke as Yuri rose and walked from the room with Rusty Wagner at his side. When he was gone, Rawleigh said, "You're a cold-blooded son of a bitch, aren't you? You know he's due for an interrogation tonight."

"He took his chances, as we all do."

"Yes. Well, he lost. You've lost. You might as well make it easy for all of us, Mr. Markham, and tell us where the others are. Where is Lyle Taney?"

The old man's gaze on him was steady, thoughtful. It made little difference if he talked tonight or tomorrow, or never, Rawleigh knew. A team of electronic experts was on the way; they would rig up the telephone, tackle the computer, find out everything that had gone into it. If anyone called, they would trace the call, dispatch another team. Everyone was ready to move very fast. They would find out what kind of car Taney had left in and put out a bulletin on it; the first of a series of announcements about espionage, Russian spies, germ warfare, God knew what, would be on the air as soon as the Russian was in a safe place. Everyone was ready to move, the first moves had been made, the rest was a matter of inevitability.

"We know she left after the storm," he said easily. "That isn't much of a lead for her, is it? Where are your insurance papers, by the way?"

Werther/Markham shrugged. "I never try to keep track of that sort of thing and my secretary quit some time ago. I'm afraid I can't help you."

"We'll find them. Doerring, take him to one of the offices and see if he can remember anything that will be of help. I'm going to bed." If no papers turned up, the state licensing department would track down the car for them.

He was glad that he no longer had to be involved in all-night interrogations; he no longer had to go through drawers, shelves, boxes of junk looking for the one item that would complete a picture. He had done all that, too many years, he thought sourly. Now he could go to bed, let others take care of it, hand him reports when the job was done. Seniority had its advantages in government service. Doerring was young and eager; let him earn his right to climb the ladder just as everyone else did over the years. Doerring was only forty, perhaps a bit too eager, too pushy, but on the other hand, he did not have a clue about what was at stake in this game, not really. He thought they were after spies, simple as that. He thought the world was made up of our agents and theirs, simple as that, and their guys deserved little consideration, no matter what their ages, their affluence, anything else. As he watched them leave the living room he was not sure which of the two men he pitied more. Werther/Markham would talk the minute he decided he wanted to and Doerring did not know that yet. His forty years had not been long enough for him to know people like Werther/Markham, to know that he was going to be under as much pressure as the old man for the rest of the night, through tomorrow, however long he kept at it. Rawleigh was convinced that all-night stints like this one exacted a terrible toll, but in this case only Doerring would have to pay, and he especially did not know that.

Sighing, he wandered down the hallway to choose one of the empty bedrooms for his own use that night. All were spacious and warm, all equipped with towels, soap, shave lotions, body lotions, toothpaste, and brushes in pristine plastic cases. He told Jules Blakeley which room he had chosen, in the annex, glanced in at the two men going through the papers in Werther's study, and at others going through books, riffling through them page by page, and again was glad he was not part of that end of it any longer. He went on to his room. A hot soaking bath, then bed, that was all he wanted now. Everything was under control here, everything being done that could be, should be done. A hot soaking bath, a bit of lotion on his hands, chapped from the frigid wind, maybe a few minutes for reading, then sleep. The distant highway noise was inaudible in the annex. There were even robes in the bedrooms, he noticed with pleasure. He would still be awake when the helicopter brought in the team of experts, see that they got started; let them envy him his comfort of a robe, a waiting bed. He began to hum under his breath as he drew the water. Maybe he would even drop in on Doerring for a moment, see how he was making out.

He heard the helicopter arrive as he was luxuriating in the oversized tub, almost falling asleep. He shook himself, got out and toweled down briskly and put on the borrowed robe. A touch short, but comfortable enough. He examined the lotions, selected one and rubbed some on his hands, and then went looking for slippers. None fitted him. His feet were slender, elegant, he liked to think. Regretfully he put his own shoes back on and went out to greet the newcomers. Blakeley had already taken them to the office with the computer setup. He did not like computers very much, did not trust them, did not understand them. He stood back watching for a moment as the computer men conferred. His attention wandered to an open closet door, and he walked over and looked inside. Shelves of supplies, reams of paper, boxes of envelopes in different sizes. A lot of empty space where supplies had been; dust still outlined box shapes.

He stared at the boxes, blinked several times, stared. Why would they need so much of this kind of stuff here? The main office was in Philadelphia, that's what Doerring had said. This was a personal computer, a laboratory computer, with a printer, and a screen . . . a telephone connection. Postage scales.

Abruptly he turned and left the office, walked down the circular stairs that wound about the center post in the building, and went to the kitchen where the radio was. The operator was dozing in a tilted chair.

"Get Scanlon!" Rawleigh said, and the man jerked awake, nearly fell. "And then get out."

They had made copies of everything Malone had done, he thought viciously, and someone had the stuff out there now, copied, printed, addressed, stamped, ready to mail.

◘ 29 ◘

MENTALLY LYLE had made an inventory of the contents of the van: the boxes of envelopes to be mailed, sleeping bag, blanket, thermos of coffee, sandwiches . . . her purse, a handful of clothes in an overnight case. There was a tire jack, of course, but under a panel, under the boxes. In the glove compartment were maps, a flashlight. No weapons, nothing that could even serve as a weapon. The flashlight? Too small, lightweight. In her purse was a nailfile, too small, too flimsy.

"Which way you headed?" Lasater asked.

"South, out of the snow."

He looked at her sharply when she spoke. "Just take it easy, Lyle," he murmured. The trouble was, she was taking it too easy; she was too cool, too remote, too much in control. Planning something, that was it, preoccupied with her plans. The traffic stopped again and he twisted in the seat, reached behind him and pulled one of the boxes within reach, opened it. Envelopes. He pulled one out and felt it, then tore it open. He could not read it in the dim light.

"What's all that stuff?"

She did not answer.

"Listen, Lyle baby. You're in such trouble, you wouldn't believe it. And so am I, sweetheart. So am I. Those choppers landed back at your little retreat. By now your sugar daddy and the Russky are in the hands of the government. How many others have been picked up already is anyone's guess. Don't hold out on me, Lyle. Not now."

She continued to gaze out the windshield with that same absent expression. He put the typed message on the floor between them and eased the van forward with the traffic that was moving once more.

The thermos, she had decided. It was heavy enough. Not here, not with so many people trapped by the snow, witnesses who could watch any little drama they might have to play out. Later, after they left the packed cars, when the highway was clear and they were not under constant observation, then she would get the thermos from the back, hit him with it enough to stun him, enough to kill him if she had to. Push him out of the car, and speed away from him. She concentrated on the problem of swinging the thermos in the confines of the front of the van.

"Were you clear of the driveway before those choppers showed up?"

"Yes."

"Good. They'll know you're gone, but not when. Listen, Lyle, I'm taking the interstate east. We'll leave it as soon as the snow lessens. I don't think anyone's stopping traffic here yet, but if they are, don't you even peep." He reached into his coat pocket and withdrew the gun he had bought in Philadelphia, not much of a gun, but sufficient. He showed it to her and pushed it back into the pocket. "I take it you have a chore to do tonight, somewhere you have to go, something you have to do, and believe me, honey, you won't be doing it with a hole in you, no matter what kind of immunity you have now. So be good, okay?"

They were almost to the cloverleaf entrance to the interstate when they had to stop again. Now he turned on the dome light and picked up the paper, started to read it. "Jesus!" he whispered. "Jesus Christ! Is this what's in all those boxes?"

She looked straight ahead. He pulled out a few more

envelopes, opened one, then another, tossed them all back into the box. No wonder she had made no attempt to get out of the van, no wonder she was sticking, had not even checked to see if her door was unlocked. He was gripping the wheel so hard his hands ached. They started to move forward.

He would not turn her in around here, she reasoned. He would try to take her back to Washington with him, take the evidence to the proper authorities, his bosses, not hand it over to local police. Washington was an all-night drive; there would be time during the night . . .

They turned onto the interstate, and here the crews had opened a lane in each direction, with mounds of snow between them. Traffic picked up speed, still single file, but definitely moving now. They headed east.

Lasater felt numbed by what was in the envelopes. They were handing it out! Just like that, they were giving it away! All the fighting he had done, all the conniving, the cheating, the money he had spent, the worry, all for nothing. Now everyone would have it. For free! There was a catch, there had to be a catch. He had read only the opening paragraph, scanned the rest. As soon as they got to the open road, with a safe place to turn out, he would read the whole thing. There had to be a catch.

The Russians had it, were using it! Scanlon and his crew were aware of it. He could not seem to keep his thoughts going forward; they kept skittering away as if what they approached was too terrifying to deal with. Grimly he started over. Scanlon and his gang knew the Russians had it and were using it. They had Werther; they were not making any announcements about what it was, what it would do. They must believe the Russians were too far ahead. He forced himself to follow the line of thought. They had to believe the Russians were secretly immunizing their own people, and when enough of them had it, the Russians would launch a strike.

He shivered. Rawleigh must have hightailed it to Scanlon; they were dealing each other in. They probably got Balinski without too much trouble, traced the Russian, just as he had done, to Monroe, New York, and from then on, it was child's play to find Werther's hideout. So they had a lot of pieces now.

Did they know what Taney had in her car? Probably not, not unless someone had talked, and he did not believe any of them would talk, no matter what kind of persuasion was used.

"Where are the samples the letter talked about?" he demanded.

She remained silent.

"Damn you, Taney! Tell me! Do you have them in the van?"

"Of course not! You saw what I have."

He believed her, but he would look anyway, as soon as they could stop somewhere. Were others out in another van, many other vans, stuffing samples in mailboxes, hand delivering them to households like samples of a new toothpaste, or catsup? Pills? Sugar cubes? How was it being given?

She was thinking hard, also. He would read the information sheets, understand finally that it was transmitted sexually, and then . . . She felt such a pervasive chill that it seemed the arctic air had penetrated the van in spite of the excellent heater. No matter what happened, she had to stay alive, able to act, and out of the hands of the government until ten in the morning when she would phone Saul, and then Carmen. She knew the call to the laboratory was futile. But maybe Saul would give the signal and tell her to come home, tell her it was being done in a more orderly way, the government was going to make it available . . .

"Fill me in," Lasater said, his voice grim and hard. "I'm going to read the stuff anyway, so tell me. What's the catch with it?"

"What do you mean?"

"Why hasn't your pal handed it out before? Why now?"

She took a deep breath and suddenly saw a way to prevent his reading the papers. "I might as well," she said. "It's all on the information sheets. It kills half of those who use it. A high fever develops and they die; others recover completely. You saw me when I was sick, when I recovered. That's how it reacts in the human body. Until the Russians discovered a way around it, it left sterility. They learned how to overcome that, but it will take years of training for most women to be able to conceive. Saul and Carmen couldn't turn it over with those two drawbacks. It would have been the death of the race. Half the people, never any children . . . It would have been a hopeless, static society.

But now that the Russians have it and they are distributing it, Saul knew we had to use it too."

"You're willing to kill half the population!"

"If they start a war it will be *all* the population before it's over," she said quietly. "Those who don't die in the first week, will die during the weeks that follow. You know that."

He did know it. He was gripping the wheel too hard again. He wanted to hit her, to hit anyone. He wanted to cry. Fifty-fifty! It wasn't fair! To have come this far, to have learned this much, to have found her, and then find it was only fifty-fifty!

"Who dies? What's the critical factor?"

"No one knows."

"Damn you! You're lying!"

"I'm not lying. They don't know. There are warnings on the samples, explanations, warnings not to let children use them, or pregnant women, or seriously ill people . . ."

"You said *use them*. What does that mean? How do you take the stuff?"

She bit her lip, then went on. It didn't really matter if he knew; as soon as the samples were distributed, everyone would know. She told him.

He cursed. "Hand lotion! For Christ's sake! Soap!" He cursed again. They had reached the end of the snowfall. He had not been noticing, but now the road was clear, with slight accumulations beyond the shoulders. The speed of the traffic had increased until it was normal.

He estimated the time it would take to drive to Washington, directly to Scanlon, directly to the top, bypass Rawleigh altogether. They would have to cut him in if he delivered Taney and her printed material. Without that her group was done for. They wanted to give the world information as well as the samples. Scanlon had the old man — his doing. He would have Taney — his doing again. It would just be a matter of time before they picked up the others, one by one. He would be on the inside then, not out in the cold with his nose mashed on the glass. And then?

They would bomb the hell out of Russia, stop the stuff in its tracks, and then take their own sweet time to find the glitch that made the stuff kill half the people.

He knew that was a lie. There would be no one left to do the research, there would be no place in which to do it. Besides, they were already trying to cover their own asses by using it . . . He remembered what Balinski had told him about the vicious flu that was loose in Washington. Like the flu that Lyle Taney had had back in Oregon last year! But would they drop bombs while this group was out threatening to start distribution? That was the tough one.

"What were you supposed to do tonight?"

When she did not answer, he glared at her. "You're to mail that stuff, aren't you?"

She nodded.

"And other people are mailing the samples, or handing them out somewhere, aren't they?"

Again she nodded.

He drove fast, overtook other cars, then slowed down. No tickets, for Christ's sake! Not now. He had thinking to do. He was cursing under his breath. "Why did they send you? You're so green you're sure to get picked up!"

"Anyone can mail a letter."

"And they can stop the mail deliveries! You bunch of idiots! You have no idea of what you're up against! The whole fucking federal government! The post office department! CIA, FBI, everyone!"

"Then I'll have to deliver them to the addressees."

"Christ!"

She was stunned by his words: they could stop the mail deliveries! She had not thought of that. No one had thought of that. Or had Saul? Some of the letters had the M&S logo for the return address; many had no return addresses; some had false addresses. Some of them were in script, others in type, some printed . . . Surely they wouldn't open every single piece of mail. They would pick out the M&S ones, they were easy to spot. She would have to mail them from many different post offices, mail drops . . . A few here, a few there, through the night, into the morning . . .

Meanwhile they were speeding toward Washington.

"There's a rest area ahead a mile or so," he said after a short silence. "I'm stopping to see what other little goodies you have stashed away in the back. Don't try anything, Lyle baby. Or I might take off without you."

"You said you didn't want police any more than I do. Why?"

"I nearly killed a man today. Maybe he's dead by now. I think you'll make up for him, though. I think it'll be a fair exchange." He grinned at her. "And if I have to take off without you, I've got the real payload in back, don't I?"

"Lasater, if you take me in, take that material in, you know what it will mean. If they can suppress this long enough, there will be war, and no one will win, no one will survive to use the samples, or even suspect what might have been."

"Just shut up, baby. I know everything you do and then some, so just shut up."

They pulled into the rest area, stopped at the end of the parking lane, and then he motioned to her to go into the back of the van before him. She slid from her seat, eased herself over the gear shift, and went to the rear in a semicrouch. He followed. There were no windows; there was a curtain that he drew between the cargo space and the front. Then he turned on the dome light.

"You saw the message," she said, kneeling on the floor. "It's basically the same, some more technical than others, depending on who is to receive them."

He opened the boxes, poked in among the letters in each one shaking his head. No samples. "You don't have a chance. They'll stop the mails."

"Why would they? They don't know I'm going to mail anything tonight. No one knows."

"If the stuff is at the building back there to print up all these, postage scales, supplies, they'll suspect. Will they find that stuff back there?"

She nodded.

Lasater sighed. He picked up one of the envelopes he had opened earlier and started to extract the sheet of paper from it.

"Look," Lyle said, holding up several other ones. "If I mail all of them with the M&S return address together, from the same post office, they'll assume they have them all. Won't they?"

"Maybe. Then what?"

"Then we keep driving and stop now and then and mail the rest a few at a time, some in post offices, some in mail drops, in shopping centers, wherever we can."

He shook his head. "Not we, baby. No way."

"Yes, we! You won't get it from them in Washington! They'll pretend no one is going to get it until they find out why it kills so many, and meanwhile they'll be trying it on themselves, or the army officers, or officials . . . But you won't get it. They don't trust you enough!" She watched him, went on. "They might even decide to kill you outright just so you won't talk, won't be a nuisance later when the war starts. You know too much."

He was holding the envelope with the letter halfway out. Now he slid it in again and tossed it down.

She reached for the thermos. "I have coffee, sandwiches. They're in that bag by your elbow."

He did not move yet. "What's the difference if a million people die from bombs, or die from your damn secret ingredient? What's the difference? Dead is dead."

"The survivors are the difference! They get to choose for themselves to use it or not. Who chooses to get killed in a war? And there's no end to the dying in that kind of war, not until we're all dead, not until every bomb has been exploded, every warhead used, every missile . . ." She was handling the thermos, watching him, tensing her muscles, getting ready.

He was looking at the boxes again, all open now, all revealing only letters, hundreds of letters, and no samples. She didn't have the stuff with her, and her time was nearly over. They would track down the van, find her, haul her in, and where would that leave him? Hauled in with her? His only chance lay with Scanlon, the agency . . . He wished suddenly that he had just stayed with his own car, driven the hell away from it all. Washington would go, New York would go, the whole fucking East Coast would go . . . and the West Coast, and the interior . . . He reached for the bag of sandwiches just as she raised the thermos and struck.

If he had not moved forward, leaned, it would have caught him in the head, but it glanced off his shoulder and he dived, avoiding the full brunt. Reflexively he jerked out the gun and rolled so that it was pointing at her. She was very pale and there were beads of sweat on her forehead.

She should try to talk him out of shooting; she thought it very distantly, almost coldly, as if she were thinking about someone else, someone not real. His face was without expression, masked, his eyes looked dead, as if he too had to withdraw first, watch himself from a safe place.

He saw her jerk, saw her drop over, twitch a little, stop moving. He saw it flashingly, and, as he saw it, he knew if he did it his last chance was gone. If she had moved, if she had spoken during that instant, his finger would have squeezed the trigger, she would have been dead. The moment passed; he began to think again, regained control over his hand, and now he felt sweat on his back. No way could she ever know how close that had been for her. No way. He pulled himself up to a sitting position, still leveling the gun at her. "Listen, Lyle baby, and listen good. You've got a little job to do and, honey, there ain't no way on God's little green earth that you can get it done alone. You called the play, now we're going to run with it. And you do as I say. I know every trick they know. They trained me, remember? We do it my way. And now, if there's any coffee left, if the thermos isn't broken, we'd better have some. It's going to be a long night, sweetheart."

She stared at him, not moving.

A long night, he repeated to himself. And more than likely they would not make it. Scanlon, the rest of them, they'd pull out all the stops now, and they had the manpower, the organization, the need to find her, have themselves a little bonfire with the stuff in the boxes. But they'd work for it, he thought grimly. They'd have to work their asses off for it. Taney was his, had been his from the start, would be his at the finish. He had some unfinished business with Lyle Taney, he thought, watching her, and he was going to keep her until it was settled.

As he looked at her he suddenly remembered a statue he had seen in India, in Calcutta, years ago. One of their crazy looking gods. A female with a great figure, breasts like apples ready to be plucked, narrow waist, and spreading, flaring hips. From her belly there was a torrent of goodies — flowers, fruits, even animals, for Christ's sake! And in her hand there was a sword. Like Taney, he thought, or Taney was like her. Take off his head with that sword in a flash if she had to. And she would try again, and again, unless they had an understanding.

Slowly he reached out with the gun and laid it on the floor between them. "After we have coffee, while I'm driving, you can sort out the stuff with the M&S addresses."

▣30▣

FOR MANY SECONDS neither of them moved. Finally Lyle said, "I don't believe you."

"I don't believe me either. Talk me out of it. It wouldn't take much."

Still she did not move. It was a trap, another one of his tricks. He shrugged and again reached for the sandwiches, took one out and unwrapped it, started to eat. He continued to watch her, now with a glint of amusement.

"You've certainly come a long way, honey. Last year you couldn't have hit me with a cream puff, you know?"

"I'll kill you if I have to."

"I know. That's why I'm offering you the gun. Symbol of a truce, or something like that. Don't like the idea of you lurking behind me with blunt objects in your hands."

She snatched up the gun and held it, not pointing it. "Is it loaded?"

"You kidding? Most dangerous thing in the world is an unloaded gun. Sure it's loaded. Probably a lousy sight. I just paid forty bucks for it. Still, at this range . . ." He finished the sandwich, picked up the thermos and shook it. "Don't hear glass. We'll see." He opened it carefully and looked inside. "Think it survived. If you'd got me in the head, you'd have to go without coffee all night."

"You're afraid too, aren't you?"

He sipped the coffee, watching her over the edge of the plastic cup. "Honey, I'm just scared shitless, that's all. You want some of this? Is there another cup?"

She shook her head and now she put the gun in her coat pocket. "I think I should mail all the M&S ones from Philadelphia where the main plant is. They might not suspect there are more."

He nodded. "Are there maps? I want to stay on the interstates until we get out of the snow range, and then get the hell off them onto state roads."

"In the glove compartment." She watched him crawl forward, her hand on the gun in her pocket. Driving toward Philadelphia was also driving toward Washington, she reminded herself.

She should kill him now and be done with it, not have to worry about him any longer. They should have killed him a year ago. But he was afraid, she reminded herself. He knew what was at stake and he was afraid. Also, he wanted to keep away from the police. She believed that, no matter if what he had told her was true or not. If he delivered her to anyone, it would have to be his bosses in Washington, not state police, or local police. And he knew about roadblocks, how to avoid them. If they got through to Philadelphia, if they actually mailed any of the envelopes, he would be as committed as she was . . . She shook her head. No. He could tell them where the envelopes had been mailed, they could still pick them up. Why had he given her the gun? Why had he told her they could stop the mail deliveries? She took out the gun and looked at it.

"Lasater, I want to see the bullets in the gun. How do I open it?"

He groaned. "Christ! Don't point it in my direction, okay?" From the front seat he told her to point it at the rear of the van, then told her how to see the bullets, where the safety catch was, how to tell if it was on or off. Satisfied, she put the safety on and replaced the gun in her pocket. He had gone back to studying the maps. She would use the gun if she had to, she told herself, and knew it was true, but as long as he was helping her get south, if he actually stopped for her to mail the envelopes, the gun would stay in her pocket. If she could use him now, that seemed only fair.

When they started again, she was in the back of the van, the

curtain closed, the dome light on. She began to sort the envelopes. About a third of them had the M&S imprint.

In a little while she heard him cursing, and their speed was
cut, cut again. She finished, and joined him in the front of the
van. It was snowing.

The snow blew against the windshield, piled up under the
wipers. It was sticking to the road, accumulating fast on the
shoulders.

"What kind of tires does this thing have?" he asked.

"They're good, heavy-duty snow tires. We should be all right."

"Yeah. Is it licensed in Pennsylvania?"

"No. Ohio."

"That's good. They won't be looking for an Ohio car for a
while, let's hope."

A truck passed them and he cursed more audibly. "Bastards!
One of them will jackknife and then we'll all have to stick it
out waiting for cops, tow trucks, God knows what."

She turned on the radio and fiddled with it until she found
a station not choked out by static. Weather news, nothing but
weather news. The storm was a full-fledged blizzard in upper
New York state; snow was falling in New York City, down the
Jersey coast. Philadelphia had escaped it so far.

The radio cackled, garble won out, and Lyle turned it off.
The snow was not getting heavier, but the accumulation was
continuing.

"We'll have to stop eventually," Lasater said. He was concentrating on the road, holding the wheel in a tight grip. The road
was getting slick; it would be treacherous before long. "Anyone
asks, we're from Toledo. Spent Christmas with my folks in Scranton, and now we're on our way to Florida for a vacation. Snow-
birds, that's us. Mr. and Mrs. Hugh Lasater on our way south
for a couple of weeks."

She nodded. No one would ask, but it was best to have something ready, in case, something they both knew in advance.

He was thinking about his mother and father in Florida, arm
in arm, strolling the beaches, sipping gin and tonic in the shade,
fishing now and then. His father had been okay, strict, but okay.
Just grew up in different times, that's all that was wrong with
him, and he was not responsible for that, for Christ's sake. What

if they took the stuff and made it? Walking arm in arm for the next ten years, fifty years, forever? Too old to work, not ready to die. Who'd support them, for Christ's sake? He chewed his lip. Maybe the old man could get a job again, he'd been a crack accountant. Maybe he could be again. Would they take it? He did not know. Would they feel they'd had theirs together, no point in going on longer? There was no answer. Married more than fifty years now, how had they managed not to kill each other? They even seemed to like each other in exactly the same way they always had. He shook his head, not understanding them a bit. Never had, he realized. Never had.

"Isn't your bleeding conscience going to bother you?" he asked harshly to turn off his own thoughts about his parents.

"Yes," she said in a low voice. It was an impossible choice, she knew. No human should have to make such a choice. No saint, no angel, no god should ever have to make such a choice. She remembered how startled she had been, and how outraged, at the concept of triage when she first came across it. In battle, if you're a doctor, you don't help those who need extensive care, who might not survive; you don't help those who will survive without your help, no matter how painful their injuries are; you help only those who will survive with help. Each person to be judged in a flash, each injury assessed in a flash, then on to the next, and the next, and the next. The doctors would come out inhuman, she had thought. Their humanity could not survive, their souls would be killed by being forced to choose like that.

They turned onto Interstate 87, and soon the snow became intermittent, then stopped again. They sped south.

She remembered lying in bed with Saul, neither of them sleepy yet, just talking in the dark of the room.

"Afterward," he had said, "if you feel differently about us, will you come back and talk about it?"

"You're not serious!"

His arm tightened about her, he drew her closer. "Carmen and I have had so much time to think about this, to talk about it, what it will mean. You know about the great discontinuities of the past? The establishment of the Christian religion was one. It changed the way people thought of themselves and their relationship with their god. The Copernican theory was another. It changed the way people thought about themselves and their relationship in space with space. Then came the proof that the world was really round. Finally we knew pretty well what our world was, where it was in the universe. From the center of it all we slipped into an insignificant position in a nondescript galaxy, on the fringe of that even. Each great change was tumultuous; each one changed our ability to perceive. Perhaps our synapses are changed with each discontinuity. First only a few people believe, then a few more, and after a very long time the rest of them follow. Many of them are still rebelling against the last two great discontinuities: the Darwinian theory and Freud's theory of the subconscious. It takes a very long time for such things to be accepted, for the adjustments to be made."

Lyle's mouth felt dry. She swallowed. "And there won't be time for this change. Not the next generation, or the one after, but this one has to adapt."

"Yes. Can they? My dear, I'm sorry. You're shivering."

They clung to each other in the dark and neither answered his question. When he and Carmen had talked, she realized, they had understood what they would do to the entire world, and, more, they had understood what this would do to the ones responsible. It was a long time before her shivering stopped.

Occasional snow flurries were driven by a brisk wind as they drove into Philadelphia. The streets were nearly empty of traffic. Lasater drove past the M&S plant out of curiosity. It would be occupied, but what would show? Nothing showed. It was a modern building with lots of glass, set back, landscaped, prosperous-looking, deserted-looking. He did not slow down.

They had decided to go to a post office substation a few miles from the plant to mail the first batch of envelopes. When he stopped the van, pulled in to the curb to park, she hesitated.

"Now what?" he asked in annoyance. It had occurred to him that they might be watching post offices. Not likely, but possible, he thought, studying the cars up and down the street.

"Let me take the key with me," she said.

He laughed harshly, yanked out the ignition key and handed

it to her, and watched her leave with a box of envelopes, watched her deposit them a few at a time in the mailbox. It was done. He was committed.

He had told her the truth that he was scared shitless. He knew that her outfit had no idea of the odds they were bucking, how slim their chances of success actually were. They were a bunch of starry-eyed innocents, and they were his only hope. Taney didn't have the stuff with her, but she sure as hell would lead him to it. And then he would decide about taking it, if they got that far.

She came back, handed him the key silently, put the empty box in the back of the van and looked straight ahead as he started, left the curb, got back into traffic, and headed south. She looked like someone in shock.

They were still heading toward Washington, now on Highway 1. He could still change his mind; this might still be a trap, she kept thinking, but she no longer believed that. He was too frightened. He had got her into it all, a year ago, and now he was her ally . . . She had hesitated at the mailbox. She had watched her hand as if she never had seen it before, doubted its function. It had refused to move for what had seemed a long time. Her ally . . . as long as she had the gun in her pocket, her hand close to it. Then she had willed her hand to move, to drop in the first of the envelopes, forced her fingers to release them . . . She would kill him if she had to, if this was a trap. Then the next batch had slid down, vanished without a sound to indicate when they hit. How many other letters had been in the box? Nearly full? Almost empty? How long to sort through them? To separate them by zip codes, start them on their way? To sort through them and pull out the ones with the M&S logo on them? To open them, in a secret room somewhere, burn them? File them? What would they do with them? Her hand had acted as if it no longer had been connected with her mind, her will, her nervous system. It had not wanted to release the envelopes.

"Taney, pay attention. I asked you if you want to mail any of them in Washington."

"No."

"Okay. We stay on One until we go through Baltimore. We'll

make as many stops as you want there, and then we get on Interstate Ninety-five and head south, bypass Washington, and back to One. Okay?"

It was easier in Baltimore. Resolutely she held the envelopes over the chute, dropped them, and went back to the van. At the next stop, he got out and mailed a batch; he took the key with him. Soon after that they stopped for gas, to use the restrooms. When she left, she took the key with her; when he left, he carried it. Partners, she thought soberly.

They skirted Washington, headed for Richmond. Lasater was getting very tired, but when she offered to drive, he refused. He did not like being driven by a woman. It was three in the morning, and it had been a very busy day for him, he thought. That morning and the trip to the clinic now seemed another lifetime, a distant past. Edging his way toward the Pennsylvania mountains seemed a dream fantasy, nothing directly connected to him. The road before him wavered, and he jerked upright.

"I came looking for a sign," he said, to keep himself from falling asleep. "Funny, that's how I thought of it, looking for a sign, and then I saw that fancy sign to the bird refuge and I knew that was it. You believe in coincidence? Fate?"

"I don't know. Sometimes."

"Look, Lyle, I'm falling asleep. Talk to me, sing, tell jokes. Something. Or listen to me talk, and now and then agree with me, or argue with me."

"Let me drive."

"I'm not that sleepy yet."

"Why did you almost kill someone?"

He told her about Rawleigh, about Alex, about working with Alex for twenty years, give or take a little. She asked questions and he answered them. No point in lying to her, he thought, no point in hiding anything from her. He told her the truth, and he grinned as he realized that she probably believed none of it. For the first time since he had met her, he was telling her the straight truth, and she doubted every word.

"Why are you staying with me?"

"Maybe I can keep you out of Rawleigh's hands, away from Scanlon, and if I do, and if the kid stays in the clear, eventually you'll head for him, and I'll tag along. He has the samples, doesn't he?" She made no response. He did not blame her. As far as she was concerned, he was still an unknown factor, not someone to hire to guard her life savings.

She was thinking that she understood him in a way she never had been able to understand Saul and Carmen. She knew Lasater's motives, his fears. He was harsh and cruel and selfish; he had nothing but contempt for anyone who got in his way, anyone he used. It was evident that nearly killing his one-time friend meant nothing to him, and yet, she understood him. He was like a child in his amoral unconcern for anyone else. He was with her now simply because he thought he had a better chance with her to get the serum than he would have had with his own agency. But now, for the first time, she felt some doubt that it was quite that simple, that he was quite that simple. He had been genuinely afraid of war, as afraid of it as she was, as Saul was, or Carmen. And he had been compelled to choose her because of that fear, not because of the serum. As far as he knew there was no chance of getting it through her, not for any foreseeable future.

"How'd you manage the switch in Amsterdam?" he asked suddenly, his voice too loud, making an obvious effort to fight his fatigue.

She told him and he laughed. "Do you want more coffee?" she asked then. "There's another sandwich, I think, if you want that."

"Yeah. Anything. The coffee's cold, but what the hell, it's still full of caffeine."

They mailed the last of the envelopes in a small town north of Raleigh, south of Richmond. Neither knew where it was. It was six-thirty in the morning. The sky was lightening, but there were thick clouds, the light was bleak and cold.

Lasater sat with his hands on the steering wheel, so tired he felt he could not lift his foot to the accelerator, could not push in on the clutch, shift gears.

"You did it, sweetheart," he said when she took her seat, locked her door. "Job's well done. Let's find someplace in the hills to hide and get some sleep."

She shook her head. "I can't. There's something else I have to do first, but not yet. Let's have some breakfast and then drive on to Raleigh and I'll finish there. You can do anything you want after that."

"When will you be finished?"

"Right after ten."

He sighed. "I'll find a café or something. You know, they serve grits with breakfast in this part of the country. Pretty good, too. Can't stand them anywhere else, but down here, they're pretty good. Must be the way they cook them."

"After we eat," she said, "I'll drive. You might kill us both, you're so sleepy."

"Kill you? Not a chance."

"You could kill me," she said. "It isn't a magic cure-all."

But it was, he knew. She looked mildly tired, nothing drastic, nothing to make anyone feel concern over her, while he, on the other hand, must be looking like death on the prowl. Breakfast would help, but not enough. "Okay, okay," he said. "I'll catch a nap and you take us on to Raleigh. Get there about nine-thirty or so, and you can do your last little chore."

It had to be a phone call, there was nothing left to mail, and she had had no set destination, no meeting with anyone in mind. Call the old man and report the job was done? Why not now, why at ten? Check to see if the mail actually got delivered? Not so soon; no one would expect delivery until another day, two days even. More if it was heading for the West Coast . . . West Coast! That was it. Ten here, seven there. A call to the lover boy? To other accomplices? Tell them this part was done, go ahead with the next step? He did not ask; he knew she would not tell him. Again, he did not blame her.

They had breakfast in a small roadside restaurant and, on the way out, he picked up an Atlanta paper. She was an okay driver, but he could not sleep, as he had known. After trying for a while, he gave it up and started to read the paper. Nothing about the flu in Washington. Nothing about the president, the vice president. Nothing about anything in particular. He flipped pages and then stopped.

The Russians had announced a major flu epidemic in the USSR. The strain had not yet been isolated and meanwhile they were curtailing travel to limit the spread of the disease, said to be the most virulent ever to surface.

He read the scant item again, then read it aloud and watched her knuckles go white as she gripped the steering wheel harder.

"That's it, isn't it?"

She nodded. "Yuri thinks so. We all think so. They can't hide the fact of death on that scale, they had to announce something."

"How much time will it take them?"

"I don't know. How many have they inoculated? How long ago? We don't know. Fever starts within hours, but it takes twenty-four hours for the illness to become really bad, and then two or three days before recovery even begins. People can die any time after the inoculation, a few hours, two days, three days . . ."

He folded the paper carefully and put it on the floor in the back of the van. Neither spoke again until they came to a stop at a mall in Raleigh.

She started to get out and he caught her wrist. "You know they have Werther under wraps. If you call him, they'll trace the call. You know that."

She nodded. "How long does it take?"

"Not as long as you think. They'll be ready, waiting."

"I have to call him," she whispered. There was still a chance that he had convinced the government people that they had to distribute it themselves, that it was the only way to avert war. She had to try.

"If anyone stalls you, says he's in the john or something, asks you to wait, hang up. You can try again in a few minutes. But don't wait on the line."

"Yes, I know."

"Do you have a signal arranged? Something that will be quick?"

"No more than a second or two."

He chewed his lip, hating it, not trusting it. Finally he released her wrist and watched her walk to the pay telephone.

She dialed the number, deposited coins, and waited. For what seemed a long time it did not even ring and the line was filled with noise. Maybe the phones were still out. Then it rang. She counted and knew they were tracing it. Saul would have answered instantly, expecting her call now, ready for it. She closed her eyes, eight . . . nine . . .

"Hello."

"Saul, it's Lyle. Are you all right?"

"My dear! How good to hear your voice. We've had the most terrible storm —"

"Welcome, chaos," she whispered, her eyes closed hard, and she hung up.

"Come on, let's get the hell out of here!" Lasater started to pull her away from the booth.

"Not yet. I have to make one more call."

"From another phone. Down the road somewhere. Come on!"

This time he drove. He stopped at a gas station that had a phone booth. "I'll fill it up while you call. It isn't that number again, is it?" She shook her head. "Good. I'm going in that little store over there and buy some stuff to eat. No more restaurants for us, no more public appearances. Come on over there when you're finished."

It was five minutes before ten. She listened to the distant phone ringing, ringing, and then stop ringing.

"Yes?" Carmen's voice.

She took a deep breath, heard a waver in her voice when she said, "Carmen, they have Saul and Yuri. I mailed the envelopes. Saul said you have to carry through."

"Oh God. Are you all right?"

"Yes. But they may have traced a call I just made to Pennsylvania."

"Okay. Hide, Lyle. Stay out of their hands if you can. I'll see you when it's over. I love you, Lyle."

"I love you!" she cried. "Be careful. Carmen, be careful!"

Everyone kept telling her to stay out of their hands. They thought she might tell everything if they caught her, and she was not certain she would not talk. If they said, watch us do this to Saul, watch him sweat, writhe . . . Lasater would tell them everything, she thought suddenly. He would have to just to save himself, get a promise from them that he could have the inoculation. He might know they would lie to him about it, but he would have to try one last time. She understood that. He had worked with her through the night, but if they failed, if they were picked up, he would have to think first of himself, pretend to believe any promise they made to him. Would he remember which post offices they had stopped at? She was afraid he might.

She found him in the store, at the check-out counter, and shook her head when he asked if she wanted anything. They were going out the door when they heard a siren, not far away, and then another more distant one.

Abruptly he turned and nearly pushed her inside the store again. "We forgot cookies for the kids. You go pick them out." Thank God she wasn't stupid, he thought, when she glanced outside and then turned quickly and went to the back of the store. A police cruiser was passing slowly, the cop in the passenger seat studying the cars parked in the small lot.

Okay, he thought darkly. They didn't know the make of the car yet; that was a plus. But they would have her description, and that was most definitely not a plus. At least Werther had had enough sense to have Ohio plates on the van, another plus. The fact that local cops were already searching was bad, very bad. The state police would cover highways leading from town; the county sheriff's department probably would take care of the country roads. That could be very bad indeed. To them an out-of-state license plate might be cause enough to stop the van. So he would switch, he decided.

He was grim when they got inside the van again. "You'll have to stay in the back," he said brusquely. "I'll get a few tools, and road maps for this county, anything I can find for south of here. You keep out of sight."

"You think they're already putting up roadblocks?"

"You bet your sweet ass. It's been over twenty minutes, plenty of time if they were ready to start the machine. And they were."

She went to the rear of the van and closed the curtain between them and made no comment at his next stops. He removed a license plate from a car parked at the edge of the vast lot at a shopping mall, the area where the employees had to park. With any luck, he thought, no one would notice until the next day; it would be dark, he hoped, by the time the clerk, or whoever, knocked off, came out to get in the old buggy, head for the stable. He backed into a parking space bordered by hedges, and there put on the stolen plate. Now he felt better.

His other purchases included a compass and a dozen county

maps. He studied one carefully and when he left town he went by way of city streets to county lanes, to a dirt road that wound westward. Once he glimpsed a police car parked behind a sign. In the distance there were sirens now and then for a short while. Pulling some poor sucker over, he thought and grinned. He pitied anyone from Pennsylvania heading south that day.

He stopped finally in a deep wood, hidden under a canopy of pine branches. She slipped into her own seat again.

"I could drive now," she said.

He shook his head. "We'll go on this afternoon. Do most of our driving at night from now on. But first some sleep. I want to give you the address of my parents, a place you can go if we get separated and you're still able to go anywhere. Tell my old man the truth. He likes the truth." He wrote out the address, handed the slip of paper to her.

"You think they're going to catch us, don't you?"

"Yeah, I think so. They've done everything but call out the Marines, and they'll probably get around to that too. I'm counting on your ignorance, honey. They know you're dumb. You don't know shit about hiding; that may save us. They won't look for you on dirt roads out in the boonies. I hope that's how they figure you. If we do see a roadblock and can't avoid it, we split. I stick with the car, you hoof it to the nearest place you can find to dig in. They'll go after the car. I'll tell them you ran out on me in Raleigh."

"What will they do to you?"

He yawned. "You must be kidding. They really hate it if their own people give them trouble. They'll look on me as one of them, one who went bad. Eventually I'll probably talk, and then I'll join the list of the missing. Simple."

"You think they'll kill you?"

He was eyeing the back of the van dubiously. The floor was carpeted; it would have to do. His coat would help some, and the blanket. He worked his way over the gear shift, to the rear.

"No, they won't kill me. They'll ask questions, day after day after day. I can imagine the scenario: year after year getting a little grayer, more stooped, more tired, while they come in fresh-cheeked and shiny-eyed and rub it in."

"You've decided you would use it?"

"Yeah, I'd try it."

And he would tell them everything, sooner rather than later, she thought distantly. His last chance at getting it, he would think, and he would make a deal with them. And then they would renege. In her mind some lines of T. S. Eliot's repeated over and over: *I grow old . . . I grow old . . . I shall wear the bottoms of my trousers rolled.*

She thought of the gun in her pocket and rejected it. Not now. Not after he had helped her. He was rearranging the bags of food, the empty boxes they had not got rid of. She swung around and joined him, sat back on her heels.

"Lasater, I have it. I can give it to you."

▣ 31 ▣

AT TEN-THIRTY Rawleigh was ordered to bring most of his men back to Washington, along with Werther/Markham. Only the computer specialists were left behind, still trying to unravel the program. In the CIA building Saul was locked in a room along with two fresh interrogators. Down the corridor Seymour Oliver was undergoing interrogation; farther down Dan Malone was still being questioned.

Scanlon and Rawleigh attended a three-hour conference with various secretaries, generals, admirals, and congressmen. It became a shouting match very quickly.

At one, Seymour Oliver was taken away to confer with the president at a secret location.

Rawleigh sat in his office at four and cursed silently. He had got up with a headache; minute by minute it had grown worse. The woman was still missing; none of the others had been located. No one knew if the letters they had found in Philadelphia were the end of that. No one knew if other letters had been mailed. None had been mailed from Raleigh, where she had stopped to make her phone call. The reports from Russia indicated that the flu epidemic was rampant in Moscow, in Leningrad, in several other major cities, that it had spread to the armed forces. Here, the vice president was seriously ill, running a high fever; the secretary of the treasury was ill; two generals had become ill . . . The Joint Chiefs were in chaotic disorder, screaming at each other like madmen. If they caught the rest of the gang of terrorists, they would go forward with their plan, but not until then, not until they found the samples the letters talked about. No announcements, no leaks . . . And the reporters were like piranhas, aware that something was happening, schooling hungrily, pressing everyone, offering rewards . . .

He turned on the closed-circuit television and studied Werther/Markham who was sitting upright in a straight chair, calm, at ease, only slightly tired from his all-night ordeal. Doerring was in bed somewhere, exhausted, feverish, the two new men were already showing twitches of weariness. The old man was serene.

He flipped to the other room where Dan Malone was being questioned. His style was different; he had been talkative from the start, only he never said anything. He bantered with his interrogators, kidded them, told them jokes, told them of his various travels throughout the world. And said nothing.

He too looked as if he had been sleeping regularly, eating regularly, got in his daily nap . . . There were slight circles under his eyes, and he was not quite as quick as he had been, had begun to stammer now and then, but it was an insignificant change.

Rawleigh turned the set off and drummed his fingers on his desk. Fifty-fifty, he thought. Not good odds, not good enough, but, by God, those two men had gambled. Others had gambled. And when the gamble paid off, it paid big, very, very big. But not for Ralph Wilders, who had been the secretary of defense. For him it had not paid off.

Scanlon was ready to bolt, he knew. This was turning out to be too much for him. He would snatch himself some of the stuff and run, stare at it until he got up his nerve to give it a go. Who else would leave, or yield to the irresistible promise of the serum? He began to sort them out, and when he finished, he knew the government would fall apart. It was too big, no one could handle this. With the president hiding, the vice president maybe dying, maybe not, who would take over? His fingers were no longer tapping, had become very quiet as he stared at the far wall thinking. The military would seize the government, he thought with incredulity. It would come to that.

The wall was moving toward him, back again. He blinked and shook his head, making it ache unbearably. His mouth was dry, his eyes burned. He had a fever, he thought fretfully, now of all times, he was coming down with something. Probably the same cold that Alex Radek had been suffering from. He closed his eyes for a minute or two, but when he opened them again, he found that he was having trouble focusing. It was time to go home, he thought distinctly. Let them bomb each other to hell and be gone, he wanted to go home. He had not been ill for years, fifteen years, twenty? He could not remember the last cold he had caught, the last time he had run a fever. Damn Alex Radek, he thought, damn his eyes; he almost hoped he had died during the day. He stood up shakily, went to his washroom and drank down a glass of water, then another.

Go home, he thought again. Aunt Jane would know what to do. If he had to die, he wanted to die at home, where his father had died, his grandfather had died, where all his family went to die, to be born, to live . . . He pulled on his coat and walked from his private office into the anteroom where Mathew Sedgehorn was speaking on the phone. Mathew looked at him in surprise.

"Going home," he said, walking across the room.

"But sir, Mr. Scanlon has called for another meeting in an hour."

"Tell him I'm going home." He walked out, let the door close itself after him.

Mathew was already dialing Mr. Scanlon's number.

At six the rumor went around that nearly every man who had gone to the Pennsylvania hideout had come down with a mysterious disease. They were taken to the communicable disease wing of Walter Reed Hospital and put under top secret security. Those who were still well began a debriefing that was to go on through the night.

The rumor started life no bigger than a whisper of air, but soon swirled to hurricane size and strength; no one in official Washington failed to hear several versions of it every fifteen minutes or so.

The first leaks made the eleven o'clock newscasts. The Russian flu was devastating Washington, the report went, and there were hints of biological warfare.

At twelve the attorney general announced to staff that the president was returning within three or four hours. His major speech writers were to prepare texts for several alternate announcements. It was not known yet which one he would decide to deliver.

Belatedly the interrogators were pulled out of Saul's room and he was left alone for the first time. Immediately he stretched out on the narrow sofa in the office and went to sleep.

The computer men were taken out of the Pennsylvania laboratory and the building was quarantined until a team of experts could be assembled to track down the source of the disease.

The radio stations had been off the air for hours. There had been no follow-up story about the flu that was raging in Washington. Lyle turned the knob back and forth, finally gave it up. Lasater was sleeping in the back of the van while she drove; now and then she could hear him groan or whisper or make an incoherent sound. His fever was very high; he was having fever dreams. She hoped they were not as frightening as hers had been, but from the sounds he made she suspected they were, or even more so.

She was desperately tired, but dared not stop now. They were so close to his parents' home, another two hours, three at the most, and she could hand him over to their care, and go someplace and sleep and sleep. She jerked her eyes wide open and turned on the radio again, welcoming even the static as a diversion. If it had not been for him, she would not have made it, she knew. He was wise about roadblocks, about back roads, county roads, dirt roads, when to get back on a real highway. He was mumbling again. He needed a bed, cool water, his face wiped off with a cool cloth . . . She drove on, forcing herself to concentrate on the road, on staying on her side, on approaching lights that came very rarely now. Today the envelopes would be delivered, the samples would be delivered, people would start using it. Today was the end of the world. The beginning of a new world. Long live the world, she whispered to herself.

She stopped at the condominium at six in the morning. The air was cold and still, the sky clear with stars shining although the sun was rising also. Pelicans flew toward the gulf; a heron lifted from the lawn before the massive building; no person was in sight anywhere.

When she got out of the van the earth seemed to continue to move under her. She was uncertain in her walk, steadied herself with a railing that had been designed for just that purpose. There was a sleepy-eyed security man who watched her suspiciously as she called the Lasater apartment, waited for an answer.

He was even more suspicious when she went back out and brought in Lasater, virtually holding him upright, supporting his weight, guiding him.

"He's been very ill," she said. "He's still weak from it."

He did not offer to help; rather, he backed away from Lasater and watched closely until they were inside the elevator, the door closed. Lasater clutched the rail in the elevator, weaving back and forth.

"I dreamed you cut your hair all the way off," he said, in a surprisingly clear voice. "I cried. It's so soft. I thought it would be, back at the coast, I thought it would be so soft." He closed his eyes and leaned his head against the wall.

Mr. and Mrs. Lasater were in their nightclothes. His hair was tousled from sleep, but she had run a comb through hers. They were white-headed, suntanned to a deep rich brown, and frightened-looking.

"Is he running from someone?" Mr. Lasater asked, helping her get him inside. "This way. There's an extra room."

"Yes, he's wanted. He's very ill. He needs care . . ."

"We'll take care of him until he's well," Mrs. Lasater said, following closely, her gaze on her son, worry and fear creasing her face. "Is he dying? He needs a doctor, the hospital."

"That won't help him. Please, just put him to bed, try to ease his pain, his fever."

When they got him to the bed, and she no longer had to support him, she swayed, and found herself being guided to the other bedroom, their room. Mr. Lasater was firm in his insistence that she sleep for a bit. She sank down to their bed gratefully and did not remember stretching out, closing her eyes.

Jeremy Troy sat at his desk in the Oval Office and scowled at Seymour Oliver, whom he had known for nearly all his life. They had gone to the same summer camps, the same prep school, had gone on to Harvard together. Hell, they had rowed on the same team. He had believed a man could trust someone he had known that long, someone who had rowed with him. The Oval Office was crowded, but he ignored most of them and concentrated on Seymour Oliver, and on Werther/Markham, whatever he was called, when he arrived. They were the only ones in the room who were not threatening to go out with a stroke any minute.

Werther bowed respectfully and waited in silence as President Troy studied him. They had brought his clothes, had allowed him a shower and shave that morning. He looked rested, and he looked calm, as if he was the one in charge, and he already knew the outcome.

"Seymour suggested I ask you directly how you infected those men in your place. And how you intend to distribute samples of your serum to the entire country."

General Strand coughed and Yancy moved in closer; otherwise everyone was quiet for the moment. Werther/Markham glanced at his watch. It was going on nine.

"If your mail has been delivered yet, you'll discover our delivery system," Werther/Markham said. "I believe the White House was on the list."

Clarendon raced to the door, left. No one else moved.

"As to how I infected your people who invaded my property, I didn't. If they stole my soap, or lotions, or shaving creams, anything of the sort and used them, they infected themselves,

I'm afraid. I did not invite them to use my personal toilet articles."

"My God," someone across the room said. He moved away from the window where he had been standing, came around the attorney general. It was Hanford Wilkes. "You mixed it with a solvent? Something to carry it into the lymphatic system?"

"Exactly," Werther/Markham said. "Hanford Wilkes? How do you do."

"I thought soap was antibacterial," someone objected.

"This isn't bacterial, it's RNA, and our soap is exquisitely pure, completely organic, a perfect medium for it."

Scanlon and Senator Fullerton were whispering together. The senator said, "We think we can stop the mail deliveries today, if we act immediately, Mr. President. It will take an executive order . . ."

Werther/Markham said gently, "The mail has been delivered up and down the entire East Coast, in most of the interior. It's much too late, I'm certain, to stop enough to matter."

"Issue a warning, then. Say it's germ warfare, terrorists have sent it out to kill the American people. You can stop this right here, Jeremy! But you have to do it now!"

Werther/Markham was eyeing him curiously. "You'd rather go to war?"

"Nobody wants war! But this may be the last chance we'll have in this generation to beat them down to their knees!"

Others were talking now, some were shouting. Wilkes was talking to Oliver; Werther was standing before the wide desk, partly facing the room, watching, listening. He turned back to the president.

"It's too late," he repeated firmly. "It's out and it can't be put back in. You can either disown the whole thing, or you can announce it for what it is, offer this country's help to all people to make it available worldwide."

Clarendon rushed back in then, carrying a small box containing samples of the soaps and lotions, each individually wrapped, the size that hotels issue to guests. He dumped the box out on the president's desk.

"It's out," Werther said once more. "There are explicit warnings on the back of each package, but I doubt that many people will pay very much attention to them."

There was a scramble for the packets. Senator Fullerton read part of the warning aloud: "This product will cause a serious reaction in the human body. There will be fever and chills that will last for a period of one to three days. Those who recover will find they are immune to bacterial and viral diseases, to diseases of aging. Approximately half of those who use this product will die of the fever." He looked at Werther venomously. "You're killing them! You're an insane mass murderer!"

"Would it be more sane to kill them with bombs?"

"You'll hang for this! Hanging's too good for you —"

"Harry!" President Troy's voice was sharp. "Knock it off, will you? How many of those samples did your people put in the mail?"

"We were aiming for five million in the States, and of course there are mailings in Europe, Asia, South America . . . Nearly ten million altogether, I think. I haven't received any figures yet."

"Five million!" President Troy repeated. He was ashen-faced. "And half of them will die?"

"They won't all use the products," Saul said. "From our previous mailings of samples, our own studies, we think that one out of five may use them right away, perhaps one out of six. People put them down, forget them, toss them out. Of course, articles will start appearing simultaneously, and they may cause more usage, or perhaps less. We had no way of knowing in advance."

"One out of five. A million. And half of them . . . God help us! And this, this immunity is passed sexually? Isn't that what your information sheets claim?"

He nodded.

"We can isolate all those who use the stuff," Fullerton said fiercely. "We can find them and put them in camps, for their own protection —"

He leaned on the president's desk, pushed the samples aside. "You can't back out now, Jeremy! For God's sake, don't go chicken on us now!"

"Fuck off, Harry! Don't you understand it's a whole new game! Everything's changed!"

"Why? Last week you were with us one hundred percent! Now you're waving a white flag. Why?"

"Last week I didn't think there was an alternative. They were going to push the button, or we were. Now, no one's going to push it. That's what's different!"

"Right now we've got a window! They're vulnerable, they're helpless with so many of their people sick. Twenty-four hours, that's all it would take! Jesus Christ, Jeremy! Twenty-four hours!"

"Get the fuck out of here!"

Fullerton stamped to the door, paused to yell at Werther, "You're not free yet, old man! I want you, and I'm going to get you! Just you wait and see!"

Before the door was closed behind him, President Troy began to give orders. "Wilkes, take these two with you, prepare a detailed statement of effects, what to do for those stricken, what to expect, the works. Brief the Surgeon General, NIH. General Strand, report back to the Joint Chiefs and tell them we're preparing a mass inoculation of our armed forces just as fast as the stuff can be prepared and shipped. You're going to need more doctors for the duration of the illness. It will have to be done in sections, figure out the optimum method. God, I have to call the Premier! I wonder if that son of a bitch has already had his."

When the office was clear, except for his aide, Clarendon, he counted the samples on his desk.

"How many were there originally?"

"Twenty. Are some missing?"

He laughed and tossed a sample of shaving lotion to Clarendon. "We have nine now, counting that one." He examined them briefly, then slipped a bar of soap into his pocket. "Well, let's get on with it."

◙ 32 ◙

IN DENVER, Mavis Oblatney heard the mail hit the floor in the hall and shuffled out in her robe and slippers to collect it. Bills. A slick advertising pamphlet. A sample of something. She carried them back to the kitchen where Mike, finished with breakfast, was tying his boots, ready to go to work.

"Anything?"

"Nope. The usual." She glanced at the advertising pamphlet. Expensive furniture, tableware . . . Nothing for them. The bills could wait for payday. She knew the amount of each one without opening them. She unwrapped the soap sample. It smelled nice. As soon as Mike left she would have her shower, get to work at ten . . . She yawned and put the soap down, gathered up the ad, and the soap wrapper, and tossed them into the trash can.

At ten minutes past ten, in the department store where she worked, she heard that the soap samples were all poison, or an immortality treatment, or part of a conspiracy . . .

In Buffalo, Stuart Poulson hooted with laughter when he read the warning on the hand lotion sample. "Hey, listen to this! You'll be immune to all kinds of disease if you use this junk!"

Ann Sneed took the sample from his hand and read it for herself. She squeezed some of the lotion from the tube and, laughing, chased him through the apartment to the bedroom where she smeared it on his cheeks, his neck, his stomach, his penis. Laughing, they tumbled back into bed together.

In Los Angeles, Terry Grimes put the lotion on her dining room table and considered it. She had heard the president's message that morning, and here was one of the samples he had talked about. She was sixty, lived alone, and wondered if she cared one way or the other. If Nicky were here with her, now that would be different. Eight years too late for Nicky. The president had warned people not to use the stuff, to turn it in if they received it. The FDA had not approved it. She laughed at that one. The FDA! All morning the sample remained on the dining room table that had not been used for eight years. In midafternoon, holding a glass of gin with one ice cube in it, she considered it yet again. Hand lotion with a nice fragrance. There was no one here to take care of her when she became ill, she thought, and shrugged that away. She could take care of herself. But was there any point in it? That was the hard one. She wandered out, sipping her gin. It was midnight when she finally rubbed the lotion on both hands, over her elbows.

In Detroit, Eugene Jones skipped first period, U.S. History, to break into old man Henson's apartment. Everyone knew the old fool kept money there, he never went to the bank, and always had cash. Eugene searched rapidly and found nothing. There were only two rooms, the search did not take long. He looked over the few pieces of mail, pocketed the sample of after-shave junk, and fled with nothing more than that to show for his trouble. His old lady would give him hell for skipping again, he'd have to forge an excuse . . . That night when he cleaned up to go out, he used the after-shave lotion, decided he didn't like the smell, and washed it off again. He kept smelling it right up until his fever tumbled him into nightmares.

In Lexington, Susan Kreschner put the sample down in the middle of the table and said dramatically, "There is our salvation!"

Her sisters, Leigh and Nancy, looked bored; her brother, Walter, did not look up at all. He was reading the paper. Their parents had left them alone for the first time ever; Susan, the youngest, was sixteen.

"It's what they were talking about on television," Susan said confidently. "Really. Look at the warning on it. It's the hand lotion they warned everyone not to use."

Walter snatched it up and examined it, read the label. "Where'd it come from?"

"It was in the mail. Just like the president said. Addressed to Occupant. That's us, or at least me."

"You crazy or something? You're not going to touch this stuff!"

"I knew you would take that attitude," she said and held up both hands. "I already used it. My plan is to be the first girl in the area to have it, and then go into business. I can sell a fuck for ten, twenty dollars . . ."

Walter knocked his chair over rising, coming at her, his face dark with anger. She ran away laughing at him.

"I will, though! Just you wait and see!"

In Atlanta, Bob and Martha Alward examined the soap without touching it, then pushed it into a plastic bag, using the wrapper, being careful not to get any on their fingers.

"What will we do with it?" Martha asked.

"Throw it away, say nothing to anyone. If we turn it in like they said on television, they'll ask questions, pry, come back again and again. Toss it out."

"Maybe we should just put it away until they tell us more about it . . ."

"You crazy or something? No more questions! Ever!" The ghost of his first wife drifted between them, invisible, silent, but there. He picked up the plastic bag and threw it into the garbage can. Later, when he went out for his walk, she pulled it out again, washed it off, and put the package away carefully in her jewelry drawer.

In Missoula, Sylvia Loos looked at the soap, studied her face in the mirror, and, sighing, threw the soap away and never gave it another thought. Her cleaning lady found it the next morning, recognized it for what it was, and took it home where her boyfriend melted it down along with half a dozen bars of regular soap and sold them all for five dollars each. He made fifty bars of soap altogether. They had not read the article that claimed that any temperature above one hundred seven degrees F. would destroy the RNA.

In San Francisco, Jimmie Lee and his girlfriend, Doris, tossed a coin to see which one would use the lotion first. The other would be nurse, and in turn be nursed. If she died, Jimmie Lee promised, he would, kill himself. Gently he helped her smooth it over her skin.

In Boston, Joseph Gartman slapped his wife Hilda when she suggested they turn it in, as the president had asked people to do. Turn in a gold mine? Turn in eternity? Turn in pills, medicines, hospitals, doctors? Turn in their whole goddam future? The problem was when, he brooded. Not this week. He had that deal with Horstt. Not next week either. Contracts would be back from the lawyers, there was the luncheon meeting to celebrate the new acquisition . . .

In Paris, in Rome, in London, Buenos Aires, Rio, La Paz, Mexico City, Beirut, Johannesburg, Madras . . . The same scenes played over and over, the same decisions were being made, the gamble accepted . . .

The next day the dying began.

◨ 33 ◨

LYLE DROVE aimlessly. Mr. and Mrs. Lasater had asked her to stay with them until their son recovered, but there had been no conviction in their voices. A friend of his, they had implied, could be no friend of theirs. They had asked no questions; she had volunteered nothing, but they had watched television, read the papers; they knew. She had left after one glance at Lasater, who had been delirious.

Now she was driving nowhere in particular. They hoped he would die, she knew, and pitied them and him. Once she stopped on the beach road, parked, and walked for several hours. The sun was shining, but a bitter wind blew and it was very cold; no one else was walking.

She listened to the radio most of the first day. They were hashing it out over and over, repeating themselves endlessly. Late in the day they began to have panels of experts. Economists, doctors, educators, politicians . . . When she turned off the radio she could not remember what she had heard.

That night when it became dark, she was in northern Florida, near no town. She found a parking spot away from the highway and crawled into the sleeping bag in the rear of the van and slept. At dawn she was driving again, her mind still blank, yesterday a blank. Sleep had been fitful, dream-ridden.

She would need food, she thought suddenly, and realized she could not remember when she had eaten. At the Lasaters' she had had something; she could not remember what.

Food. And a stove to cook on, a pan or two, dishes. Blue jeans and boots. Warm jacket. She might as well spend the paper money; everything was going to smash, very soon no one would want it. She shook her head at the idea, but could not deny that she believed it. She turned on the radio again, and this time she listened.

". . . orderly sequence. Hospitals, police stations, schools will all be used to dispense the serum. An effort will be made to ensure that no more than one family member at a time receive the inoculation —" She switched the station.

". . . riots. In Rome the crowd has continued to swell, but it is an orderly crowd, not a mob. The Pope will speak in two hours —"

". . . martial law. The fires are still out of control, but the National Guard has manned the fire-fighting equipment now —"

". . . repeat, not. Do not allow any child under eight to touch the lotions or the soap. Seriously ill people should not use the material until they are recovered. If you develop a fever, go to bed, rest, take fluids. During the first days of the illness aspirins should be used to fight the fever —"

She turned it off. She was on an interstate highway. The sun was behind her now; she was driving west. It was as good a direction as any.

She stopped in Tallahassee for gas and found a supermarket. There had not been a run on food yet, but there would be. When people began to realize that truckers would be ill and dying, airlines not functioning, trains stalled because the crews were feverish . . . She stocked up on everything she could think of for the next month. She bought a camp stove and fuel, and an icebox and ice. At a shopping center she bought jeans and shirts, a sweater, jacket, warm socks . . . Her last purchase was a coffeepot that plugged into the cigarette lighter. It was on sale, half price, after-Christmas clearance. The clerk was flushed-looking. Lyle nearly ran from the store, shoved the coffeepot back with the clutter of boxes and bags, and began driving again.

Now she knew why she had purchased the kinds of things she had. She would not enter another city if she could avoid it. By tomorrow it would be chaotic.

". . . special prosecutor. The investigation will proceed along the lines suggested earlier by Senator Fullerton. To date there has been no agreement about who the special prosecutor should be. We switch now to Stanley Wyman in Washington for more on this development —"

". . . toll continues to rise. The official count is now nine hundred forty-seven. In Topeka the entire family of Jackson Merrick —"

In Pensacola she found a stereo shop that was open, and bought a tape deck and many tapes.

Tristan and Isolde got her across Louisiana.

". . . regret this inconvenience, and we all hope our disruption will be of short duration. Meanwhile, all you guys and gals out there, you take care, you hear? —"

There was no open gas station in Beaumont. She waited all night, and when someone appeared, he was a policeman. He gave her directions to a station that would be open from ten until two that afternoon. He advised her to get a couple of five-gallon cans and fill them, also.

She was charged four dollars a gallon for the gas they pumped into her car, and five dollars a gallon for the gas they put in the two five-gallon cans. It had started.

Under the carpet in the back of the van, under the metal floor, there was a box with twenty thousand dollars in gold and silver coins. Saul had insisted that everyone have a stake in gold and silver. Spend the paper first, as long as people will take it, and then use the real money, he had said. Right again, she thought, and realized how little she had thought about him, about Carmen, the others. Maybe they had all been picked up, had given themselves up. She had an address in San Francisco where she could go, to await Carmen, or orders, or something. She would not go there.

Stabat Mater and the *Pachelbel Canon* got her to San Antonio.

". . . and Adam lived a hundred and thirty years, and he

begat a son in his own likeness . . . And the days of Adam after he had begotten Seth were eight hundred. All the days of Seth were nine hundred and twelve. All the days of Enos were nine hundred and five; Mahalaleel, eight hundred ninety-five; Jared, nine hundred sixty-two! I say to you that the Lord gave man those long years in the beginning and He took them away in His wrath! Now He has given them back to us! Praise the Lord, brothers and sisters! Praise —"

Would they all be imprisoned for life? Would they be executed?

". . . toll now stands at sixteen thousand —"

". . . this insanity. There will be a return to order rather quickly when the government begins distribution. The plan that is evolving is designed to space out the inoculations over the next ten years, you see, and that will prevent another —"

That day she saw the first bumper sticker: FUCK THE FLU! Later she saw another: GIVE A FUCK! PASS IT ON!

". . . say how sorry I am for being late. I was busy at the office, trying to sell my stock in the Dispos-A-Diaper Company —"

". . . of course, doctors won't be put out of business. There will always be accidents, broken bones, the like. The people I'm concerned about are the children's furniture producers, baby food companies, infant and children's clothing. And elementary school teachers, on up to the college level. We anticipate a lot of new entrants to the universities —"

The Tales of Hoffman saw her through to El Paso.

". . . forty thousand. In Boston today the police arrested nine men and women for what was called public prostitution. All nine had recovered from the fever and were engaging in the act of prostitution for amounts in the five hundred dollar range and up —"

In Albuquerque the toll jumped. Two hundred thousand or more.

". . . explain it. Many people waited a day or two to hear what was happening before they used the stuff. Some of it was late in getting delivered, no doubt. If it is true that five million samples were distributed, and if it is true that the mortality rate is one half, it will get much, much worse. In every state the National Guard is being put on the alert to help with this crisis, but, of course, many of those men also received samples. The government urges you, if you have those samples on hand, do not use them! The crisis is worldwide —"

What would they do when they ran out of space at the cemetery? She had to pull off the road to wait for her vision to clear. For the next three days she remained in New Mexico, away from any radio station, away from people. Then she started to drive again.

She yearned for a night of unbroken sleep. Every night was the same: she could fall asleep, but she could not stay asleep more than a few hours. She jerked wide awake again and again, with no memory of dreams or nightmares. She wished she could take a pill, sink into oblivion for twenty-four hours, not think, not hear the wind in the window, the radio voices that echoed in her head after the radio was turned off, not hear her own body noises. Simple oblivion. She did not feel especially tired; she felt virtually nothing. She had withdrawn so far that she could not find herself again. She was out there watching, waiting. Maybe she never would come back. Maybe that was the only safe way.

Beethoven's symphonies got her to Phoenix. She did not turn on the radio, listened instead to the Mormon Tabernacle Choir singing Bach cantatas.

In Phoenix many businesses were closed, people looked like zombies. They were in shock, she thought, and drove on.

Las Vegas, Reno, Alturas. She stopped in Alturas and called John Donleavy to ask if his house on the coast was available. It was. He would turn on the electricity, get some wood stacked, leave the key under the loose board on the bottom step.

Now her movements all seemed to have been planned although she had not thought about a destination, had not used a map. She did not even know how long she had been driving.

For the past few days, ever since Phoenix, she had been using the silver for her purchases. In Alturas no one had received a sample, but they had been cut off from the world effectively by the failure of the truckers to keep them supplied. She had to pay ten dollars a gallon for gas. When the attendant saw that she had silver, he gave her a different figure: four dollars eight cents, total. She had not seen a paper, had no idea what the current price of silver was. She paid, and that night when she stopped, she got out some of the gold coins and a hundred dollars in silver.

She would need a poncho, rain pants, rain boots . . . Now that she knew where she was going, she wanted to be there, perhaps never to leave again. She would want her own bedding, towels . . . She drove and made her list and then she listened to Debussy.

Klamath Falls, Chemult, Eugene.

". . . open again in a week or ten days. The Emergency Mortgage Act survived its first hurdle today when the spokesman for the Savings and Loan Associations conceded that the organization would not challenge it. And today the New York State Supreme Court ruled that the victims of the serum are not accidental death cases, but suicides. The attorney for the class action suit has already announced that the decision will be appealed immediately to the Supreme Court, as soon as that body reconvenes. In other financial —"

". . . thirty million people have died in wars since nineteen forty-five, and twenty million Russians —"

". . . hospitals. They cannot accept any more patients. Go to bed —"

". . . town of Andrea where the mass burial —"

". . . estimated that in the Soviet Union that figure is approaching five mil—"

She shopped in Eugene where the department store was open half days only. She consulted the silver announcement board before she paid for her purchases. When the clerk asked where she was going, she said she was going home.

Nothing had changed in the house, or outside it. Hard rain pounded the roof, the surf sounded close by and loud, the wood stove emitted billows of smoke before it settled down, everything felt clammy and cold.

It was nearly eleven at night before the house was heated enough to open the door to the bedroom, let some of the warmth enter. She had unpacked the van in the rain, and had her clothes draped on chairs drying. She had bought a warm robe and slippers, and now sat near the stove sipping coffee. The world seemed very far away.

Now she surrendered herself to timelessness. Every day she walked the beaches, or climbed the hills until she was exhausted, until her muscles throbbed, until she was certain that this night she would be able to sleep through.

The eagles returned; she watched them briefly, turned and walked away. After that she avoided that section of the hills. She avoided the charred spot where the other house had burned down. If she saw people on the beach, she always turned and walked in the opposite direction.

When her food ran out, she shopped in the village. It was like attending a funeral; she bought enough to last a long time. There were few choices, many of the shelves were empty; she did not care what she ate. At the check-out counter she saw stacks of news magazines. She picked up one of each, and bought a newspaper also.

"You need stamps for the milk and the coffee," the checker said.

"I'll put them back. I don't have stamps."

"You better sign up pretty fast. It'll be everything by next month. Gas rationing starts Monday, you know."

The checker was a survivor; she had the bright eyes, the vivid coloring of those who survived. Eddy, the middle-aged man in an apron who swept up, helped load groceries, he was another survivor. Lyle drove off thinking of Eddy. Would he be sweeping up in ten years, twenty years, a hundred years? She felt her muscles tense with anger at the thought.

The storms came with the frequency she remembered; sometimes she stood on her cliff and watched, sometimes she was inside, sometimes on the beach, or on one of the hills.

It took her many days to read all the magazines and the newspaper. The government was not sending out checks; there was a moratorium on credit collection, on the use of paper money. People had to sign each week for ration coupons and scrip, entire families had to be present in order to be issued both. Deserters who reported back to their units within thirty days would not be prosecuted. The list of senators and representatives who had died was long, and growing; there was no government, only executive orders. The vice president had died; the president had promised not to use the serum during the crisis. Daniel Malone had been named the president's press secretary, and Seymour Oliver his science advisor . . .

There were pleas for volunteer survivors to come forward, to assist in caring for the ill, to perform police duties, to form day-care centers . . .

She stopped reading midway through an article that described the worldwide chaos that had paralyzed nation after nation, caused governments to fall, threatened new horrors if the nuclear facilities were not maintained . . .

She began to take her notebook with her on her walks; she wrote in it on the beach, or under a tree, on the cliffs. One day she saw a group of young people playing on the beach, flying kites, throwing sand at each other. Survivors, unmistakably so. A second group, larger, chased them with sticks and even a rifle. That had started. Saul had predicted that the survivors would be at terrible risk for a time. Those who had not yet used the serum, those who feared it, might try to stop its use, might try to harm, even kill, those who had survived.

The next time she went to the village, the store was closed. The gas station was closed. She found two old men in the tackle shop. They glared at her.

"They're all leaving," one of them said. "Won't be no tourists for a long time, no way to make a living here."

"If I was you, lady," the other one said brusquely, "I'd get out too. Your kind ain't too popular around here."

She drove away slowly. It was time to go, but where? To do what? Start a day-care center? She shook her head angrily. That would simply be another dodge, she knew, and the time had come for her to stop refusing her responsibility. She thought longingly of tramping through the woods with her camera, turning her back on the world again until it had become sane once more. She had reached the campsite overlooking the lagoon and abruptly turned into the drive. She parked and walked to the rail and stood looking at the water far below. A new storm was blowing in, driving the surf high up on the beach, howling through the rocks, but the storm lacked the fury of the winter storms; it was an imitation storm, a feeble attempt after all. Spring had come.

In her mind's eye there came a glimpse of her New York apartment, empty, waiting for her return. She could finish the history of Saul's group. She rejected that also. Another year, another decade even.

All her adult life had revolved around history, and then art, humanity's two attempts to conquer time. We used art, she thought, to carry our present into the future. And we used history to try to give order to what was always chaos. Always. We used history in an attempt to unite memory, to make our collective memory tangible, give it permanence, bestow it with authority, as if the act of writing, the magic of print was enough to make human memory in all its frailty somehow real, to make our existence now somehow more real. We always forget, or refuse to believe, that our history is little more than the nuggets that fall through our psychic filters. And the nuggets themselves are reshaped in the passage, made larger or smaller, prettier or uglier than the experiences they represent. We draw a bold line to separate myth from history, and pretend we no longer know that the line marches through time with us.

And yet, she thought reluctantly, there was a use for history. There was a very real need to be anchored, to know where we have been. She thought of her own survival, the help she had needed, the confusion she had felt. It had taken her more than a year to accept this new reality. Suddenly the rain started, but she did not move yet. She remembered Yuri's response to the question: How do you get people who don't want power to take command, lead? "You make them, that's all." A world traumatized, dazed, in shock, and a few people who had had enough time to accept the changes. You make them, she repeated to herself. *Something* makes them. She returned to the van and started to drive.

That afternoon she went to see the eagles. She stopped short of where her blind had been last year. They would be too startled, she knew, if she got that close now. Rain was falling, as silent as snow here in the woods where the lichen and mosses glowed and the ferns were high and freshly green. She could not see either of the eagles until suddenly one of them cried, flew into sight, carrying a fish in its talons, and she realized the eggs had hatched.

The sea was restoring the beach now, bringing back the scrubbed sand, rearranging it, a cycle completed. And high in the spur of the dead tree another cycle was completing itself. Suddenly Lyle felt as if she were being overwhelmed, invaded almost, and she knew that her other self that had remained so distant, so untouchable had come back. She no longer could see herself as someone apart, alone, meaningless. She was back. The eagle rose on the side of the nest and stretched his wide wings, lifted into the air, circled, and flew away with such ease and grace that Lyle felt tears start in her eyes. She lifted her face to the rain. It was time to go home.

She began to hurry back down the hillside, running by the 'time she reached the spot where Saul's house had burned. She had to find him, call him, tell him she was coming home. She splashed through the creek, clambered up the bank, and stopped. Saul was there, hurrying toward her. She flew the rest of the distance. He held her in the rain and there was the sound of the white water hissing over rocks, and the rhythmic booming of the surf and, high above it all, the cry of the eagle as it flew to its nest. All ordered, necessary, unavoidable.